The Reaver Chronicles: Raziel

A Novel

1

Table of Contents

Dedication

To my best friend Mike

Thank you
for believing in me when I had a
crazy idea to write a book
for letting me bounce ideas off you
even if I just bounced them off myself
for telling me that I was going to finish the book
even when I thought I never would
for supporting me regardless of what I named my characters
or how it was spelled
for literally just being there
through this entire insane process
for dealing with me currently through book 2 as well
for being a huge part of this book
Thank you

Chapter 1

"Damn… you are so beautiful. Are you even Human?" Eric asked, as he trailed his fingers and lips down the side of my cheek. I will admit I was guilty of lying to my boyfriend… I am definitely not Human… I am a Werewolf, but I am not forced to shift, therefore I can keep it a secret. He can't hear my Wolf, Wynter, speaking to me in my mind either. I never meant to lie to him… but not all Humans know about us. That, and the topic just never came up.

Not that I think he would have looked at me differently had I told him. But why go through all of the drama? I knew this relationship wouldn't last. They never do, not with… him, the Demon, watching my every move. In fact, I was surprised he hadn't already showed up.

"Rayne, you know you shouldn't be doing this… You know what happens when he gets mad." Wynter whimpered in my mind. I ignored her when Eric's lips met mine. Any thought of the Demon who watches me in the night was lost, along with my willpower. I moaned softly against Eric's lips, allowing him to pull me closer.

Eric lived in the Human town across the river. I met him at a frat party that I wasn't supposed to be attending, but I snuck out and showed up anyway. The entire place was full of Humans, and then there was me. Not that any of them could distinguish my species, but still, Humans always seemed to flock to me.

Making friends was just too easy. Eric was gorgeous with his big blue eyes, his muscular build, and neatly styled blonde hair. His smile was full of perfectly straight, white, teeth and his voice was angelic. He was part of the football team, and the moment we locked eyes from across the room I knew I had him if I wanted him... and I definitely wanted him. What I didn't know was how quickly he was going to sweep me off my feet. He was charming, funny, and witty. He made me laugh and kept me interested the entire night in all the conversations we had.

He introduced me to his friends and ensured that my drink was never more than half empty. He didn't even try to make any real moves on me, except the sensual kiss he placed upon my lips right before he got out of the car and opened my door, walking me to the river bridge.

I gave him my number, much to Wynters dismay, but I had no idea we would ever get this far. We had been seeing each other for the past few months. Nothing serious, but dinner here and there, and texting all day. I also sent him some risky photos and maybe a video or two. He had never once in that time tried anything that I wasn't comfortable with.

But tonight was a bit different... he had drank far more alcohol than I had ever seen him drink before. Something about shot for shot with his best friend. He did it, but he was way past wasted. "I love you, Rayne. I love you so fucking much." He mumbled against my lips. I froze, he had never said that before. This was the first time. I pulled away and we locked eyes. He was smiling, and even as drunk as he was, he looked so sincere staring at me like I was the prettiest woman he had ever laid his eyes on.

"Eric, I..." I began, trying to avoid saying it back, when he cut me off. "Shh, babe. You don't have to say it back. I just wanted you to know how I feel. You've invaded my life in the best way. You are the woman I've always dreamt about. I can't stop imagining what it would be like to make you mine, fully mine..." He said, before bringing his lips back to mine.

"Rayne... you have to stop him!" Wynter cried as he pulled my shirt off over my head. "I know, I will." I replied to my Wolf. Eric peppered kisses down my throat and onto my chest, before attempting to undo my bra. I pulled back at

8

his advance, causing him to look up and meet my gaze. "Hey, this isn't a good idea. I can't go further. I'm sorry, I just…" I started to say, but he cut me off again with his lips on mine. I pulled away again. "Eric, I'm serious!" I growled. "Shh, babe, just let me touch you, let me taste you. Please." He begged, looking up at me through his long, perfect, lashes.

"Listen, Eric. I want nothing more than to let you do whatever it is that you want to do… but I can't. I can't let you… or something really bad is going to happen." I tried to warn him. He laughed, taking my hand and placing it directly on his hardened cock. "What bad thing would happen?" He asked, rubbing his hand over mine along the length of his shaft through his jeans.

"The only thing that is going to happen is I'm going to show you what a real man is packing and just how to use it. I'll have you screaming my name before you even know what hit you." He growled, then he slipped his hand up and unclasped my bra. I was starting to get nervous now, I knew this was a bad idea and Wynter's internal dialogue wasn't helping. "Eric, I'm serious… stop." I said, pushing him off of me.

I had never used any of my Wolf strength on him before. He was surprised when I was able to move him with ease, but he was too drunk to really comprehend what had just happened. I attempted to clasp my bra back on but I didn't succeed before he was back on top of me. "Come on, babe. I promise you will enjoy it." He murmured in my ear before taking the lobe in his mouth. "Don't you dare fucking do it, Rayne." Wynter growled. I sighed, pushing Eric off of me, once again. "I said no." I replied, reaching for my bra strap once more.

"No? Ha, I'm going to take what I want from you and you are going to enjoy every second of it. I'm not going to stop until you are screaming my name." He growled, pushing me back down onto the bed. He slammed his lips back onto mine as I fought to climb out from underneath him. "Eric, fucking stop! You are going to regret this!" I cried. I, honestly, was just giving him one last chance to stop on his own before I took matters into my own hands. As fucked up as he was acting, I didn't want to hurt him. My feelings were beyond hurt at his disrespect, but I still cared... Alcohol is never an excuse, but I knew deep down that he would never act like this had he not been drinking like he was.

A justification, but I needed something to try and save the small sliver of respect that was left for him. I watched as he pulled his belt from his pants and threw it aside. I was glaring up at him, and if looks could kill... "Oh, come on baby. Don't tell me you don't want it. Look at me..." He said.

"Eric, I have told you already. I can't... Please, trust me, don't do this." I pleaded, trying to spare him. After what he said to me I shouldn't have cared if anything happened to him, but I did... I do. He looked at me, matched the daggers in my eyes, and then snaked his hand through my hair and forced me up to my knees so I was kneeling on the bed in front of him, and he was standing on the floor before me.

"I have been more than patient with you, Rayne. I have allowed you more than enough time to be ready for this. You do not want to piss me off. Now you're going to do every single thing that I say, and you're not going to complain about it. Do you understand me?" He growled.

More than the absolute heart shattering pain that was radiating through my chest at his betrayal, was flaming, red hot, anger. So much fucking anger because I knew that not only was this the end of us, it was about to be the end of him at my hand.

"Don't say I didn't fucking warn you." I growled. The next events happened so quickly that I had little time to comprehend them. I slid back on the bed and instantly pulled my shirt up over my partially bare breasts. I still hadn't been able to clasp my bra so I was trying to cover myself as much as possible with what little material I had to work with. Panic began to set in as I comprehended just what had happened. The Demon turned his head and

10

looked directly at me. I tried, and failed, not to flinch under his murderous glare. His golden eyes were burning holes into my face with a gaze that was haunting and deadly.

He was absolutely, breathtakingly, gorgeous, with his porcelain skin, strong jawline and high cheekbones paired with medium length golden blonde hair. Wynter, howled in my mind. Anytime he had gotten close to us since I shifted for the first time when I was 15, she's gone absolutely wild. She is completely and utterly obsessed with him. I, however, was nothing but terrified.

I wasn't blind, but still, the only emotion I could ever feel around him was fear. I shut Wynter out of my mind and I glanced over at Eric's lifeless body lying there on the floor. I was in shock, disbelief that he was quite possibly dead. No, I knew he was dead. I didn't see him breathing at all. I felt as if I was going to be sick and fought to keep the bile from rising any higher in my throat. I know that he royally fucked up, but still, I never wanted him to die for it.

I wouldn't say that I particularly loved Eric, but more than sadness, I was feeling guilt. Guilt... because it was my fault that he was dead. No, I didn't choose his actions tonight, but I knew where this would lead. Eventually, I knew it would come to this. I just didn't think it would be so severe.

I felt the tears begin to form in the back of my eyes but forced myself to push them away. My face began to go numb as I let out a breath I wasn't even aware I was holding. I was trying my best to comprehend what had just happened. It all seemed so surreal.

After a few deep breaths, my mind finally cleared some and I was able to focus. I could hear the music from the party downstairs booming. Judging by the way I was still alone up here with my Demon, no one must have heard anything.

I did not want to deal with this... with him. I was contemplating an escape, a way out of this mess without conflict, but there was no saving myself, not this time. I flinched as the Demon, who I've only known as Mr. Kane, closed the gap between us with an unnatural speed and

11

took my chin in his hand. He pushed my chin up, forcing me to look directly into his burning golden eyes.

"No one may take your innocence but me. Don't think I will not kill again to prove how serious I am." He purred, licking the blood off his still elongated fangs. A single tear fell down my cheek as I fought like hell to keep the flood that had been brewing at bay. No fucking way was I going to show weakness. Not here, not now, and *never* in front of him. I broke eye contact, trying to look anywhere else. That, in and of itself, was a risky move, and I knew it, but I didn't care.

I could feel Wynter trying to push her way back through in my mind, but I forced her back. I wasn't anyone's property, but I was too afraid to say that to him. I knew My Demon had put a claim on me all those years ago, but I never thought he would go to this extent. "I'm sorr..." I started to say, but he put his finger to my lips. "Do not apologize, Rayne." He said, with almost a sadness to his voice. But then his eyes darkened and he narrowed his gaze on me. "You will not disobey me again." He spat. The venom slipped off his words and sank into my veins. Every hair on the back of my neck stood up when I looked up and we locked eyes.

If I wasn't already scared shitless, I swear the gold in his eyes looked a lot darker than it previously did... and that terrified me even worse. I had to fight to keep what little was left of my composure, to keep my body from shaking. "Yes, sir." I said. "Good girl, Rayne." He replied.

He was the most terrifying man I had ever met, and I hated the way my name rolled off his tongue like liquid gold. Wynter, however, was absolutely losing her mind. She was trying to release a low growl and I pushed it back as he turned to leave the room. She just didn't get it.

She wanted him more than anything else in this entire world, and was willing to completely look past anything and everything he did... even this. The thought of being with him paralyzed me with fear. Could I ever forgive him? I was torn from my thoughts when his golden voice rang out through the room. "Anthony, come clean this mess up." He snapped from the doorway. Seconds later my friend's bedroom looked as if it hadn't just been a murder scene.

I locked eyes with my Demon one last time. His expression was stoic and forced. It seemed as if he was holding something back. Something I wasn't sure I was interested in knowing about. I swallowed hard and broke our gaze, holding my head high in an attempt to contain my emotions.

"Please... allow his body to be found... He has many who love and care for him." I said softly. But when I glanced back over, they were both gone and my request fell upon deaf ears. Maybe he didn't deserve it, but I couldn't shake the fact that I still didn't think he would ever act this way had he not been white girl wasted.

I exhaled and was unable to hold back the flood any longer. I lost it. Tears began streaming down my face and onto my shirt, which was still in my hands.. Wynter was howling in the back of my mind, and I was doing my best to just ignore her. I didn't need her commentary, I already knew how much I fucked up...

I clasped my bra and put my tear-stained shirt back on before heading towards the window. I didn't want anyone else at the party to see me in this state.
I also had no idea how to explain where Eric had gone. I would have to deal with that later because everyone at this Frat party knew we were up here together... I just wanted out of here, and away from it all.

I had just slid the window pane open when I heard the door handle jiggle. "Fuck." I mumbled under my breath. I turned around as tears continued to stream down my face.

"Rayne? Oh my god, girl, are you ok?" What happened?" Jae cried.

Chapter 2

*J*ae was probably one of the only Humans I had met while dating Eric, that I actually liked. She was of Japanese origin, with long black hair and deep brown eyes. She was shorter than me standing about 5 foot 4 inches and she had pouty lips that always seemed to help her get her way anytime she protruded them the tiniest bit. I inhaled her scent of lavender and cherry blossom as she wrapped her arms around me.

Somehow, her being here and hugging me made me cry even harder. Though, that didn't help the burning panic from creeping into my veins. I had to lie, and I had to lie fast. "I got into a fight with Eric, he wanted to have sex and… and I… I wasn't ready yet." I stammered, hoping my lie was believable. At least my tears were real.

"Ugh! Goddamn Eric! He's such a douche!" She cried. I knew there was no escaping now. Jae would never let me leave this party no matter how much I begged. "I'm sorry he did that to you, he's such an asshole. He always has been." She growled. I pulled away, wiping the remaining tears from my pink cheeks.

"I don't know where he went, he left and slammed the door." I mumbled softly. "Fuck him! You need a shot! Let's go downstairs and find the Crown." She said. I nodded, knowing that I was trapped, at least for the next little while. My plan was to drink a little more myself, and in turn, get Jae so drunk that she wouldn't notice me slipping away from the party. It was the perfect plan. "Just keep your shit together, Rayne." Wynter said, trying to comfort me. I nodded to my Wolf and followed Jae back downstairs and into the kitchen. My silver combat boots slapped against the sticky tile as we made our way to the island where all the alcohol sat. The stench of stale beer that had been sitting spilled on the counter before us infiltrated my nostrils.

I held back a gag, beer was never really my go to. I have drank it before, but if I could choose, I'm choosing something else. I ignored the mess because if I start to clean this then I'm going to clean the whole house. It might get my mind off of my Demon, and Eric...

I was snapped from my thoughts when Jae held out a shot glass full of dark amber liquid. It was only seconds before a hint of cinnamon wafted through the air. This was Fireball. Jae clinked her glass to mine and with a twinkle in her brown eyes she tipped her head back and took the shot. I followed suit and had barely set my glass down before she was pouring another. Good, she needed to get absolutely smashed so I could escape this hell I found myself caught in.

We both tipped back another and then she began to make us both a mixed drink. I didn't care what was in it, so long as it was strong. "Put a double shot in there." I said with a half smile. "That's more like it!" She cackled, cracking a perfectly straight toothed smile as she poured far more than 2 shots into each glass.

Jae was always down to party. I had found this out upon our first meetup a few months ago. She was doing a handstand while shotgunning a beer from a beer bong, and still, to this day, it has me wondering just how she was able to succeed in doing that. I knew talking her into a few drinks heavy handed like this would be an easy feat. I just had to hold my composure until then.

She handed me the glass and clinked hers to mine again before we both took a drink. Well, hers was a drink, mine was more like a sip, though it didn't matter. She would be smashed far before I even felt the alcohol. A flash of blonde hair to my left as we walked through the crowd, caused pain to ricochet through my chest. Memories of

15

what had just happened charged their way back into my frontal lobe and I took another sip of my drink to try and calm myself down. Fresh air, that's what I needed. The second we stepped outside, I took a deep breath of the crisp air. I allowed the burn to engulf me as it infiltrated my lungs.

My hearing regulated due to the lack of loud music out here and I felt some of my stress begin to dissipate. I knew it wouldn't actually go away, but it was nice not to feel suffocated for a brief moment. "Hmm, and what exactly are you doing here?" A snooty voice from behind me screeched. I didn't even have to turn around to know this was going to be Sarah. Jae rolled her eyes at me before we both turned around to face her. I had to stifle a laugh because the floral printed dress she was wearing was absolutely atrocious.

It had large flowers spanning across the entire thing. It was white and gaudy with some frilly shit on the shoulders. Her dyed, partially black, partially gray hair, was done up in a fancy updo with some pieces falling out on the sides. Her makeup at least matched her hair, but not even the large hot pink heels she was wearing matched that atrocity she called a dress. A large green stone sat right in the hollow of her neck and it looked even worse with her bright green bracelet. I crunched my nose up when the scent of blueberries and something musky forced its way in.

"Sarah, what kind of stupid ass question is that?" I replied, folding my arms. She knew full well who I was dating and why I was here. She hummed as if my answer was subpar. I didn't care what she thought. "So where is he then?" She questioned. I began to panic internally. "Lie, Rayne! Make something up!" Wynter hissed. I was the worst liar in the world, and I knew this.

"It's none of your fucking business, Sarah. Go the fuck away." Jae said, just before I opened my mouth to speak. I sighed internally, relieved that I didn't have to say anything. Sarah's snark fell from her face and was replaced by anger. I snickered out loud, unable to control it this time. "He's

16

cheating on you, you know… He was with me last night."
Sarah said, and then turned her back to walk away. I tried
to ignore the way my heart sank straight into the pit of my
stomach as I stepped forward and grabbed Sarah by the
hair. I yanked her back towards me causing her to stumble
and fall.

"What the fuck did you say?" I growled, putting the heel
of my boot on her hand that was splayed out on the ground
before us. "I… I…" She stammered, unsure of what to say. I
handed my drink to Jae and leaned down so we were face
to face. "I never want to hear his name come out of your
slutty fucking mouth, ever a-fucking-gain. Do you
understand me?" I growled.

She looked up at me with pure, unbridled hatred in her
eyes. I ignored the energy shift in the area as the poison
emanating from her glare surrounded me. I thought she
was going to cower down and agree with me, which would
have been the smart move. But instead, she raked her
sharp nails across the side of my face. I heard gasps as
blood trickled down my cheek. I was fucking pissed now. I
looked up at Jae who had a look of horror on her face, and
then I rolled my head back, cracking my neck on one side,
before looking back down at Sarah.

"Wrong move, bitch." I snapped, before I slammed my
fist right into her nose. I felt it crack under my knuckles. She
screamed and attempted to scratch at me, but I dodged out
of her grasp. She was already basically underneath me, but
I pushed forward, slamming my hand around her throat.

Her head made a sickening crack as it hit the tile
beneath us. She was only Human, and I want to say I was
trying to go easy on her, but I was seeing more red than
anything.

"You're fucking insane!" Sarah cried, digging her nails
into my forearm. I didn't even feel the flesh break open, nor
did I feel the blood running down my arm through all the
adrenaline. "You need to leave, right fucking now!" I
growled, trying to save her more than anything. "Ok, ok...
God, fucking psycho." Sarah muttered as I got off the top of

her. I shook my head, and turned towards Jae when the wind was completely knocked out of me. Surprised, I attempted to roll as I fell to the ground. It worked, but I didn't have time to get back up to my feet before Sarah took her place on top of me and attempted to dagger my eyes out.

Her nails were her only form of defense against me, and I think she realized it when I reached up and grabbed her wrists, stopping her mid swipe. A much larger crowd had gathered around us at this point, and even though the music was still blaring inside, I could hear everyone chanting. "Fight, fight, fight." Being a Wolf, this was a completely unfair fight, but no one here knew I was Supernatural, and I planned to keep it that way.

I yanked Sarah's wrists and used my knees to push her off the top of me. She went tumbling over my head and into the crowd that surrounded us. I was on my feet, and within seconds my fist clashed with the side of Sarah's face. She screamed and fell backwards, but the boys in the crowd didn't let her fall again. They pushed her back towards me. I knew she couldn't throw a punch, not with those nails, so I had little to worry about.

She circled me for a moment, and I allowed her to do it, anticipating her next move. She ran towards me but I stopped her with a hand straight to her throat. I lifted her and threw her to the ground at my feet. The crowd gasped and then started cheering as I put my boot down on her heavily heaving chest.

"You'd do best to stay the fuck down." I growled. I wasn't holding back any of my strength at this point. Sarah had blood coming out of her nose and the corner of her mouth, but she refused to back down. She grabbed my calf and yanked me, causing me to lose my balance and fall to the ground. "Kick her fucking ass!" Wynter cried.

I regained my composure, diving into the back of Sarah's knees as she attempted to get up and away from me. She was too slow as I latched onto her legs and she fell to the ground. I crawled up on top of her and laid 3 good

18

slams to her face. Blood was flying everywhere but I only had 1 goal in mind, and that was stopping her from running her big fucking mouth. "Rayne, stop!" Jae cried, pulling me off of Sarah. I was so lost in the commotion I barely realized where I was. The red began to filter out of my vision as I got to my feet and looked at my friend. She was daring to put her hands on me, but I understood why.

I shook my head and looked back at Sarah. Her friends were helping her up and she was bleeding pretty badly. I used my hand to wipe my brow and attempted to steady my erratic breathing. "You're fucking crazy!" Sarah sneered as she walked past me holding some tissues her friend had given her up to her nose to stop the bleeding. She bumped my shoulder as she passed but I only got 1 step in her direction before I felt a large hand on my bicep.

I turned and glared at the man who had the audacity to touch me. It was Brett, he was the Quarterback of the football team. Brett's imposing figure loomed before me, his piercing hazel eyes seeming to see right through me.

The quarterback's rugged charm was undeniable, from the chiseled lines of his athletic build to the unruly mess of dark hair that framed his strong features. The overwhelming scent of Axe body spray clung to him like a cloud, an unmistakable signature that seemed to announce his presence. As he stood there, clad in his worn quarterback jersey, I couldn't help but feel a little intimidated by the sheer force of his personality.

He held my glare for a moment before I ripped my arm from his grip. He nodded to me to follow him. I looked back at Jae and sighed. "It's ok, I'll be right here!" She hollered as Brett began to walk off towards the stairs. I mumbled to myself and followed him.

He was probably going to chew my head off for fighting in his house… that was fair. The adrenaline was beginning to wear off by this time and the pain of what happened earlier with Eric began to creep back in. I did my best to ignore it. I had other issues to deal with now. Brett headed upstairs and to the bathroom before ushering me inside. He

19

closed the door and clicked the lock shut, drowning out some of the noise from downstairs. He then reached towards me and I stopped him, instinctively, latching onto his wrist before he could get close enough to touch my face.

Chapter 3

"Rayne, knock it off. I need to examine your wounds." He snapped, pulling his wrist from my grip and grabbing onto my chin. I allowed him to look, but I knew they wouldn't be there anymore. I had no idea how to explain that to him. "Just lie, tell him that it wasn't your blood it was from Sarah, it was just on her nails." Wynter said, which was a great idea.

I opened my mouth to spit out the lie, but he spoke over me. "What pack are you from?" He asked. Panic flooded through my chest as I backpedaled, trying to avoid this conversation. "Rayne, don't fucking play with me, I know you are a Wolf. What fucking pack?" He growled. *Fuck...* I had to tell him now, I couldn't keep denying it, not when there were so many damn indicators.

Finally, I sighed and looked down. "The Obsidian pack." I mumbled, hoping he didn't hear me and would just forget about it. I couldn't be so lucky. His breathing hitched in his throat. "Alpha Drake?" He snapped. I nodded my head. He inhaled slowly. "Jesus Christ, does he know you are here?" He hissed.

I shook my head. He then put his thumb and forefinger to the bridge of his nose. "You are playing with fire, you know this, right?" He hissed. "How in the fuck do you know about any of this?" I interrupted, not caring that I completely ignored his question.

He raised his hand and elongated 5 Wolf claws, spinning them around between us. I gasped. "You're a Wolf?" He turned from me and clinked his claws on the sink. "I'm a Hybrid, half Wolf, half Human. My mother had an affair, but we all pretend that she didn't. Luckily, I still look like my 'dad' enough not to cause concern. But... well, you know. I'm surprised you didn't realize it the first time we spoke." He said. I just shook my head. "I wasn't paying enough attention to notice." I retorted, offended that he would take a jab at me like that. He ignored me with a snort.

"So now what?" I asked. He shrugged. "We both have a secret, so we both need to keep it. We are going to go back downstairs and get fucking trashed. Everyone is going to cheer because you kicked Sarah's ass, and you are going to appreciate the recognition. After tonight, we both just keep our fucking mouth's shut and you stop kicking Human's asses. Deal?" He said.

I didn't agree, I rolled my eyes. "Rayne, I'm serious! Knock your shit off. Where is Eric anyways? Weren't you with him earlier?" He asked. My stomach felt like it fell straight out of me onto the floor. Pain, sharp and furious, clawed its way into my chest, and tears attempted to make their way out of the silver prisons that caged them.

"I... I don't know where he is. We got into a fight earlier and he left... I thought... I thought he would be back, but..." I said softly, before the cages failed to hold their prisoners, allowing burning hot tears to escape down my cheeks.

"Fuck... I'm sorry. I didn't mean to... fuck it, you need a drink." He said, pulling a bottle of Crown out of his inside jacket pocket. "Rayne, are you ok?" I could hear Jae's voice outside of the door, faintly.

I looked at Brett who nodded for me to open the door just as his claws rescinded into his fingertips. I unclicked the lock and opened it. She eyeballed Brett, who was standing behind me, for a bit longer than I think she wanted to, before looking back at me.

I knew I still had tears cascading down my cheeks but I had taken the Crown and tipped the bottle back. I looked at Jae and shrugged. She started laughing nervously but took the bottle from me and followed suit. Brett pushed his way past us both, and only shot me a glance as he headed back down the stairs. He didn't even bother to take the Crown with him. "Ok girl, SPILL!" Jae cried. I shook my head. "It was nothing, he was just asking me about Eric, which is why I'm now crying..." I said softly. "Brett didn't try anything?" She asked. I shook my head. "No, he just asked about Eric, that's all." She sighed out loud. "Fuck him. Let's go, we need more drinks."

She pulled on my arm as we headed back down into the crowd. The second I stepped down off the stairs the entire crowd erupted in cheers. Startled, I stood there like a deer in headlights. I could feel the redness digging its way onto my cheeks. A feeling that was unwelcome at best. I looked at Jae who was laughing her ass off.

Her brown eyes were a bit glazed over and I knew she was drunk enough now that I could have escaped without her noticing, but it seemed that I was not going to be able to escape everyone. I sighed, and then tipped the Crown back. More cheers erupted and clapping. What better way to grieve than drink the pain away? Maybe if I drank enough I could actually get drunk.

The feat was easier than I expected to achieve. It didn't help that everyone I passed was handing me shots and drinks. 2 hours or so went by, and I will say I was definitely feeling the alcohol. Brett had rejoined the party by this time and was pouring a cheap beer into the funnel above me, and the funnel above one of his Frat boys at the same time.

"Chug, chug, chug!" The crowd chanted, as I downed the entire thing in record speed. I wiped the dribble from my chin as everyone cheered. The Frat boy had finished his but I was already done and ready for round 2. I turned to Brett to get him to find me another contestant I could beat at the beer bong, but I stopped dead in my tracks when I noticed a small commotion directly in front of us.

It took me only seconds to realize it was surrounding a man who looked *very* out of place here. Every single female and most of the males in this room were gravitating towards him. He was leaning against the doorway between the kitchen and living room with his arms folded across his large chest. The gold surrounding his attire seemed suffocating, as I, once again, fought to regain what was left of my composure. It had been hours since I had felt a single thing except pure, unbridled joy, and I wasn't about to let my Demon ruin this. We locked eyes and he shook his head slowly, as if to forbid me from whatever the fuck he thought I was going to do next. I raised an eyebrow at him, before I turned my back and got ready to annihilate the next contestant.

I know I should be upset, annoyed, or humiliated that he thinks I need a fucking babysitter. But with this much alcohol running through my veins I wasn't even scared. What would he do, kill me too? Bring it...

"Rayne, you need to listen to him! We should go." Wynter whimpered, but I pushed her away. I wasn't going anywhere. It wasn't until I was just about ready to take another beer that I heard the golden tone of his voice. "You are done. We are leaving." He ripped the beer bong from my hand and tossed it aside. I looked up at Brett, who had already taken 4 steps back. He had to know what a Reaver was to act this way. It was a subtle movement on his part that no one else here would understand, but it made sense to me.

No one was safe here, not even me... not anymore. The moment of clarity I had was gone in a flash, and my usual snark replaced it. "I am not leaving." I huffed. I watched anger flash through my Demon's eyes before he reached for me. I stepped back, just out of his grasp. "Rayne, I'm not fucking around. Do not make a scene." He hissed.

In my drunken state I have no idea why I thought this was a good idea, but I turned and took off running through the house. The Humans at the party parted to allow me through, which in turn, allowed my Demon to follow much too easily. I took off up the stairs and into the first room I came to, slamming the door behind me.

My heart was hammering in my chest as I fumbled with the lock, though I knew it was no use. He could get in, regardless of what I did. He slammed his fist into the door, further startling the couple that was making out in the bed behind me. "Rayne, open this goddamn door right fucking now." He hissed. Anger rolled through his words, engulfing me through the measly slab of wood that separated us. In any normal circumstance I would have been absolutely shaking with fear, but I was shitfaced drunk, and couldn't feel anything but excitement.

"Make me!" I replied, backing away from the door when I heard the lock click. The couple in the bed were slightly panicking as the door slowly opened, but I saw their demeanors change drastically when they saw the man standing behind the flashy gold attire.

He did not look amused. I only dared to meet his gaze for a brief second before I attempted to dart past him and out the door. My attempt failed, and he basically clotheslined me with his arm hooked around my waist. Panic finally broke through my drunken euphoria, and began to seep deep into my bones. He pulled my back to his chest and held me there. I could feel his warm breath as it danced along my jawline.

"Enough is enough. We are leaving. Don't tell me you have already forgotten our meetup from earlier. I will kill every single person in this house and not even think twice about it. Don't fucking test me, Rayne." The tone was calm, too calm. I didn't know much about the man in gold, but I had a feeling that he was not actually calm at all. "Listen to him, Rayne! Stop being stupid!" Wynter snapped. "Shut the fucking door!" One of the Humans in the bed hollered, breaking me from my internal panic.

My Demon released his ironclad grip on me just enough for me to step to the side and exit the room. He followed and closed the door behind us. I turned and locked eyes with him, and then took off on a dead run down the stairs. I heard him growl under his breath as he pursued me. I only made it to the second to last stair before he had a hold of me.

He grabbed me and threw me over his shoulder. I pounded on his back, screeching for him to release me. I could hear the gasps of the Humans who split the way for

25

us to leave. "You motherfucker! Let me go! You can't control me!" I hissed. I attempted to kick him in the balls, but I couldn't get my foot down that far. Instead, I kept assaulting him and continued to scream and holler the entire way out of the house and outside. It was childish. I ignored the feel of his large hand as it pressed into the side of my thick thigh. I could feel the bruises beginning to form already.

It wasn't until we got to a solid gold sports car that he stopped and finally let me down. He dropped me to my feet in front of him and immediately I began to pound my fists into his chest. He grabbed my wrists, stopping me. He was gripping them so tightly I was sure I would bruise here too. I finally calmed down enough to look up at him. He was glaring at me, and for the first time since he had shown up, I could feel the terror grabbing hold of me and dragging me down into its inky depths.

I previously had opened my mouth to say something snarky, but chose not to follow through with my retort. Instead, I closed my mouth and swallowed hard. "Get. In. The. Car." We were so close I could taste the mint on his breath as he slowly spoke, over enunciating each word. I was vaguely aware of the crowd that had gathered outside to watch our shenanigans. I'm sure the fancy suit and sports car wasn't helping. It was rare to see something this fancy in the Human side of town so naturally, they were curious. Even those with money didn't drive Bugattis. I ripped my wrists from his grip, surprised that he let me, and took a step back away from him.

I fixed my shirt that was falling down over my shoulder and stormed past him to the car. He snapped and the door opened as I walked up to it. I turned to look back at the crowd and locked eyes with Brett who was standing right out in front.

I rolled my eyes and stuck my fingers to my head pretending to shoot myself. The crowd began to laugh, but not Brett. He knew the severity of what I had done, and I was starting to realize it too. "In the car, Rayne." My Demon's silky voice echoed throughout my inner ear. I snapped back to the task at hand, slipping into the car without another glance at the crowd. I shut the door and heard the lock click. My jaw dropped as I tried to open the door to find that it was locked from the outside. Offended, I turned and looked at my captor. He was already in the car, and I let my jaw drop in offense.

"You locked me in? Are you fucking kidding me?" I huffed. "Tell me you weren't going to try and run." He replied, starting the sports car. The rumble of the horses did little to calm me. *Fuck,* he had me there... I remained silent, unsure of how to answer him.

He leaned over and I instantly placed my hands up to shield myself. He pulled away briefly with the seatbelt in his hand and gave me an annoyed look while clicking the seatbelt across my chest. I would be lying if I said the black interior peppered with gold wasn't bringing out the shades of gold in my Demons hair and eyes.

Even as pissed as I knew he was, somehow, it made him that much more enticing to look at. Regardless of his God-like beauty, I was still upset that he had the goddamn audacity to kidnap me from a frat party. He acted like I was a child who needed to be watched at all times.

The fucking audacity of this man!

Chapter 4

"What the fuck were you doing?" He growled, pulling me from my erratic thoughts. Suddenly, my courage returned, pulling me back from the dark. "Well, it's not everyday that your boyfriend gets murdered in cold blood, right in front of you after trying to rape you... which, by the way, I could have handled that myself, thank you. What was I doing? I was grieving." I snapped, folding my arms in front of me.

I could feel his annoyance surrounding me, suffocating me. The purr of the horses underneath the hood suddenly seemed much easier to focus on. "Grieving what? He didn't deserve you and you know it." He replied. I scoffed. "Oh, and you do?" He hummed his disapproval but ignored my question. "There is a way to stop your erratic behavior." He finally said after a few moments of silence passed between us. "Not likely." I retorted.

He stopped the fancy car in front of my house but didn't let me out yet. Instead, he turned to face me. "You know, you can't escape me. No matter how much you may try, I will always find you. One simple touch, and my mark will adorn your face... and when it does, you will be helpless to tell me no, ever again." He said, caressing my cheek with his hand.

Goosebumps sprouted along both of my arms and settled themselves deep into my spine. The thought of being marked by him was terrifying. I knew very little of Reavers, but I knew they were able to choose their own mates. He had chosen me long ago, and he made sure I was very aware of his intentions. Why he hadn't just marked me yet is a question I do not have an answer for. But it seemed the more I acted out, the closer he got to just doing it. "Please… don't…" I stammered, as another break in my euphoria rushed through. "I am generously allowing you your freedom. The more you take advantage of this fact, the closer I become to taking it all away. Don't force my hand, Rayne. You have seen firsthand how far I am willing to go."

The thought of him marking me and forcing me to be with him made my stomach turn. Not that I don't find him incredibly attractive. I'm not blind, but being forced into it is not how I envisioned my story turning out. I had always thought I would find my mate someday and we would be able to experience the mate bond in all its glory. If I am marked by a Reaver... I would never have that option.

I swallowed, hard, and pulled from the copious amounts of liquid courage that scourged my veins. "I'm not mated to you." I said firmly. He looked out the window for a brief moment, then turned back to look at me. I inhaled slowly as I took in the mischief dancing though his eyes. "Oh? And you know this, how?" He asked. I raised an eyebrow and folded my arms across my chest.

"You are of age, you would feel it if we were." I snapped, knowing that I would have to be 21 to feel it, but he was past that age already so he could feel the bond if it were present. He took my chin in his hand causing me to flinch slightly as he turned my face towards his. "And how do you know that I don't?" He whispered. I could feel Wynter running rampant within my mind. She wanted nothing more than to be mated to this monster. The saliva instantly dried in my mouth, almost causing me to choke when I tried to swallow.

"You're lying!" I croaked, but still, it came out as cracked as my throat was beginning to feel. "Am I?" He said, getting impossibly closer to me. I pushed myself back as far as I could, but the black and gold bucket seat did little to allow me to shrink into the nothing like I was hoping I would. He was so close to me now that our lips were almost touching.

He allowed his hand to slide from my chin, gripping onto my neck and pressing it further into the seat back, if that were even possible. "Explain to me just why my presence affects you like it does. The thrill, the fear... the way a strategic squeeze of your inner thigh, like this, causes you to gasp out loud, like that... do explain to me why my lips being this close to yours has your heart rate increasing by the moment. Tell me, little Wolf... if I am lying, then why do my words cause shivers to run up and down your spine?"

I was completely and utterly shaken. In the state of mind that I found myself in, and against all of my previous conceptions, I wanted nothing more than for him to completely and utterly devour me. The thought of his lips upon mine, and the way I imagined he would taste... the way his tongue would dance along the edges of my lips, begging to be let in. The feel of his large hands as they claimed parts of my body that the light didn't see often.

My breath hitched in my throat when he removed his hand from my throat suddenly, and took his place in his seat, ripping me from my thoughts and leaving me begging for more. I squeezed my legs together, trying to calm the heat that had been building between them, but not without a snicker from the peanut gallery. "Tell me, little Wolf, am I lying?" He asked.

I couldn't even look at him. I could feel the redness grasping onto my cheeks for dear life. "I... I don't know." I mumbled, fighting over words because my mind was not in its right state. Not in the slightest. Even Wynter had gone quiet, which was an eerie feeling.

"Then I guess you will just have to wait and find out." He said. I grasped onto my courage momentarily. "Find out? I won't have a chance, you're going to mark me far before I get that chance." I huffed, clasping my hands together in my lap in frustration. "Am I?" He asked.

I glared at him. "Ughhh, you infuriate me!" I growled, and attempted to open the door, forgetting I was locked in like a fucking child. "I wonder how many days you'd have to be missing before someone came looking for you..." He said, nonchalantly, causing my heart to stop beating in my chest momentarily. I turned and we locked eyes. The disbelief was clear on my face as I glared at my captor.

"You wouldn't dare." I growled, realizing that daring this man to do anything was just as good as a death threat, but the words had already left my lips before I could stop them. He reached for my arm, but I wasn't fast enough to avoid his death grip. Panic gripped onto my wrist and yanked me through space and time. I was falling and tumbling, disoriented and confused. I landed on the ground, hard, and then had to close my eyes to fight a bout of nausea that threatened to swallow me whole.

"What the fuck was that?!" I cried as soon as I was able to form a coherent sentence. I opened my eyes and noticed that we were no longer in the gold sports car in front of my house. No, we were much further away than that.
The ocean crashed in furious waves against the rocky shore below the cliff I found myself lying on top of. To my right was a dense forest full of evergreens spanning hundreds of feet into the sky. I could hear birds chirping and singing in the distance. The smell of pine was strong as it wrapped itself around every fiber of my being. As I sat up I cringed, pulling small rocks and twigs from the skin on my elbow. "How fast can you run?" He asked, pulling my attention from the breathtaking scenery that surrounded us and directing it straight onto himself.

"What?" I replied, confused as I got up from the floor and brushed myself off. "I will not repeat myself." He said, nodding towards the tree line. I turned, but before I could even take a step I heard him snap his fingers, and then my ankles were suddenly bound together. I turned and looked back at him. "What the fuck?" I growled. "You and that mouth of yours." He tsked.

Another snap, and the golden rope that bound my ankles made its way to my mouth. It slithered around my face and wrapped around my lips, closing them as it constricted. Anger burned its way through my veins as he made his very fucking clear point. Another snap and the

31

rope made its way down to my wrists, wrapping them up like a golden silk cocoon. The golden rope was glittering in the absence of sunlight, and albeit beautiful, it only pissed me off more. He then walked up to me and took my restrained wrists in his hand. Slinking his fingers around the ropes that bound me, he pulled me to his chest, forcing me to look up at him.

"Tell me again how you think I wouldn't kidnap you... tie you up, just like this, and keep you as my pet for all of eternity." His fingertips danced along the edge of the ropes that silenced me causing heat to build in places I knew it shouldn't.

"Explain to me just exactly how you think I wouldn't force you to do anything I ever wanted... get on your knees." He said, as he yanked me down by my wrists. The small whimper that left my lips as small rocks and twigs dug into my soft skin, was more than pathetic. He pulled my chin up so I was looking at him.

"How perfect you look down on your knees for me." He hummed. The alcohol was beginning to wear off by this point, and my snarky attitude was starting to fade right along with it. I concluded that he enjoyed fucking with my feelings, which should have upset me, but it only scared me. "Do you enjoy being able to speak freely?" A snap, and I felt the golden ropes that bound my mouth begin to unwind. "Do you enjoy being able to go anywhere you please?" Another snap and the ones around my ankles loosened and snaked their way off.

He reached down, clasping his fingers around the ropes that still bound my wrists. He pulled me up until I was standing before him once again. "Do you enjoy being able to use those pretty little hands of yours to pleasure yourself after our meetups?" A snap, and the ropes binding my wrists began to untangle.

I gasped, horrified that he would watch me like that... but why was I surprised? "You didn't..." I stammered, fully aware that I sounded like an idiot. "Oh trust me, darling, I did. You are very skilled with those hands. And you are absolutely breathtaking when you come undone. Maybe, just maybe, I'll tell you my first name so I can hear you moan it next time." He purred, while running his fingers along my collarbone and down my chest.

He stopped just before the edge of my shirt, allowing his fingertips to dance along the swell of my cleavage. He didn't go further. I was standing there, frozen, horrified, and unable to make a coherent thought. He circled me like prey, but I didn't dare to move a single muscle. "Feeling violated yet?" He hissed, causing me to flinch. The alcohol had all but worn off and I was beginning to panic. He stopped directly in front of me and pulled me close.

"This is your one and only warning, Rayne. Behave, or mark my fucking words I will come for you... I will not be gentle, and I will not be kind when I do. I will break every single deal I have made with your Alpha. And at that point, no one will stop me from collecting what is mine." He whispered in my ear.

My feelings of horror and disgust quickly turned into fear. He wasn't fucking around, not at all, and I knew this. I took a few steps back away from him, surprised that he allowed it. Fear and unease swam through my chest, allowing me one brief moment to call Wynter forward. I turned and began to run when Wynter broke through.

I exhaled in relief when I felt us begin to shift and then 4 paws hit the forest floor. She ran like our lives depended on it. Maybe they did. It was sunrise before we finally slowed down enough for me to comprehend where we were. The clearing was unfamiliar, regardless, I knew we were outside of pack lands.

A forest full of towering pines was behind us and there was a clearing adorned with small wildflowers in varying colors to the side of us. I still had no idea exactly where we were, but the sun was just rising up over the horizon, casting a beautiful orange glow over the valley.

Living here in Maine my entire life, I could tell you that it never lacked a beautiful landscape no matter which way I turned. Looking down into the city below us, the cityscape

33

was immaculate. Skyscrapers reached through the air, and you could clearly see the outline of the entire city, block by block from up here. Even as early as it was, there were plenty of vehicles on the roads. That must be a Human town, as we rarely used vehicles in the pack, but only because we never left the pack… it wasn't allowed.

There was only 1 Human town that bordered our pack, and it was directly across the river… The town that Eric lived in. We had come much further than that. I looked down at the grass under my paws, noting how green and lush it seemed to be. It was almost springy underneath my weight. I could feel the dewdrops that clung to the blades of grass surrounding us as they soaked into the fur around the pads of my paws.

I shook the thoughts. I knew I was only distracting myself with the small details. I knew damn well we weren't supposed to be here, or anywhere for that matter. The rules are simple. You don't leave the pack territory without the Alpha's permission… but no one ever got permission from Alpha Drake. I doubt many dared to even ask him for it.

He was intimidating, to say the least. That's even an understatement… a big understatement. He was 6 feet tall, dark complexion, and had large muscles that cascaded throughout his entire form. The man never left the gym, I swear. He had black hair that was always kept short and a little messy, with dark blue eyes like the depths of the ocean. His facial hair was always kept neat and tidy, as if one hair out of place would ruin him. And maybe it would…

He had a long scar that ran down the right side of his face down onto his neck, and many similar scars on both of his arms and back. He never spoke of how he got them, but there were rumors. A smile never fell on this man's lips. He had a husky voice that demanded respect and attention. And he got it… good God did he get it.

Even just the venom in his voice alone was enough to make a grown man shudder. No one ever disobeyed Alpha Drake, or lived to tell about it… "Rayne, we need to go back… we are so far outside of pack lands. Alpha Drake is going to kill us." Wynter whined. "It doesn't even matter now, we've already disobeyed, we are already dead. Why even go back?" I snipped. It wasn't her fault. Sure, she was in control in this form, but we were both hurting.

I get why she wanted to get back. It was for good reason, really. But I honestly could care less if we ever returned... Alpha Drake looming or not. I will admit that while Wynter was in control, I should have had a chance to process what happened with Eric. Should have... but my mind continued to betray me, forcing me to focus directly on my Demon and the sexual tension that sat so thick between us that you could cut it with a knife. Still, it was going to take time to get over Eric whether I processed the situation or not. I needed to compartmentalize it and work through it.

I couldn't do that under Alpha Drake's tight rule. If we survived this he would have us doing extra rounds for weeks... unacceptable, because I needed to grieve. I tried not to focus on it, which was harder than it seemed. The main issue on my mind was the next year and what my life would be like until then. Or even after.

I was only 20, if my Demon was willing to literally kill my boyfriend for touching me, stalk me at a frat party, and kidnap me, promising to hold me hostage forever, what else was he capable of? The thoughts made me shudder.

Not that I hadn't thought he would do something like this... but he had never actually hurt anyone before. Sure, he had scared other romantic interests of mine away, but never to the extent of hurting someone, let alone killing them. I guess it didn't help that Eric was Human. In all my time being haunted by my Demon, I never thought he would become so crazed. I was struggling to understand the true reasons behind his insane behavior.

'Do you enjoy being able to use those pretty little hands of yours to please yourself after our meetups?' His words floated through my mind, settling right behind my eyes.

Embarrassment dug its way into my chest and onto my face. The thought of him watching me was haunting. I pushed away the spicy thoughts and tried to focus on anything except his erratic behavior but my thoughts then began to run a bit wild. What would he do to my other friends? Jae? What if I ran away? I was already this far, why go back now? Why not just continue running? What if I never looked back? Maybe he wouldn't find me. I could start over, somewhere new and far, far, the fuck away from here… and him.

Wynter let out a growl at my intrusive thoughts because she was infatuated with the man. I never understood just why. He may be gorgeous and God-like, but the man was absolutely fucking terrifying. I ignored her.

My mind flitted back to when Eric was killed. Once I started to think about it, I couldn't help but replay it over and over until it drove me mad.

My Demon, ripping Eric's throat out with his Vampire fangs… the blood was dripping off his fangs as he closed in on me… I wasn't sure if I was next. Me, attempting to cover myself with the sheet, with anything. Attempting to hold back the tears, the pain, the guilt…

Reavers were terrifying because of all the powers they possessed by nature. Honestly, I felt there wasn't anything he couldn't do. It all made sense why every other Supernatural creature was afraid of Reavers… yet I was supposed to, what? Just forget that I was claimed by one of the most ruthless creatures in the world? Or worse, accept it? I don't think so...

I was snapped from my internal panic when I heard Alpha Drake's powerful voice snaking through my mind link. "Rayne, get your ass back to the pack lands, immediately." Venom snaked its way through his words. I could feel it seeping into my very bones. Then he ended the mind link. "Son of a bitch." I growled. Wynter whimpered like a hurt pup in my mind.

"He's going to fucking kill us, Rayne. Straight up kill us. We will be just as fucking dead as Eric when we return." Wynter scolded. "Jesus, Wynter! Too soon. Too fucking soon!" I huffed. She didn't apologize, she just went silent. I mean, she was right. What did we expect? A homecoming?

Balloons? A party? Ha… I knew this was coming, I just sort of hoped that he wouldn't even notice. But I couldn't be so lucky.

With everything else going on, I wasn't anywhere near ready to face Alpha Drake, and I knew this… but it didn't matter. What he says, goes. And that includes whatever punishment he has in mind for everything that I've done in the past however many hours.

I exhaled an annoyed breath before Wynter turned back. We started running but every single step was absolute pain and agony, bringing us forever closer to what was sure to be our imminent doom…

Chapter 5

On the way back my mind was racing. I couldn't keep it quiet even if I had tried. On top of my insistent guilt over Eric's death, I was also thinking about my Demon. We passed an old abandoned wishing well in the forest, and I couldn't help but remember the first experience I ever had with him.

I was 9 years old. I was living with my mother in a small, cozy cottage just on the edge of the Obsidian pack. It was close to where I currently live now. We weren't part of a pack back then, it was just us. Me and her. Thinking back, it was a little strange that we didn't live in a pack, being Wolves and all.

I never knew my father and my mother never bothered to bring him up. I figured if she never did I wouldn't either. He was a forgotten staple in our household, but I preferred it that way. My mother always used to say that we were strong and didn't need anyone to protect us. I always believed her. Honestly, what I wouldn't give to be able to hear her words of wisdom just one more time.

She always told me I was forbidden to go to the well. She said it was too far away from our cottage, and to go alone would surely mean death. I never felt unsafe a day in my life as a child, but she insisted that we were never truly safe. Not out here. She'd always say we weren't safe living outside of a pack to begin with, but would never approach any pack to try and join. It never made sense to me. She always used to say that we'd be fine around the house, but there were many creatures lurking in the forest.

Most of which wouldn't hesitate to kill me. I believed her, even though I had never personally seen another soul around here, creature or not. I couldn't help my curiosity, and would always try to sneak away to the wishing well… unsuccessfully, I might add. My mother was around 5 and half feet tall and had long blonde hair to the middle of her back. Her facial features were soft and alluring, which matched her personality. She was always kind hearted, willing to help anyone who ever needed it. Always the first to offer her services. She had an athletic build, as most Wolves do, and the most beautiful platinum silver eyes I had ever seen.

They were even prettier than my own. I swear though, those silver eyes were like hawk eyes, because she caught me every single time I tried to sneak off, and made me come back to the safety of our home. One time I somehow managed to escape her watch. I cried out in surprise when I reached the wishing well, alone, and realized that she hadn't caught me.

I stood there in awe, admiring the scene before me. The wishing well was absolutely beautiful up close. Stunning, large, multicolored stones made up the main shaft of the well. Complete with a dark stained wooden arch, harnessing a single rope and a matching stained bucket which could be lowered down into the well. It looked as if the elements had never touched it. I could smell the clear, crisp, stream not far away which fed the well.

The trickling water sounded like heaven as it danced through my ears. I knew that the water flowing in the stream was a light turquoise blue, my favorite color, so it would make sense that the water in the well would be the same color.

But my curious child mind had to know for sure. I walked over to the well and allowed my fingers to run along the smooth surface as I peered down inside. I was leaning over the edge to try and get a better look and see if my theory was right, when I pushed up a little too hard and fell straight down into the well. I felt my head go under the cool water and I held my breath. I opened my eyes underwater to realize it, in fact, was turquoise as I had thought. I smiled and surfaced soon after. I knew how to swim so I wasn't in any danger of drowning, at least not right away. In fact, I knew a lot of things, including how to defend myself. My mother never let me be unprepared for anything. I can't recall a time when we weren't training or learning something new. She overcompensated in that fact a little.

At least I used to think so, back then. I guess when you live alone outside of a pack, you never truly feel safe. Even with the abilities she had, there were always risks and I was always made aware of them. As I bobbed up and down keeping myself afloat in the crystal-clear turquoise water, my mind was racing. I was stressed out and trying to contemplate a way to get myself out of here.

I looked at the walls surrounding me, and they were all perfectly flat, as if molded that way intentionally. As if all the years of corrosion and elements hadn't laid a finger on a single stone. There were no hand holds, or jutted stones I could use to put my feet on. Nothing that could possibly help me escape this watery prison I found myself in. Panic began to flood through my chest. I swam to the base of the well, running my hand along the outside edges just to see if there might be some sort of secret way I could escape. But it was no use, just as I had expected. The edges were perfectly smooth.

I held my breath and dove back underwater, swimming down as far as I could, but even with my eyes open, I couldn't see any type of exit down here. I couldn't even really see to the bottom of the well. I surfaced and caught my breath, trying not to panic further. I was trapped. "My mom is going to straight kill me if I survive this." I said out loud. My voice sounded meek and frail, muted out by the large stone structure I was entrapped within.

"Then we might as well get you up and out of there, don't you think, little one?" A voice that sounded like liquid gold, purred from somewhere above me. I froze. That sheer and utter terror that grips onto you when something unexpected happens, tore through my chest like a freight train. I thought I was alone... but apparently not. The shock and terror that flooded my chest quickly started to dissipate, and I snapped out of it just long enough to look up. Standing at the top of the well was the most gorgeous man I had ever in my life laid eyes on. At the time I didn't appreciate his beauty as I was too young to care about trivial things like that. But looking back I can see now what I missed back then. I also knew he was tall but not specifics, he's actually 6' 3".

He had golden blonde hair that was cut into different lengths down to his shoulders and it seemed to sparkle in the sunshine. His body was chiseled and defined, I could see parts of his muscles peeking through the black button down shirt he was wearing. His facial features were perfectly symmetrical, high cheekbones and perfect porcelain skin free of any marks or blemishes.

He had the most beautiful golden colored eyes that seemed to glint and shine, even as far away as I was from him. I had no idea who or what he was, but I knew I should be afraid... I was afraid. Just the way he was standing there, silently, screamed power. I watched as he set down a gold suit jacket, which he had just taken off as he started to lower the bucket down to me. He was going to save me... I think...

Once the initial shock began to wear off, and I actually registered the color of his eyes, the panic came flooding back full force. He wasn't just a strangely beautiful man, he was a Reaver... I should have known immediately, but I knew now. I could tell by the way he was literally dripping in gold, that should have been my first clue. All Reavers have eyes the colors of precious metals and voices just as silky and smooth. They usually tended to wear their chosen color as well, which this one had definitely chosen gold.

It's like everything about them was made to entrance you and lower your inhibitions... Reavers weren't only powerful, they were the most powerful creatures in this world. It was said that they possessed some of the powers of all the Supernatural beings, plus a few of their very own. My mother hadn't told me many stories of Reavers, but

41

when she did speak of them, it was always in a hushed tone. Almost a reverence, and I never understood why. She never explained when I would question it, either. Who was I to question such things at my age?

My mind flitted back to the dangerous man up above and I looked again to realize the bucket was almost down to me. My heart was racing, beating completely out of my chest. I swear if I had stayed still long enough, you could have seen the ripples in the water from how hard it was thumping. I wondered if Reavers ate children. Or if they liked to eat scared children.

Being 9 years old your mind tends to run a bit rampant, and I had watched too many scary movies to think anything but the absolute worst. The closer the bucket got to me, the worse the tightness in my chest became. Even through all of my stress and panic, the only thing I could focus on was the fact that I was trapped down here, in a beautiful watery grave.

Trapped in an impossible situation, and one of the most deadly creatures in the entire world was waiting for me. He was either going to be my savior, or my demise... and I wasn't sure I wanted to find out which. The bucket finally reached me but I was spinning. My mind wouldn't quiet down long enough for me to make a rational decision. I didn't have to get inside... I could just stay down here. Right? I knew I was trapped no matter what I did... And if the Reaver didn't kill me, my mother would. At that moment, I didn't know which thought was scarier. It was a lose-lose situation.

I hesitated and looked back up at the Reaver who was waiting for me. I hadn't even reached for the rope and bucket yet. I still wasn't sure if I even would. He seemed to be waiting patiently, but why wouldn't he? He knew I had no other way out. "Take the rope." He said. The way his voice sounded as it echoed between the flat stones and nestled its way into my ears, struck enough fear into my small body that I listened. Immediately, I grabbed the rope and climbed into the bucket. I had no other option and we both knew this. I guess if this sealed my fate to death, then I was dying today. All these thoughts, and many even more irrational than those, flashed through my mind as I was being pulled up. My fear started to rage out of control as I was getting closer to the top.

I inhaled slowly and looked up, catching his eyes again before quickly looking away. I had never seen a Reaver in person before, and definitely hadn't ever been this close to one. From everything my mother had taught me about Reavers, I never wanted to be this close. I just kept replaying my death over and over while trying to hold back the tears that were threatening to fall down my cheeks.

After what seemed like forever, I got to the top and the Reaver reached his hand out to grab me. I had no idea what to do. It was like all of my lessons my mother had taught me went straight out the window. I completely froze up. I swear I wanted to fight and protect myself, but I didn't even flinch at his touch as he grabbed my arm and helped me down from the bucket gently.

Surprise overtook me when both feet hit the ground and I was still very much alive. *So much for being able to take care of myself,* I thought. "There you go, little one." He said softly, ignoring my very obvious fear towards him. I didn't reply, unsure of just what I was supposed to say. Thank you for not killing me? I mean, what do you even say? What do you even do? I was pulled from my internal panic when the Reaver spoke again.

"Now how did you manage to get all the way out here anyway?" His voice was soft and gentle. I assumed he was trying not to scare me even worse, which confused me as I was expecting my throat to be ripped out.

I knew better than to believe his silky lies though, this was how they get you… fake trust. I couldn't even bring my mouth to speak. I just stood there, staring at him, fear struck, still trying to hold back the tears that I could feel trying to burst through. I should have ran… I wanted to run, I wanted to scream, or cry or yell… fight… anything but stand there frozen in time like a helpless idiot. I was torn from my panic when he turned around after putting his suit jacket back on, and locked those deadly golden eyes straight onto mine. I shuddered under his fiery gaze. He was so fucking intense. He may not even have to touch me to cause my death. Can you die from panic or shock? My heart was beating so hard I thought it might rip through my ribcage and escape.

Once I snapped out of my temporary stupor, I realized that his eyes were like molten gold. The color seemed to be moving within itself as if his eyes themselves were actually molten gold, and it was being poured back into itself. His expression when getting a good look at me was confused at first.

He raised one eyebrow as if he was trying to figure something out. Then something that resembled realization crossed his features, followed by surprise, as he looked past me into the woods behind us. I had no idea why he was surprised, so I turned to look at what he was looking at, when I heard a deafening growl.

I covered my ears just as a huge silver Wolf with eyes just like mine, platinum, jumped from the trees and charged straight at the Reaver. Panic, again, flooded my chest as I realized that this was my mother. How did she find me? I mean, she had to have known, this was the only place I would have gone. But still, I was very shocked.

I wanted to scream, and yell at her to run, or do anything to stop my mother from attacking from fear of what he would do to her. But I was frozen in place, riddled with fear, once again. I was completely terrified, and forced to stand there and watch, helplessly. To my surprise the Reaver didn't move an inch. Instead, his face hardened.

Every feature he had was outlined as if he were chiseled straight from stone. His golden eyes darkened to almost black. He put out his right hand, open palm, and threw what looked to me like a fluorescent green fireball at my mother. It engulfed her, and the force of impact knocked me back onto my ass. A green string of light and fire stayed attached

44

to his hand as if it were a rope. Wherever his hand moved, my mother inside of the fireball, moved with it.

Just as I thought he was going to throw her back towards the forest with a flick of his wrist, I finally gained my composure and screamed as loud as my 9-year-old self could. My scream wasn't filled with legible words. Instead, it was only a sound. One full of raw emotion, laced with fear and despair. He stopped and looked directly at me. We locked eyes and I knew this was my only chance to try and save her... I overcame my fear in order to beg for my mother's life.

"Stop!!" I cried, taking a step towards him. His hand stopped mid throw, as he narrowed his eyes onto mine. I had no idea where I got the courage to continue to speak, but I knew it was life or death at this point.

"Please, no... please put her down. She's all I have! It's my fault she's here! I snuck away from home... Please don't hurt her." I pleaded. I knew I was rambling, but I tended to do that when I was panicking.

I forced back the lump in my throat, as a single tear rolled down my cheek.

Chapter 6

As if he was forced, he slowly set my mother down and released his fiery hold. I had no idea what he was thinking or feeling because his face was stoic, and no emotion seemed to cross his features. It was only a brief second that he caught me looking at him before I turned and ran to her side.

She had already shifted back into her Human form, and before I could realize what was going on she had grabbed me and was holding me tightly to her chest. Her platinum eyes were darker than I have ever seen them as her Wolf fought to get back out.

"Are you ok Rayne?? Did he hurt you?!" She tore her hardened gaze from the Reaver to inspect me and when I turned to look back at him, he was gone. He saved my life and listened to my pleas, allowing my mother to live… all of this, and I had no idea who he was at the time.

Why would a Reaver do that? It never made any sense to me after all the stories I was told about them. I questioned my mother for months after that, but she refused to tell me anything except it was a fluke. She had every excuse as to why he didn't kill me, but not one of those excuses made any sense. Nothing about that night made any sense to me… it still doesn't. "Rayne? Rayne!"

Wynter called out, snapping me from my memory. I looked up to see that we were already in my backyard. It was so easy to get lost in my own mind when I wasn't the one in control of my body. I wondered if this is how Wynter felt, often being in the background of my mind.

I looked up at my house, the house I had grown up in since I was 12. It was a dark gray with white trim and the door was painted a bright turquoise blue. The house was 2 stories tall, and it was a cookie cutter, much like the rest of them here. It looked just like the one next to it, and the one next to that. The door was the only difference, and it was the only thing that I requested they change when I came here.

I wanted it because the door on my home back on the outskirts of the pack was the same color. My mother and I painted that door together... I spilled paint everywhere, and most of it was still on the porch of my old home. Another memory threatened to pop back into my head regarding it, but I pushed it away. I didn't have time to get lost in my head right now.

"Shit, sorry I was lost in an old memory." I said to Wynter breathlessly, as I changed back into my Human form. I threw on the black sports bra and matching pair of sweatpants I always had stored outside for times like this. Once I was dressed, I sat cross legged on the grass hoping to get just a minute to myself. Thoughts of Eric passed through my mind, causing me to cringe.

I tried not to think about it, which was difficult. Instead, I let the cool breeze flow through my long silver hair, relaxing me a bit. Unfortunately, I knew we wouldn't be here long. I knew my Alpha wanted to speak to me, and he would know exactly when I stepped foot back in pack territory. He probably knew I was here already. I was right, because seconds later I felt the prickle of Alpha Drake as he came through my mind link. "Rayne, my office, now." He spat. I could practically feel the venom coursing through my veins. "We are so dead..." Wynter chimed in, and for the first time I agreed.

After disobeying Alpha Drake, I wasn't sure we would make it out alive... most don't. He wouldn't kill me though, right? I mean, I tried to come up with any reason why he wouldn't. He needs me, I am one of the pack's best fighters... he couldn't sacrifice me...

I was trying to reassure myself, but it wasn't working at all because I knew I was feeding myself lies. Alpha Drake

47

wouldn't have cared if I was Beta Sean, his second in command, in the flesh. I had broken pack rules, and the punishment remains the same regardless of your rank. I inhaled slowly and headed towards town.

The pack house loomed before me, a towering presence in the heart of the town. Its sleek, modern design stretched six stories high, its solid black exterior giving it a very intimidating appearance. Although it had a contemporary look, it had undergone many renovations over the years. As I approached the entrance, the sun's rays danced across the dark windows, creating a dazzling display of light that forced me to squint.

The glare was intense, making it difficult to see as I made my way to the front doors. Two of our pack guards motioned for me to pass through once I reached them. They looked alike in size and stature. They both had large builds, one with dark hair the other with light, both with multiple scars and tattoos. There was no mistaking it, you could tell they were warriors. Most of our pack looked like this, which is what made them so scary.

The Obsidian pack was known for their no mercy attitudes. We were taught this from day one. Had it drilled into our heads. This is how we maintained our elite status. Our pack was absolutely ruthless and we looked the part. I shuddered as the thought of crossing one of the warriors of our pack made its way through my mind. "Hard pass." Wynter snickered. I agreed.

I made my way down the hallway, admiring the photos of the previous Alphas and the warrior memorabilia on my way to Alpha Drake's office. I thought it was really neat that we kept these things up, and I briefly wondered just what might be adorning the hallways in the upper levels. Everything I had ever had to do was on the first level, so I had never been anywhere else inside.

Mostly, I was trying to distract myself because I was shaking like a leaf. Wynter started trembling too as we approached Alpha Drakes office door. My heart was beating out of my chest, and I knew this might be the last time I ever saw the light of day. I tried to cherish our adventure, and all of the scenery we saw today, focusing on the sheer beauty of the last sunrise I may have ever seen.

I swallowed the fear that had been building as I stood outside the door and knocked. No one ever just went into Alpha Drakes office without an invite, that was a death sentence in and of itself. "You may enter." He snarled. He even sounded fucking pissed.

Wynter started to whimper, but I wasn't about to show weakness. I wouldn't give Alpha Drake the pleasure of seeing me unraveled. Especially if this was my last day alive. No one would ever get that pleasure, especially not him. Call me hardheaded, but I didn't care. I inhaled slowly, put on my strongest face, and walked into his office acting like I was completely ready for whatever was coming next. Even if that meant death.

Alpha Drake was facing me in his chair. He was wearing a black and silver suit jacket with a black button down shirt underneath. His Obsidian black hair was perfectly slicked back, as usual. His fingers were intertwined within one another sitting on top of his desk in front of him. His dark blue eyes were darker than I had ever seen them. The different colors of blues were swirling like the waves in the deep.

Power, that was one word I could use to describe him. Complete and utter power was emanating from him in nauseating waves. They washed over me, threatening to consume me. I didn't say a word and neither did he. The air was heavy with tension so thick it was nearly choking me. The silence between us was so intense it had my mind running in every direction, my erratic thoughts threatening to drive me mad.

"Where were you?" He finally asked. I almost thought I heard worry in his voice but was proven wrong when I didn't answer him fast enough. And by fast enough, I mean that very second. He hardly gave me a chance to speak before he exploded. He stood from his chair and slammed his hand down on the desk so hard, he knocked over a glass full of pens which scattered across the desk, causing me to flinch while Wynter let out a yip.

"I will not ask you again, Rayne." He growled, and this time the venom in his voice was deadly. It prickled into my brain, numbing my senses. I panicked internally trying to think of something to say. "I... I was trying to blow off some steam, Alpha." I stuttered, hoping it would suffice. It was the first thing that popped into my head, but we both knew I was a terrible liar.

Unfortunately, I knew my answer wouldn't be good enough for him, but it was too late to take it back now. I saw his face harden and that's when I knew that he knew my answer was complete bullshit. There was no way I was telling him what happened with my Demon and Eric. No possible way... I couldn't even gather the words if I wanted to. In fact, I wasn't sure if I could ever speak about Eric... ever again.

"Tell him the fucking truth, Rayne! Jesus Christ! Why are you so hard headed?!" Wynter screamed. *Not a chance in hell,* I thought. I pushed her out of my mind just as Alpha Drake closed the gap between us. I flinched at his advance which just seemed to piss him off even more. He snarled as he grabbed onto my upper arm. His grip was so fucking tight I couldn't have escaped if I tried. But I didn't try. He yanked on me, causing me to gasp as he basically dragged me through the pack house and outside.

My Alpha had manhandled me on occasion, mostly during training sessions or when he was trying to get his point across, but this was different, this *felt* different. I wasn't even sure that he was in his right mind at this point. The rage emanating from him as he dragged me outside tore through my chest like a flaming sword.

I had seen him upset, but never anything like this. Nothing on this level. I whimpered as I fought to keep up with his long strides. He didn't care, nor did he slow down a single bit. Even though I was tripping on my own feet, and his, he kept going. He didn't stop until we were outside and in the pack training grounds. He threw me away from him, causing me to stumble but I kept my balance, barely. "You want to blow off steam? Let's blow off some fucking steam." He roared.

Wynter was howling at the thought of what was sure to be our death. Her internal banter gave me cold chills. No one ever fought Alpha Drake and lived to tell about it. He was only 26, but he was the most ruthless and powerful Alpha I had ever known. He had started the Obsidian pack years ago when the Red Ace pack had taken his old pack over. They were another larger and stronger pack at the time. They killed his entire family, including his little sister, Reya. He broke from his new Alpha, refusing to bow to him after such monstrosities. He did so bringing a handful of equally pissed off warriors from his old pack with.

Together, they spent the next 8 years building, growing and making a name for themselves, The Obsidian pack. Then Alpha Drake took them and got retaliation for the deaths of his family. He, basically, single handedly slaughtered the Red Ace pack. From the stories, Alpha Drake didn't leave a single soul alive. They say he killed the entire pack one by one. Men, women, and children. They say he made Alpha Jared watch the whole entire thing while the warriors from The Obsidian pack held them all hostage. Then Alpha Drake killed him too.

He then took over his old stomping grounds turning it into his new pack land, which is where we live now. The stories change every time they are retold, and so do the time frames. Sometimes they say 5 years, sometimes 8. I've also heard that he let the children live, same with the women. I've recently heard that he killed the children first to make the families suffer. But regardless, no one fucks with Alpha Drake. So, to say that I was terrified would be an understatement.

"Give him hell." Wynter snarled, snapping me from my thoughts. We were standing across from each other in the training grounds, and from the look of my Alpha, He definitely wanted to fight. "Here we go." I said to Wynter, as I lunged at Alpha Drake. I may have been fucking terrified, but I wasn't about to let him strike first. I trained with him often, and I knew better. I was fast and I knew how to fight. Alpha Drake swung back to deliver what was sure to be a very painful punch to the stomach. I slid underneath his fist and swept his legs out from under him. As he fell, I jumped up and slammed my elbow straight into his sternum. It was a decent hit, but I knew this was the only good hit I would get. I almost wondered if he let me get it, knowing he was going to end me.

He didn't even make a sound as he pushed me off him, sending me flying backwards. He pushed me so hard that I rolled back into a nearby tree on the edge of the training grounds. I heard a crunch as the ribs in my back cracked from the pressure. I choked, trying to catch the wind that was knocked from my lungs as he jumped back to his feet and headed towards me.

Wynter's growl was deep and intense as we got to our feet. I could already feel my ribs knitting themselves back together. And with it came the air I so desperately craved. A rustle in the trees to the side of me made me turn my head, distracted, just as Alpha Drake slammed into me with the force of a freight train.

The back of my head hit the ground with a loud smack, and he was on top of me pinning both of my hands above my head. I tried to escape but it was no use, I couldn't even move under his muscular build. I was 5 foot 7, and muscular built myself due to the daily training, but I was nowhere near strong enough to push him off me. Wynter was snarling in my mind. Alpha Drake locked his ocean blues onto my platinum silvers, and if looks could kill I would have already been dead.

"You are a beautiful little thing aren't you." Alpha Drake murmured while tracing my jawline with his free hand. I turned away from his touch, disgusted, but he grabbed my jaw, forcing me to look at him. Then he leaned down and laid his lips onto mine softly. I froze, and then tried to turn away from him but he had a death grip on my jaw forcing me to stay put. What the fuck was he doing? "It's a shame I have to kill you." He whispered against my lips. "Jesus Christ." Wynter shook. I felt cold chills run down my spine at her words. This was it, everything we had been dreading… everything that I knew was going to happen, was happening… and it was all my fault.

I kept my eyes open, trying to drown out the memories of Eric, my mother, my Demon, training, my pack, everything, as they flashed through my mind over and over, as if on repeat… all of these things haunted me when my eyes were closed. I decided if I was going to die, I wasn't going to shy away from it. I was going to look it straight in the face, even if my reaper had dark blue, ocean colored eyes.

Just as Alpha Drake moved to rip my throat out, a green flash of light hit him, sending him flying off me. I looked up and saw him engulfed in green flames.

Confusion and panic crossed my face, but it was only a brief couple of seconds before I realized what had just happened. I turned towards the tree line where the blast had come from and watched in horror as my Demon stepped out of the trees and lifted Alpha Drake into the sky.

Chapter 7

"Oh my fucking God, it's him!" Wynter shrieked. She was going absolutely insane in my mind. I was overwhelmed with her emotions, causing my heart to flutter in my chest. My mind instantly settled on the events of yesterday and all the things he said to me... I sat up and tried to gather my bearings. I took a breath in trying to comprehend the events that were unfolding.

I should have known that he would be watching. He was *always* watching. My head was pounding, and I could feel warm blood trickling down my brow. The wound would heal, so I wasn't worried about it as it dripped down onto the ground before me.

It hadn't even been 24 hours yet and the words he spoke never rang so true. Panic began to seep into my bones when I realized that if he doesn't think I'm safe here he could just break the contract and take me. My thoughts were jumbled and confused.

"Wait, did Alpha Drake just kiss me, and then try to kill me? What the fuck?" I said to Wynter in a daze. "Who cares, Mr. Kane is literally right there! He saved you!" Wynter swooned. Her emotions were so strong they were making me dizzy. I rolled my eyes at her and then I turned to look at him again, my Demon. As if he knew I was looking, he turned and locked those golden, molten orbs onto mine.

He was standing there looking like a fucking God-like being. The sun was glinting off his golden hair casting shimmers that danced around his high cheekbones. With the way the sun was shining behind him, I half expected him to sprout golden angel wings and fly away.

His dark red suit jacket was partially open, and I could see the gold suit vest underneath. The muscles he tried so hard to hide under his clothes were peeking through, as every piece of fabric clung to them like magnets. There was a fire in his eyes, much like when he killed Eric... the thought made me shudder.

He was fucking pissed then... and he was fucking pissed now. But this time he wasn't mad at me... I hoped. There was no doubt that he was absolutely breathtaking in every way, shape, and form, but he was the scariest man I had ever met.

He still had Alpha Drake suspended in midair, engulfed in a green fireball. "Rayne, come here." He snapped. My name rolled off his tongue like velvet. Wynter yipped with pleasure hearing his voice, and once her infatuation passed through my gut, the terror hit me. I knew I had no choice but to listen and obey him... once again. He would only force me if I refused.

Fear gripped me, and seemed to hold me down. Even when I tried to move, my body wasn't cooperating. This seemed to be a normal response when I was around him. "What the fuck are you waiting for?? Go!" Wynter begged.

He narrowed his eyes at me which was all it took to kick my ass into motion. Reluctantly, I got up and started walking towards him. Wynter's emotions were stronger the closer we got to him, almost overwhelming me with a mixture of butterflies, excitement, and lust. I had to push her out of my mind to escape the emotional tendrils that threatened to consume us both. As soon as she was out of my mind and no longer influencing my thoughts, all of those emotions were suddenly replaced with just one. Mind numbing fear.

As I closed the gap between us, my Demon reached out and grabbed me by the waist, pulling me closer. I could feel the hard ridges of his muscles as his chest pressed against mine. As a reaction, I put both of my hands on his chest, but quickly moved them away. I whimpered quietly, unsure if he would be upset or not. I knew he was already pissed off and I didn't want to make it worse. I know what happens when he's mad.

Wynter was threatening to push her way back through. I fought against her to keep her down. Her emotional rampage was not helping. I forced her, again, to the back of my mind. I couldn't let her to the forefront, just in case she tried something stupid, like shifting right here in front of him. I wouldn't put it past her. My focus was all over the place, but once I had a few moments to breathe I honed in on the fact that his touch was electrifying. It always was. It sent chills down my arms and spine. I fought to hide my reaction so he wouldn't see. I was absolutely terrified, but my body seemed to have a reaction of its own.

"Are you hurt?" He growled. Concern and anger were clear in the molten gold of his eyes, but nowhere else on his face did he show a singular emotion. Still, I could tell he was furious. The rage emanated from his energy like waves of angry golden mist.

"No, I'm fine." I said, wiping the blood from my brow. His face hardened at the sight, and he turned his death glare onto Alpha Drake who was still suspended midair.
He then flung his wrist and threw Alpha Drake down right at our feet. His body slammed into the ground so hard, I heard bones breaking.

"Get up, Wolf." He spat. Alpha Drake looked at the golden God before him with rage and fear mixed in his eyes. He got to his feet, but he never broke eye contact.
"And just what the fuck do you think you were doing out here?" My Demon spat. His silky voice sounded like poison sliding through the air between them. He never let go of my waist. I was afraid to do anything but stand there, frozen, and hoping that I survived this ordeal.

"She disobeyed the pack rules and left the territory, she needed to be punished." Alpha Drake spewed. Honestly, by the way Alpha Drake said those words, I couldn't help but wonder if we were about to need a new Alpha. Wynter snickered in my mind at the thought.

"You will pay for this Rayne, do not think this is over." Alpha Drake sneered through our mind link. His words replaced my fear with anger. I was definitely hotheaded, and I had a one track mind when it came to my anger. I glared in my Alpha's direction and took a step forward, out of my Demon's arms. I wasn't completely sure what I planned to do just yet, but Alpha or not, he can't just treat me like that.

"Please stop Rayne, it's not worth it!" Wynter pleaded.

"Yes, it is." I growled, not caring what happened next. I was only seeing red and I knew I would possibly regret it later, but it didn't matter right now. I had only taken 2 steps forward when I felt a stiff arm blocking my path.

"This is over, Wolf. You will not touch her again. If you lay a singular finger on her I will have it removed, along with your tongue." The words flew from my Demon's lips with such force and fluidity, that even I stepped back.

Did he hear the mind link? How did he know what Alpha Drake had said? Did he just give me permission to disobey my Alpha? Not that I would dare… but damn. I was beginning to panic again.

When Alpha Drake didn't respond, I was nervous about the outcome. "Do not make me remind you of our agreement, Wolf." My Demon said, enunciating that last word as if it tasted bad coming out of his mouth. It seemed that he did not like Wolves… and I just so happened to be one, so that stressed me out even more.

The agreement… it always floated in my mind reminding me that I actually belonged to my Demon, and Alpha Drake was essentially babysitting me until then. Insert eyeroll here. I'm not a child anymore. "One more year is all you have left, Wolf. Remember, what I have given you I can very easily take back. Do not test me." My Demon purred, with an evil look in his fire ridden eyes. Then he waved his hand as if to shoo my Alpha away. I watched as Alpha

Drake turned from us, transformed into his Wolf, and ran, leaving us alone on the training grounds.

When I was 12 years old my mother was killed. My Demon found me and he took me to The Obsidian pack, where he made a deal with the most feared Alpha in the world, Alpha Drake. The terms of our arrangement were starkly clear: my protection. But what my Demon had offered Alpha Drake in return, I could only speculate. All I knew was I had less than a year left and he would be back to collect his prize... me... and there was absolutely nothing I could do to stop it...

Chapter 8

I couldn't help but stare at my Demon's exquisite beauty noticing how chiseled his features were. His jawline was perfectly straight, even though I could see he was clenching and unclenching it as he watched Alpha Drake run off into the trees. I should be upset with him. I should be hurt and angry over what he did to me yesterday, and over Eric, but my mind was so distracted. I could barely breathe, let alone think straight.

His words flooded back into my mind and it had me wondering if he was right about us being mated. Of all the stories I've heard of Reavers, I still didn't understand how one creature could be so alluring, but equally terrifying.

He brought the type of fear that gripped onto your very soul, ripping it from your body at the time of his own choosing. Yet, on most occasions our encounters left me wanting more. Wynter had her own dialogue going in my mind and I quickly snapped out of it as he turned to face me.

He raised his right hand and put it over the wound on my brow, healing it instantly with a slight purple light. It felt tingly but the pain was suddenly gone. I knew Reavers had healing powers, I had heard this before. Still, it was strange to see it in action. It had me curious as to what else they could do. "I would looove to find out." Wynter chimed in with a snort. She was always answering my thoughts, even when they weren't directed at her. "I'm sure you would." I exclaimed.

"If he so much as breathes in your general direction I demand to know about it. I will cut the lungs from his chest." My Demon spat, enunciating the last few words. I tried not to flinch at the anger in his voice. I wanted to ask him why me? I wanted answers, I wanted more than just a cryptic sentence out of him. But I also didn't... I was more terrified of him than I was curious as to his actions. And with the lack of alcohol in my system, I wasn't daring enough to speak up. I chose to remain still and push my fear down so he couldn't see it… hopefully.

He seemed as if he was having an internal battle before his eyes flashed black, and he closed them in a threatening way. His jaw tightened while he held back, what I assumed to be an outburst of sorts, which caused a new wave of terror to ripple through me. Then my mind link was activated, but it wasn't the venom of Alpha Drake that I felt. The link was smoother, like liquid gold.

"I will take his fucking hands should he touch you again." My Demon's silky golden voice infiltrated my mind, making my Wolf go wild. So he does have a Wolf! I had heard stories but never experienced it before. Though I didn't think a Reaver could actually shift, not that he had, but I was running through so many scenarios of what the extent of his powers could actually be.

My thoughts were running rampant through my mind. He suddenly closed the already small gap between us with infinite speed. I jumped back defensively, but he pulled me close and grabbed my chin like he had before, tilting my head so I was looking directly into his golden eyes. There was something new burning in them, something different.

"These lips." He growled while running this thumb along the fullness of my bottom lip. I ignored the fire coursing through my veins as he did this. "They belong to me. Along with the rest of you." His eyes darkened as I followed his gaze to my partially parted lips. "No one will ever taste you again." His words were more of a warning, and I completely understood the message.

Rage, fierce and free, boiled through my body. It coursed through my veins taking my freedom with it. The freedom that I have never truly had, but that I fight so fucking hard for. I tried to keep the anger from my face, but

I wasn't as skilled as my Demon in that department. He snickered under his breath and at that was my snapping point. I was done being submissive. "What?" I growled. "I love when you get angry." He replied, which made my blood boil even hotter.

"No, you love inciting my anger!" I hissed. Somehow, he stepped closer to me, enveloping me in his forest musk. The edge of citrus that danced along my nostrils calmed me, settling into my chest which then calmed my erratic breathing, but that also annoyed me because I didn't want it to calm me.

The amusement danced within his eyes as he looked down at me as if I were a fragile doll that he was afraid to break. "What I love is the immense power I hold over you." He paused, just long enough for my lips to part, but the snarky retort I was thinking never made its way out because he began speaking again.

"The way a simple touch along your jawline, immediately transforms all of that fiery rage into burning desire, leaving you completely vulnerable to me. The way you look up at me as if begging me to completely devour you... and you haven't said a word. The way you haven't taken a single breath since I started talking. What I love... is the way my words completely destroy you, yet, you want to hear more, you wish for me to do more despite your attitude and verbal refusals. That... that is what I love." He purred.

I sucked air into my lungs, pissed that his words were so spot on. The fact that I hadn't taken a single breath while he was talking was infuriating because I didn't even realize it until that very moment. The insane hold he has on me does nothing but piss me off further, but he is not wrong... I want more and we both know it. Even through my fear I can't deny that he puts me in a trance everytime he opens his mouth.

I stepped away from him, trying anything to calm the heat between my thighs. I exhaled and closed my mouth. "You're wrong." I snipped. "And you're lying." He retorted, stepping near me again. I put my hand out to stop him from coming closer, but my attempt was futile when he reached out and pulled me to him by my waist.

"Stop me then." He said, before leaning in towards me. My breath hitched in my throat as he closed the miniscule gap between us. Heat flushed my face and Wynter began squealing as he moved in closer. I felt his hand snake around the back of my head, wrapping into my hair but I couldn't even move. His lips were so close to mine, a single movement forward would have sealed the entire deal, but he stopped just before we touched. "Stop me..." He purred. His minty breath danced along my lips. "I...I..." I stammered, pissed off that we both knew there was no way in hell I was actually going to do it.

"Who's lying now?" He whispered so close to me that I felt his lips brush against mine slightly. "Ugh!" I growled, pushing him away from me. "You are the fucking worst!" I snapped and turned from him, finally able to grip back onto my anger. He snickered which made me even more upset. It felt like hellfire coursing through my entire body.

"Regardless of how you may feel or not feel about me, I mean it, Rayne. He so much as looks at you wrong and I will pluck his eyes from their sockets. Do you understand?" I turned to speak but didn't get the chance before he was gone.

I exhaled a breath I only then realized I was holding. I ran my fingers along my bottom lip, absentmindedly. My head was swimming, trying to piece everything together. I was still shaken up and left trying to put the pieces back together of my latest encounter with my Demon. He was so quick to change the subject, so quick to destroy me and leave... I was afraid that maybe he wasn't actually gone. Maybe he was standing behind me now, but the way I was finally able to breathe told me differently. It only took me seconds to gather my composure and push any confusion and mixed feelings from my mind.

Once I was able to gather myself, I started walking back towards my house which was about a mile away. I couldn't help but feel strange at our interaction. As afraid of him as I was, and as upset about many things, especially what he did to Eric, he did save my life. In fact, he had never actually hurt me, now that I think about it... I know for a fact that Alpha Drake was going to kill me, but my Demon wouldn't let him. Had it not been for that arrangement I believe Alpha Drake would have gone through with it. And Eric? Well, he would have gone through with it for sure. He told me as much.

I was finally starting to compartmentalize my feelings and be able to sort them out. I would have been raped, had my Demon not intervened. I would have been killed, had he also not intervened... maybe I just haven't given him a chance, a real chance. Except I tend to forget one small fact, he owns me. He fucking owns me... It's not like I would ever have a choice in the matter.

Frustration bubbled through my veins as a chill came over my body. Anger, sticky and rough, tangled its way through those thoughts. I exhaled in frustration and slammed my front door as I stormed inside. I would never truly be free.

"I don't know why you fight him so hard. He clearly has a thing for you, and don't act like you wouldn't bow the fuck down and do whatever the hell that man asked. Have you seen him? I mean, open your fucking eyes, woman! He's a goddamn heartthrob. Any female would be begging on their knees for him to even look in their general direction and here he is practically throwing himself at you! Stop resisting!" Wynter exclaimed.

I shook my head. She truly had no idea how I was feeling. Even being inside of my mind 24/7. She was completely oblivious to my feelings. I knew arguing with her wasn't going to help either of us, but I had to get my point across.

"Well, I'm not fucking blind, Wynter. I can see that he's sexy as fuck. I mean no one in their right mind would deny that fact, but looks aren't everything! He's going to keep me locked up like a fucking prisoner, and don't think for one second that he wont. You heard what he said about taking

Alpha Drake's organs. He won't let me out of his sight and we both know it." I growled.

"Then don't leave his sight. Who the fuck cares, Rayne? You're going to push him away and then you're going to be sorry that you did." Wynter replied. Annoyance bubbled into my chest causing me to exhale out loud. "Ok, and explain to me how not being haunted by a Demon 24/7 is a bad thing?" I scoffed.

"Jesus, I can't believe you are being so dumb right now! Because then Alpha Drake will have his way with you! You know, just as well as I know that he's in love with you. And without Mr. Kane, you are so fucked. You think you'll be locked up with him? Wait until Alpha Drake gets his hands on you... Rayne, you'll never see the light of day again. You know it's true, he will make you Luna whether you want it or not. Now stop acting like you're brand new and get the fuck over yourself." Wynter scolded.

I didn't want to admit that she was right. I knew what would happen if I didn't have my Demon... more than he haunted me, he protected me. I was just upset and trying to avoid the truth. I sighed out loud before flopping down on my bed. "Ugh! I know, Wynter. I fucking know, but I don't know what to do! I fucking loathe being told what I can and can't do. Whatever happened to freedom?" I growled.

She was just about to answer when I felt the all too familiar Venom from the mind link of Alpha Drake. It danced along the edges of my mind, settling straight into the pit of my stomach. I knew it was coming... and I feared the repercussions after everything that happened today.

"Rayne, report to my office, immediately." He hissed. I could tell he was holding his anger back, trying to sound less venomous with his words, but it didn't really help.

I fought back the bile rising in my throat and sat up. I looked at myself in the mirror and rolled my eyes so fucking hard it actually hurt.

"Oh boy." Wynter scoffed.

Chapter 9

espite the fact that I knew Alpha Drake couldn't hurt me anymore, my legs were still shaking like a leaf when I got to his office door. I squared my shoulders and held my head high, waiting to be called inside. Not that it would change my outcome at all. I was only outside of his door only a few agonizing seconds before I heard him. "You may enter, Rayne." His tone was rough, and he didn't sound happy in the least bit. I cringed, and Wynter whined when she heard the straight acid seeping through his words.

Alpha Drake exudes power. You could feel it rolling off him in waves at all times. Even when my Demon had saved me earlier, Alpha Drake had still exuded immense power. He was looking him dead in the eyes, not knowing if that would be the last sight he ever saw. Still, even faced with possible death, he never backed down. It was terrifying, really. The man was fearless, and I knew from the stories that he was also ruthless. Those two combinations are volatile. At that moment I wasn't sure who I was more afraid of... Alpha Drake or my Demon

I swallowed the lump that was sitting in my throat, took a deep breath, and stepped inside the door shutting it softly behind me. "Yes, Alpha?" I said, trying, and failing, to keep the snark from my voice. I wasn't planning on being such a bitch, but the second I was back in the room with him I got upset, and couldn't help it. I was met with a hardened glare filled with anger.

I could see signs of an internal struggle emanating from Alpha Drake's facial expression. I had never seen him this way before. It was like he was struggling to keep his composure. He was a hardened, ruthless, murderer. He didn't show fear, he didn't show emotion... but I could see it, and I could see he was trying to hide it. "I just wanted to... " He stopped, and readjusted the diamond encrusted watch on his left wrist before continuing. "Apologize for today." He said softly, while exhaling a ragged breath. He was struggling to get the words out.

I was dumbfounded. Wynter gasped in my mind at his words, causing my eyes to widen in shock. Did he just apologize to me? I swear he had never apologized to anyone a day in his life, I couldn't believe my ears. This surely wasn't the Alpha Drake that I knew... the Alpha Drake that killed people for less. "I really was going to kill you, Rayne, and I know you know it as well." His words sent a wave of pain down my chest.

Wynter chimed in. "Why are you feeling guilty? He's the one who tried to kill you!" I pushed her out of my mind with a frustrated groan. Why was I feeling guilty? Yea, sure, I disobeyed my Alpha and left pack territory, but it's not like I killed anyone or betrayed the pack. I just... left. I never planned to actually stay gone. I didn't actually run away like I had thought about. I was always planning to come back. I just needed... time.

I hated how his words turned on me, making me feel like the bad guy. Just something about the look in his eyes was really getting to me. Like he was disappointed in me. Like out of everyone in this pack, I should have known better. But that's the thing, I did know better. I do... and somehow, his sheer disappointment in me hurts worse than anything else.

He startled me, pulling me from my self pity when he closed the gap between us and grabbed me by the throat, slamming me into the wall behind us. It knocked the wind out of me. I was determined not to show weakness, so I did my best to keep my composure. Alpha Drake was always handsy and cruel, so this type of treatment I was a lot more used to. He held me there for a few minutes leaving me just enough room to breathe, barely. He lightly ran his finger along my jawline like he had before, this time ending on my bottom lip pulling it down a little. Wynter howled in disgust. I didn't dare move a muscle.

Not that he wasn't attractive and didn't have all the girls in the pack swooning over him, but personality wise? He was the fucking worst. I could never be with him. I would kick, claw, scream, and fight until he killed me, should I ever be put in that situation. "I don't want you to think what you did was ok though, because it wasn't." He said softly in my ear, his face nearly touching mine.

"For your punishment you will do extra rounds all next week." He growled. Less emotion, more Alpha in his tone. He released his hold on my neck shortly after, causing me to gasp for air. "Yes, Alpha Drake." I choked out, and saw the corner of his lip curl into what looked like the start of a devious smile. The man never smiled and I wasn't sure what he was even almost smiling for, but I didn't have time to think about it before he continued.

"You may have that filthy Reaver on your side... for now. But I have you for the next year, and that's all I need to ensure I get everything I want. He can't have you, not yet. I don't care how much he begs, pleads, or bargains... watching him suffer will be the ultimate payback." He stated, matter of factly.

Immediately, the guilt from earlier faded from my chest and was replaced with burning rage. I was furious at the thought of being used to hurt my Demon. "Let me out, Rayne! Let me shift! I'm going to kill him for that!" Wynter was furious, screaming for me to let her have her revenge. She was so protective over my Demon, she saw red often when it came to him. I took a slow breath in, closed my eyes and exhaled. "Yes Alpha." I hoped the words stung him as much as they did leaving my lips. I wanted to say so many more things but I knew better.

"Oh and Rayne?" Alpha Drake said. I shot him the best glare I could muster. "I *will* have everything I want." He enunciated each word with a fierce growl, looking directly into my eyes when he said it. I could feel the absolute possessiveness rolling off him. "Fuck that! You're not getting shit!" Wynter cried in my mind. I cringed at the thought of being with Alpha Drake. I wanted so badly to tell him to fuck right the fuck off. I was so disgusted I wanted to scream, I wanted to do literally anything but stand there at attention… but I was frozen in place, trying to hide my anger. It wasn't worth poking the wasps' nest. Then with a wave of his hand, I was dismissed. Of course he would shoo me away like a fly that was bothering him when he was done with me. I turned around and burst out of his door, fuming.

As I stomped my way down the hallway, I fought to keep my emotions at bay. I have never had a good experience with Alpha Drake, and I was surprised that he even let me stay in his pack for as long as I had. We butted heads from the first day I arrived here, and it has only gotten worse over the years.

"What a manipulative piece of shit! What game is he playing at?" Wynter spat. "I'm not sure, but if he keeps touching me my Demon is going to end him!" I snarled, then I cringed at the thought. Did I want my Demon to end him? Take his hands and deliver them to his doorstep. Rip his lungs from his chest? Pluck his eyes from their very sockets? The thought made me shudder. *Wait, why wouldn't I want him to?* My thoughts were a fucking mess.

"Didn't Alpha Drake already get everything he wanted? Isn't that why there was an agreement in the first place? He got his revenge, he got his pack, his territory, what else could he possibly need?! Ugh… besides me, anything but me." I whined to Wynter. She agreed. "I swear if I have to hear his goddamn venomy voice one more time I might just kill over." She cackled, but I didn't laugh. The questions swirled in my head as I headed home. I was so distracted and lost in my thoughts conversing with Wynter I didn't even realize where I was walking until I slammed into something solid.

Dazed, I stumbled back and looked up into a large pair of crystal-clear, neon green eyes. "Shit, I'm sorry! Are you ok?" He stammered trying to collect himself. His voice was husky and deep but he had a baby face. "Yea, yea, I'm fine, no worries." I said, snapping out of my own thoughts. He was only a little taller than me, about 5 foot 9 inches. Dark, short, clean-cut hair and a muscular build. I noticed he didn't have any scars on his arms or face. He must not be part of Alpha Drake's minions. *Thank god.* I thought. That's all I needed tonight was to deal with more Alpha Drake. Wynter made a gagging sound at Alpha Drake's name, and I giggled internally.

He stuck his hand out. "Hi Rayne. I'm Roman." I looked at him curiously. "How do you know my name?" I asked. He chuckled. "Everyone knows your name. You're the girl protected by the Reaver." He said. I rolled my eyes. "More like imprisoned." I huffed. He started to chuckle again.

"Well don't let him know I plowed you over... I value my life, thanks." He was laughing as he said it, but he shifted uncomfortably, so I knew he was partially serious. I snorted. "It's not like that." I said to him, but I didn't really care if he believed me or not. No one else did so what did it matter?

"Don't even think about it, mister. Our man will tear you limb from limb." Wynter growled. She seemed all too happy to claim him. "Shush, he's not our man, he's terrifying!" I exclaimed. She rolled her eyes. "Speak for yourself!" I ignored her and pushed her out of my mind. Roman was looking at me with a weird look.

"Sorry, trying to calm my Wolf. We have had one hell of a night." I said. "Well, I will leave you guys to it then, have a good night!" He sighed. "Thanks, you too." I said. I could tell he wanted to say more but refrained, and I was thankful he did. A brief flash of Eric made me cringe. I quickly pushed the vision away. There was no way I was going to let a cute baby face become Eric number 2. I had to get home anyway, I had training in the morning.

"Speaking of training, we have to be on extra patrol duty for the next week. Barf." I gagged. Wynter mimicked my gagging noises and we laughed hysterically all the way back to my house. It was nice to laugh and forget the drama for a bit. Once I got home, I checked my cell phone. I never took it with me anywhere, defeating the whole point of having one, I know. But it was so annoying going off all the time. I really hated it. There were 2 messages. I clicked open the first one, it was from Jae.

'Hey girl, have you heard from Eric? I know you probably don't want to talk about it after the other night, but he didn't show up for football practice this morning and the guys are worried. I figured if he would talk to anyone it would be you.'

My heart sank. You know that feeling of sheer panic that latches onto you and threatens to eat you alive? The one that takes your breath away has you feeling like you are falling from the highest peak? Well, it engulfed me, sinking its sharp canines straight into the back of my neck. Tears began to fill my eyes as I typed out a reply.

'I haven't heard from him at all. Now I'm worried, do you think he's ok?'

I was a terrible liar but I had no idea what I was supposed to do. I had a feeling that Eric's body would never be found, but I couldn't give anything away. He was dead because of me, after all. My guilt was already at an all-time high over it.

'I don't know... I don't want to jump to any conclusions, but I think his family is going to file a police report if they can't locate him by tomorrow.' She replied.

The tears fell as I fought to think of something to say in return. This was all my fucking fault, all of it...

'Fuck, I'm still mad at him but I really hope he's ok. Please, keep me informed.'

I didn't even read the second message, it was from Brett, and I had a feeling it was about Eric as well. I rushed through my bedroom door and straight to my shower. The hot water did little to ease the ball of pain I noticed sitting in the middle of my stomach, or stifle the tears that streamed down my face in waves. What a fucking mess I had gotten myself into. I stayed in the shower a bit longer than I anticipated, letting all of my tears fall. I hated to cry so if I was already crying I figured I'd better let it all out. Ugly crying was not my favorite thing to do. Once I was out of the shower and ready for bed, finally, I picked up my phone and clicked open Brett's message. My hands were shaking as I read his words.

'We need to talk about the Reaver who dragged you out of my party the other night.'

Of course he would want to talk about the literal only thing I didn't want to talk about ever again. I sighed and pulled the covers up before replying.

'What about him?' I replied, barely able to type.

'You tell me. Explain to me first, how are you still alive? And second, where the fuck is Eric?'

I inhaled slowly. How exactly would I explain this? Brett knew, he had to know. He knew I was a Wolf, he knew about the Reavers, he had to put two and two together.

'Look, it's a long story with the Reaver, but I do not know where Eric is. Jae already asked me the same question.'

I knew my answer wouldn't suffice, but I didn't know what else to say. I had to keep it simple…

'He was looking at you like you were a piece of meat, Rayne. Don't play stupid with me. You shouldn't be alive… the Humans may not know shit, but I am not a simple Human.' He replied.

I waited a few minutes while trying to calm my erratically beating heart before I finally replied.

'I know, Brett. But I can't help you.'
My words were pointless, I knew he wouldn't let up.

'You can't or you won't?'
My hands were shaking so badly at this point that I physically dropped my phone. The wind chimes that were my text tone went off again, and it was the first time that I thought they were the most annoying thing I had ever heard before. It had me wondering why I even chose that to begin with?

"I don't want to say you can trust him, Rayne, because I have no idea… but he is a Wolf…" Wynter said, briefly breaking me from my panic ridden state. While she was right, it meant nothing. Wolf of not, I couldn't trust anyone. I ignored her and clicked back open Brett's message so I could reply. With shaking fingers I began to type.

'Do you value your life? Because if you do, you will stop interrogating me and leave this well enough alone.'

Unfortunately, my response was partially incriminating, but I didn't know how else to get him off my back. Luckily, he didn't reply after that.

I spent the next 3 hours of tossing and turning in a panic ridden state. My mind was racing and replaying the entire scene with Eric over and over again, before I finally drifted off to sleep.

Chapter 10

was in my room, except it wasn't my room… It looked different, somehow… I got up and went to my closet to find something to wear. As I opened the closet door and peered inside I noticed that everything in my wardrobe was not mine… The closet was full of frilly dresses, blouses with frilly sleeves, some sort of professional looking pencil dresses, and jeans. Tons of jeans. It seemed that none of these items of clothing were anything I would have actually bought for myself.

After looking through all the items available, I picked out a black and silver shimmery dress. It was short and had only one shoulder. It was tight fitting and accentuated all of my curves. I picked it because it seemed like the most *me* styled thing in there.

A pair of black and silver, sparkly, six-inch heels followed. They looked like they were made for this dress. I didn't normally wear heels, but these were just calling out to me. Plus the rest of the shoes in this closet were flats or very pointy ugly heels. I never would have worn heels like that, and flats don't go with club dresses.

After looking in the mirror I noticed that my long silver hair flowed down my back in beachy waves. That is strange... my hair was always pin straight. I've never worn it wavy before. It looked nice though, maybe a change was needed. I took another glance at myself in the mirror before I left, admiring the way the colors of my dress and shoes accented my hair.

Plus, something about this dress just brought out the platinum in my silver eyes. I took one last glance, still thinking something was off, but I just couldn't put my finger on it. I headed downstairs to my kitchen and grabbed a bagel. I threw some jalapeno cream cheese from my fridge on it, and then I headed out the door. I wasn't even sure where I was heading but my feet just seemed to know.

I was surprised when I ended up stopping in front of the pack house. I had no idea why I would ever want to be there. The thought of coming here of my own volition made me want to hurl. I was just about to turn around and head the other way when Alpha Drake walked out the front door. I froze in a mixture of terror and disgust.

My emotions were all over the place at the sight of him. No doubt he was gorgeous with his dark skin, dark hair, and dark blue eyes. No one ever said he wasn't attractive. It was his personality that I hated. He had on a black suit jacket, and pants. Platinum silver shoes with a matching suit vest and tie. His dark hair was tousled and rough.

He matched my dress, eyes, and hair, perfectly. It was as if we had planned this outfit. I had very mixed feelings as he walked towards me with his arm out. I grabbed onto his arm automatically, as he greeted me. This was not at all what I expected from him, or me.

"Good morning my Luna." He said, kissing my lips softly. He tasted like the ocean waves and something else I couldn't quite place. For some reason I reciprocated, but I would never do that. He pulled away and locked his eyes onto mine, which pulled me from my thoughts.

Looking up at him I could see what looked like... love, possibly, radiating from them. My eyes widened in shock as his words finally registered in my brain. *His Luna? Oh, hell no!* I thought. Something isn't right, this didn't feel right. First off, I have never seen any emotion emanating from Alpha Drake. None, besides anger and the conflict from last night, of course.

And second off, I would never be his Luna. This was too weird, and I was suddenly terrified. "Are you ready for The Edge tonight?" He asked, distracting me momentarily. There wasn't even a slight hint of acid in his voice. The

74

Edge was a nightclub that was just 20 minutes off the pack lands. It was a place where a lot of Wolves, Humans, and other Supernatural creatures frequented. We had our ins with a special key phrase and stamp. It let the bartenders and bouncers know who we were, and more importantly, who our Alpha was.

I had never been there before. You had to be 19 before Alpha Drake would allow permission, and nobody was allowed to go there unless Alpha Drake was going as well. He rarely went, so that meant this was going to be a big event, and a lot of our pack would be attending. The rules were put in place as a precaution to prevent any unnecessary drama.

With a mix of Humans and Supernatural creatures, anything could go wrong. I was feeling nervous and wondering what in the fuck was going on. I attempted to reach out to Wynter, noting that she had been quiet this entire time. That wasn't at all like her. I was met with silence.

Wynter wasn't in my mind and no matter how much I tried to reach out to her she never replied. Just the mere thought of being here alone without her, scared the shit out of me. Where was my Wolf? I was in a silent panic. I knew something was wrong, I just couldn't put my finger on it.

I was in a full blown panic. I didn't want to have to resort to this, but I had no other choice. So, for the first time since my Demon had saved me and threatened Alpha Drake, I used my mind link and contacted him. I was too nervous and confused to really have a full-on conversation. Instead, I left him with one uneasy phrase. "I… I need you." Then I ended the link.

The amount of speed in which my Demon instantly appeared in front of us had me rattled. I would never get used to the materialization, but I knew that's how he traveled on most occasions. Alpha Drake stopped, frozen, in what seemed like fear and anger. I could feel the muscles on his arm flexing at the sight. He was grinding his teeth so loudly I thought they might crack. The silence didn't last long before Alpha Drake spoke.

"Reaver, to what do we owe the pleasure?" The venom was clear in his words. His ridicule was too much because the next thing I knew Alpha Drake was flying across the street and slammed into the house nearby. My Demon then stepped directly in front of me and grabbed my shoulders.

"Are you ok, darling?" I could hear the worry dripping off his words. Something about him felt different. It felt familiar... solid maybe? Like he may have been the only real thing around me. "No, something is wrong. I don't know why I'm here. I don't know what I'm doing with him, and I can't hear Wynter." I stammered, as tears began to form in my eyes.

He brought me into a bear hug, immediately pulling me to his chest. An intense feeling of safety washed over me like a soothing blanket, which was very different from my usual fear of him. Everything here was different though... wherever 'here' was.

"Rayne, darling. I'm here, you're alright. Shhh." His silky voice washed over me, stilling my ever beating heart. He had never spoken so kindly before. He softly ran his hand through my hair until my breathing calmed down and returned to normal. I pulled out of his arms only partially so I could look up at him. I had been this close to him more times than I could count, but never without an immense feeling of terror and fear. This was... different.

Slowly, as if he realized I was looking, he smirked and slid his hand around my neck. I was expecting pain, but instead I was met with an intense fire coursing through my veins. With the absence of Wynter's internal dialogue, this was very foreign.

"Do... do you really think I'm your mate?" I asked, suddenly getting a grip on my scattered emotions. I have no idea why I asked this instead of any of the other hundred burning questions running through my mind. He tightened his grip on my throat, but not enough to truly hurt me, just enough to assert dominance, which he didn't even need to do because I was already feeling very cornered even though I wasn't in a corner at all.

"I don't give a single fuck who your mate is. I challenge anyone who thinks they could take you from me." He snarled. In any regular situation I would have instantly gotten pissed that he thinks I'm a belonging to be owned, but for some reason his words made me feel like I was the most important person in his life, and maybe I was. "Do you promise?" I replied, still unsure where my newfound bravery was coming from. He hadn't taken his eyes off mine since I pulled away and looked up at him, but the molten gold seemed to darken as he articulated his next sentence.

"Oh, I promise, darling. No one will ever lay a single finger on you. You belong to me and no one touches what is mine." He said, and then he slid his hand from my neck and wrapped it around the back of my head, tangling his fingers through my hair. I gasped as he tilted my head up and pulled me in close. My heart began to beat completely out of control. My bravery began to waver the moment I felt his lips brush against mine, but rather than kissing me like I thought he was going to, he spoke.

"Wake up, Rayne, wake up…" His golden voice echoed in my mind as I shot up out of bed panting heavily. Oh, my good fucking God, it was just a dream. Relief flooded into my chest, overthrowing the panic and distress I was currently feeling. I looked up and I swear I saw my Demon standing at the foot of my bed, but I think I was just discombobulated.

I was still trying to discern fact from fiction. This wasn't like any dream I had ever dreamt. It felt foggy, almost like it wasn't my own. Like I may have been watching it from the sidelines, but somehow was also able to interact with it. Lucid dreaming maybe? I know I sounded crazy, but I was feeling crazy. Wynter stirred lazily, not remembering my dream at all, she must have been in one of her own.

Why would I, in my dream, be with Alpha Drake? Why would I even do that? I hated him, so fucking much. Just the thoughts of Alpha Drake's lips on mine made me want to hurl. It didn't matter what he looked like, or that every mated and unmated She-Wolf in this pack swooned over him… I didn't, and I never would. It made absolutely no sense to me, but still, left me shook.

My mind flitted to my Demon. I know why I called him, but the fear that was absent? The fact that I made him promise to ensure that I would remain only his… I would never have gotten the balls to do something like that. Sometimes I think that having as vivid of dreams as I did was more of a curse than a gift. At times, I can't even tell the difference between what is a dream and what is reality.

I got up and ran to my closet to find all of my regular everyday wear. It was mostly sports bras, cut off tees, yoga pants, and flats. I exhaled in relief. I just had to be sure that it was truly a dream. I think I own two pairs of heels, which were seated in their respective spots on my shoe rack. I definitely would have worn one of them, had we been going to The Edge. However, I was more of a fan of my combat boots for everyday wear.

I picked up my phone, relieved to see no messages from either Jae or Brett. I sighed in relief then threw on a crop tank and some black yoga pants, before slipping into my favorite black combat boots. It was a good combination for training. I ran downstairs, grabbed a bagel and jalapeno cream cheese, then stopped.

This was a bit too much like my dream. I put the jalapeno cream cheese back in the fridge, and instead, grabbed a strawberry spread. I used a knife and covered my bagel before running out the door. Training better just be absolutely normal today because my mind was still reeling over my dream.

Chapter 11

~

(Raziel)

"**A**nthony, what do you have to report?" I asked curiously. Anthony was my second in command. He was tall and muscular like any Reaver. He sported dark hair, dark bronze eyes, and a straight expression almost always. He had a crescent moon tattooed on the right side of his face with vines going down his neck. He handled all my dirty work, the cleanup, the reports. He did literally anything and everything I asked with complete obedience. Absolutely no questions asked and this is why I keep him around.

Reavers did not run or live in packs like the Wolves did. We were more solitary keeping to our small Covens of 13 or less and just branching off from there. I, however, ran 23 Covens. Much of those Covens are intertwined together, living in the same areas. We inhabited more areas than I think anyone realized.

With our sheer numbers and our multitude of powers, we really had no enemies worthwhile. I have a title, High Priest. The High Priests do not report to anyone higher up. There are 4 of us, and while we don't always see eye to eye, we are the top of the food chain. I can't say that I would prefer if we always agreed, the controversy makes things interesting. Being alive for so long we tend to get bored. Regardless, each of us has a multitude of Covens under our control. Together, we four rule the Underworld.

"The Alpha Wolf thinks he's going to make Rayne his Luna, sir." Anthony said reluctantly, snapping me from my thoughts. I felt a wave of rage flood through me. "She is mine." I spat possessively through gritted teeth. "I know, sir. He only thinks that. He will not succeed in his endeavor." Anthony replied. His words did little to calm me. I had a tendency to lose my temper and no, I'm not working on it. Though, I always tried my best not to let my anger show around Rayne. She just knows how to push all of my fucking buttons.

I know she was already terrified of me. Which was partially… ok, entirely my own fault… ripping her boyfriend's throat out and all. I will admit, I lost control for a moment there. But the things he said to her. The crack of my neck was deafening as I relived the day. Rayne wasn't of age to find her mate yet. But I had an inkling since that day I met her in the forest, there at the wishing well, that she may be mine. I had let her know this a few days ago and she tried to fight me on it, but there were signs even she couldn't deny.

Being a Reaver, the mate bond worked differently for me. I couldn't feel it like she said. Not that I felt nothing, I have always felt something around her, but I have never been able to pinpoint exactly what it is. It could very well be an inkling of the mate bond slipping through, or it could be my need to possess that which I have claimed as mine… and she *is* mine. Both are possibilities.

Not that I truly ever had to worry about mates. As a Reaver I could choose my own mate. I wasn't bound by the Gods, or subject to their silly matchmaking games. But I had a Wolf, and with a Wolf comes a Wolf mate bond… of sorts. There was no true way to be sure regarding Rayne, besides keeping an eye on her until she was of age. It had proven to be a feat harder than I expected.

I stifled a smile when I remembered the way her breath hitched in her throat with my words. Her heart was beating completely out of her chest. Though, with me being me, and Eric's death being so fresh, I may have only made things worse for her. The thing is, I didn't care, and I still don't. No one ever said I was a good person, and I'll never claim to be one. I was now reeling with the thoughts that

Alpha Drake seems to think he has any kind of permission to lay a single finger on her. She belongs to me, and I had half a mind to remove his fucking hands for it. I had already told Rayne as much. I shook the thought, knowing that he had to keep her safe for the next year, and if I took his hands he would probably kill her out of spite.

I held back a chuckle at the thought of Alpha Drake starting all out war over Rayne. Because that is exactly what would happen. My brother's and I would eat him and his entire pack for fucking lunch. He knew better than to truly trifle with me, even over someone as important as Rayne. The thought of taking his hands was looking better and better... I pulled myself from my internal banter.

"Anthony, I need someone on the inside of that pack, someone who will befriend Rayne. She needs company, she needs interaction with others besides those filthy Humans, to keep her distracted and away from that motherfucking Alpha." I spat. "Yes, sir." Anthony stated, and he vanished, no doubt to fulfill my will. I'm sure he would have no trouble finding her a suitable friend, or even two.

A twinge of guilt flooded into my chest when I realized that I was the reason she hadn't let anyone get close. I had always been there to scare her potential love interests away, but I never realized this would also stop her from having meaningful friendships. My intention was never to stop her from having relationships of her own, but I couldn't let another man take her innocence. The very thought made my blood boil.

I am the only man she would ever be with. My cock will be the only one she will beg on her knees for. My hands, the only ones to force her legs apart. My tongue, the only one to make her legs shake and force a scream from her perfect lips. My Wolf growled in agreement. "Ours." He said. I nodded to him. "I don't care what the cost is, I will have her, even if I have to take her." I replied.

I recalled my first interaction with Rayne. She was 9 years old at the time, a clumsy little thing. I had heard her victory cry when she made it to the wishing well without her parent's pursuit, which made me chuckle. I carefully watched her through the trees, so as not to make my appearance known.

I had a feeling that she was going to fall over the edge the second I saw her approach. She was being careful, but not careful enough. I waited, and sure enough, she fell right in trying to look over the edge. I fully intended to leave her there to drown. It wasn't my problem. Her parents should be watching her. I started to walk away when I realized she was not drowning but swimming, and talking to herself. I couldn't just walk away then as my interest was piqued. I knew she was terrified when I pulled her out. The second I looked into her platinum silver eyes I knew what she was… but it was clear to me that she had no idea, and I planned to keep it that way.

A Reaver would *never* come into their full powers unless they were raised in a Coven and taught to unlock them. I knew I had nothing to worry about with her, as she lived in a cottage on the edge of the Red Ace pack. She was too young to have shifted for her first time, and I knew she didn't have a Wolf spirit yet, I would have heard her Wolf if she had. Too bad she would never shift…

Reavers can't shift, but we do have a Wolf spirit and she wouldn't be exempt. Though I had heard myths and stories of Reavers honing in on one certain ability and being able to utilize it in full, unlike the partial abilities we usually are granted. Call it a Reaver with Wolf focused abilities. Would this be her fate? Would she shift? And her mother? She had the same eyes, and while I never asked her, I had always wondered if she was a Reaver with Wolf focused abilities too.

My Wolf, Nero, pushed through, breaking me from my memory. "She is ours." He growled, clearly still thinking about my claim from earlier. I agreed. She would be ours regardless. *I can be very persuasive when it comes to something I want.* I thought, with a sly smile. I got up and continued on with my business. I had Covens to run but I was distracted. The memories of Rayne were always flitting in and out of my mind.

I felt a pang of guilt again when I remembered what happened when she was 16. She was out at the swimming hole with some of the other Wolves. I knew she had been sort of seeing a young Wolf named Brad at the time. It bothered me, but I knew she was too young, and far too proud for anything serious. She was the type who didn't need anyone to take care of her. If she chose the company of another, it's because she wanted it, not needed it. Still, the thought of Brad putting his hands on her irked me, and continually lived rent free in the back of my mind. I got word from my men that her and Brad had disappeared away from the other Wolves during that outing.

So, I, of course, being me, materialized right in front of them. Brad had his arms around her, and she was laying in his lap. They were just talking, but it made my Wolf uneasy to see him holding her like that. I locked eyes with Rayne and calmly asked her if she remembered what I had said when I brought her here. She was shaking with terror, but it was her who put herself in this position to begin with. "Yes." She said softly, and I loved the way it sounded escaping from her lips. "Good girl." I replied, then I vanished.

I scared the young Brad shitless, apparently, and from what I was told he never spoke to her again. Not that scaring him completely away was my intention… but it just so happened to work that way. Since then, I had never seen her with another person until recently, and that was Eric, whom I killed anyway. But he definitely crossed a line, or was about to.

Hmm, I thought. No wonder she is the way she is with me. I've given her every reason to fear me, and even hate me. But it didn't matter. She could hate me for the rest of our lives, it wouldn't change a singular thing. She could run from me too, but that would just make me want her more. The chase is most of the fun. I would follow her unto the ends of the earth, over and over again and through every lifetime, just to prove my devotion to her. I snapped back to reality. I knew she was not in the safest spot with Alpha Drake. But it was much safer than here with me or in any of my Covens, for now at least.

She didn't know it, but since our first encounter I have had her followed. She will be outraged when she finds out, but it's for her own good. My men know never to be seen and are very agile. I only chose the best of my men to watch her when I personally couldn't. Plus, they knew I would end their lives without question, should anything happen to her under their watch. My thoughts had been running rampant. I hadn't realized how much time had passed until I glanced up and out of the enormous picture window in my library.

It was after nightfall now. I could see the twilight glow had almost faded and the darkness had already begun to take over, swallowing any remnant of light that remained. This was my favorite time of the day, when darkness engulfs the world. I've never cared much for people. I prefer to keep to myself and travel by night where I do not have to deal with the constant stares and murmurs. You'd think I'd be used to it by now, but it still irks me. I am fully aware of my genetic makeup and how enticing I look to others.

Anthony appeared in my doorway and knocked a short 2 knocks. I looked up and we locked eyes as he walked inside my room. "It has been handled, sir." He said, and I could tell he believed that. I was content with his answer. Never had he disappointed me before. "Good." I replied and stood from my desk.

That's when I felt it, the flutter of silver glitter falling softly around me. The mind link that I had so longed to feel. It had my body aching and my Wolf howling, begging to hear her voice. "I... I need you." She stammered through the link, and I was gone, leaving Anthony alone and wondering.

Chapter 12

I materialized directly in front of Rayne. We locked eyes and I could see her confusion. She had no idea where she was or what she was doing. I knew where we were though. We were in a dream, her dream. She was standing next to Alpha Drake. My Wolf howled at the sight of her this close to him.

I, however, was much too distracted by how she looked to even really notice their proximity. The sight of her completely took my breath away. Not that she didn't always take my breath away, but I had never seen her done up like this before. I had no idea how someone who was already so beautiful could become even more enticing.

The dress was absolutely perfect and hugged her in all the right places, accentuating her beautiful curves perfectly. The silver and black heels put her even with Alpha Drake in height. Her long silver hair was in loose waves flowing down her back. I couldn't help but notice how the colors of that gorgeous dress made her eyes pop.

Nero was absolutely howling and begging to take her right here, right now. I wasn't necessarily opposed and couldn't stop the immediate barrage of terrible, dirty, filthy fucking things both Nero and I wanted to do to her delicate body from entering my thoughts. I inhaled and pushed Nero to the furthest recesses of my mind with a sharp growl. I needed to stay calm and assess the situation. With my mind much more clear, I looked over at Alpha Drake who was perfectly matching Rayne in silver and black, which made me cringe.

I wanted to rip him to shreds. That's when I actually noticed the placement of her arm around his bicep. I had overlooked it when her beauty had me distracted, but the fact that I realized she was touching him now made my blood straight fucking boil. The Alpha said something, but I was too busy seeing red to even hear him. Before Rayne could even utter a single word, I used magic and threw him across the street into a nearby house. He slammed into it and I just smirked. Dream or not, that felt good. I stepped up in front of Rayne to check on her and I realized she knew something wasn't right. She didn't know it, but she was dreamwalking. This was one of the many powers of a Reaver.

We learn this at a young age and can infiltrate the dreams of others... or in her case, manipulate our own. We can walk in and out of dreams as if it were real life. When you are first learning though, it's hard to differentiate between what is real and what is the dream. For her, she would have no idea what was going on. I can see how that would be extremely confusing. She still had all of her memories and was able to access them here, while dreamwalking. This is why everything seemed so weird to her.

Not knowing or understanding how to manipulate the dream would cause her to become disoriented and confused. I grabbed her shoulders. "Are you ok, darling?" I asked. She said no, and was mumbling mostly incoherently, and then she said something about not hearing her Wolf. That was probably the most disconcerting part for her. Wynter's absence anytime would raise red flags, but especially now. However, until Rayne learned to actually dreamwalk, she wouldn't hear Wynter in here.

Honestly, I was more worried about her coming into her powers than I was about her silly dream worries at that moment. A Reaver never comes into their powers unless they grew up in a Coven. It wasn't normal for her to be coming into them now. I noticed the tears beginning to form in her eyes and I pulled her to my chest in hopes to calm her down. "Rayne, darling. I'm here, you're alright. Shhh." I said softly, running my fingers through her hair. It didn't take long for her to pull away from me, but I was surprised when it was only partially. She looked up at me and she looked so innocent, I couldn't stop myself from sliding my hand around her neck.

I wanted to pull her to me and kiss her, but I refrained when she started to speak. "Do... do you really think I'm your mate?" Her words were shaky, unsure, as if she was afraid to even speak them. I tightened my grip on her throat slightly, it was a reaction to my thoughts regarding her question. "I don't give a single fuck who your mate is. I challenge anyone who thinks they could take you from me." I snarled.

"Do you promise?" She asked so softly I wouldn't have heard her be it not for my Vampiric hearing. My eyes had never left hers, but I knew the intensity behind my gaze was making her very uneasy. I didn't care. "Oh, I promise, darling. No one will ever lay a single finger on you. You belong to me." I said, and then slid my hand from her neck and wrapped it around the back of her head, tangling my fingers through her hair.

She gasped as I tilted her head up and pulled her in close. My lips brushed against hers but a kiss wasn't my goal. Not this time. I wanted to completely ravage her. Destroy her in the most beautiful ways. Leave her a blustering panting mess on the floor... leave her begging for my touch. However, I had more pressing matters.

"Wake up, Rayne, wake up." I hummed, then I stood at the foot of her bed to make sure she did, in fact, wake up. There have been times when even an experienced dreamwalker can get stuck in a dream, and I wanted to ensure that didn't happen to her. She had never done this before to my knowledge, and her inexperience would be her downfall.

She shot up out of bed in a flurry, her platinum silver eyes full of worry and surprise. I thought about sticking around and tormenting her for a bit before leaving... But I had too much on my mind to play games at this very moment. Instead, I materialized home before she realized I was there.

Once I was home my mind went straight to the fact that she was developing Reaver powers without the aid of a Coven. In fact, she had never even been in the vicinity of a Coven. Not close enough to activate any of her Reaver powers. So why were they coming through now? Could it be because of my proximity to her since she was 9? I scolded myself silently. There was no way to be sure, but what other explanation made any sense? "She's progressing faster than we expected, dreamwalking already?" Nero howled, snapping me out of my thoughts. "I know. I know, Nero." I snapped. My mind was running in circles.

"It's going to keep happening unless she gets the training she needs." He growled. I pursed my lips together and narrowed my eyes at my Wolf. I was completely aware of what needed to happen, and his commentary wasn't fucking helping.

"How can we prevent this? There has to be a way. If she doesn't use our mind link, I may not realize she's dreamwalking again and she might be on her own." I shot, worry snaking its way through each and every word. Nero remained silent. I knew he didn't know the answer. I didn't know it either. "I can't protect her if I don't know she's in danger!" My voice was rising as my panic level increased.

"Now let's be logical. It might be time to bring her here…" Nero said, trailing off. I shook my head. "No, we had a deal. She still has a year. I can't go back on my promise. I threaten it, and often at that. But a deal is a deal, and if I am anything, I am a man of my word." I replied.

Nero groaned in frustration. I began to pace my office, scouring the knowledge base in my mind for any answer I could muster. There was none. I had never experienced this before. A Reaver growing up outside of a Coven would never develop their powers, and if any did… we were to handle it. Panic shot through my chest as I recalled that specific conversation between myself and the other High

Priests. "It's impossible." Rowen said, running a hand through his brown hair. His rose gold eyes glinted as he locked them onto me. "How do we know it's impossible? Have you ever experienced it?" Raphael asked while adjusting the cufflinks on his silver suit.

"You realize you guys are really overthinking this shit. Who fuckin' cares if a Reaver comes into their powers outside of a Coven? What does it matter?" Ramses asked, raising his eyebrows at me specifically. I had yet to say a single word, listening to them bicker like children.

"Who cares?? Oh, only the entire village that gets destroyed by some random child who throws a temper tantrum. I'm sure they will have much to say on the subject... or would, had they still had the privilege of their lives." Rowen retorted. "You are speaking of this as if it has already happened. We have yet to even see a Reaver coming into their powers outside of a Coven. Who's to say we will ever have to deal with it?" Raphael asked.

"You know we will be dealing with it. It's inevitable. Can't we train them, teach them to harness their powers?" Ramses asked. "You know the extent of which a Reaver begins to learn to harness and control their powers... it starts almost at birth. Do you really think someone untrained could just pick it up as easily? It would be a bloodbath." Raphael replied while Rowen nodded his head in agreement.

I tuned them out briefly, while discussing the options with Nero. He seemed to be much more level headed than any of the other High Priests in this moment. "I know you don't want to hear it, Raziel, but unchecked power like that is dangerous and destructive. You know what needs to be done should we ever encounter this situation." Those were the only words Nero had to say for me to understand. I agreed and cleared my throat causing the other High Priests to stop bickering and turn their attention to me.

"We've yet to deal with this situation, but should the chance arise we only have 1 choice... and I shall be the one to do it. Problem solved." I said nonchalantly, as if the prospect of taking an innocent life meant nothing to me.

"No, Raziel. There has to be another way." Rowen cried. Ramses folded his arms in front of his chest, but remained silent. Raphael looked at me with concern in his silver eyes, and also remained still. "You know as well as I do that unchecked magic as powerful as ours will do nothing but become a burden on this world. We are in charge, we make the rules, and we cannot afford to risk the safety of our people over something that may never even happen.

Enough bickering. If any of you find out a Reaver is developing powers outside of a Coven, I demand to know, immediately. I will handle it and we can further convene. This is the last I will say on this subject. Understood?"

Rowen opened his mouth to speak but thought better of it, closing his lips and nodded to me instead. I looked at Raphael who sent a singular nod in my direction, then I looked to Ramses. He sighed out loud while shaking his head. "Fine. We find them, you kill them." He said. I didn't afford them another word on the subject.

A sound to my left jarred me from my memory. I looked to see what had caused it to find Anthony pouring 2 glasses of Bourbon at the mini bar. He walked over and handed me a glass. I took it, turning it gold immediately before taking a sip. He followed suit.

"You looked like you could use a drink, sir." I loved his uncanny ability to read me. I looked up at him, letting my eyes linger on the crescent moon adorning the side of his face. His dark hair was slick back and his bronze eyes accentuated his dark olive skin.

"Anthony, get me every piece of literature you can find on dreamwalking." I snapped. "Yes, sir." He replied. Then he vanished, leaving me to Nero's internal dialogue. "You need to speak to them, the other High Priests." Nero said. I was trying to ignore him, but I knew he spoke the truth. But how could I bring it to them? I was the one who made it perfectly clear that any Reaver coming into their powers outside of a Coven would be taken care of... and that I would be the one to do it.

A fierce protectiveness surged through my veins, igniting a burning rage that threatened to consume me whole. The mere idea of harm befalling her was intolerable. I would never lay a single finger on her, and I would kill anyone who thought they could in my stead. My instincts screamed for me to take action, to assert my dominance and defend what was mine.

The thought of the other High Priests interfering in this matter on the premise that I couldn't fulfill my millennia old oath, only fueled my determination to handle it alone, to keep her safe from them as I knew they would seek to rid this world of the abomination they believed she was.

I would never let them harm her, would never let them extinguish the radiant light that she embodied. She was not an abomination, but an ethereal being of beauty, of wonder, and of magic. She could burn this entire world down and I would stand at her side in the very heart of the flames, and together, we would face the inferno.

Consequences be damned... I would defy the laws of gods and men, I would shatter the chains of convention, I would brave the depths of hell itself, if that's what it took to shield her from harm. My duty, my honor, my very existence was bound to her protection, and I would stop at nothing to ensure that she remained unscathed, unbroken, and untouchable.

Chapter 13

~
(Rayne)

We train four times a week Monday through Thursday, every morning for 4 hours. It was rigorous training. Alpha Drake shows no mercy, and we were expected to do the same. The only reason I knew how to fight and protect myself the way I did, was because of him and the training he makes us complete.

He pairs us off with different members of the pack to gauge and strengthen our skills. We normally never fought the same person twice within the week. We had enough pack members to be able to accommodate that. So basically, we just kicked a new person's ass every day.

As much as I loathed Alpha Drake, he definitely knew what he was doing. Today, I was paired off with Roman. Strange that I had never once fought him before, or even seen him, now that I think about it. It made me wonder if he was new to our pack? Or have I just not noticed him until now?

To be honest, I never noticed anyone. I kept to myself in fear that my Demon would do something. His track record wasn't very good with me and other men. Thoughts of Eric fluttered into my mind briefly. It was easier for me to just stay away.

Roman wasn't much bigger than me in height and stature, but I was a lot faster. He still landed a couple of good blows. I have to give him props, for sure, but as fast as we heal it didn't affect me much. He was definitely the one worse off. When we were done sparring, I got a weird feeling that someone was watching me, I looked over and locked eyes with Alpha Drake.

He was giving me a venomous glare. I shot the dirtiest look that I could muster back to him, and then looked away. After the events of yesterday, and my stupid dream, I wanted nothing to do with him. We switched partners for the next set of training and Alpha Drake must have taken offense to my dirty look because he paired me up with one of his cronies.

This guy was fucking huge, almost as big as Alpha Drake himself. He had rippling muscles full of scars, tattoos… the works. *Oh boy.* I thought. "Here we go!" Wynter snipped. He may have been strong, but he was not fast. I was successfully able to dodge most of his attacks but the ones that did connect were brutal. I felt a couple ribs break on two occasions. He definitely was more of a match for me than Roman. But honestly, I liked fighting people who were more of a match for me.

I feel like because I'm small people don't think that I can fight, or they take it easy on me, but I really can hold my own. I had been training since I was a kid. I suppose I have to give my mother credit for some of my training as well. She used to teach me before I came to stay in The Obsidian pack. She wanted to make sure I was never left unprepared for anything. I, on the other hand, never understood what was so scary out there.

Until, of course, I met my Demon. And I realized if there are more things out there like him, then I definitely had something to be afraid of. I took my training with my mother a little more seriously after that, which obviously, served me well. I never wanted to be unprepared after how I froze up and panicked like a fool when encountering my Demon for the first time.

My wounds had healed, and training was just ending. I was gathering my stuff when I noticed Roman heading my way. "Hey, you fight pretty good, for a girl." He said, as he nudged me with his elbow and laughed. "So do you for being my same size." I retorted with a chuckle. "Hey, that's not fair! I can't choose my size." Roman said, taking fake offense. "I call it like I see it." I replied, raising an eyebrow.

He just laughed. "Hey, do you want to go grab lunch?" He asked reluctantly. I could see a hopeful look in his neon green eyes. I hesitated. Then decided, *fuck it.* "Sure, I'm starving! I do, however, need to go home and shower first. Meet you at the diner in 45 minutes?" I replied. "Sure, I'll be there!" He said, and I could see the excitement in his eyes.

He waved while flashing a million-dollar smile with a set of perfectly straight teeth in my direction. How did I never notice those before? We parted ways and I jogged the rest of the way to my house. "Don't even think about it, Rayne." Wynter's internal dialogue made me blush. "I'm not, Jesus!" I huffed. "You don't want Eric #2." She said with an exasperated sigh. Her words had my stomach curdling.

"Ugh, don't remind me, Wynter, I was there." I said, sadness snaking through my voice as I recalled my Demon licking the blood off his fangs with a shudder. "You think I wasn't? I just don't want it to happen again, ok?" She said with concern.

Yea, she's probably right. I thought. *But it's just lunch. No big deal.* I arrived at the diner perfectly on time. Roman was already there waiting. We got seated and he ordered some sort of junk food, a big hamburger with fries. I ordered an avocado salad.

It's not like we had to worry about what we ate, our Wolf genes would devour any calories we consumed anyway. We were basically all muscle, and even if we didn't work out, we still had a muscular build. So, I could have eaten a greasy hamburger, I just wasn't in the mood. In fact, I never seemed to be in the mood. I guess I liked my healthy food.

"So how long have you been a part of The Obsidian pack?" Roman asked while we waited for our food. "Since I was 12. I was brought here after my mother was killed and I have been here ever since." I replied. "Oh, I'm sorry about your mother… that's terrible." He said. "Thank you. It's ok, it was a long time ago." I replied. "Still, deep wounds don't always heal quickly." He said. He was right, but I wasn't willing to admit just how right he was. I pushed the pain away from my chest and tried to change the subject. "What about you? I swear I haven't seen you around." I said. "It's only been a few weeks here. I am pretty new." He replied. Just then the waitress brought our drinks. "Food will be coming shortly." She said with a smile. I smiled back at her, she seemed nice, and then I focused back on Roman.

"So, Alpha Drake? How is he?" He asked. I scoffed. "He's like stabbing a red ant hill. And then just when you think you've escaped, you realized that you were running the wrong direction the whole time and now you're covered in red ants and they are all biting you." I said. Romans eyes went wide as saucers. "That bad, huh?" He said. "You have no idea." I replied.

"I have heard all of the rumors about this pack, am I to believe they are all true then?" He asked. I nodded. "As far as I know, every single one of them is true. All the way down to the minute details." He shook his head. "Good God, Alpha Drake is ruthless." He replied. I nodded, again. "You're telling me."

My phone went off and I grabbed it from my pocket and peered down at the text preview. It was Brett.

'We need to talk, when can you meet me?'
Panic clawed its way through my chest but I ignored it for now, I could meet with him later. Or never… that would be better. I shoved my phone back into my pocket and pushed the thoughts from my mind. "Do you need to take that?" Roman asked. I shook my head and spent the rest of lunch talking about training and how things were going in the pack with Roman. It was nice to just have someone there to talk to who wasn't drilling me about Eric. It allowed me to forget, briefly.

Once we were done with lunch, we were about to part ways. "I'll see you tonight at Patrol?" He questioned. "You're patrolling the East quarter?" I asked. "Yes ma'am, six to midnight!" He chirped. "Oh, then I guess I'll see you there!" I replied with a wave, and we headed our separate ways. That was strange though. He knew I would be there, but how would he know? I just barely got put on the extra patrol duty when I got in trouble. I usually patrol the West quarter, never the East. So really, I barely even knew where I was patrolling.

Wynter was whining in the back of my mind, telling me that something wasn't right... I didn't feel like I was in danger, but something was strange about Roman. I couldn't quite put my finger on it, but I was determined to find out what it was. It would have to wait though. I pulled my phone from my pocket and replied to Brett.

'I'm free now if you want to meet up.'

I had hoped he would be busy as it was short notice, but of course, I couldn't be so lucky. My phone went off immediately, as if he was waiting for my response with his phone in his hand.

'Now is good. Where are you? I'll come to you.'

I groaned in frustration. I couldn't hide from him forever and I knew this.

'I'm heading towards your house, meet me at the river bridge?' I replied.

Honestly, I was crawling with stress. I had hoped that he would change his mind but running from this wasn't going to happen either. No matter how much I wanted it to.

'Be there in 5.' He said.

I knew with 100 percent certainty that this was about Eric, but I also knew that I had no idea what to do or say about it. This was going to be interesting, to say the least. He was already at the bridge when I walked up and folded my arms across my chest. "What do you want?" I snapped. He rolled his eyes at me and then followed suit, folding his arms across his chest as well.

He looked far more intimidating in this stance, even wearing his red and white football jersey. "Look, I'm not stupid. I put it all together. The Reaver has decided that you belong to him. Eric basically trespassed on the Reavers property, and he killed him for it. That is the only explanation to how you are still alive and Eric is missing." He said using air quotes over the word missing. He got right down to it, and didn't even give me a chance to deny it. My heart was hammering in my chest so hard, I thought it might rip through the fabric of my top. "What proof do you have?" I asked, hoping to throw him off.

"I'm not here to prosecute you for it. But we have to do something. Eric's parents are filthy fucking rich and huge staples in the community. They will not just let this go. They already plan to have search crews sent out for the next week at least. They plan to scour every single inch of this place and you know how bad it's going to look if they find him and your DNA is *anywhere* on his body. I am not trying to scare you, but I don't think you realize the severity of it all."

The thing is, I did. I *really* did. I didn't confirm nor deny, but I did put my face in my hands, trying to calm some of the absolute panic that was shredding its way through my otherwise snarky demeanor. "What do we do?" I finally croaked through my fingers, hoping that those few words wouldn't give it away.

"First, you go talk to that fucking Reaver and make sure that he didn't half ass a single fucking thing. Then you join the search party because his parents know that you and him are dating. And then you attend his funeral when they finally declare him deceased. And don't for even a half a second think that you will get out of any of this. If you want to keep from becoming a suspect, then you make yourself known and willing to do anything you fucking can to help bring him home." Brett explained.

Guilt. That was the only emotion I couldn't suppress. It blew through me like a fucking tornado, sweeping up everything in its path of destruction. It gnashed its sharp teeth at my heart and ripped it into pieces, leaving it lying on the ground before me. I wanted to bend down and pick up the pieces in a feeble attempt to put myself back together, but I couldn't bring myself to even move.

"I never meant for this to happen... you have to believe me." I said softly after a few moments of deafening silence. I wasn't planning on admitting it to him, but we had come too far now to turn back. "You and I, we are the same in many ways. Both hiding ourselves from the Humans, keeping secrets, living in a world that most don't even believe exists. Eric was a fucking pig, and he deserved what he got. We both know it. But it doesn't change the fact that he's gone and his parents will stop at nothing to find his killer."

His words rang very true, and justification was relative, no one truly would believe that he tried to rape me. And from the way Brett was talking, I had an inkling this wasn't the first time he had done it. Not that I ever told Brett what happened, but it seemed like he already somehow knew. I was starting to think that my Demon had done the world a favor. Now, if there was just a way to get out of the repercussions.

Then I had a crazy fucking idea. "I know you are here, watching, like you always are. You can come out... we need to talk." I said to my Demon without breaking eye contact with Brett. He froze when he realized what I had done. The look on his face went from confusion to absolute panic when my Demon walked out of the trees adjusting his golden cufflinks, before coming to stand by my side.

I turned to him and tried to keep my composure. The way his hair was falling in perfectly curved wisps, framing his strong jawline and sparkling in the sunlight caused my heart to stop beating. The words I meant to say fell short, and disappeared like smoke dancing along my lips. Wynter was clawing and scratching her way to the forefront of my mind and I wanted nothing more than to let her. But I knew now was not the time.

I gathered my courage, pulling it seemingly from the air around us before I spoke. "This is Brett. No, he is not romantically involved with me in any way shape or form, and you are not allowed to kill him." The words were shaky as I pulled them from the quicksand they were sinking in. Composure or not, I called him out here and I wasn't planning on wasting his time. "You called me out here to tell me this?" He inquired. "I... no..." I stammered before Brett finally cut in. "No, she called you out here because we have a problem." I was glad that he took initiative because apparently, I could barely form a coherent thought, let alone put those thoughts into sentences.

The man dripping in gold had much more of an effect on me than even I wanted to admit.

Chapter 14

~

(Raziel)

The Human/Wolf Hybrid standing before me was brave, I'll give him that much. But my focus wasn't on him, it was on the rapidly increasing heart rate of my little Wolf standing next to me. She looked panicked. I already knew why she called me out, and exactly what the problem was. I had been listening to the entire conversation, of course.

I scoffed internally when the boy insinuated that I would have left a singular shred of evidence. I know how Humans and their laws work. I have been around for many years, enough to know how to avoid being caught. I held out my hand in response to his inquiry. "Your phone."

He was reluctant, but he handed it over. I opened the maps and pinned him a location. "Here you will find a very tall cliff. The fence along the sharp curve is destroyed, and there will be a vehicle that was recently on fire at the bottom. Evidence of losing control and crashing will be found, along with dental records which do not burn, and a license plate to verify the vehicle's owner, one Eric Stalling. How you relay this information is up to you, but she stays out of it. I know how to make much more than a simple car crash look like an accident. Are we clear?" I growled the last few words to make my point as clear as newly cleaned glass.

"We are clear." He said, and then with one last look at Rayne, he headed off the bridge and towards the Human town. I turned towards Rayne. She stepped back, just one step, to which I smirked. "Getting bold are we?" My words danced around her pretty little head as she met my fiery gaze. "I… no, I… I just knew you were there and that you would have a solution." She finally said, but her words were uneasy, as if she didn't even believe them herself.

I stepped towards her, causing her to back up more until she was flush with the edge of the bridge. I caged her in with both arms on either side as I grasped the railings behind her. She sucked in a breath and I reveled in the fact that she was internally squirming due to our sheer proximity.

"And if I wasn't?" I asked. Her Wolf was screaming in her mind. As scared as Rayne was of me, Wynter never had been, and I took advantage of that fact every time I had the chance. She didn't speak, but how could she? I was suffocating her with my mere presence. "What? Cat got your tongue?" I whispered, running my fingers up her neck and under her chin, forcing her to look up into my eyes.

"No, I didn't think that far ahead because I knew you would be there… you are always there." She huffed. Good that she knows this by now. "Am I?" I hummed, knowing this would piss her off. I loved to get under her skin. "Yes, and maybe I will just call on you all the time, for no reason, just to prove my point." She snapped.

There it is… the snarky attitude I was waiting for. My lips slowly curved into a wicked smile as I articulated my well thought out response. "You do that, and when I come I'll be leaving with much more than just the air filtering through your pretty little lungs, and that erratic little heartbeat of yours."

She froze in place but I knew she was thinking about it. "You can act like you don't want it all you want, but your body will always give you away. The way you instantly get wet for me shows just how much you truly want everything I have to give." I purred, allowing my hand to trail down her chest and stomach, brushing ever so slightly along her clit as I made my way to her inner thigh.

I could feel my cock getting rock hard in my suit pants and I didn't even care that it would be completely visible.

These pants left me little room for movement, let alone what I'm packing. "I... I don't want y-you." She stammered, but it came out so quietly that had I not been the creature that I am, I wouldn't have even heard it. I hummed in response.

I took her hand and pulled it down to her side, rubbing it across my thigh and placing it directly on my cock. She gasped in surprise causing me to smirk. "Does this help to change your mind?" I purred in her ear, grinding against her hand. She hadn't tried to pull away, and for a brief moment I thought she might actually grip onto it. Instead, she pulled her hand away slowly, dragging her fingers along my shaft a bit too slowly. She looked up at me, eyes wide with surprise.

"That thing is going to kill me..." she mumbled. I tilted my head. "Quite possibly." I murmured. She gasped and then punched my chest, pushing me off of her. "You can't just keep doing this to me!" She hissed. Her eyes kept looking down at my very noticeable package, and I fought to hide my cocky grin.

"Doing what, little Wolf? Enticing you with promises of mind blowing pleasure? You seem to be enjoying it." I replied, nipping her earlobe with my teeth. She pushed me away again and folded her arms in an attempt to become more intimidating, but it did little for her in that aspect.

The redness danced along her cheeks as her Wolf fought her to just give in to me. I agreed with her Wolf. "Well I'm not. So..." she huffed. "Oh? In that case let me clarify your wants then. Are you saying you no longer want me to touch you, here, like this?" I said, running my hand through her hair from the side and using my thumb to pull down on her bottom lip. "You no longer wish me to hold you close, like this?" I growled, as I flipped her around and snaked my fingers around her slender neck, pulling her back to my chest.

"And let me guess, you would prefer it if I didn't do this, right here, in this specific spot..." I whispered, blowing my hot breath on the spot just behind her ear that I knew was her major turn on point. She gasped. "And last but not least. I'm sure you definitely do not want me placing my lips on you, right here, like this..." I purred, allowing my lips to touch down gently on the delicate skin behind her ear.

Shivers tore through her small body, and if she planned to listen to her Wolf at all, I would be ravaging her right here on this bridge. I wasn't opposed, but she never listened to her Wolf. I released her and stepped away, allowing her to catch her breath. "I care not how many times you tell me no, little Wolf. Until my presence fails to make your heart beat completely out of your chest, then I will not stop pursuing you." I placed her hand on her own chest so she could feel the thundering of adrenaline through her ribcage.

"Fuck it. Take her right now. Mark her and make her ours!" Nero barked. I had been doing a good job at keeping him at bay, but he was beginning to win the fight. I didn't say goodbye, but had I stayed a moment longer, I may have pushed her up against the bridge and fucked her until she came so hard she wouln't even be able to remember her own name. I needed to calm myself down, possibly more than she did.

~

(Rayne)

I exhaled in relief when he materialized away from me. My heart couldn't handle another second of torture. I was absolutely pissed because he was right. My words did not match my actions in the slightest. Telling him no and pushing him away was pointless. I was only doing it because I had this insistent need to be independent, and I felt like he was working so fucking hard to take that from me. I refused to allow anyone to take my independence, not even him...

Forget the fact that I was hopelessly attracted to him, and deep down I had the slightest feeling he may be my mate. I would fight it until I turned 21 and we found out for sure. But until then all he would get is defiance. I sighed and pulled my composure together, heading back towards my house. I kept replaying the scene in my mind as I walked.

My hand on his cock. It was big... too big. He had never been that bold before and I should have pulled away immediately, but I *wanted* to touch him. And I had the sneaking suspicion he wouldn't have let me pull away, even if I tried. Wynter had her own dialogue that mostly consisted of chewing me out for being defiant and how dreamy was. She was #TeamDemon and there was nothing I could do to sway her opinion. It was almost as if she knew something I didn't know. My mind kept going back to the mate bond. Not that she could feel it, but did Wolves have some sort of sixth sense about it? I would have to ask her later, though I had another sneaking suspicion that even if they did, she wouldn't tell me. Maybe she wasn't allowed.

Once my mind cleared some I realized just how tired I actually was. Training earlier had really kicked my ass. It was rigorous on any regular day, but I only now noticed how badly it was affecting me. I was already tired, but after that interaction with my Demon, I was going to need a nap or there was no way I was going to stay awake for patrol tonight. I still had a few hours before I had to report to the East quarter.

My mind flitted back to my Demon the entire way home, running through all of the things he said and the way he made me feel. Redness invaded my cheeks again as I thought about his sheer size under my small palm. Someday, he was going to kill me with that thing... I was sure of it.

As soon as I got home I headed upstairs and jumped into bed. I pulled the covers up over my head and tried to clear my mind. My alarm was already set so I wasn't worried about missing patrol. I thought I would never fall asleep after the adrenaline rush but it felt like as soon as my head hit the pillow I was out.

I found myself standing in front of what looked like a medieval castle. That would be the only way to truly describe what I was seeing. The estate was vast, sprawling across acres and acres of land like a sovereign kingdom.

The mansion itself was magnificent, its solid black architecture punctuated by gold accents that seemed to dance across the many spires and pillars with precision. Upon them, golden gargoyle statues stood watchful guard, their presence felt in every direction. The windows, a marvel in their own right, were enormous, dwarfing any I had ever seen, even in the grandest of homes. This was no mere residence, but a palace of unbridled extravagance. The estate's grounds were a labyrinthe, a sheer wonderland, with acres of serpentine paths winding through lush greenery that seemed to stretch on forever.

Some paths whispered to me, calling me into secluded enclaves, where lush shrubbery cascaded downwards, and rich gardens stretched out as far as the eye could see. A stunning pond caught my eye, its turquoise waters flowing gently, a reminder of the wishing well and stream of my childhood memories.

As I stood at the front gates of the home I noticed a large crescent moon connecting the two gates. Golden filigree wrapped the moon and strung itself down both sides of the gate. The air surrounding me felt almost electrified, seemingly alive and whispering secrets to those who dared to explore. The scene before me was like a macabre masterpiece, a chilling memoir that seemed to have been plucked straight from a terrifying horror film. And yet, paradoxically, it exuded an unsettling elegance, one my brain struggled to wrap itself around.

I stood there in awe, when the gates began to open on their own. Of course, my curiosity was always getting the best of me, so I decided to walk in. I wanted to explore the property but I knew it would take all day to adequately survey this magnificent place. I reached out to Wynter but I couldn't hear her, which I thought was really strange.

Usually, she's in my mind trying to stop me from doing dumb shit, but I was much too distracted to worry about it right now. I walked down the long gravel pathway, resisting the urge to turn down literally any of the pathways promising to lead me into the excitement of the unknown. Instead, I remained on the main pathway headed towards the front of the mansion. Soon, I came upon a set of very large black and gold double doors. I knocked, but no one answered. I figured if the gates to the home were open, maybe the front door would be too?

I stepped forward and pushed on the door. It opened so easily, almost too easily… but I decided to go inside anyway. No one ever said I had any type of common sense when it came to my curiosity. I mean, I had a feeling I shouldn't be here, but it was too late to turn back now. That was my justification. It opened up into a giant foyer. Black walls with gold filigree and empty golden picture frames littered the walls.

There was a spiral staircase in the middle with a sparkling black and gold crystal chandelier above my head. The feel of the home was dark and elegant, with a thrum of magic bursting through the silence. The sight took my breath away, it was the most beautiful place I had ever seen. I had three options before me. I could either go forward up the spiral staircase, to the left into an unknown hallway, or to the right into another unknown hallway. I decided to just go forward and up the spiral staircase.

As I got almost to the top I turned into the most breathtaking view of the city through the enormous window above the front door. The sun was setting, casting a pink and orange glow across the entire town. I must have been up high, somewhere up on a peak of some sort… somewhere the entire city could be viewed below me.

I thought it was strange that I had never been up here before or even noticed it. Why wouldn't I have seen a mansion like this sitting on top of a peak that can see the whole city? When I'm in the city looking up I should have been able to see it. As massive as it was, there was no hiding it. The gold would absolutely blind the entire city under the afternoon sunlight. I got to the top of the stairs and there was just one single hallway, leaving me only one pathway. Looking around, every surface seemed to be adorned with gold accents from the delicate filigree of the chandeliers to the subtle patterns woven into the rugs.

Immense power echoed through the architecture. You could feel it dancing along the edges of your consciousness, begging to be allowed entry. An array of black doors with delicate gold designs littered the hallway on both sides. So many doors, so many secrets. I resisted the urge to open them trying to stay focused at the task at hand. But what was the task? My mind was cloudy, but also clear. I seemed to be focused on something that I didn't understand. A pull to a place that I couldn't see. I shook it off and continued. At the very end of the hallway there was one set of beautiful, golden double doors with the word 'Raziel' across the top in large solid gold letters with a black outline. The letters were huge, spanning the width of both doors.

The doors looked to me as if they were actually made of solid gold, and they looked heavy. I really wanted to knock… but I also just kind of wanted to walk in. I mean the other doors were open, why not this one? Panic flooded my chest and I suddenly felt like maybe I shouldn't even be here… like something was different about this place. Like maybe it wasn't real? I didn't even know how I got here and I couldn't put my finger on where I was before this.

Somehow though, I was eerily calm even with the panic accelerating the adrenaline that rushed through my veins. It was the strangest mix of contradicting feelings. I reached out to Wynter again, forgetting she wasn't there. I was met with no response. I felt a twinge of fear being here alone, but pushed it out of my mind. I figured she would be back, eventually. I looked up at the double doors before me and decided, against my better judgment, that I was going to open them.

107

Suddenly, they started to open slowly on their own, as if they had heard my thoughts. I gasped and took a step back, but then gathered my bearings and stepped inside. I was met with a room much like the doors, literally gold everywhere. If anything wasn't solid gold it was accented gold.

There was a four-poster bed in the middle back of the room that had gold netting going up each of the four posters. The frame, headboard, and footboard were black with gold accents. The sheets were gold silk, the comforter was black with gold filigree strewn throughout. There were two nightstands, one on each side of the bed. They were black with gold drawers, which really brought out the black in the feather down comforter.

On one of the nightstands there was a gold hand statue resembling what I figured to be the hand of Midas. *Fitting,* I thought with a chuckle. I wanted to touch it, but I wasn't too keen on being turned to gold. The rug in front of the bed was black with intricate gold stitching. The curtains around the room were all black with golden swirls dancing throughout causing a slight mystical feel in the air.

The walls were black and adorned with gold paintings and gold painted animal skulls. It made a nice color pop on the solid black walls. A part of me wondered if they were actually painted with real gold.

In the right-hand corner of the room there was a fireplace and a black velvet Victorian style chaise lounge with golden stitching and legs. I could see a golden blanket draped over the back. The fire crackling in the fireplace was burning golden flames. I wasn't sure how that was possible, but it did match the room.

There was a gold pool table with black felt lining on the opposite side of the room. Gold and black pool sticks hung on the wall behind it neatly. To the side of the pool sticks was a full bar stocked with every spirit and champagne you could ever want. Of course, it was gold and black, just like everything else in the room. I noticed a decanter full of some sort of golden liquid. I'm assuming it was alcohol, but I don't know what alcohol would be that color.

Four crystal glasses were neatly surrounding it atop an octagon mirror, which was reflecting the golden liquid in a perfect shimmer on the ceiling above it. The last thing I noticed was the scent of musk and citrus tones wafting through the air. It was a familiar smell and I was racking my brain trying to remember where I had smelled it before. It was very soothing.

As I stood there, I couldn't help but be captivated by the sheer perfection of the room. Every item, every ornament, every detail seemed to have been carefully considered and placed with precision. The space was immaculate, with not a single speck of dust or imperfection to be seen. The level of meticulousness was almost surreal, and yet, it only added to the room's enchanting allure.

I felt an overwhelming desire to reach out and touch every object, to explore every nook and cranny, but I knew better. My curiosity had gotten me into trouble before, and I wasn't about to let it happen again. So, instead, I took a mental snapshot of the room, committing every inch of it to memory, from the subtle patterns on the walls to the delicate curves of the furniture.

As I stood there, a sudden, inexplicable sensation washed over me, like being enveloped in a warm, liquid gold. It was a feeling I knew intimately, one that stirred a deep, primal response within me. I turned my head, and my eyes met his – the piercing, golden gaze of my Demon. I gasped, transfixed by the shifting, molten hues of gold in his eyes, like a mesmerizing dance of light and shadow.

"Mr. Kane!" I breathed, my voice barely above a whisper, as a thrill of excitement mixed with a hint of fear coursed through my veins.

Chapter 15

~

(Raziel)

nthony brought me a whole stack of books, everything that he could find, every piece of literature known to the Underworld about dreamwalking. I had spent hours pouring over every book, committing everything I read to memory. I didn't want to miss a single thing.

There had to be a way I could help Rayne. I was already so exhausted after the day I had endured. That, and all of this reading on top of it, had me fighting to stay awake. I swear I only closed my eyes one time and the next thing I know I'm dreamwalking.

This was nothing new to a Reaver though, no big deal. I'm dreamwalking my own dream. Perfect, I could use this time to study more while my body rested. I was in my room where I had originally fallen asleep, when I heard a noise. How could there be something unexpected here? I control my own dreams...

I wanted to let it play out, so I stepped just behind the drapes as Rayne walked into my room. I was so surprised to see her, my heart skipped a beat, or maybe two. Nero started going crazy at the aspect of her in our bedroom. Even if it was a dream bedroom, still. I had just seen her a few hours ago but I would never pass up the opportunity to make her squirm. I watched as her face lit up when she took in the sight. She was impressed, likely, by the array of gold surrounding her.

I think it's safe to say that I prefer the color gold. Everything in this room was made of solid gold. Literally everything, all the way down to the stitching in the rug. I wouldn't have it any other way. Some might say it's extreme, but I've never cared what others think and I'm not about to start now.

Looking back at Rayne, even though I knew this was just a dream I couldn't help but revel in the fact that she was this near. What she didn't know though, is that when you dreamwalk you are actually there. Your spirit leaves your body in a physical form to dreamwalk, and her spirit's physical form was standing here now.

If you want to dreamwalk you have to concentrate on the person who's dream you want to infiltrate, that creates a link between the two of you. Your physical form can use that link to find the dream. It's something you must practice and is very difficult to master.

While I would like to know just how she found my dream by sheer accident, I couldn't help but smirk when I realized she was thinking of me when she fell asleep. I loved that thought. But of course she was, I had left her earlier in a flustered mess. For her to be thinking of anything except my hands on her perfect little body would be a travesty. I let her wander around for a few more minutes before I decided it was now or never. I materialized right next to her. She heard me, turned her head, and we locked eyes.

"Mr. Kane!" She said with a tone of extreme surprise. I took a moment to take in her expression, then searched her beautiful platinum eyes for any signs of fear. What I saw instead, was overwhelming excitement.

Might be selfish of me, but I couldn't wake her yet. I fully planned on taking full advantage of the time I had with her while she wasn't feeling her usual emotions regarding me.

"Is this your room? Is this your house?" She asked in awe. "Yes, little Wolf. This is my home." I stated, while reading her facial expressions. "Is it to your liking?" I questioned. As much as my decor was chosen and strategically placed for me and *only* me, I was hoping she would say yes. "It's incredible, and it's so... you, with the gold and all." She smiled as she said that last part.

I did always wear something gold, she must have noticed, though, it would be hard for her not too. I fought the smile that was itching to form behind my lips. That's strange, I never felt like smiling... not like this. Maybe a smirk here and there, or something a bit more sinister... but this? A *real* smile because I felt... happy? I then realized that she was waiting for my reply. "It is, how would you say? My color, after all." I smirked, turning with my arms open wide to show off the room.

She reached up and placed her hand on my forearm. Her touch sent sparks of lightning shooting through my body, re-igniting the fire she had instilled just moments prior. I turned to face her again, and I could see she had a dreamy sort of look in her eyes. It was different from her usual hardened, protective, glare. This was different.

I was shocked because she had never willingly touched me before. Her hand moved up my arm and onto my chest. I was the one in control, not her... yet, here I was, allowing this behavior, and completely willing to let her do anything she damn well pleased.

She was tracing my muscles with her fingers sending small shocks of pleasure to my core. I was fighting to keep Nero under control at her every advance. I hadn't even realized I wasn't wearing a shirt...

Wait, why wasn't I wearing a shirt? It wasn't until we suddenly materialized onto the bed, and she was straddling me, that I realized she was manipulating my dream. She took my shirt off. She put us on the bed. Absolutely not! I was willing to let her take the lead for a moment, but all in all, I control things, period.

I sat up and pulled her to my chest as I scooted us back against the headboard. She looked down at me with a breathtaking smile. "Did someone decide they were going to be bold today?" I snipped with a raised eyebrow. It was time to take back control. She giggled and it was absolute music to my ears. "How are you so fucking breathtaking?" Her breathy voice danced along the edges of my mind, threatening to sink me into the madness that was Rayne.

112

"I appreciate the sentiment, little Wolf. But in the world of beauty, you are the only contestant here." She smiled and moved a piece of my hair behind my ear. "Do you know you drive me absolutely mad?" I confessed, pulling her close and whispering in her ear. "Is that so?" She replied.

"Yes. I watch you all the time, imagining what it would be like to taste you anytime I wanted. I breathe only you. You are my every reason and purpose for existing... you are all I ever think about." I purred while tracing my fingers along her collarbone.

"Then why don't you do something about it?" She replied. She was getting even bolder. "Something like this?" I asked, pulling her close to me so our lips were almost touching. Her breath hitched in her throat but I would be lying if I said I didn't live for the moments where I could take her breath away.

"Yes... s-something like that." She whispered. I let my tongue dart out and taste her top lip, closing my eyes when the taste of coconuts and candy infiltrated my taste buds. It was faint, but it was fucking intoxicating and I waned more. But I wanted it while she was awake.

I pulled away as she shot me a look of confusion. I cupped her face with my hands and looked deep into her eyes. I was looking for any sign of her not wanting this or fighting it. There was none, just a hunger that I had never witnessed. One that I had longed to experience for so many years...

Unfortunately, I knew it was time to wake her up. I couldn't continue to entertain her, no matter how much I wanted to. It was times like these that I allowed my *very* small moral compass to point me in the right direction even though I wanted to smash it. I silently scolded myself because this would be the second time I had woken her up and sent her away...

"I'm sorry, little Wolf, but when I taste you... truly taste you, I will do it when you are awake. Rayne... wake up." I whispered, sending Nero and I straight into withdrawal. I knew she was awake when she disappeared from my arms.

I sat there for a moment, remembering how her body felt pressed against mine, and internally kicking myself.

The selfish side of me wanted nothing more than to take advantage of her boldness. Take her breath away again and again, sink my fangs into her neck and taste her blood as it flowed into my mouth. The other side of me, the more logical side, knew she would remember it as only a dream. And I refused to allow her to think that it wasn't real, not after I had finally been allowed to do with her as I wished...

I was secretly hoping that she would start to change the way she thinks and feels for me if we could have more meetings like this. Not that I was opposed to forcing her to love me. She has never had a choice in the matter.

She's been mine since the day I laid my eyes on her fragile form. But knowing how independent she is, I knew it would work much better if she *thought* she had made the choice on her own. I knew she would fall for me, if given time. I just had to be patient enough to allow it, rather than force it. I sighed. I was beginning to see just how impatient I truly was.

This small, yet feisty woman, had taken my mind, body, and soul hostage. She had unknowingly inserted herself into every waking thought, every dream, and every fiber of my being. Her presence was a constant, thrumming hum, a vibration that resonated deep within my chest. I was no longer my own, but a captive of her spirit, her fire. She completely devoured me without her even knowing it... and for the first time, I thought maybe her dreamwalking wasn't so bad.

Chapter 16

~
(Rayne)

J woke up suddenly before my alarm. I sat up and was confused about my recent dream. It felt so real. I touched my top lip and realized the feeling of his soft tongue was lingering. Wynter had dreamt with me as well, while she wasn't there in my dream for some reason, but she remembers it all.

She was howling about my Demon and how close we were to him. In any normal situation the thought of him would have sent a spike of fear shooting straight through my chest. But for some reason I found myself almost missing him… I blamed the dream for my sudden change of heart, though I knew the feeling wouldn't last. Wynter's approval was prevalent in her howls.

"Maybe we should get to know him?" Wynter stated with a pout. That thought made me nervous and excited. *Maybe.* I thought, as I got ready and headed out the door to patrol. But when I turned to close my front door I froze. Taped dead center to my door was a flier with Eric's face plastered right on it. He was smiling, a genuine smile, showing his perfect teeth. It was a smile that used to melt my heart.

The picture was huge, covering almost the entire page. His blonde hair was a bit messy, but that was his normal style. My heart ached as I read, 'MISSING' in large red letters that spanned the top of the flier.

Bile immediately rose in my throat at the thought of his family and friends looking for him. I thought I was compartmentalizing this, and dealing with it. I thought I had concluded that he was going to rape me, and accepted that he was gone… but the way my gut involuntarily reacted at the sight of him, told me I was very wrong. Guilt flooded into my chest as I ripped the flier down and crumpled it in my hands.

It would seem that Brett hadn't delivered the location of Eric's body just yet, he was probably waiting on a good time. If he was smart. he would wait until a few days of searching had happened and then reveal it. I wasn't sure just how I felt about that, not yet. But I had no time to stress over a dead boy, I had patrols to get to.

I tossed the flier in the trash on my way past my outdoor garbage can and tried some steady breathing to calm my nerves. Once I get to patrol I have to act like nothing's wrong, and that would be impossible if I didn't try to forget Eric right now.

"No more guilt, Rayne. It wasn't your fault." Wynter said. "Yeah, but it was. If he hadn't been with me then nothing would have happened." I said. "And whoever he was with would have gotten raped because you know that no one would have stopped him." She replied. I sighed. She was right.

"Ok, fair. It's better this way. He will never hurt another soul, ever again." I said, hoping my conviction would reassure me. It did little in that aspect. "Now get your head in the game, it's patrol time!" Wynter said. I nodded to my Wolf and tried to follow her advice.

I may have been a bit shaken seeing Eric's face on that flier, but it didn't matter. He was never coming back and it wasn't my fault… I pushed the thoughts from my mind and tried to focus on the task ahead.

Patrol would be slow, like always. We watch the grounds, and make sure there aren't any threats. There usually aren't any. Hell, no other pack dares go against Alpha Drake due to his reputation. I can't blame them. He wouldn't hesitate for a second to kill another Alpha and absorb his entire pack, or just slaughter them all. Due to that, we have a lot of free time on patrol. It's nice when we patrol because I can let Wynter loose.

Our Wolves love to have free reign once in a while. They are cooped up in our heads 90 percent of the time anyway, so whenever we can let loose it's beneficial. We communicate with our peers through our mind link in our Wolf form. Tonight, it was Roman and I, patrolling the East quarter.

Roman's Wolf was bigger than mine. He had dark brown, long fur that was scruffy. My Wolf was more petite. She has platinum silver fur that was a medium length, and her fur shimmers in the sun. My mothers did too. I inherited a lot of attributes from my mother, including her platinum silver eyes. But where my platinum hair came from? I couldn't tell you because my mother was as blonde as you could get.

"Did you hear that Alpha Drake plans to make a trip to The Edge this weekend?" Roman said through our mind link, pulling me from my thoughts. "I hadn't heard, but if that is his plan then you know it's going to be packed. Are you going?" I asked Roman.

"Damn straight I am! We never get to go from what I've been told, so you can bet your sweet ass that I'll be there. What about you?" He questioned. I shrugged. "I'll think about it." I replied. Truth is, I really wanted to go. This was the first time since I was of age that Alpha Drake was actually going. It was the first time I had the chance to go without disobeying my Alpha... I definitely wanted to go.

My dream from the other day popped back into my Mind. *Ugh.* Alpha Drake was insufferable to say the least. I had felt lucky that he had left me alone after our last interaction, but I know he was gone on business too, so that's probably the only reason he hasn't tormented me. I guess I'm speaking of it like it's been ages, when in reality, it's just happened. Still, even an hour without him tormenting me felt like heaven.

After patrol, I was still deciding on what to do. Wynter, however, was already going over outfits for us, so she had her mind made up. It didn't really take that much persuasion from her, for me to finally just agree as well. She barely pushed before I caved. In a normal situation I would have gone to bed after patrol, but since I napped earlier, I was wide awake.

My mind was racing between going to The Edge and thinking about my Demon. In dreams, anything can happen but something about that dream just struck me differently. Something wasn't… I don't know, it was too real to just be a dream… but I had woken up in my own bed, so it had to have been a dream, right?

My thoughts, as usual, were a mess. I decided to head to the library and see if I could find any books on Reavers. My curiosity was piqued. That, or was I just using it as an excuse to think about him… maybe a little of both.

I scoured what seemed like every shelf, and there was literally nothing on Reavers. I finally found a book with a few passages stating that Reavers were the most dangerous creatures in the Underworld due to their vast abilities.

It also said there were 4 Reavers that ruled the Underworld, High Priests it called them. Ramses, Raphael, Rowen, and Raziel. So I knew he was one of the 4, but which one? Any of these names could be his. He refused to tell me his name, opting to keep it secret because he thinks it funny that I don't know it.

My dream fluttered through my mind again, to the name above the door… Raziel. But it was just a dream, though how curious that the exact name above the door was also in this book. Then I remembered the large castle-like home sitting above the city, and just to appease my curiosity, I ran outside and looked up at all of the mountains and peaks. I was straining to see if there might be an enormous castle anywhere that I missed. I was met with nothing. Maybe it really was just a dream. I sighed, and then went back in and read the rest of the passages.

I learned that each High Priest runs multiple Covens of up to 13 Reavers, thus making me think there were quite a bit more of them around than I anticipated. In that case, it would seem that they kept to themselves. That struck me as weird, since all I ever heard of them was how bloodthirsty they were. If they were such monsters, then why would they keep to themselves? You'd think they would surround themselves with prey.

I shook my head and looked back down at the book in my hand. There was literally nothing else in the book about Reavers at all. Those few short paragraphs is all I was able to find. Annoyed, I put the book back on the shelf and left. It was pointless. Short of asking my Demon myself, which would *never* happen, I would probably never find the answers I seeked.

On the way home I had made up my mind, I was definitely going to The Edge and I needed to find something to wear. I was in my room and sifting through my closet already when I felt that all too familiar venomous link into my mind. "We will be going to The Edge this weekend. I thought I would leave the spot on my arm open for you, if you're interested." Alpha Drake said, his voice was less acidic than usual.

I rolled my eyes. I'd had enough of his bullshit and wasn't afraid to talk back anymore knowing my Demon was on my side. "I'd rather die." I spat, trying to be as catty as possible with my words. "That can be arranged, you know." He said with a smirk. "I fucking dare you." I shot, not caring how pissed I was making him. I heard him snicker. "Very well. But I will be dressed in black and silver, I expect you to match me if you change your mind." And he ended the mind link.

Wynter made gagging noises and I couldn't help but laugh. *He thought I was planning on wearing Silver and Black? Ha, little did he know I had a new color in mind.*

Those thoughts infiltrated my head as I left to do a little shopping.

Chapter 17

I took one last look at myself in the mirror, satisfied with my appearance. I had found the most perfect dress for tonight. It was solid gold and shimmered in the light with a set of black chains hanging off the single shoulder. I decided even though it was scarily close to the dress from my dream, it was not the same color so it would suffice. Plus, I really liked that whole one shoulder thing. It was shorter than I intended, but it fit well, accentuating my curves.

I paired it with some gold 6 inch heels. They had black and gold straps that went up over my ankle, also very similar to my dream. My hair fell to my waist in waves. I decided it was time for a new style. Plus I really liked my hair in that dream, so why not? Gold eyeshadow adorned my eyelids, with black in the creases, and black mascara to match. On my lips was a glitter gold gloss. Not too overpowering, just enough to show a hint of glitter in the right lighting. I felt bangin' hot and ready to go. Wynter let out an approving howl at our reflection in the mirror. Roman was picking me up in 20 minutes but I was ready early.

I wondered if I should invite my Demon. But what would a Reaver care to go to a club for? I shouldn't be bothering him with such trivial things, but honestly, I yearned for him to trap me into a corner and say something that would take my breath away…

I couldn't help but wonder if he would like my outfit. He always wore something gold in his attire. I couldn't hide my smile though when I realized how mad Alpha Drake was going to be to see me in gold, and not my usual silver... I smiled even bigger when I pictured his face, especially after he realizes that I wasn't matching him on purpose. The thought made Wynter bust out laughing right as we heard Roman's car honking. Looks like he was early too. Roman had offered to give me a ride even though I didn't need it. I tried to decline, but he insisted. I was still leery of him. I couldn't help but wonder if there was more to his story, but I agreed.

I was still determined to figure out why he was suddenly in my life and so persistent to accompany me literally everywhere I went. He had no idea how bad of an idea it was to be in my life. No one did, and that's exactly how I kept them safe… by keeping them far the fuck away.

Roman was wearing solid black, his button down shirt was not buttoned all the way, exposing part of his muscular chest. He had a neon green pocket square matching his neon green eyes, and his dark hair was a little tousled. *Fitting club attire.* I thought to myself as I got into his neon orange Toyota Supra. He smiled at me and withheld the compliment I knew he was wanting to give. I'm glad he did, it was best for him to not even say it. I was sure my Demon was watching and he could hear everything. It was safer this way. I smiled at him in return, and we headed to The Edge.

"Alpha Drake from Obsidian will be here shortly." I said to the bouncer at the door. That was our code so they would know that we are Wolves. This also told them who our Alpha was and what pack we belonged to. The doorman swallowed hard when I mentioned Alpha Drake, but that was nothing new. Everyone knew of our Alpha, and everyone was afraid of him. Even the Humans who were aware of our existence were afraid.

He put a neon stamp in the shape of a Wolf on our hands. It was invisible, but lit up under the black light at the bar. That told the bartenders who we were, and allowed us to drink underage. Alcohol didn't affect us like Humans anyway, so it didn't really matter.

When we got inside the club, it was swarming with people. There was a mixture of Humans, Wolves,

Vampires, and some other species. Maybe Witches? I wasn't all too familiar with the other Supernatural species and could barely tell Wolves apart from Humans. That was pathetic on its own. We rarely had to deal with any other species, so I was very much in the dark.

I must have really looked good though, judging by the looks I kept getting from literally everyone as we walked by. I ignored the whispers and sideways glances, but I could tell Roman wasn't as intent on letting it go by the way his low growls echoed through my ears. There was no way for anyone to tell just what pack we were from, but I'll bet if they knew who my Alpha was they would think twice before trying to pursue me... even with their eyes alone. Still, my confidence was high.

The club had three levels. On the main level was a big dance floor with a DJ playing dubstep and dance remixes. This was my favorite type of music. I could see many people dressed in bright colors and wearing items that were so furry it looked as if I could get lost in the soft fibers, or things that flashed and glowed. There was a sweet floral scent wafting through the air, which made no sense, but I didn't question it. And everywhere you looked there were lasers and colored lights flashing to the beat.

The light show was incredible, and easily one of the best I had seen, even though we didn't stick around to see the majority of it. The second floor was more of a chill floor with a lot of slow dancing and choreography. This floor boasted a very soft nautical type theme. Fishnets hung around the walls, strategically placed to hang off of the many ship helms and glass fishing bubbles that adorned the area.

Seahorses, turtles, and other fish swam along the base of the walls in dreamy pinks, silvers, and blues. The staff here was dressed in boating attire, some in swimsuits, others in captain apparel, and I swear I could smell saltwater misting around us. I noticed the bar up there was significantly less busy compared to the first floor.

The third floor was essentially a balcony looking out over the dancing lights of the city below. It was covered, but not enclosed. I saw no fancy decorations, no flashing lights or lasers. Instead, many strings of soft white lights hung above us casting a soft dreamy glow that seemed to engulf us.

There were couches, tables, and chairs set up all over with a plethora of people surrounding them. Something about the glow of the lights as you looked over the edge of the balcony at the city lights below, felt very surreal. There was not a DJ on this floor, but you could hear the music from the floor below, so it wasn't needed.

The bar up here was crowded and peeking through the plethora of people standing before it, I could see a faint sparkle of color. A neon blue, but I couldn't make out any decorations from where we stood.

The crisp, cool, outside air infiltrated my nose as I turned to Roman. "This place is awesome." I said. He nodded in agreement. "Drinks?" He questioned. "Yes please." I replied, and we headed to the second floor where the bar wasn't as packed. I ordered a dragon fruit margarita on the rocks, with salt on the rim and a sidecar of tequila. Roman ordered a whiskey and coke.

I thought it was a little strange that he didn't want to leave my side. But honestly, being alone here probably wouldn't have been the best choice. Not with so many other species around. Plus, he knew we were going simply as friends. We didn't even coordinate outfits for that reason. I did not want anyone to get the wrong idea, and have the info somehow get back to him… my Demon.

I was afraid of what he would do if someone told him the completely wrong thing out of context. I knew he would know that I was here. He was always watching me anyway. I just didn't want to give the wrong impression. I could just imagine having an Eric #2 situation right here, in the middle of the club. The thought made me shudder.

But also the idea of him being here excited me. As terrified of my Demon as I was, he exhilarated me. The way he was always so intense, too intense. Always forcing me into impossible situations and causing my body to involuntarily react to the delicately dirty words he weaves. My body began to heat in areas it shouldn't and I pushed the thoughts away before Wynter chimed in and made it worse.

I brought my attention back to Roman, instead. I thought maybe he would meet up with some friends, but it seemed like the only person he knew here was me.

We were just hanging out, talking about patrol and watching the crowd from the bar when Alpha Drake walked in… and of course, he locked eyes with me immediately. I let out a growl.

Roman looked between us with a confused look. I shook my head knowing that shit was about to go down. "Here we go." I said with an eye roll, as Alpha Drake headed our way.

Chapter 18

~

(Alpha Drake)

J headed into the club knowing that more than half of my pack would be there or following shortly. The Edge was a place where the creatures of the Underworld frequented, along with Humans. It made an interesting collaboration, for lack of a better word.

I forbid my pack from going here without myself present, as we have had issues with the other species before. When I'm here, no one dares step to me or my pack. Perks of being who I am. With everyone knowing my history, it makes it easy to be left alone. They know that I would do anything for those loyal in my pack, but those who disobey don't end up so lucky.

It's easier for me to kill them than punish them, and wonder if they will do it again or not. I had complete control over everyone. Everyone… except Rayne. She was my problem child. Escaping death previously for disobeying because of that damn Reaver. And since then, she's been far from obedient. I could feel her slipping from my control and I hated it… but a part of me also reveled in it.

Knowing I couldn't harm her made me feel like I had no control. But I didn't realize just how much having no control over her would make me want her. It was like she was pushing every button I had. She was threatening to push me over the edge with every dirty look and every conflict… all on fucking purpose. But still, I found myself continually wishing for more. Something about her just had me hooked, regardless of how disobedient she was. I was determined to get my control back, no matter the cost. I had told her there was a spot on my arm for her tonight and she rejected it, of course. I expected nothing less, but I was on a mission to find her and try and talk some sense into her pretty little head.

I got word she was on the second floor at the bar with a young Wolf newer to the pack, so I headed that way. She was with Roman, I assumed. He was only new because he was requested by the Reaver to join us. I agreed, only because If I wanted to keep what's rightfully mine then I had to honor our agreement... no matter how reluctant I was to do so.

I didn't ask why the Reaver wanted Roman around. But now I'm wondering if he's been instructed to watch over Rayne, as it seems he never wants to leave her side. My Wolf, Samael, growled at this fact. He also wanted dibs on Rayne, stating that she was ours from the get-go.

I stepped onto the second floor, looked over at the bar, and instantly locked eyes with Rayne. She absolutely took my breath away. The gold dress she was wearing accentuated all of her curves perfectly. I hardly noticed her heels but the gold on her eyes and lips popped.

Not to mention her hair was different... it was in waves instead of straight. I was bothered that she wasn't wearing her go to silver and black, causing us not to match as I had planned. But looking at her, the gold really was a fitting color on her. I gave her a devious look and headed that way as she rolled her eyes at me. That singular movement had my Wolf howling. I had to fight to calm him down.

On my way to the bar, I snapped my fingers, and the short haired blonde bartender already had my crown and coke waiting. I mind linked her since she was a Wolf, and asked her to refill Rayne's drink as well. Of course, she did as she was told. She set both of our drinks down on the bar just as I arrived there.

"Alpha Drake, to what do we owe the pleasure?" Rayne said sarcastically, a gesture that had me pushed against the edge. I slid her drink towards her. She looked at me as if I had poisoned it, but took it anyway. *Good girl.* I thought.

126

That ounce of obedience had my lip almost turning up into a smile. "Would you like to dance?" I asked her, knowing she would refuse. A chill ran down my spine at her next words. "Fuck off, Alpha." She was always playing hard to get lately. I smirked, she was so goddamn sexy. "Oh, Rayne. You don't have to play hard to get. I'm already here and willing." I said, taking a sip of my drink.

She looked disgusted which made me chuckle. She rolled her eyes and took a sip of her drink, set it down, then looked away from me.

"You know, it's better to show a united front between us now. It will make things much easier later on down the road when you become Luna of The Obsidian pack." I said. She snapped her head towards me so fast I thought her neck might break. "I don't know what you're playing at Alpha, but you should know I will *never* be your Luna!" She spat the words as if they were venomous, burning her lips as they left, and spewing right into my ears.

The rush of her anger and disobedience was too much to handle, and Samael took over. I closed the gap between us grabbing her by the throat and slamming her into the wall next to the bar. My eyes were solid black and I could tell she was afraid but trying not to show it. My emotions, unstable at best, were bursting through. I was practically begging to be disobeyed again, yet my primal side wanted to punish her for it.

It was all I had to control my Wolf long enough to put my thumb softly on her bottom lip. My hand was shaking. "You will *not* talk back to me again." I enunciated every word through gritted teeth. I could feel her blood boiling at my words, igniting my passion and pushing my rage even further.

"I will do whatever I choose." She spat, slamming her hand on my chest. That's when I felt it. That familiar burning/tingling sensation I remember from being suspended in the Reavers fireball. Surprised, I looked down just in time to see that Raynes hand was engulfed in a bright green flame. The next thing I know I'm flying into the adjacent wall with the force of a freight train. Everyone on the dance floor stopped and gasped in shock. I hit the wall so hard that the decorations above me fell and crashed to the ground all around me. Growling, I stood up, brushed my suit off, and locked eyes with Rayne. She looked terrified and confused.

Her hand was no longer engulfed in flames, and it made me wonder if I had imagined that part, but I knew better. I knew what she was. I've always known. I just didn't realize she was coming into her power.

She wasn't in a Coven, and she had only been around one Reaver... none of this made any sense according to what I was told by that exact filthy fucking Reaver.

Samael was fighting hard to get back out, but I didn't let him because I knew she'd had enough for tonight.

Re-playing the Reavers' words in my mind, I decided to let it go. This was something I wasn't good at normally. But the circumstances required it.

I gave her a murderous glare and turned to walk away when I locked eyes with him, the fucking Reaver, standing in the doorway.

Chapter 19

~
(Rayne)

My blood was boiling, how could Alpha Drake expect me to want anything to do with him after how he's always acted towards me? His hand against my throat, my back against the wall, such a familiar position we always found ourselves in. He was unpredictable, and I guess this is what made him so terrifying.

He couldn't keep his temper under control, in turn causing his Wolf to lose it. And he couldn't control his Wolf either. To say he was hot headed was an understatement. His temper just didn't mesh well with my newfound cockiness towards him, thanks to my Demon.

"You will *not* talk back to me again." The venom in his voice was oozing as he enunciated every word. I was fucking raging at this point, and I just lost it. I wasn't even sure what I was doing but it was like my hand knew exactly what to do. "I will do whatever I choose." I spat, and as if instinct took over, I slammed my hand into the middle of his chest.

Alpha Drake then went flying into the adjacent wall. I could feel a burning/tingling sensation in my hand when I did that but when I looked down my hand looked normal. I was so confused. How did I just do that? I was strong, but there's no way I could have flung anyone, let alone my Alpha, into a wall with that much force.

Wynter was howling at the fact in my mind, telling me to run, but I would never show that kind of fear. I would stand there and take whatever was coming to me and I would do it with a straight face. I knew he couldn't kill me, but I also knew that this would make him want to kill me even more than he previously did. I heard everyone at the club gasp and step a few feet back.

I stood there in shock and terror, all eyes burning on me, as I watched my Alpha stand up. He brushed himself off and shot me a murderous glare. I thought I was dead. Even though he isn't supposed to kill me, he was never one to follow the rules. I felt like he was definitely not going to spare me this time.

My panic was building, and the fear was coursing through my chest when he turned as if to walk out of the room. He froze instantly. I followed his gaze to figure out why, and gasped when I saw that my Demon was standing in the doorway. His golden eyes were as dark as could be, and his intense gaze was locked straight on Alpha Drake.

My heart fluttered at the sight of him, taking in his every inch. He looked like a villain standing there, partially in the shadows, as the lights danced around his mostly black attire. His golden hair was tousled in a way that seemed as if he had left in a hurry, but not tousled enough not to match the golden chains that hung from his jacket pocket and danced along his cufflinks.

I could see the outline of his muscles along his biceps showing through his shirt as his arms were folded. Anger, then worry shot across his face as he took in the room and locked his eyes on me. I could see surprise, which turned into desire as he began to stalk his way towards me.

Everyone in the room had taken multiple steps back at this time, not moving, afraid to even breathe at the sight of a Reaver. This cleared him a path straight to me, with the exception of Alpha Drake.

My Demon muttered something to my Alpha as he stalked by, but he didn't stop. Alpha Drake clenched his jaw but acted like he heard nothing as he stormed out of the second floor. I was so distracted by the God that stalked me in the night, that I didn't even notice that Roman was still right by my side. He hadn't moved an inch. Even with a

Reaver stalking towards us, he stayed put with a determined glare on his face. At this moment I appreciated his loyalty, though I was instantly worried that he would be the next target, considering the fact that he was standing much too close to me.

My Demon snapped his fingers and the whole club came alive and acted as if they didn't just witness a Wolf disobeying her Alpha. They all were acting as if there were no Reaver standing right here. He snapped again and the bartender refilled mine and Roman's drinks, which I appreciated, because I had spilled mine in the tousle. She then slid a brandy on the rocks across the bar and right into My Demon's hand. I watched as the liquid inside the cup instantly turned gold under his touch, as if on command.

All of this was unfolding by the time he reached the bar, which was only seconds. It seemed as if it all played out in slow motion to me though. He was standing directly in front of me. His golden eyes were full of different emotions, seeming to change every second. His gaze never left mine. "Thank you Roman, you may be dismissed for now." He snapped.

"Yes sir, I will be downstairs when I'm needed again." Roman replied, not an ounce of fear or wavering could be heard in his voice. My friend shot me a million-dollar smile, grabbed his drink and headed downstairs. "How the hell does Roman know Mr. Kane?" Wynter questioned, but I was too lost in my Demon's molten golden orbs to even hear her, or care what she was saying. I felt as if I could get lost in his eyes forever. They were like a chasm that I longed to fall headfirst into.

"You look fucking incredible in my color." He smirked. I smiled, of course he would approve. "I refused to match Alpha Drake, and what better color to piss him off than yours?" I replied with a chuckle. "Good girl," he purred, his words causing wetness to dance between my legs.

I watched as my Demon looked down the entire length of my body and then met my eyes again, slowly and deliberately, as if I were his last meal and he hadn't eaten in days. "You know, there is no way to deny your feelings for me now." He said. I raised an eyebrow. "My feelings?" I scoffed, knowing full well that he knew I was about to deny everything, even though we both knew I would be lying. He narrowed his intense gaze on me and hummed to himself before sipping his brandy.

I watched as he set the glass down and took a step closer to me. I swallowed hard, but didn't move. My heart was beating a million miles per second and I knew he could hear it. "Look at you… so quick to deny yourself when we both know the truth." He purred, running his fingers up my arm. His touch instantly gave me cold chills.

"No, the truth is that you are very…" I began, but the words fell from my tongue as soon as I saw the sparkle in his eyes that followed the slight smirk that danced along his God-like features. "I am very what? Sexy? Intimidating? Persistent? Suffocating… intense?" He whispered each word while inserting himself right into my personal bubble. Had he been an inch closer he could have swallowed me, and I would have let him.

"Um, yes…" I stammered, suddenly unable to breathe, let alone think with his proximity devouring me. "No, Rayne… I am a man who knows what he wants, and I'm not afraid to take it. Lucky for you, that is not why I'm here." He said, snaking his arm around my waist and pulling me to his chest, completely draining me of any personal space I thought I may have had.

I looked down, panic engulfing my small form. I felt so tiny next to him, but we both knew that he was here because of what I had done to Alpha Drake. My hands were on his chest and I looked at them before intertwining my fingers together, unsure of what to even say. "I… I didn't mean to hurt him… I'm not sure what even happened…" I said softly.

Even though I was slightly feeling the alcohol, the fear was still creeping its way through my chest. It had me wondering if it would ever truly disappear around him. "I know. But tonight, the only worry I want you to have is what the rumors are going to sound like tomorrow." He said. I crinkled both of my eyebrows as I looked back up at him and we locked eyes. "The rumors?" I questioned.

He smiled at me, and I had to fight to keep my knees from caving in. "Yes, little Wolf. The rumors. Do you know how fucking beautiful you are? How enticing and utterly breathtaking you look tonight?" He said, running his fingers along the side of my face softly. Shivers ran down my spine with his touch. I thought I was breathing, but I don't think I could remember how if you had paid me. My Demon always said things that took my breath away, but a compliment? This was different, it felt more personal than the things he's said before…

I didn't have time to sort through my jumbled thoughts, nor did I have time to even hear what Wynter was trying to say to me before he twisted his fingers through my hair and forced me to look up at him. He licked his lips while looking down at me. "Mmm, my God… I could devour you." He growled, and allowed his free fingers to run down the side of my neck. Any breath I thought I had was gone. "You know, my self control is usually much better, but… I've waited a long time to do this." He purred, before he leaned in closing the inch between us.

There is no possible verblage to explain the way my entire heart, body, and soul exploded into ecstasy when his lips met mine. Time completely stood still. Every single ounce of stress and worry that I had been holding onto, melted. I never realized just how much I truly wanted him to do this until this very moment. He was the epitome of perfection.

His lips tasted like something dark and forbidden, begging me to run away with him and never return. And I wanted to, God's I wanted to. Cold chills racked my entire body and my head began to swim, lost in utter bliss. The way I allowed him to deepen the kiss without so much as a hesitation, told me that he was right all along. I never belonged to anyone else… and I never would. He was my past, my present, and is my future. There was no fighting it.

133

Not anymore. I may pretend, but we both know exactly where I belong. Wynter's internal banter was all but ignored while I fought to pull myself back from the stars. Our lips parted, but only because air is crucial, and neither of us wanted to pass out in the middle of the club.

I sucked air in slowly, trying to quench the burn, but he didn't pull away. Instead, he leaned in slightly and placed his lips back on mine softly. What was supposed to be a small peck turned into more, and I drug my teeth over his bottom lip gently, before allowing him to pull completely away. I looked up and we locked eyes as redness engulfed my cheeks.

Tingles ravaged my entire body as my heart pounded completely out of my chest. Even breathing as regularly as I was, I couldn't seem to pull in enough oxygen. He ran his thumb over my cheek gently. "Those rumors." He said with a smirk. My mouth dropped open, pulling me from the absolute stupor that I found myself in.

"You did that on purpose?!" I cried, astonished that he would purposefully make everyone talk. Of course he would! He was just the type to entice the rumors, if not start them his damn self. He snickered, which enraged me. "Oh little Wolf, do you truly think I would ever do something without a purpose?" I took a step back, to which he allowed, surprisingly.

Instantly, every thought I previously had was null and void. I was no longer swimming in a pool of confused emotions. My thoughts were crystal fucking clear. This man was going to be the death of me. "You are the fucking worst!" I cried, attempting to turn from him.
He stopped me with a single hand around my wrist. I looked back at him with raised eyebrows. "You wouldn't leave your date standing here like that, now would you? Not without sharing at least 1 dance." He purred, holding his free hand out to me.

I wanted to slap it away and tell him to go fuck himself, but we both knew I wasn't going to decline his ask. As much as the man terrified and infuriated me, my body was still dancing in the stratosphere. "Fine, but you're not my date!" I snapped. "Oh? Do you allow everyone you meet at the club to show you the beauty of the stars then?" He purred. I was astonished that he would ask me that. He always watches me, he knows what I'm doing at all times. "Really? You know the answer to that." I huffed. He smirked in response, and pulled me back into his arms by my wrist.

"Of course I do, little Wolf. But what fun is it if I can't absolutely infuriate you every chance I get?" He replied with a wicked smile. I shook my head but I couldn't stop the smile that began to involuntarily form on my lips.

"You are absolutely horrible." I said. "There's no one worse than me, little Wolf." He concurred. "So long as we agree." I snipped.

Chapter 20

~

(Raziel)

J had felt the pull of magic coming from Rayne as it was materializing in her palm. Being a High Priest had its advantages. I could zone in on any Reaver and know what powers they were using at any given time. I could do it to any creature, but why waste my time? It wasn't something I really used often, or even cared about. But since Rayne started dreamwalking I had kept my eye on her in case other powers started to emerge. It's a good thing I did.

As soon as I felt it, I instantly focused on her and materialized where she was. I ended up at The Edge, in the doorway of the second floor. I scoffed. *A night club huh? Lovely.* Our kind rarely frequented places such as these. We had, what you could call, a reputation... I looked up just in time to see her throw Alpha Drake into the adjacent wall in a fury of green flames.

It took me a minute to register what had happened as I was in awe at her appearance. She was wearing my color, gold. And I had not influenced her to do it in the slightest. She chose to wear it on her own accord. I couldn't help but delight in the extreme pleasure just seeing her in my color showered over me.

The shimmering gold of her dress was sparkling in the low lighting of the club. On her eyelids was a brilliant golden eyeshadow with black crease, and in her hair were those beautiful beachy waves I loved. Nero was distracting me, howling in approval and primal lust. I had to push him out of my mind to focus. I, of course, matched her perfectly, all the way down to the very last accessory. It looked as if we had planned it. That thought appeased me.

As much as I was worried about her coming into her powers, I was more interested in gauging her feelings for me and if they had changed. Call it selfish, but she was wearing gold, after all.... her feelings were my first and only priority right now. We could deal with the powers later.

I was torn from my thoughts when a very fucking pissed Alpha Drake stood up, brushed himself off and turned to walk out. *Good,* I thought, as he wasn't going to torment Rayne for her behavior. He had taken what I said to heart, it seemed. That thought also appeased me. Today was full of surprises. We locked eyes, he never let his gaze falter as I stalked his way.

He may be a sorry excuse for an Alpha, in my opinion, but even I couldn't deny he had balls. He never backed down from me when others in his position would have easily bowed down. "Don't forget our agreement, Wolf." I spat quietly enough that only he could hear as I strode by him heading in Raynes direction. He didn't reply and kept walking, which is exactly what I wanted him to do.

I was perfectly fine with that. I noticed the entire club had stopped and backed up against the walls, staring at me in awe and fear. It wasn't everyday a Reaver stepped into The Edge. It wasn't everyday a Wolf threw their Alpha across the room without punishment either. Today was full of firsts. I snapped my fingers, forcing everyone to carry on with their business as if nothing had happened. I wasn't going to make them forget about it this time. Instead, I chose to make them ignore it.

I wanted them to know not to fuck with Rayne. Not that they would try, but it was more of an insurance policy than anything. I snapped again to get the bartender's attention, and with my mind link had her refill Rayne and Roman's drinks, plus make one of my own.

She slid mine to the bar just as I stepped up, the cup sliding directly into my hand. As soon as I touched the glass the liquid inside turned gold, my preferred color, of

137

course. Turning things gold was my forte. In fact, all things magic were. I didn't hesitate to take advantage of an opportunity to use my magic, no matter how trivial the reason was.

Rayne watched my actions in awe as we locked eyes. I was trying to gauge her fear level, but to my satisfaction, I found that it was minimal. I excused Roman as his services at this time were not needed. He obeyed like a good little pup and left the room. He was obedient to a fault. Anthony did a great job finding him. If he could just keep his Wolf's thoughts under control around Rayne, then he would be perfect.

He had the audacity to crush on her… I know he didn't mean to. Not that he could help it, I doubted anyone could… but my jealousy was pushing through. I had every thought of taking his eyes so he couldn't look at her again, but I refrained. My focus was on her now.

Of course, I took this chance and multiple others to infuriate her, and then take her breath away. But all of that was done in good fun, like usual. What I struggled with was keeping Nero tame enough to place my lips onto hers and not completely lose every ounce of self control I had been clinging onto. All by a thread, of course. I would never admit it, but the second our lips collided and the full extent of coconuts and candy touched my tongue, I almost allowed Nero to have the control he so desperately craves.

Had I allowed that, I would have taken her far from this club and all of its prying eyes while I completely and utterly devoured her. Hours, if not days, locked in my red-room with no hope of ever escaping…

She wouldn't leave without my mark adoring her face, and my bite marks adorning every inch of her perfect body. Her slender neck, bruised and swollen in shades of blues and purples from my lips and hands. Her wrists and ankles indented from my intricate rope work. The array of crop welts I would leave along the swells of her perfect breasts and curve of her banging ass… I could never allow her to leave if that were to happen. I had to stop the thoughts, stop the intensity in order to calm my Wolf. So, of course, I infuriated her. What better way? My plan world perfectly and I smirked as she attempted to rid herself of me.

Of course, I stopped her, and I wooed her again, reveling in the feeling of her head lying against my chest. Though she had just tried to escape me, and told me I was the absolute worst, here she was, in my arms.

I smiled internally at the position we found ourselves in. One that I hoped would become a permanent staple, eventually. I had planned to win her over around 18 but that didn't work as well as I had hoped. Probably my own fault anyway, you know, scaring off all those people she cared about, and furthermore, killing Eric.

Nero scoffed, they deserved it anyway but that doesn't necessarily make it right. No one ever said I cared about what was right. It didn't really matter. I'd been waiting for someone like her for thousands of years, I could stand to wait a little longer... I hoped.

I was distracted from my internal banter when I could hear Wynter speaking to Rayne. "Omg, we are dancing with HIM!" She swooned. "Can we just stay here forever in his arms? I never want to leave!" Wynter's pleas appeased Nero and myself.

I couldn't hear what Rayne said in response to Wynter. Reading normal thoughts was not something a Reaver could do, which really was surprising, given the rest of our powers. We could hear any Wolves speaking through mind links, as well as any internal dialogue if we were close enough and focused on it. We usually pushed the chatter from our minds as it made things noisy.

I, however, was always listening to Wynter. It gave me an idea of what Rayne was thinking and feeling since she always hid her emotions from me. I wondered why... maybe she didn't want to seem vulnerable in my presence. My little Wolf...

I traced my fingers across her arm and shoulder. I could feel how her body was reacting to my simple touch, a hidden fire burning underneath her mostly collected exterior. My thoughts wandered to Rayne and our inevitable future together. I wanted nothing more in this moment than to take my claim and mark my chosen mate. The mark must be reciprocated though, otherwise, over time it fades and will disappear, taking the mate bond with it.

If the chosen mate accepts, and they complete the mating process, the mark will become permanent, thus solidifying their bond. As often as I thought about forcing it on her, I refrained, and would refrain, no matter how often I threatened it. I imagined what she would look like with a delicate gold crescent moon adorned in glittering, swirling, filigree and vines running down her cheek onto her neck. Nero approved this thought, picturing it in his mind. She looked absolutely stunning, like a Goddess.

I took her hand and spun her around then pulled her back into my arms.She must have calmed down and she definitely wasn't as angry with me because she flashed me a smile full of perfect teeth, something she's never done before, then put her head back on my chest. It seemed that she was getting used to me. I may not have to force her to love me after all.

I tried to conceal my yearning for her. She smelled like coconuts and amber, a smell I found myself missing often. I was able to get a small glimpse of what she was thinking through Wynter's dialogue. I could tell she was still a little scared of me but was ignoring her instincts. Ignoring her primal need to self-preserve in the face of the enemy.

She was determined not to show weakness in front of me. This was something she exhibited often in my presence, thinking I couldn't tell, but I knew. I was her enemy, or so she thought. She was raised to be afraid of us, all creatures of the Underworld were. We were the top of the food chain, after all.

She had no idea just how dangerous I really was, but her instinct was correct in her fear. Honestly, I wasn't sure if I ever wanted her to find out the truth. It was inevitable though, and eventually she would... I pushed the thought from my mind. Nero was complacent for once, not howling or whining to be let loose. He was just enjoying the feel of her body against ours. This was a behavior I could get used to from him.

Nero was extremely primal, for lack of a better word. A trait I found myself trying to control often. More of an annoyance in certain situations, than anything. The song was nearing its end, shaking me from my thoughts. I hated the fact that it was almost over. I took in every last second I had with her, not taking one moment for granted.

We may not be speaking to each other at this moment, but I didn't need her words to satisfy my cravings. Once the song was over, I reluctantly called to Roman through the mind link. My heart ached and Nero howled in anguish as I saw Roman come through the door, knowing our time was up.

I moved the wave of silver hair from the side of Rayne's face to behind her ear. "Until next time, little Wolf." I purred. She knew I was about to go, and I swear I saw her heart shatter through her eyes. My heart was breaking at the sight. I wanted to take her with me, I just couldn't risk the word getting out yet. A Reaver who was coming into her powers... naturally, and without training or living in a Coven? It was unheard of.

Our kind was quick to kill what didn't serve us. And while I knew with every fiber of my being that she was to be mine, others may not share the same feelings. The other High Priests would understand, but the rest of the Priests who would hear the startling news, may not be so forgiving. I knew I had to protect her any possible way I could. I couldn't risk anyone finding out, not yet... not even if it meant I was going against them all, my people included. I didn't even care.

I kissed the back of her hand and just as I was about to let go and vanish, she grabbed my arm and stopped me dead in my tracks. "Don't go... " she pleaded. Her silky voice sent shocks of pain through my chest. I could hear Wynter's whining and sadness at my parting. I wish she knew just how much I truly didn't want to go. But she wasn't safe so long as she spent time with me. Not yet... I snapped my fingers and produced a single, solid 14kt gold rose. I handed it to her gently. "Not even this rose could contain your beauty, little Wolf. See you soon." I purred, and then I vanished just as Roman stepped to her side.

Chapter 21

~

(Rayne)

J was definitely feeling the alcohol after my drink, the partial amount of Alpha Drake's drink, and Raziel's drink. They didn't go light on us Wolves knowing that we didn't get drunk like Humans. I probably had the equivalent of 10 shots, if I were to guess.

Not that I was even drunk, but definitely feeling good. You know, that lowered inhibition feeling good. I looked up into Raziel's eyes and I wasn't even afraid of him. Probably the alcohol talking... definitely the alcohol talking. I was still somewhat in shock after the events that unfolded. Actually, I was in denial mostly. I had launched Alpha Drake across the room with only my hand. I acted like I didn't see the green flames, but I did, and I've seen them before from Raziel... I was just too afraid to bring it up.

I vaguely remembered my mother and Alpha Drake being suspended in green flames. A twinge of realization hit me. I may be more than just a Wolf... at this time it was probably due to the alcohol, but I didn't even freak out. My emotions seemed to be weirdly calm given the situation. I decided I was going to pretend I didn't notice and revel in this moment.

I was definitely going to try and use the powers later and see what I could really do. But right now, I just pushed the thoughts out of my mind, we could deal with it later. Wynter's dialogue snapped me back to reality, she was going wild as I danced with my Demon.

I swear the time seemed to slow down as we were living in this moment, him and I. I laid my head on his chest and a sliver of fear tried to push its way back through. He may be gorgeous, mysterious, and alluring…. but he was my enemy, and every being of my body knew it. He was a killer… and what about me? What if we are the same? Would I be a killer too? The thoughts swam in my mind, but luckily Wynter did not comment on my erratic thoughts. Not those ones.

I was still feeling somewhat foggy from the alcohol when Raziel suddenly spun me around on the dance floor and swung me back into his arms. I loved this, everything about it was dangerous, tempting, forbidden… all things I had only just realized that I craved more of.

This man has literally killed for me, and would again in an instant if I asked. My smile confirmed my acceptance of the current situation. I closed my eyes, listening to his heartbeat and trying to take in every ounce of this moment. Maybe I should drink more often when he's around. I was feeling a mixture of fear and excitement through my cloudy mind, but reveled in it.

As the song came to an end, I knew it was time for him to go. Wynter whined and I just lost it. It may have been the alcohol, but I never wanted to be out of his arms again. I boldly reached out and grabbed his arm, something I would have never dared to do before. It didn't stop there… I begged him not to go.

It seemed as if I could see the hurt in his eyes as the prospect of leaving me. He snapped his fingers and produced a long stem gold rose, handed it to me, purring in my ear something about my beauty and seeing me soon, before he vanished.

I was too entranced by the mere thought of being in his arms again that I wasn't even sure what he had said. As if instinct kicked in, I smelled the rose expecting it to be scentless because it was solid gold. But to my surprise a sweet aroma filled my nose, in turn filling my stomach with butterflies. I had all but forgotten how infuriated I was with him earlier. I knew then that I had to pursue this… him. Forbidden or not, I was being pulled in his direction. And I had no ability to be able to control it. It was as if nothing else in the world mattered when he was near. As much as I physically feared him, my body wanted him... my Wolf wanted him... and my heart wanted him, leaving me with a mixture of fear, desire, and excitement at his every whim.

"Stop fighting it, Rayne. You know how this ends. We both do." Wynter chimed in. I was lost in my thoughts when a rush of realization washed over me. He had me from the first time he ever laid those golden orbs on mine.

He always had me... he knew it... and now I knew it too...

~

(Roman)

"I wonder how much longer I will have to be Raynes' bodyguard with her powers breaking through." I said to my Wolf, Ace, as I sulked down the stairs to the first floor of The Edge. I was trying not to be bitter, but this was just too much. I was headed to the bar to get a few shots. I was not drunk enough for this. I wasn't even drunk at all, actually... and that had to change. "I'll take five Jager shots." I said to the pretty Wolf behind the bar. "That bad huh?" She smirked.

"You have no idea." I replied, as I downed all five shots in a row and turned my back to her. I wasn't in the mood for talking. Rayne looked so goddamn beautiful tonight. It was everything I had to hold myself back. Ace sat in silence because he could feel my turmoil. I guess when you make a deal with the devil, you pay for it... little did I know I would be paying like this.

I shut my eyes, trying to tune out the slamming of the bass and the noise of the dancing around me. I recalled how I got myself here to begin with. A nearby Vampire clan had eradicated my old pack lands. They killed a lot of my pack and held many others hostage. I was one of only four to escape with my life intact. I knew there was no way I

145

could just run and leave them like the other 3 had. They were my pack, my family.

It may not mean much to the others, but my pack meant everything to me. I tried for weeks to infiltrate and save them, but I failed every single time. I just wasn't strong enough alone. That's when I decided to swallow my pride and ask for help.

I put the feelers out there and within hours I was approached by a Reaver named Anthony. Said he would save my pack and take care of my little Vampire issue if I did something for him in return. Befriend a She-Wolf in a pack a lot further away. I would have to transfer packs and live there. I would have to keep a close eye on her, keep her out of trouble... a simple task, how hard could it be? It was for 1 year, and then I was free to do whatever I wanted.

"Ha, until you fucking fell in love with her!" Ace scoffed. "You started it, dude! I wasn't even looking because I knew better! And then your internal dialogue wouldn't stop, and then my brain wouldn't stop, and now look what we've gotten ourselves into." I sighed.

It was no use arguing with Ace, he was stubborn to the core. The one damn thing Anthony said that was forbidden... a relationship. If I valued my life, I would push any feelings like that clear out of my mind. Believe me, I've tried, and tried, and fucking tried...

It was like the first time she laid those silver beauties on me, when I purposefully slammed into her that day, she had me. She could have had me in an instant had she even attempted it. I would have given in to her every want without a fight. I would have allowed her to take me off into the forest and sacrifice me to the Gods if she wanted. I wouldn't have even made 1 snarky comment about it. I knew she was 100 percent off limits, but that just made me want her more.

And now I'm stuck here, falling in love with a girl I definitely can't have, but am forced to be around on the daily. "Blah blah blah, just nut up and get over it. You have not even a year left and then you're free!" Ace snarled. "Dude, shut the fuck up. You are such a dick! This is all your fault to begin with!" I snapped.

"You're just being a sappy fuck. Go out there and hit on that hot blonde over there." Ace cackled. I attempted to argue, but he stopped me. "I don't want to hear excuses, motherfucker." He scowled. I rolled my eyes. I wasn't about to get up and speak to her. He was always kind of douchey, my Wolf, but he was my douche.

"You're right, but I'm not talking to her... let's just get through this next year." I said with fake ass enthusiasm in my voice. I turned to the bartender and took another 2 Jager Bombs. Whatever Ace was saying, I ignored it hoping the alcohol would start to kick in, luckily it had.

That's when I felt liquid gold pouring over me. It was the mind link from Mr. Kane, letting me know I was again needed.

"Here we go, Ace." I stated, and headed back upstairs.

Chapter 22

~

(Rayne)

Roman had dropped me off a little early, I blamed it on the night's events. But really, I didn't even mind because I was eager to get home. The whispers were deafening after my Demon left the club and I was just waiting for someone to dare to come up and ask me about him. Only the Gods know how I would have reacted. His words infiltrated my mind again, as they had for the 3,000th time. The rumors he started, deliberately. I tried to ignore it and shift my focus to my newfound powers, or whatever this was.

I had always wondered why my mother and I had platinum, a precious metal, colored eyes, when no one else I had ever met did. I had always heard the stories of Reavers and their precious metal obsessions. How their eyes and voices matched, but never put it together until now. I can't be just a Wolf, I had to be something more. This made me wonder, for the first time in a very long time, if my father was a Reaver, and if I was actually a Hybrid.

I could do the things my Demon did. Well, some of them, sort of. I know I didn't imagine the green flames, and I know he saw them too. Curiosity always got the best of me, and I was determined to try and produce them again. I changed out of my dress into a gold sports bra and sweatpants. I was becoming fond of the color. I may be a little biased though because gold reminded me of him… I smiled at the thought as a twinge of fear shot through my chest. I shook it off. I sat on my bed and closed my eyes. I was determined to make a flaming green fireball. I concentrated as hard as I could and tried to force it to form, but nothing happened. I tried focusing on everything I could think of to upset me or annoy me, but still, nothing.

"Maybe there really wasn't any fire? Maybe we did just push him across the room out of anger." Wynter said. "I saw the fire. I know I saw it and I felt it! Why isn't it working?" I sighed. I swear I wasn't seeing things, but no matter how hard I tried I could not get a fireball to happen. I couldn't get it to even kind of happen. I tried for so long that I drifted off to sleep, while wondering if I had truly imagined the entire thing.

I found myself standing in front of an exquisite castle. This one was a little less gothic looking than you'd expect from a mansion of this magnitude. It had a sleek modern style that blended seamlessly into the natural surroundings. The mansion's exterior was black, dark enough to mimic the night sky, with a touch of silver traced throughout that seemed to shimmer and ripple like the moon's reflection on a vast, yet still, lake.

The windows, framed in silver, gleamed like stars in the night sky, casting an ethereal glow around the surrounding landscape. There were no statues on its magnificent spires or pillars, and I expected there to be vines growing up along the sides of the walls, but I saw none. Even so, it seemed familiar... somehow.

I was standing in front of the main gate to the whimsical property, which was solid silver. I could see a large infinity symbol standing diagonally, covered in vines and filigree running down the middle of the gate. I could see the separation in the symbol where the gate would open, splitting it into 2 pieces, one on each side as you walked through.

"Open." I said, and to my surprise, it creaked open slowly. I walked inside and down the trail following the main trodden path. Winding pathways, lined with silver tipped bushes and black stone lanterns, called to me like a Siren at sea. I swear if I listened close enough, I could hear its actual song. I wanted to follow the call and explore as I

149

could see the gardens and what seemed like an orchard in the back, but I refrained. I was more interested to see the bedroom in this castle. I had no idea why I was interested to see that, but it seemed to be the only thing pushing me forward.

I reached the front doors of the castle. They were the largest doors I had ever seen, black and intricately designed, adorned in silver accents. It looked as if someone had hand carved every single curvature of vine and leaf of filigree. I stood in awe, admiring it as I ran my fingers along the smooth edges of the design.

After taking in the beauty, I realized the door was cracked open, so I walked in. The layout of this home was intricate and breathtakingly gorgeous. The interior revealed a grand, high-ceilinged space filled with silver-spined books that seemed to stretch up to the heavens. Towering shelves, crafted from a rich, dark wood, supported the tomes, their silver lettering glinting in the soft, ambient light.

Grand architecture dominated the space, with sweeping curves and angular lines that seemed to defy gravity. 3 majestic staircases, their banisters forged from silver, curved like a swan's neck, leading to the upper floors. Behind those, a dark hallway that led visitors to the unknown. Black and silver encased the entire home, giving the illusion of space and the night sky. It was breathtaking. After a moment of pondering, I decided to take the right spiral staircase, following my instincts.

When I got to the top of the staircase it opened up into a giant foyer with more magical books adorning every wall. Most of them were silver spined, sparkling in the sunlight that was glinting through the large picture window opposite of the room. I ran my fingers across the spines as I walked through the foyer, noting how silver glitter fell softly off every book.

I looked down and saw the ground was littered with sparkling silver dust. It was strange dust though, it didn't stick to my boots. It seemed to just stay in place, sparkling and taunting me, as if beckoning me to lean down and attempt to wipe it with my own fingers. I refrained in fear that if I touched it there, it might whisk me away from this magical place.

As I ventured deeper, I found myself in a sprawling hallway, surrounded by another astonishing array of books. The sheer scale of the full collection left me breathless. Row upon row of bookshelves stretched out before me, the books' silver spines glinting in the soft light. The haunting book collection seemed to stretch on beyond my line of sight. From what little I was able to read as I walked by, their topics ranged from ancient Grimoires bound in black leather to modern volumes, bound by machines with glossy edges.

I finally reached the end of the corridor, stopping before a magnificent silver door, its surface etched with intricate black accents. The name 'Raphael' was emblazoned across the top in bold, Old English calligraphy, seeming to shimmer with a light of its own. I felt a shiver run down my spine as anticipation built within my chest. "Raphael." I said out loud, reading the door, and to my surprise, the door opened. Albeit, slowly, it didn't even make a single sound.

My mind instantly trailed back to the book I had previously read in the pack library. 'There are 4 Reavers that rule the Underworld.' Raphael was one of the names in the book. I was snapped from my thoughts when I looked up and found myself face to face with an eerily gorgeous man.

We locked eyes and I noticed his eyes were a darker silver than my lighter platinum, but the color in his irises were swirling as if they were made of molten metal. I recognized that from my Demon, his eyes looked like molten gold often. This mysterious man had black hair, dark like obsidian.

It was semi short and neatly kept. He had light stubble which accentuated his strong jawline and tanned olive skin. He was taller than me, so I assumed about 6 feet, if not taller, with rippling muscles cascading down his arms. He was absolutely breathtaking in every way. In fact, he was too gorgeous… almost ethereal.

"Well, hello there beautiful, and how exactly did you get here?" He said, holding his hand out to me. Fear danced along the edge of my mind, but curiosity pushed it from the ledge. As if instinct, I took his hand and my heart fluttered as he bent down and kissed the back of it, sending a chill down my spine.

The only thing I could think of was how pissed my Demon was going to be when he found out that another man put his lips on me, even if it was just on the back of my hand. The man's voice was smooth and silky, like molten silver. The sound of it was like music to my ears. I felt myself wanting to hear it again even though I knew I shouldn't. But who was he? Raphael, like the door said?

I didn't answer him, I was too enthralled in my whole situation to be able to really comprehend what was actually going on. He didn't seem to care, and instead, led me inside the room. I should have been afraid, but this was my goal the entire time. I wanted to know what this bedroom looked like, and here I was. I wasn't about to back down now. Not when I was so damn close.

The room was a masterpiece of elegance and mystique, leaving me utterly enchanted. My gaze was drawn to the far left corner, where a stunning four-poster bed stood, its silver and black accents gleaming in the soft light. Next to the bed, a towering wall of silver spined books stretched up to the vaulted ceiling, their leather-bound covers seeming to shimmer before me. I had no idea how one could have such a large book collection.

On the right side of the room sat a sleek mini bar, fully stocked and accompanied by a decanter of silver liquid that seemed to glow as if it were the source of magic itself. Next to it, a beautiful silver and black globe of the world sat in between two plush armchairs that invited me to linger and explore.

In the center of the room, a magnificent black and silver area rug seemed to anchor the space, its intricate patterns captivating my senses. A solitary couch faced the right side wall, where a large television hung flush. My eyes were drawn to the infinity symbol from the front gate, now hanging on the wall beside the main door which seemed to complete the look. The room was absolutely beautiful, breathtaking even. I noticed the man, Raphael, I assumed, was watching my every move.

"This is a beautiful room." I said with a gasp. I saw a flicker in his eye, amusement maybe? He seemed to approve of my approval, causing a small smile to creep onto his lips. "I'm glad you approve." He smirked.

"Now what is your name, beautiful?" He asked, his silver eyes sparkling. "Rayne." I replied, matter of factly. "Rayne." He repeated out loud. My name rolled off his tongue so easily… too fucking easily. "Well Rayne, you may call me Raphael." He said with a bow. He was extremely formal.

"Would you like to sit and read with me?" He asked, with one eyebrow raised. He didn't give me much time to answer before he snapped his fingers and two books appeared in his hands. He handed me one and I followed him to the two armchairs as we sat down. I didn't say anything, but I was at a loss for words. He didn't seem to care that I was basically mute, or if he did, he didn't let me know.

I opened the book, and to my surprise, it was a chapter regarding Reavers. How coincidental… I reached out to Wynter, to find her absent and that was what triggered my memories of my dream before. The black and gold castle that belonged to my Demon… it was so fucking similar to this place. Different colors, but so eerily similar you'd think he and Raphael designed them together.

Was I dreaming? There was no other explanation, but dream or not, my interest was piqued. I wanted to read what was in this book before I woke up and missed out on anything that could help me. I ignored the strangeness of this whole thing and began to read. I got about 2 paragraphs in when my alarm went off and my eyes fluttered open slowly. Wynter was waking groggily as well.

I sat up. "What in the fuck." I said, as Wynter reveled in my thoughts, re-living my dream. "Damn, Rayne, you've been having some weird ass dreams lately." She chuckled. "I don't really understand what in the fuck is going on, or why I keep having these dreams. This one was just like my last but different. And who the hell is Raphael?" I mumbled.

"I have no idea, but maybe you're dreaming this because of the book you read in the pack library?" She replied. I nodded, she was probably right. I had read stuff in that book and I had been thinking about it all recently, trying to decipher it.

I couldn't help but be upset that I didn't get to read through the book from my dream though. I tried to remember the 2 paragraphs I did read, but I was struggling to recall. It was like everytime I had one small piece of the memory, it was snatched away, just out of my grasp.

Something about a mark and being chosen. Something else about the 4 High Priests that rule the Underworld… It was too blurry to piece together anything relevant.

I was definitely going to try and get back there and read it again. Dream or not, it could give me some insight. All those thoughts were swirling in my mind as I got up and got ready for training.

Chapter 23

~

(Raphael)

I was dreamwalking my own dream to get some peace and quiet and let myself read a bit. I never really got much time to myself, running a multitude of Covens and all. So my escape was in my dreams. I had just downed a second glass of brandy, which I had just turned silver, when I felt a presence.

"Strange... now who would be daring enough to enter my dreams?" I questioned Axel, my Wolf. "It feels like a woman, sir." He said. "Curious... shall we go see, or let her find us?" I inquired. "Looks like she's already on her way up, sir." Axel said.

I set my glass down and headed towards my bedroom door just as I heard a stunning voice say my name. "Raphael." I was surprised. I opened the door and locked eyes with the most beautiful pair of platinum silver eyes I had ever seen.

This woman standing before me was stunning, to say the least. I took a minute to take in her beauty. Axel was howling his approval in my mind. She was wearing a simple gold sports bra and sweats, paired with black combat boots. She was exquisite, even in such relaxed attire. Although it was an atrocious color scheme. I scoffed internally. You'd think she'd have better taste given her color was also silver.

I took in her every feature. The way her pouty lips protruded just under her button nose. Perfect eyebrows, shaped and filled in, along with long, luscious, eyelashes.

A small amount of mascara to make them pop. Her silver hair falling pin straight to her waist, and a look of wonder in her sparkling eyes. She was about 5 foot 7 inches. I was a bit taller than her and she had a petite, but muscular stature. No doubt she was a Reaver.

"Well, hello there, beautiful. And how exactly did you get here?" I asked her. I held my hand out and she put hers into mine with no hesitation. I bent down and kissed her hand. I could feel her body reacting to my touch, this pleased me. No Reaver would ever have dared to dreamwalk into *my* dream. She was ballsy as hell.

I realized that she didn't know who I was, and I couldn't help but wonder just how she had gotten here if that was the case. And then it hit me, she didn't know she was dreamwalking… I wondered if she even knew she was a Reaver.

Regardless of the possibility that she could destroy my entire home with a strategically placed temper tantrum, I led her inside. I smirked as her face lit up. She was in complete awe as she took in every inch of my dwelling. I could see her look of approval as she looked throughout my room into each section, committing it all to memory.

"This is a beautiful room." She said with a gasp, and I approved that she approved. I asked her what her name was. "Rayne…" *What a beautiful name.* The way she said it was with conviction, she was proud of who she was.

I asked her if she would like to sit and read with me, as that was my intention to begin with, to sit and read. She didn't say yes or no, but I had already snapped my fingers and materialized two books. I handed her one, and started walking towards my nook.

I glanced back to see she was following me. *Excellent, I* thought. We sat down and she started to read. I had purposefully given her a book about Reavers because I had the inclination that she probably didn't know what dreamwalking was. I thought maybe a little history lesson might help her. A Reaver coming into her powers, without knowing she was… a very small sliver of panic coursed through my chest as I recalled that conversation from what felt like an eon ago.

I needed to tell Raziel about her, but knowing that he would kill her with no remorse was something that didn't sit right with me. I was very aware of how volatile and dangerous unchecked Reaver powers would be. But for some reason, unknown to me, I wanted to protect her.

I looked down for a split second to collect my thoughts, and when I looked up she was gone, and the book was sitting on the chair. She must have woken up and thought this was all a dream, I'm sure. I left my dream in order to speak with my second in command, Atreyu. "Find me anything you can about a silver haired, platinum eyed woman named Rayne." I snapped.

I knew I was giving him hardly any information to work with, but that was his forte, finding out things. He was extremely skilled in this aspect. "Yes sir." He said, and he vanished.

Before I alerted my brother and caused a huge scene, I wanted to ensure that she really was a threat. I wanted to be sure that her powers were truly unchecked, and she really was in the dark about it all.

~

(Rayne)

Training today was normal. I was working with a few different Wolves on new techniques that Alpha Drake was teaching us. I was trying to just get through the lesson because I had patrol tonight and I was eager to get back home. I needed enough time to try to work on my powers again. I was determined to get these powers to come out. You could say I was definitely distracted.

Alpha Drake noticed my lack of attention and I rolled my eyes as he stalked my way. "Here we go." I said to Wynter as he approached. "Struggling today are we?" He snarled. He was clearly still upset about the club. The club.... then it hit me! I was upset at the club because of Alpha Drake. So it's possible that if he could piss me off again, I may be able to reproduce the fire!

"Well, I wasn't, but just seeing your lovely face has ruined my whole day." I spat to my Alpha. I could see his face turning red as he fought to hold in the boiling anger threatening to rise up. I wondered just how far I could push him before he exploded. Which hopefully, would cause me to explode too. I locked eyes with my Alpha and I could see something else besides the rage stirring in those ocean blue orbs. Was that desire? "Oh my god, I think I'm going to be sick." Wynter retched in my mind.

"Good God, he gets off on me tormenting him!" I exclaimed to Wynter. This clearly wasn't going to work in my favor. "So glad to see you too." He scoffed after what seemed like a longer than normal pause. And just like that he turned and walked away. *Damnit!* I thought.

Just when I thought our hate/hate or apparently hate/love relationship would be beneficial, he had to go and pull that shit. *Ugh!* There had to be a way to get these powers to unlock!

"Why don't you just ask your Demon? I'm sure he would be oh so willing to help." Wynter snorted. I scoffed at her, but to be honest, I was afraid of what he would say or do if I told him. I couldn't risk ruining what we had. *But what did we have anyway? It was something... right?* It felt like something... I hoped it was something.

Whatever it was, I wanted it... no, I *needed* it. I wasn't about to risk losing everything, so I decided to keep my mouth shut. "I can figure it out on my own, but thanks." I said to Wynter. The rest of the training wasn't bad, but nothing triggered me. I was a better fighter than the others I was paired with, and plus, they weren't pissing me off.

I did contemplate asking my Demon for help, even after I said I wouldn't. But I had something else on my mind before I possibly ruined everything I had with him... I knew I had patrol later tonight, but rather than working on my fireball, I headed home, popped some melatonin and climbed into bed. One thing at a time, and right now I was determined to get back to that silver castle and finish my reading.

Chapter 24

~
(Raziel)

J had been tracking Rayne for weeks now, in case she was using her powers unknowingly again. She could do some real damage to herself, and possibly others, being untrained. I made it my personal business to keep track of her unsolicited magic usage. Whether she liked it or not, her whole life was my personal business, so why not?

Nevermind the fact that she should have been dead the moment I found her in my dream. I should have crushed her windpipe without hesitation, and had it been anyone else, I would have. Never had I found myself in such a conundrum before.

She had access to a plethora of powers that she really had no idea about, and any of those powers could start to form at any time. She already was using fireballs and dreamwalking. What would be next? Materializing, freezing an entire town? Overreacting and causing an explosion the equivalent of a nuclear blast?

I should have taken her heart from her chest the moment I found her using unchecked powers. I know this, and I have no justification for it which makes it worse. I'm the level headed one, the one that makes the rules and enforces them. I set an example for my brothers. Yet, here I was, determined to throw it all away and keep her safe… no matter the cost.

I had never felt so weak, so utterly helpless. The rules were the rules and even I couldn't go around breaking them. Fuck the fact that I made the fucking rule, which I was beginning to regret my previous actions. Had I put more thought into this we wouldn't be standing here trying to figure a way out. I had been watching her so carefully and everything had been calm the last little while.

I assumed that Alpha Drake being out of town multiple times in the past few weeks, definitely helped. Unfortunately, he had returned a day or so ago, and I had been waiting for her to snap again. He undoubtedly would not leave her alone, I was sure of it. He made it very clear to me by his actions that he wanted to make her Luna of The Obsidian pack.

The thought enraged me and made me want to do very stupid, reckless things. Over my dead body would I ever allow him to take advantage of her in such a way. The Obsidian pack didn't need an Alpha... I could replace him in an instant and I had half a mind to do just that. "Let's not focus on him, we know his outcome." Nero said, pulling me from my internal flames. "You're right." I replied, and pulled my thoughts back to Rayne.

I had contemplated telling her what she is, and helping her with her powers... but I knew how that would turn out. She should have been learning this from birth, not 20 years later. She is volatile, her powers unchecked, unbridled. She could level this entire continent if she had a bad enough meltdown...

I knew the risks but I just couldn't fathom the other High Priests finding out about her... not yet. We were so quick to kill... and they would know something was up immediately should I tell them about her and tell them that she is still alive... I just couldn't trust that one of them wouldn't decide that it's not worth the risk and take her life for me. That would start a fucking war. One in which I wouldn't even hesitate to kill anyone who laid a single finger on her. Family or not.

Pay no mind to the fact that none of us can actually be killed, but that wouldn't stop me from doing as much damage as I possibly could. That was a thought that terrified me... and I don't get scared. Just the thought of her being harmed or even killed by one of the other High Priests was enough to make my goddamn blood boil. No sooner than those thoughts entered my mind, so did the familiar feeling of falling silver glitter. The feeling of Rayne using magic.

It was similar to her mind link, but I felt it over my entire body, not just in my mind. I focused on her and materialized, except when I opened my eyes I was still in my room. I hadn't gone anywhere. "What the fuck just happened?" Nero spat. He was just as upset as I was.

"She's just dreamwalking, why can't I reach her?" I questioned. Instantly, worry flooded my mind. I tried again, and nothing. I materialized outside of my home to make sure my abilities hadn't somehow been affected, and that worked just fine. I materialized back and started pacing in my room. I was racking my brain, talking with Nero and trying to piece together anything and everything that could make her not accessible to me.

It was possible that she figured out how to use a shield. But who would teach her that type of magic? A shield isn't something she would learn accidentally... or could she? Honestly, with her, anything was possible. Even if she did, why would she shield from me? Unless she didn't realize she was doing it. I started to wonder if maybe she knew more than she was letting on, and she had been practicing her skills secretly.

I honestly wouldn't put it past her at all, but I would have felt it if she had. I would have felt her utilizing her skills and I have felt nothing. The problem is, even if she figured it out and tried to learn, there are still certain things that only another Reaver can teach. That literally left only one other option... she was dreamwalking in one of the other High Priests' dreams.

As a High Priest you cannot dreamwalk another High Priest's dream unless you are invited to do so. Any regular Reaver could dreamwalk our dreams, but none dare... and that's the way we like it. We would most likely kill them if they did anyway. I believe that's why they choose to stay away. So it's possible for her to be dreamwalking one of the other three High Priests' dreams, just as she did my own.

Now the question is, how the hell did she find out about them? You can't dreamwalk someone's dreams unless you are thinking about them. So unless she found out about them, somehow, she couldn't be thinking about them. I decided to go to her house to see if she was in bed. I could feel her dreamwalking, but I wanted to ensure her safety, at least that's what I told myself.

I materialized in her bedroom. I didn't care if she was awake, or if she would be pissed that I showed up so abruptly and invaded her privacy. Her safety was my only concern, but given the chance I'd torture her and take her breath away this very moment. I didn't have to do any of those things though, as she was there, in her bed, sleeping peacefully. I admired her beauty.

She was lying there so vulnerable and unknowing. I wanted to climb in bed next to her, wrap her in my arms, and never fucking let her go. I sat on the bed next to her and ran my fingers through her silky silver hair.

She looked so serene as she dreamed, and I wanted to wake her with my lips on hers. In fact, I wanted my lips to touch every single inch of her flawless body… but I refrained, because waking someone inexperienced while in a dreamwalk could be dire. Especially for her with her unchecked power. I decided not to risk it for everyone's sake. She was safer while she slept.

I tried to ignore the ping of anger that flooded into my chest when I thought about the reasons I couldn't materialize straight to her and my thoughts turned dark. She had to be dreamwalking another of the High Priests' dreams… it was the only explanation as to why I couldn't reach her, and that fucking irked me.

Nero growled in my mind at the thought. None of them better lie their slimy hands on her, or there is going to be hell to pay. I half expected whoever is currently entertaining her to reach out to me and question why I hadn't handled her yet, but so far I had heard nothing. I reluctantly materialized back home. I guess it was time to let them know about her, unwillingly, of course. I was going to have to explain why I hadn't killed her yet, and that was a conversation I did not want to have. I am nothing if not a man of my word, and yet, I couldn't keep it... not this time.

I sighed out loud, frustration coating the sound. I didn't give a single fuck if they understood my reasoning either. I made it my plan to confront each of the High Priests tomorrow and see just who was experiencing the pleasure of her presence.

The argument of sparing her life would follow. But, I swear to God, if any of them touched her, there would be hell to fucking pay.

Chapter 25

~

(Rayne)

"Raphael?" I said softly, as I opened the silver door to his bedroom. He was inside at his bar getting a drink. "Well, hello beautiful." He said, as he turned around with two drinks in his hand. His was silver, of course. But to my surprise mine was gold, which made me think of my Demon.

He started walking towards me as I walked further into the room. We met halfway at the globe and chairs where we had started to read last time. He handed me my drink and motioned for me to sit down. I couldn't help but admire Raphael's sheer beauty.

He was wearing a solid silver suit jacket and suit pants, which I thought would definitely be too much silver, but it really wasn't, not on him. He had a black suit vest underneath, a black tie and black shoes. The silver suit jacket had black accents, but the pants didn't, and that made up just enough offset to work. I noted how the color brought out the dark tones in his golden skin.

His hair was neat but a little tousled in the front, and his shining silver eyes seemed to sparkle with his outfit. The whole entire thing was flashy, but somehow seemed to suit him. I could feel him watching me, probably noticing that I was admiring him. I took my drink from him and sat down as instructed. "To what do I owe the pleasure?" Raphael said. Something about his voice gave me chills every time he spoke, and this time was no different.

He was always so calm and collected. It was almost eerie. He had such an even demeanor it was hard to read him. It seemed as if the only emotion he ever showed was sparkling in his eyes. Even then, I wondered if they may not be showing it voluntarily.

He was different from my Demon in many ways, but the way he looked at me was the same. I ignored the fear that instantly engulfed me, taking a sip of my drink. He reminded me so much of my Demon that it was hard not to be slightly afraid. I sucked it up quickly, and decided it was pointless to beat around the bush.

"I was hoping that I would be able to read a book with information on Reavers. I don't know much about them, but if I may be one, I think I have a right to know more." I said, hoping he would know what book I meant, this being a dream and all. "You mean the book from the other day?" He questioned, as he snapped his fingers and produced a book with a silver spine. It was the exact book from my last dream. I longed to get my hands on it.

"Drink." He commanded, while eyeballing the gold liquid in my hand. I did as instructed even though I had already taken a sip. The liquid was definitely alcohol, but of course, it doesn't affect us like it does Humans. I drank the whole glass in a shot form, tipping the gold liquid back and swallowing the rest of it in one gulp. I was surprised when the liquid didn't burn at all like alcohol usually does. Instead, it was sweet, and had a hint of something tropical. A flavor I've never tasted.

I instantly felt the effects of the alcohol and found myself wanting more. I wasn't drunk by any means, but I was feeling buzzed, and that was strange after only one shot. Then I remembered Raphael said the book from the other day...

How would he even remember that? It never even happened, it was a dream. *Was it a dream?* Is it possible that this was real? I was snapped from my thoughts when Raphael set the book in my hand. I had to know what the book said. This was my first priority, the rest I could deal with after. I crossed my legs on my chair and opened the book in my lap. I could tell that Raphael was watching me curiously, but I didn't care. Hopefully, I was about to find out a lot of information, so I didn't let anything else bother me.

It started out talking about the four Reaver High Priests who essentially ruled the Underworld. I was somewhat familiar with this as I had read it in a previous book. I knew from my reading that my Demon, if his name really was Raziel, was a High Priest, and Raphael was as well. So I was definitely messing with some powerful beings. It went on to talk about the history and how the Reavers were made.

'The origins of the Reaver remain shrouded in mystery, leaving us with only origin stories to piece together. The predominant tale tells us that, in a time of great turmoil and chaos among the species, a Coven of Witches sought to impose order by creating a supreme being. This being, the Reaver, was imbued with the combined powers of various Supernatural entities, as well as some unique abilities of the Witches' own devising. This made them formidable and dangerous. While the Witches' plan succeeded in that the Reavers now rule the Underworld, it ultimately failed to achieve true peace. Instead, the other species live in fear of the Reavers, and though open conflict has ceased, genuine harmony and coexistence remain elusive.'

Hmm. I thought. So they wanted this creation to bring order to a chaotically mixed species world, and end the fighting and destruction between species. Too bad it didn't work. But of course it didn't, they really didn't think it through… *giving this much magic to one species, what did they think would happen?* Raphael stopped me, picked the book up from my hands and set it down gently on the side table.

"Would you like to see my garden?" He asked, holding his hand out to me. I so badly wanted to say no and keep reading. But I was feeling tipsy, and something about him just made me want to say yes.

As I took his hand, he guided me through the winding corridors of his home, leading me to a hidden back door that I hadn't noticed before. We stepped out into a breathtakingly beautiful garden, a vibrant oasis that took my breath away. The garden was a kaleidoscope of colors, with every imaginable hue of flower blooming in harmony. Lush vines cascaded over an intricate network of arches, trellises, and fencing, creating a sense of enchantment that surrounded us on all sides.

The walkways were adorned with a lush tapestry of trees and plants, their vibrant foliage spilling onto the paths. Shrubbery and colorful bushes carpeted the ground, softening the edges of the walkways and creating a sense of serenity. As we strolled along, I was delighted to discover a dedicated haven for my favorite flower, lilies!

An entire section of the garden was devoted to showcasing a stunning variety of lilies, their elegant blooms swaying gently in the breeze. I was in absolute heaven! We came to a delicate opening with a silver bench in the middle of it and we sat down. Raphael snapped his fingers and produced the book I was reading.

"I thought you might like a better type of scenery for your reading." Raphael said. It may have been the strangely strong alcohol, but I was really wishing Raphael would just talk to me and never stop so I could listen to his silvery voice and melt. "Thank you! I love this garden, it's beautiful." I said, and watched as a smile formed on his lips. I ignored the flutter in my heart and kept reading.

'Dreamwalking is a mastery possessed by Reavers, enabling them to seamlessly enter and exit the dreams of others, as if they were physically present. This extraordinary ability also allows them to navigate and manipulate their own dreams, shaping the narrative and environment with precision. Many Reavers utilize their dreams as a mirrored reflection of their waking lives, creating a sanctuary where they can escape the mundane routines of daily existence. In this realm, they can find respite, allowing their physical forms to recharge while their minds roam free.'

"Dreamwalking?" I asked Raphael. "Yes beautiful, it is something we can do easily, and we rather enjoy it." He

168

said. "Am I dreamwalking right now?!" I gasped. "You are, which is why you are here. You were last time as well." He replied softly. "Last time? You mean, I was actually here before? So you are real..." I said. He chuckled. "Very much so, beautiful." He said. "And you are a High Priest, a King of the Underworld?"

"In the flesh." Raphael replied, swirling the single ball of ice that sat in the middle of his half empty drink. It made a slight clinking sound as it rolled against the crystal glass. "I'm sorry, I'm sure you don't want to spend your time entertaining me." I said, shutting the book, but holding it in my hands still.

We locked eyes. Raphael's gaze was deep and fiery. He took the book from my hands and set it down on the silver bench beside me. "I would rather be doing nothing more than entertaining you, beautiful. Why don't you allow me to come and visit you, wherever you live?" He asked. Butterflies swarmed my stomach at his ask, but I knew I couldn't accept his offer.

I shook my head. "I... I'm sorry, Raphael. I can't allow that. I'm sort of seeing someone." I mumbled, unsure if you could really call it that... I mean, we had spent so little time together, I just am not sure what we really were.

"Oh? And is he as... charming as I?" Raphael asked Knowing that I was referring to Raziel, I was afraid to mention his name.

"Well... he is much more... fiery." I began, but stopped when Raphael took his hand and cupped the right side of my face. "It doesn't matter who he is. He can't compare to me. No, I have decided that you will be mine, beautiful." His sultry voice dripped with confidence and a hint of arrogance, sending a shiver down my spine.

The words themselves were a bold declaration, a claim of ownership that was both captivating and unsettling. There was something undeniably alluring about the possessiveness in his tone, the unapologetic assertion that I belonged to him, and him alone. Yet, at the same time, a spark of defiance flared within me, resisting the idea of

169

being won, or claimed, or possessed by anyone. I was torn from my thoughts as a warm, fuzzy sensation spread across my cheek, emanating from beneath his hand.

It was as if his touch had awakened a gentle electric hum. The feeling was difficult to put into words, but it was akin to magic flowing through my veins. When he withdrew his hand, an intense longing surged within me, a deep desire to be even closer to him. Though I was already by his side, I longed to be even closer.

It was like I couldn't control myself, not even a tiny bit. I grabbed him and pulled him to me. Our lips collided in a kiss that was like being struck by lightning. A fiery passion coursed through my veins, licking at every nerve ending it touched.

I had never experienced such an intense, all-consuming connection. Every part of my body wanted to feel his touch. It was almost agony even thinking about our skin parting. He moaned against my lips, wrapping his hand in my hair. I grazed my teeth along his lower lip playfully before smiling against him.

"Fuck, Rayne." He growled, and the sound of my name rolling off his tongue sent a static shock throughout my whole body. The sensation was so extreme that it woke me up.

I shot straight out of bed in a panic and my sudden exit left me longing for his touch.

Chapter 26

"**D**reamwalking?!" Wynter screeched after we woke up and she re-lived my dream. "So it wasn't a dream after all. Shit..." I huffed.

Raphael clearly said dreamwalking was real, it was something a Reaver could do easily and enjoyed it.

It would make sense that I could do it as well. I knew now that I was much more than just a Wolf. That would mean I dreamwalked to Raziel's dream too. And when I summoned him to my dream with Alpha Drake, that was also real. Well, he was, at least.

I wondered how often I had unknowingly done this in the past. I started to panic thinking I had unknowingly trespassed in other people's dreams. Then I noticed I still had that tingly feeling on my face where Raphael had cupped it last night. I got up and went into my bathroom to check the mirror but before I could make it in there my phone went off. I groaned and turned around to grab it. It was Brett.

'Search party to look for Eric in 2 hours, I'll pick you up at your house. You are not missing this.'

My stomach sank to my feet, and every thought of what I had just encountered with Raphael was out the window. I tried to hold back the tears as I thought about what was going to happen during the search and why Brett hadn't given the location of Eric's body yet. A wave of nausea rolled over me as I thought about it and I ran to the bathroom because I felt like I was actually going to hurl.

I placed both hands on the sink and bowed my head with closed eyes, trying to breathe and prevent myself from losing the non-existent food in my stomach. I swallowed, hard, and then looked up at myself in the mirror. That's when I saw it...

A stunning silver infinity symbol, adorned with delicate vines and intricate filigree, stood diagonally across my face, its glittering surface sparkling radiantly against my skin. The symbol's elegant lines and curves seemed to dance across my temple, as if infused with a mesmerizing light, leaving me breathless with its beauty.

I followed the filigree and vines down onto my neck and crook of my shoulder, wincing as they disappeared under my hair. The design was not small, covering the space from my temple to my jawline, and flowing gracefully down onto my neck.

"What the Fuck is that?" Wynter screamed. "Fuck." I mumbled. "Hell, it's huge!!! Good luck covering it up." She cackled. I gave her a dirty look. The symbol was exactly like the one in Raphael's room, and on the front gate. A silver infinity symbol standing diagonally.

As stressed as I was, my heart still fluttered as I looked at it, pulling all the stress and worry regarding Eric from my mind. What replaced it was a physical ache in the center of my chest, all because I was away from Raphael. "Son of a bitch! Rayne! What the fuck did you do?? This is all your fault! You chose to go back there!" Wynter cried.

"Ugh! I know!! I know, Wynter, but how the hell was I supposed to know that was going to happen? Yet another time my damn curiosity got the better of me." I snapped. I didn't mean to lose my cool but I was panicking.

I splashed water on my face and attempted to scrub it off to no avail. It was there, and it wasn't going anywhere. "We have to find a way to get rid of this!" Wynter howled, her words stung a little. "What if I don't want it gone?" I said to Wynter, as I traced the symbol with my fingers, recalling the lightning between myself and Raphael.

"No Rayne, just fucking no. We are going to be with Raziel! No one else!" She spat. As much as I knew she was right, I just couldn't shake what I was feeling for Raphael. "Look, we will figure this out... I'll just go back there and talk to him. He can explain." I said as I walked back into my room and looked up. I gasped out loud when I came face to face with Raziel.

"Rayne, what have you done?!" He sneered as he grabbed my chin roughly to inspect my newfound artwork. My stomach sank as his tone sent a chill down my spine. Fear surged through me like a tidal wave, and I knew he was beyond mere anger... he was fucking furious. I'd never witnessed him this angry, not even when he'd ended Eric's life. "Holy shit Rayne, you've really outdone yourself this time." Wynter spat. "Fuck, Wynter, can you calm down? I'm very aware of the situation I put us in..." I shot.

Despite the anger in his voice, and the tears beginning to form in my eyes, Raziel grabbed me and wrapped me in a tight bear hug. A feeling of security washed over me and Wynter swooned. He pulled away just enough to lock his golden eyes onto mine.

I could see a mixture of pain and desire in his eyes, which ignited a fire inside my veins. In that instant, my feelings for Raziel came flooding back, and everything else faded into insignificance. But as I surrendered to the rush of emotions, a searing sensation erupted on my cheek, like a branding iron.

It was as if my new artwork had come to life, sensing my betrayal and warning me of my disloyalty. The pain was a reminder of where my loyalty *should* lie, and that was with Raphael. I looked back up at Raziel, willing the tears in my eyes not to fall.

"What is this, what did Raphael do to me?" I asked. I swear I saw hurt in his eyes when I said Raphael's name, followed by rage. "Darling, he marked you. He claimed you as his own... and as long as his mark remains, you will have trouble fighting your feelings for him." He said softly, but through gritted teeth.

He sat down on my bed and pulled me into his lap. I knew he was fucking furious, but he was trying his best not to overreact. He traced the mark on my face lightly, and as much as he tried to keep it together, I could see the rage in his golden eyes. They were actually a lot closer to black now.

"My mark does not adorn your face because no matter how often I threaten it, I do not take it lightly. A mark is not something you play with. It's not something you throw around because you think it's fun. The mark is sacred, and when I leave my mark on someone, it will be there forever. To me, it's never been about control, and instead a bond that will be absolutely unbreakable. When I leave my mark, that's it... my chosen mate will *never* leave my side." He explained softly.

His words sent a pain searing through my chest. I was only now truly realizing that this whole time he could have just marked me, and I wouldn't have even realized that I didn't want him. He could have had me at literally any moment in time, and I wouldn't have even put up a fight if I were marked by him, but he didn't... He, for once, didn't force it upon me.

Guilt clawed its way through my chest, how could I be so stupid? Wynter was whimpering at our situation. "But I do choose you! I want you!." I shot, not realizing the force of my words. As I said that a sharp burning pain inched its way through my mark. It was as if I wasn't allowed to want anyone else, and it was an annoying reminder of that very fact.

I grabbed my face and took a deep breath in. Raziel's eyes lit up at my words but were burning with fury at the sight of my mark causing me pain. He closed his eyes for a brief moment, and then exhaled slowly as he opened them and trained his gaze directly back onto me.

"The mark will fade, darling, so long as the mating process isn't completed. I can't say how much time it will take, as it varies. But I do know the mark will fade faster the less of a connection you share with him." Raziel huffed. I could tell he was annoyed explaining this to me, and I felt absolutely awful about it.

"But no matter what you do, you can't complete the mating process. If you do, the mark will be permanent... Do

174

you understand me, Rayne? Permanent. Forever." He spat those last words, and I fully understood what he was saying. No fucking way I wanted to be permanently mated to Raphael.

The mark, seemingly alive, ached and throbbed like it knew what I was trying to do, and it was going to stop me from doing it at any cost. I didn't want this fucking mark, I wanted it gone, now. "You'll be ok, darling. Just stay away from the dreams. We will figure this out. I'm not going to let you do it alone." My Demon said. I could feel the sincerity in his voice. This was much different than our usual interactions and I think I preferred when he infuriated me over all of this guilt.

"Ok... I'm sorry about all of this." I mumbled, forcing away the tears that threatened to spill over. "Do not apologize to me, I'm not mad at you. You had no way to know that any of this was even possible, let alone would happen. But it doesn't matter, because you belong to me, and *nothing* is going to stop me from claiming what is mine." He growled.

My mark was burning out of control with his words. I gasped slightly, surprised that he was being so forward. Though, what did I expect? I knew I was his, I always had been and I was just starting to accept this fact. He grabbed me again, and this time he pulled me to him and smashed his lips into mine. Jealousy and possessiveness riddled his hungry kiss. I reciprocated, and as if on command, I could feel the mark burning and stinging along the side of my face. I didn't even care.

Raziel awoke something deep inside of me, deep within my core. Something Raphael could *never* touch, mark or not. My mind may not know what I want, but my body does. And it doesn't allow me to ever forget, even when I'm trembling with fear. My Demon pushed against me, backing us up until I felt the bed against my legs behind me. He then threw me down on my bed. My thoughts were out of control, knowing that I would not stop him from doing literally anything he wanted. As if he could read my mind, he ripped my shirt from my body.

He looked down at me as if I were the last dessert at the dinner table, and he had been waiting all night to devour me. Just the look in his eyes caused warmth to spread to all of my extremities. He positioned himself on top of me. I could feel his girth through his suit pants. It was rubbing against my core, stirring up emotions I didn't know I had. Our lips met again.

I could feel his desire, his passion, washing over me like liquid gold. I wanted more. I grabbed him and pulled him closer to me. I wanted him closer. My mark was burning with rage at my disobedience to what it wanted... good. He sat up and pulled me onto his lap facing him. With one hand, he felt every part of my upper body, cupping my full breasts before he made his way down into my panties. Then using his thumb, he started circling my clit.

A soft moan escaped my lips as his hand twisted into my long silver locks, gently but firmly pulling my head back to reveal the delicate curve of my neck. His lips descended upon the tender skin, sending shivers down my spine as he kissed and caressed the sensitive area, his touch sending waves of pleasure coursing through me. His actions had the pressure in my panties threatening to explode. I could feel his fangs elongating as he brushed against my neck with them.

"Do it." I said with a moan. "You want it darling? Say it. I want to hear you say it." He purred. His words were fueled with desire. "I want it, please." I gasped. "I want to hear you say my name. Raziel... say it." He growled. I moaned out as he nibbled on my neck.

"I... I want it, please, Raziel." I moaned. "Good fucking girl." He murmured against my neck, sinking his fangs in just as I climaxed. As he drank my blood, the rush of pleasure intensified my orgasm to unbearable heights, and I couldn't contain the primal scream that tore from my lips. The sensation was overwhelming, amplifying every pleasure receptor in my body tenfold. It was as if my very life force was being ignited, propelling me into a realm of ecstasy I'd never known before. I had never had a more mind blowing orgasm.

He didn't stop as my screams of pleasure seemed to make him more feral. He increased the pressure on my clit, while still drinking. Listening to my breathless moans and feeling my body spasms. He didn't stop until I had ridden out the entire orgasm and then some.

Once I finally finished, he softly placed his hand on my neck and healed it, then he pulled away and looked at me. "Wow..." Was the only word I could muster. My brain was covered in a thick fog and I was still dancing in the clouds. He smirked and our lips met again, but softly this time. Almost like he was savoring the last moments of something he had waited so long for.

"You will always be mine, do not forget it, Rayne." He whispered against my lips. Wynter swooned in my mind, and if she had made a singular other sound before, I didn't even hear it.

He pulled away and I could see many emotions dancing along the molten gold in his eyes. I didn't know what to say, but I knew he was right, even if my mark refused to let up. I attempted to catch my breath, noting that the mark on my face was furious with his last words, burning worse than it ever had. It was a sign that my defiance was, indeed, forbidden. Yet, that just made me want to do it even more.

I looked down at my intertwined hands, and then back up, locking eyes with Raziel. I could see a possessiveness in them as he pulled me close to him again. This time he softly ran his fingers through my hair.

"Raziel, your name is beautiful..." I mumbled, hoping it didn't sound dumb. "It is the only name you shall ever call me from here on out, little Wolf." He replied softly. He pulled away so he could look down at me and we locked eyes.

"When you are struggling with the mark, and your feelings for him, just remember who you belong to. Remember who made you scream." He purred. He kissed my forehead and then vanished leaving me a flustered, breathless mess. "Holy shit!" Wynter gasped. "We need to remove this fucking mark, now." And for the first time since it appeared, I agreed.

Chapter 27

Shaking, I got up off my bed and went to my closet to change. I looked at the time and realized I had only about 30 minutes until Brett would be here. Raziel and I had spent more time than I anticipated together, leaving me in a rush. I didn't care. I wasn't particularly looking forward to the next set of events that were coming. Knowing exactly what happened to Eric, but having to pretend that I didn't know, and worse, pretend that I was upset over his disappearance, was going to kill me.

I had never been a good liar, so I was practicing what I would do and say while I got ready. I knew a search crew would consist of walking and covering ground so I decided to wear my combat boots, along with some black spandex shorts and a lighter gray colored loose t-shirt. I threw on a baseball cap, opting to bunch my hair into a loose ponytail at the nape of my neck. I was trying to fit in, look as Human as I could. I never cared before, but Eric's parents would be there and I knew this. I wanted to stay out of the spotlight.

My mind was scattered between thoughts of Raziel and what we had just done, to thoughts of Raphael and how pissed he was going to be over it, to what Eric's family would say when I arrived. None of these situations gave me any peace, and before I knew it Brett was messaging me that he was outside. "You'll be fine, Rayne. Just keep up the sad girl approach. No one will suspect a thing." Wynter said, trying to console me.

I hoped she was right. I headed outside and walked up to Brett's fancy black sports car, opening the door and getting in the passenger seat. He turned and looked at me, locking his eyes onto my mark, immediately. I saw him brush his tongue along his back teeth before he sighed out loud. "Really, Rayne? A Reaver mark?" He huffed. Surprise caught me by the throat, causing me to choke on my next words. "How… how did you kn…" But before I could finish he put his hand up to stop me.

"Do you even have to ask? The real question is how fucking pissed is the Reaver with the golden eyes?" He asked. I was shook. How could he even know any of this? I know he is a Wolf, but just being a Wolf and hiding as a Human doesn't give him unlimited knowledge. I wanted to know how he knew so much about Reavers, when I knew next to nothing, and I was the one who grew up in a damn pack!

"Why would he be pissed? It's his mark." I shot, hoping my lie would be believable. Brett threw his car into drive and floored it while laughing out loud. "I don't know who you're trying to fool, me or yourself." Brett snapped. I pinched the bridge of my nose and sighed in frustration, throwing my head back against the seat of the car. "It doesn't fucking matter, Brett! Jesus!" I grumbled. He looked over at me, rolled his eyes and chuckled.

"The mark is the wrong color, if you must know." He said, causing my jaw to drop open. Of course it was… fucking common sense. I silently scolded myself for being so stupid and Brett didn't say another word the rest of the entire drive.

I wanted to ask him how he knew so much but I decided against it. We pulled up to a parking area at the bottom of the Gulf Hagas canyon, and parked next to what seemed like a hundred other cars. Once we got out I followed Brett towards the crowd of people that had begun to gather at the trailhead just inside the canyon's entrance.

Jae ran up to me and hugged me so hard I thought she might break a rib. She was visibly upset and seeing her sad actually made me feel like shit. I thought I would have to fake my feelings this entire time, but just being here around so many people who loved and cared for Eric had me in a very upset and conflicted mood. When the tears began to form I didn't even stop them.

Forget the fact that he was a piece of shit who was going to rape me, and possibly had raped other women, or would. He was surrounded by people who truly cared for him. I shouldn't have cared, but it was hard not to when so many others did. I had never met Eric's family, so when his mother stopped everyone so she could speak, I was surprised. She was a very tall, slender woman, with short blonde hair and piercing blue eyes that looked just like Eric's. Her voice demanded respect and as she spoke no one said a singular word.

I tuned her out because I was distracted by the sheer amount of people who had shown up here to search for him. Everywhere I turned it seemed like there were more and more people. My mind began to wander and I replayed the last memories I had of Eric.

Did I really, truly think he would have raped me had Raziel not stopped him? The worst part is I wasn't even able to, without a shadow of a doubt, confirm this. Yes, he was being a drunk pig. But would he have stopped? Did he deserve to die for it? These were the questions that plagued me as we began our search.

"Rayne, what's that on your face?" Jae finally asked me after about 30 minutes of searching in silence. I was surprised at just how many people had come up to me, given me a hug, and sent words of encouragement. People I didn't even know, people I had never spoken to before.

Eric must have told more people about us than I had anticipated. And out of them, not a single one mentioned the mark on my face. I could see them all looking at it, but no one dared say a word about it. Leave it to Jae to bring it up.

"It was part of a costume I had on last night, Temporary tattoo. It has to wear off." I whispered. "Oh… ok." She replied, but I knew she didn't believe me but she didn't pry further. It was 4 hours of muffled words, strangers hugging me and telling me how sorry they were, and enough footsteps to make my feet hurt for a month, before we reached a sharp curvature in the road.

As we made our way up the steep incline towards it we could see the tire tracks indicating that someone slammed on their brakes. "Over here!" Brett said, running up to the remnants of the barrier that was supposed to prevent a vehicle from going over.

Everyone piled around the broken pieces of cement and rebar as we peered down the edge of the cliff into the ravine below. It was too far down to see the vehicle clearly, but we could see that there was something there. There's no way anyone could have survived a crash from this far up, even if the car hadn't burned.

"It's a shot in the dark, but we need to get the local police involved." A burly man's voice said from somewhere behind us. I didn't turn around, fighting the bile that was rising in my throat. I knew Eric's body and car were down there. I knew they wouldn't find anything but dental records. What I didn't understand was why I was reacting like this.

I could hear the murmurs from those around us speculating if it was Eric. Some thought it was for sure, others were weary. Jae turned to me and she said something but my head was spinning and I couldn't make out anything coming from her mouth.

Rather than try to hear her, I darted away from the crowd, dropped to my knees behind some trees nearby and threw up what little stomach acid was sloshing around in my gut. Tears, hot and heavy, fell from my eyes, running down my now reddened cheeks. I threw up again just as Jae came running over to me.

"Oh my god, Rayne... I'm so fucking sorry. Do you think it's him?? He always drives up the canyon when he's mad, and you said you guys got in a fight... fuck. I'm so sorry." She stammered. I know she wasn't meaning to make things worse, but Humans never seemed to get the social queues. Plus, they always had trouble controlling their emotions, and apparently in this situation, I did too. "I just need a moment… please." I croaked which did the trick, she immediately got up and headed back towards the gathering crowd.

I exhaled slowly and tried to gather my thoughts. I don't know if I was more sick because Eric was dead and I was finally processing the fact, or because I knew it was my fault he was dead. I had pushed Wynter to the back of my mind to escape her internal banter.

Telling me it wasn't my fault and that he was a shitty Human wasn't helping. I don't care how many times I'm told it wasn't my fault, I know that it was, at least partially. And yes, the world might be a better place without him but does that mean everyone who is shitty deserves to be killed?

He never would have been had he not met me, and that, right there, is why I was sick and throwing up. I eventually made my way back to the crowd. I had pulled myself together and decided that it was better to be seen than not.

The police had already shown up and were setting up a team to recover the remnants of whatever was down there. Once the police marked the area off as a crime scene they urged us all to go home. Some people pushed back, opting to stay but Brett was not one of them. He walked up to me and stood behind me until I turned around and looked up at him. He then moved his head slightly towards the road.

I was standing with Jae, although neither of us had really said much. I looked at her and she gave me a hug. "I'm so sorry, Rayne." She said softly. "Thanks. I don't know if I hope it's him, or not at this point. Is it worse to find him or not find him?" I said softly. She shrugged.

"I don't know, but I'm going to stay a little longer and I'll update you if I find anything out." She said, I nodded to her and turned to follow Brett who had already started walking away. I caught up but he didn't say anything. We walked in silence for a bit which I thought would be more awkward, but it actually seemed to help.

My thoughts were erratic but also somewhat calm. It was as if the events that had unfolded had actually helped the coping process, even though I knew I was only coping with the guilt that I held, and would forever hold over this. It was Brett who spoke first and he was clearly not interested in speaking about Eric. "Who was it? The other Reaver?" I knew he was talking about my mark and since he seemed to know so much about Reavers already, I only answered because I thought maybe I could get some information out of him.

"It was Raphael." I mumbled quietly, but I knew he heard me. He stopped dead in his tracks and looked over at me. "What?" I asked. "Raphael Kane?" He asked. "Uh, I don't know his last name... I assume so?" I stammered. Why would he have the same last name as Raziel? That seemed a little strange to me. Brett just shook his head and kept walking. "You do realize that Raphael and Raziel are brothers... right?" He said, knocking the air completely from my lungs.

I had to stop for a moment to gather my bearings and try to breathe. "They are *what?*" I demanded once I had processed what he said. "Yea, Rayne. Brothers... so again, how fucking pissed was he?" My head was absolutely spinning. Brothers? I had been marked by Raziel's brother... his family? No wonder he was so distraught. It was all starting to make sense to me now. I couildn't believe how fucking stupid I felt in this moment.

"You already know the answer to that, Brett. And how do you know so much about them?" I snipped, hoping he would stop playing games and just give me the answers I desperately seeked.

He chuckled which pissed me off. But then he spoke. "I'm not supposed to know my father, Aries, or his side of the family... but I've been spending time with him in secret for years. He had a run in with the Reavers back in Rome. This was years ago, but the story goes that he was in a mess with the Vampires and the Reaver with the rose gold eyes, goes by the name of Rowen, who is also Raziel's brother, stepped in to his aid. Don't ask me why a Reaver would have batted an eye to help a Wolf, but he did. And since then they have become relatively close. In fact,

184

Rowen made him 3rd in command, he allowed it even though my father is a Wolf. There are a lot of things about the brothers that I know that most people don't." He explained.

"So wait, there are 3 of them?" I asked, pulling only the pertinent information from his story. "4 actually. All 4 of them are brothers who rule the Underworld together. Ramses is the other brother and he lives in the French Quarter in New Orleans." I looked at Brett as we walked and my head was swimming with this new knowledge. I had so many questions but I didn't even know where to start asking. I had read about all 4, but never pieced it together. Not even once. How could I be so naive?

"Look, we can go over a Reaver history lesson another time. We need to figure out what you're going to do about that mark." He said, throwing me off. "What do you mean about this mark? Raziel said it would go away as long as I don't complete the mating ritual." I said, as if it was the most obvious thing in the world. Brett laughed so hard he tripped over his own feet and almost fell on his face.

I raised an eyebrow at him. "What? What is so fucking funny?" I snapped. It took him a full minute before he calmed down enough to look back at me and be serious.

"You have no clue what powers you're messing with, do you?" He said. "Well, seeing as Raziel inserted himself in my life when I was 9 years old, I think I have a pretty good idea how powerful a Reaver is." I huffed. Brett just shook his head. "Wait, since you were 9?" He questioned. I nodded.

"Raziel, the Reaver in gold... he saved me from drowning as a child and has been stalking me ever since." I huffed, remembering how annoyed that thought made me. "He saved you? Why in the world would he have bothered?" Brett questioned.

"Why in the hell does that man do anything he does?" I snipped. "That's fair, but still, it's strange for a Reaver to intervene... But anyway, I'm not talking about him when I reference the powers. I'm talking about the mark, Rayne.

The fucking marks powers." He said, bringing the conversation back to clarify his point.

His words caught me off guard, again. For some reason I hadn't once thought about the mark itself having powers. I mean, I knew it did, how else could it magically make me want to be right next to Raphael like it did? And the feelings of euphoria, the rush of sheer need it blasted into my psyche. But it was just a mark, what damage could it honestly do?

I thought back to its insistent burning and spatial awareness, as if it knew who I was with and why... it started to click in my mind that I was truly messing with forces I didn't understand.

"Rayne, the mark *forces* feelings for the other party... whether you have them or not. If you do have feelings then it will enhance what's there, but if you don't, it will fabricate them. The mark will force you to love its owner, no matter the cost. And you? You'd never know the difference. If your feelings ever start to falter, you will be none the wiser. In fact, I'll bet you've been thinking about him all day. Every other thought, even. This is how it works. It digs its clawed lies deep into your psyche. So bad, to the point where you don't know where the feeling starts or ends. And you never will. If you think for a single second that Raphael isn't going to come for you, and that you aren't going to run straight into his arms, willingly, then you've got a rude awakening heading your way."

Lead coated my gut, causing a deep sinking feeling to wash over me as he spoke.

"You... you don't think he would? Come for me?" I stammered, really feeling uneasy over this entire conversation.

Brett stopped and looked me in the eyes. "No, Rayne. I don't think he will come for you, I *know* he will. In fact, I'm surprised he hasn't already."

Chapter 28

~

(Raziel)

After my meetup with Rayne, I attempted to keep my emotions under control. I really did, but they got the best of me, as per usual. So I materialized in front of the silver gate to Raphael's home. I narrowed my eyes at the infinity symbol standing vertically on the gate, trying to hold back the rage that was bubbling at the sheer sight of it. "Fuck it, bust that motherfucker down." Nero snarled. I took a single fireball and blew the gate apart. I stalked onto Raphael's property up to his front door. "Raphael!" I roared, as I threw another fireball into his front door and blew it off the hinges.

"I'm going to fucking kill you." I yelled, as I threw fireball after fireball destroying everything around me. I stalked up the stairs using magic to unshelve every book in his library. It sent silver glitter flying around the entire room. This reminded me of Rayne, and that made me even more enraged.

I finally got to the silver double doors. I knew they were just like my own, which meant they were spelled, and they could not be penetrated. That didn't stop me from trying though. I threw a double fireball into the door, and it didn't even budge. I threw another, and another, it was no use. I even tried using a spell to open it with no avail.

"Raphael!!" I roared again, with no reply. I was done fucking around. I elongated one of my fingers into a Wolf claw and sliced my hand open. "Shadows, come to me." I snarled. In an instant, the room was shrouded in an inky blackness, as if The Shadows themselves had come to life.

These were no ordinary Shadows, but dark, silken entities that writhe and twist like living things. They erupted from every corner, pouring in like a tidal wave of darkness, and slithered across the floor with an unnerving, serpentine grace.

As they swirled around my feet, their tendrils danced across the tile, casting an eerie, mesmerizing spell. The air was heavy with the sound of their soft, sinister hissing, as if they were alive and watching me with cold, calculating intent.

"Drink." I said, as I held my bloody hand out. The serpentine tendrils slid up my arm, their slick bodies gliding effortlessly through the pooling blood. As The Shadows drank their fill, I surrendered to the familiar, chilling embrace that seeped into my very marrow. The icy coldness enveloped me, a bone-deep chill that was both unsettling and comforting.

I felt their darkness wrap around me like a shroud, its frigid tendrils curling around my heart, yet somehow, I found solace in its eerie, shadowy grasp. "What isss it you need, Master?" They whispered in a multitude of voices.

"I need you to bring me the Reaver, Raphael, name your price!" I spat. The tendrils started shaking with anticipation. "The priccceee isss the blood of the marked, Massster." The multitude of voices whispered.

I stifled a wince as a sharp pang pierced my chest in response to their question, but I pushed through the discomfort, refusing to let it distract me. "Absolutely not, you will not touch Rayne." I sneered, before taking a breath to calm myself. "Name another price!" I shouted. "There isss no other priccceee." They whispered. "So be it." I said, and with a wave of my hand I dismissed them.

I tried to release some of my anger as I watched The serpentine tendrils that were The Shadows slither back into the nothing and everything from which they came. I inhaled slowly and I was almost at a loss when Nero said. "Have you thought about just knocking on the door?" I hadn't... but Raphael had such a calm and collected demeanor, it wouldn't surprise me if he's just sitting there waiting for me to calm the fuck down. In fact, I scoffed to myself when I realized that he probably was doing that exact thing.

I've always had a bit of a temper. Exploding and destroying everything in my path was typical behavior for me. "I guess it can't hurt to try." I told Nero. I took another deep breath to try and calm some more of my anger. It wasn't really working, but it couldn't hurt, right?

I stepped to the door and knocked. Then, to my surprise the doors cracked open. I pushed them and they both opened to reveal Raphael sitting in the middle of the room. He was drinking silver brandy and had a silver spined book in his other hand. He looked up from his book and we locked eyes. "Hello, brother." He said calmly. I glared at him, upset that he was, in fact, doing exactly as I had thought he would be.

"To what do I owe the pleasure?" He said coyly, as if I hadn't just destroyed half of his home in a fit of rage. "You know why I'm here." I spat. Raphael raised one eyebrow at me in confusion. "I'm not sure that I do, brother. Why don't you enlighten me?"

"Rayne." I snapped, and acknowledgement flashed through his eyes, followed by mischief and then fury. Still, he didn't move a muscle.

He slowly took a sip of his brandy, set his book down on the side table, and we locked eyes. "Oh, Rayne… you mean the young Reaver who is coming into her powers *outside* of a Coven? The young Reaver who is still *very* much alive, and dreamwalking without even knowing it. That Rayne? Yes, what about her?" He said nonchalantly.

My anger simmered just below the surface, its fiery tendrils threatening to erupt once more, and I struggled to maintain a fragile grip on my composure, fighting to keep the storm of rage from breaking free.

He had a point, she was still alive and I had failed in that aspect. But she was not to be touched. I should have had a more level head about this, but I was in no position to bargain. "She is mine! You keep your filthy hands off her!

189

You may have marked her, but she doesn't belong to you." I spat, ignoring his very blatant observation.

I could see the emotions flashing through his eyes. Confusion, anger, possessiveness, and then fury. "Brother, she belongs 6 feet under and you know it!" He growled. His words infuriated me even worse and I wasn't even sure how that was even possible.

"I don't give a fuck if she lights this entire world on fire and destroys every single inhabitant within it. Nothing will happen to her. She belongs to me, end of fucking story!" I snarled. "Do you realize how fucking ignorant you sound right now? She is dangerous!" He snapped.

"I don't care. I've been watching over here since she was a child, I've already made my claim." I snapped. Raphael scoffed, standing from his chair. "You've been what?! And you didn't bring her into a Coven? You fucking knew she was a Reaver, and didn't take the appropriate steps to prevent this?" He growled.

Anger filled my chest because yet again, my brother was right, but I refused to admit it. "Raphael, when in our entire existence has a Reaver *EVER* come into their powers without a Coven? In all of our Millenia's of being here, tell me… have you ever once seen it?" I snapped. He looked at me but didn't reply and I knew it was because he couldn't. "Exactly. There was no way for me to know!" I said.

"So instead, you stalk her and what? Force her to be yours when she is of age?" Raphael questioned. I cracked my neck trying to release pressure because his accusations were not helping. "Raphael, you need to watch your fucking tongue." I growled. "Or what, brother? If she was to be yours, then why doesn't *your* mark adorn her beautiful face?" Raphael snipped with a little smirk.

Now I knew he was only saying shit to piss me off, and it was working. I took a step back and tried to calm my rising anger before I spoke. "That mark will fade, and as soon as it does my mark will replace it, permanently. She has already made her choice." I spat, dodging his question. He looked at me with a glint in his silver eyes.

"And you think our brothers will be ok with her and her unbridled powers wandering about this world, volatile, and free flowing? You think they will allow her to live?" He questioned. "Are you saying you would kill her?" I inquired.

"I guess we shall see." Raphael said with a devious sparkle in his eye. I couldn't tell if he was serious or not, but I suddenly realized that I would have a hell of a time protecting her if he was.

"Stay the fuck away from her, Raphael, or so help me, you will be fucking sorry." I spewed. His eyes betrayed a flurry of emotions, a window to the turmoil my words had unleashed within him. "And just what will you do if she chooses me, brother?" He questioned. "Whatever it fucking takes. Your mark is already fading after our little escapade earlier." I scoffed. I watched his eyes go from amused to furious.

And while he could keep his composure under literally any circumstance, his eyes always gave him away. I could tell that I had hit a nerve, so of course, I just kept pushing it. "You should have been there, the way she convulses when her body is reaching its climax. The way her moans sound as I ran my fingers across her delicate skin, the way her blood tasted flowing into my mouth." I was definitely trying to rub it in at this point. I guess I went too far, because Raphael lunged at me with a burning fire cascading through his eyes.

He was fucking furious that I had my way with her, and I was glad. Judging by his reaction he wouldn't kill her, and now I knew this for sure. I dodged his lunge and spun around throwing a green fireball straight at him. He, of course, used magic to block it, and shot one back at me. I did the same thing and dissipated the fire.

I, once again, used magic to unshelve every book off the shelves in his room. Silver spined books and glitter went flying everywhere in a whirlwind of fury as if the very air itself had erupted in a frenzy of chaos. Raphael used magic to part the whirlwind sending a silver glitter and book mess flying into all the adjacent walls. He snapped and produced

191

a double-bladed staff. "Oh, playing dirty, are we?" I scoffed, as I snapped and produced a double set of samurai swords.

Raphael was skilled, but I was faster. I dodged a stab to the abdomen, a slice to the shoulder, and a sweep of my feet from under me. I swung my swords parallel and did a spin jump around in the air, hoping to connect with his ribcage, but was blocked. "Smooth, brother. But you've been keeping Rayne a secret from us…" Raphael snapped.

Then he sent his staff down onto me like a sledgehammer. I used my swords crisscrossed to block the hit, which took me to my knees from the force. "I only just found out about it all… she only just started coming into her powers." I growled, then I opened my arms with swords intact, flinging his staff from his hands and across the room.

I got to my feet and pointed one sword at Raphael. "What now, Brother?" I said, still pointing my blade just under his chin. "You may have won this fight, but nothing will change the fact that she is a Reaver coming into her powers without a Coven. Regardless of your feelings or even mine… you know as well as I do how detrimental this can be!" He spat.

He was right. I honestly wasn't sure what to do about it. At least not yet. "I'm aware, and I will speak to Ramses and Rowen regarding it. But for now, you need to back the fuck off." I growled.

I snapped my swords away and tried to rack my brain on how to get rid of the mark faster. "The Shadows?" Nero said. *Perfect.* I thought, and without hesitation I sliced my hand open again. I did it right in front of Raphael, and called The Shadows. "Drink." I said, as the familiar bone chilling ice washed over me. I watched as the icy tendrils swarmed at my feet. I saw Raphael's eyes widen.

While The Shadows were something we had full control of, my brothers rarely used them. They were mostly afraid of the price that was asked for. I, on the other hand, was usually willing to pay the price, and I didn't hesitate to use them at will.

"I need Raphael's mark removed from Rayne! What is your price?" I snarled, my eyes never leaving my brother's. The tendrils swirled and twisted at my feet as if they were waiting for my next command, waiting for me to allow them to rip the life from someone.

"The priccceee isss steep. A mark for a mark, bond for a bond." They slithered. "What mark do you ask for?" I questioned. "The mate bond from Rayne. She will be 21 soon and it will be revealed. Give usss the bond she keepsss, and we will remove the bond between them." They whispered.

"How does she have a mate bond? She is a Reaver? Reavers can choose their mates?" I said, confusion etched in my voice. "Rayne wasss never raisssed within a Coven. She never learned the waysss of a Reaver. That side of her hasss been suppressssed for all thessse yearsss making her Wolf side more dominant, and thusss granting her a mate bond. Her Wolf side isss dominant, because that isss all she hasss ever known." They slithered.

"Who is her intended mate?" I snapped. "That information isss not oursss to tell, Master. Do you accept the price? Her bond for their bond?" They said. Their voices, like silk sliding over frozen steel, sent shivers coursing through my already glacial bones. On one hand, it wouldn't matter if she lost her mate bond. I was going to mark her, and fully intended to complete the mating process to make it permanent anyway.

On the other hand though, to take something like that away from her? She would hate me. I would be fine if she never found out… but if she did find out… The thoughts circled my mind. Nero remained still as he didn't want any part of this. "I reject your offer." I spat, and with a wave of my hand they slithered back to nothingness. I couldn't do it.

There was no way I could give up her mate bond. My only worry regarding this was whether I would be her mate, or whether we would have to deal with someone else. We would figure that out when the time comes. I turned back to look Raphael dead in the eyes again. "We will have to rid her of this wretched mark the hard way. Mark my words, brother, if you try anything, I will not hesitate to start a fucking war." I sneered, hoping he could feel the rage coursing through my voice.

Out of all four of us brothers, I was the most ruthless one and we all knew it. I was hoping he would take my warning to heart because he knew me and how I was.

Then I vanished, leaving Raphael in a mess of fury.

Chapter 29

~

(Rayne)

M y sleep was restless, if you could even call it sleep. My mind was swimming with everything Brett had told me, and all of the new knowledge I had gained. I was still stressed about Eric, expecting to hear anytime that they had found his remains. I didn't even check my phone this morning because I slept in so anyone could have messaged me already. Likely though, it would be Jae or Brett. I still had to get to training this morning and was now about to be late. "Shit!" I cried out loud when I realized just how late it actually was.

I threw on a gold sports bra, black leggings and my new gold tennis shoes I recently bought to match. I quickly threw my hair up in a high pony and ran out the door. I contemplated not even showing up…

I knew Alpha Drake was back from his travels this week and I was really enjoying my time not having to deal with him. But I knew he would kill me if I ditched out. He wouldn't care what I was going through, and I also hadn't even told him so he would now think I was just lying to avoid training. Figures.

I ran into the outside stadium for training at the same time as Roman. "Hey." I said, as I was trying to catch my breath from running. I looked up at Roman since he hadn't said anything. I had completely forgotten about the mark. He was eyeballing it in awe. "What is that? It's beautiful, oh my god." He stammered. His words made the mark burn. It seemed that anyone else around me, admiring me or the mark would cause it to react. *What a stupid mark,* I thought. *Ugh.*

"Oh this? Yea uh, so let's just not talk about it ok?" I asked, knowing the costume trick wouldn't work on him. He agreed, but I could tell he was still looking at it. It seemed that he couldn't really stop. In fact, it seemed like he was attracted to it like a moth to a flame, and that struck me as strange.

I realized that no one else had seen it besides myself, Raziel, and Raphael. I didn't know how it affected other people, or that it even would at all. We walked to the middle of the stadium where everyone else was, and it was like all eyes were on me. Well, my mark. It was burning under everyone's gaze.

Literally, all the males in the room seemed attracted to it. They just kept walking over to me and trying to talk to me as if I hadn't ignored every single one of them for the past 8 years. It was actually rather annoying, and I was trying to find a way to prevent it. They were making so much unnecessary commotion. It was too much, and I knew that Alpha Drake was bound to notice.

Sure enough, within seconds Alpha Drake walked out to see what the fuss was. Of course, he spotted me immediately. I rolled my eyes like I always do, and got ready for impact. He stalked his way towards me in a very threatening way. If looks could kill, I would be dead, or rather, the mark on my face would be.

He stopped directly in front of me, grabbed my jaw, and turned my head to get a better look. "Well, this isn't *his* mark." He said quietly. And then, as if he realized something, I saw anger flash through his eyes. His face hardened.

"Who did this to you?" He said through gritted teeth. He was fucking furious. "That makes 2 for 2 on furious men in our life this week." Wynter snickered. I hushed her. "I... uh, sooo... it's a long story?" I stuttered, not really sure how to respond. He took his hand and ran it across my face lightly tracing my mark. I tried not to flinch as it burned like hell

196

under his touch. It definitely did not like Alpha Drake anywhere near me. I felt the same.

"Rayne, who fucking did it?" He spat. This time I knew I had to answer. "Raphael." I said quietly, not really wanting anyone else to hear me. "Oh hell no! We had an agreement! When you turn 21, if you are not mated to Mr. Kane then you are to be Luna of this pack whether you want to or not." He roared.

And now I was pissed. How could they sit and make deals with me as collateral and assume that I just had no say? "Excuse me? I belong to *NO ONE*! And as I have said before, I will *NEVER* be the Luna of your pack! Fuck you, Alpha." I spat, and this time the venom was coming from my own voice. I turned to walk away but Alpha Drake grabbed my arm and pulled me back. He spun me around and pulled me to his chest so he was behind me speaking directly into my ear.

"The more defiant you are, the more I want you, Rayne. I promise, you will not get in the way of what I want, the deal stands. I don't care if I have to kill every single other supernatural creature to get my way, I will have you." He growled, fury and lust was rolling off him in sickening waves. He then nibbled on my ear and kissed the side of my face causing me to flinch in disgust. My mark was burning like hell to get me away from him. I wanted nothing more than to disappear right now.

I was so flustered that I'm not even sure what happened next. It all just happened so fast. It must have been the mark, the bond, or something. Suddenly, Alpha Drake released his hold on me and stepped back, not saying a word. Confused, I turned to see what had caused his change in behavior and I locked eyes with Raphael.

The other Wolves in training gasped and backed up as far as they dared. Lightning shot through my mark just like the night we had kissed in the dreamwalk. It awakened all of my senses, begging to be touched, held… anything but what was happening now. It was like just his presence alone soothed all my ailments. "Come here, Rayne."

Raphael purred. It was like my legs had a mind of their own and I started walking towards him. As much as I tried to fight it, I couldn't. I couldn't stop it. I walked straight to him, and he pulled me into his arms.

The lightning was insane, and it felt like I was supposed to be there. This was where I *had* to be, where I *needed* to be. I snuggled my head into his shoulder.

"Take me away from here." I mumbled. My body was perfectly content being in his arms, but my thoughts were a whole nother story. I'm not sure who was asking. Why would I ask that? I don't want to be with him… I *can't* be with him! All the thoughts were racing through my mind but there were none that I could control.

Wynter was even feeling the lightning. She wasn't even arguing, she was agreeing! But I can't… I shouldn't… but I fucking wanted to. My mind and body were in a battle, and I was going to lose either way.

Before I could make a conscious decision about anything, we materialized in Raphael's room. My mark was exploding with content, as if I was exactly where I was supposed to be. This was fucking insanity.

Raphael let me go and I looked at his room. Things seemed different from what I remember. The bookshelf was the same, but the bed was in a different spot. And the reading nook was gone. I swear the bar was a mini bar too, not a full bar. So strange, maybe that's the difference between a dream and real life? "Yes, beautiful, I did some… redecorating, you could call it." He said, reading the confused look on my face.

Wynter was going insane, and my mark was sending pulses of ecstasy shooting through my body every time he spoke. I just kept thinking, *I can't be here. I shouldn't be here.* But my body was saying the complete and utter opposite. I was losing the battle.

I watched as Raphael walked over to the bar and got us both drinks. I grazed his fingers as I grabbed mine from his hand. This action sent extreme sparks of lightning coursing through my entire body. I took the shot of alcohol and set my glass down. Then I turned to face Raphael, and before I could say anything he pulled me into his arms. He snapped his fingers, turned on a slow song, and we danced. I laid my head on his shoulder and let him lead.

My mind was fighting it, trying to tell me something. It was trying to tell me I wasn't supposed to be here, tell me to leave, to go... but my entire body was begging for more of his touch, his voice, his smell... his everything.

I knew I shouldn't be here, but I couldn't, for the life of me, get away. I couldn't get my legs to move in the opposite direction. He pulled away briefly to look at me. His gaze was deep, as if he was taking in every inch of me, every feature, and committing it straight to memory.

He leaned down and gently pressed his lips to mine. The lightning from my mark fucking exploded, sending sparks through my entire body again. But something was missing, something deep in my soul. At that moment I realized the mark was a physical thing. It makes my physical being weak to him. My body wanted him, but he doesn't feed my soul, he doesn't feed the deeper side of me, only the carnal, physical side.

I closed my eyes as a memory surfaced. "When you are struggling with the mark, and your feelings for him, just remember who you belong to. Remember who made you scream." said Raziel, his golden eyes full of lust and possessiveness. Flashbacks of him with his hand in my panties, and him sinking his fangs into my neck.

It all came flooding back, stirring something deep inside me, something beyond the physical, something on the soul level. The tingling in the palms of my hands pulled me from my incoherent stupor.

"No!" I shouted, as I put my hand on Raphael's chest, and pushed him away from me in a fury of green flames. I sent him hurtling completely back and into the wall.

Chapter 30

"I'm not where I belong, I don't belong with you!" I screamed. My mark blazed with a fiery passion, fueled by my defiant words. I looked down briefly, and both of my hands were now engulfed in green flames. Raphael looked back at me as he got up off the floor. Surprise, and then hurt filled his eyes which sent a pang of guilt through me. I didn't mean to hurt his feelings, but this guilt was, no doubt, influenced by the mark.

Honestly, I was surprised. I couldn't believe I was able to resist the marks pull. My memories came in jumbled sections. Everything was second to the mark and my need to be close to Raphael, even when I knew I shouldn't be.

"How… how did you do that, Rayne? How are you resisting the marks pull? That is impossible!" He stammered as he started walking back my way. "No Raphael, stay away from me." I said with conviction. Little did he know I was absolutely shaking inside. I knew that if he came even 1 step closer that I wouldn't be able to resist him again.

Every nerve ending in my body was on fire, begging me to just run into his arms. Every single thought running through my head was telling me that I *needed* him. My mark was burning at my disobedience, but I knew where I belonged… who I belonged to. That's when I got pissed.

"What the fuck kind of magic is this mark?" I sneered. I saw fear flash through Raphael's silver eyes. It was brief, but very much there. I kept my composure but wondered just how I had scared him. He put his hands up in front of him as if to calm me before he spoke. It worked, and I blamed that on this god forsaken mark. "It's a very powerful type of magic, can't be broken, can't be resisted. Well... couldn't be, apparently... until now." Raphael stated.

The tingling in my hands persisted, refusing to subside, while my mind raced with all of these unrelenting thoughts. Then, without warning, the room plummeted into an unforgiving chill, the coldest temperature I had ever experienced. An arctic blast seemed to seep into my very marrow, leaving me shivering and breathless. I could see my own misty exhalations, and a creeping sense of panic began to take hold. Raphael's eyes widened and I could see a much deeper look of fear in them than before, even though he wasn't outwardly showing it.

"Rayne.... Rayne, beautiful... what are you doing...?" Raphael stammered. As fear convulsed his voice, the room was abruptly consumed by an inky blackness, as if the very fabric of darkness had come alive. Shadows, more profound than any I had ever witnessed, erupted from every direction and nowhere simultaneously, like a living entity unfolding itself.

Their sinuous tendrils, akin to snakes, danced menacingly at my feet, spreading across the floor with an eerie, almost sentient, purpose. The Shadows seemed to vibrate with restless anticipation, as if straining to be unleashed, their dark energy coiled and waiting for my command.

I could hear their voices slithering through my ears. Multiple different voices, in different tones, snaking and whispering all at once. "What do you need, Massster?" They slithered. "Tell ussss, we will oblige for a price." They whispered.

Their ethereal whispers sent shivers down my spine, and the room's sudden darkness made me feel like I was part of a horror movie. Logically, I should have been scared, terrified even, but I was so intrigued by them.

"Rayne, fuck no! This is a horrible idea!" Wynter cursed, but I couldn't help but feel a very welcome serenity while surrounded by these slithering beings. As terrifying as they seemed, they weren't hurting me, they were just waiting for me to control them. It was as if they wouldn't do anything without my permission, which gave me power over them, and with it, a sense of security. Almost as if they were bound to me, in a way.

"What are you?" I asked them. "We are The Shadowssss, Massster. We are here to ssserve, for a priccceee of courssseee." They slithered. "I want this mark gone! Name your price!" I stammered, trying to sound confident in my ask. The Shadows started writhing and moving anxiously at my feet, as well as all around the room. "A bond for a bond... Give usss your mate bond and we will remove the mark." They whispered.

A shiver coursed through my veins. *So, I did still have a mate bond, even though I am a Reaver...* I wondered how that all worked. I had only ever known a Wolf mate bond my whole life, but upon finding out that I was a Reaver I had assumed I wouldn't have one...

I had assumed I never had one and just didn't know... "My mate bond?" I questioned. I thought about it for a minute. If I were actually mated to Raziel, I would be giving up something so incredible... something I've heard so much about for years from all my elders. I would be giving up a bond that cannot be broken, a bond that the Gods choose for me... a bond that was forever.

But, if I wasn't mated to him, then I would be giving up a bond with someone else. Someone that I, at this time, didn't even want. No matter who it was. "Don't fucking do it Rayne! Don't give them our mate bond, please." Wynter begged.

The mate bond was something a Wolf looked forward to their whole lives. Even if we were mated with someone we didn't know or have feelings for, it was still worth the wait to just experience the bond in all of its glory. In my mind I knew that no matter who my mate was, I was going to be with Raziel. So, I didn't care about the bond... but I couldn't do it, I couldn't shatter Wynter's heart like that. "I decline your price." I said to The Shadows. "Asss we expected,

Massster. Raziel did the same thing. We can alwaysss be called if you need usss. We require an offering of blood from here on out, Massster." They whispered.

And just as suddenly as they appeared, The Shadows vanished, their dark, icy tendrils retracting into the very fabric of existence, leaving behind only a lingering whisper of their presence. It was as if they had merged back into the abyss from which they slithered out of.

Raphael was still standing in the same spot, starstruck by what had just happened. I took it that he didn't mess with The Shadows much, and I could see why. They definitely had their prices, and I wasn't sure how much I would be willing to pay for their help in the future.

"Rayne... are you ok?" Raphael questioned. I locked eyes with him, and I could see the concern swimming in those beautiful silver orbs. It took everything I had to look away. My mark was pulsing with desire, pushing me to him. I wanted nothing more than to just feel his arms around me, but I refrained.

All of those feelings had subsided when The Shadows were around. Now, I was back in my internal battle, and Wynter was not helping in any way, shape, or form. I did the only other thing I could think of short of calling The Shadows again, I mind linked Raziel.

I knew he would be fucking furious, but I was willing to risk it, knowing I wouldn't be able to force myself to walk away from Raphael a second time. I was barely hanging on enough to resist him thus far. If I didn't get away soon, who knows what would happen.

Just like that, Raziel materialized in front of me. We locked eyes and worry flooded through his beautiful golden gaze. He was wearing gold sweatpants and no shirt. I couldn't help but gasp a little at the sight of his chiseled body. His golden blonde hair was tousled as if he was in bed previously.

I couldn't help but admire his beauty. Raphael was gorgeous, but he was *nothing* compared to Raziel. Honestly, Raziel may have been the most gorgeous man I had ever laid my eyes on. Raziel grabbed me and pulled me close to him. My bare skin touching his caused my mark to burn uncomfortably. "I remembered! I know who I'm supposed to be with." I said with tears in my eyes. He remained calm and quiet, quelling my erratic energy.

"I hate this mark, it's so inviting! It makes me feel like I'm right where I should be, but I know it's a lie. It's not real. Deep down, I know this is not where I belong." I cried into Raziel's shoulder.

He ran his fingers through the hair in my ponytail. I inhaled slowly while gathering my next thoughts. "I called The Shadows, and I didn't even mean to! I threw Raphael into the wall with fireballs… I can't control anything! I'm a fucking mess!" I stammered.

He held me with a desperate intensity, his arms wrapping around me like a lifeline, as if he feared that if he relaxed his grip even a fraction, I would vanish into thin air, leaving him with nothing but a memory.

He then turned to Raphael who had just started to speak. "It's only going to get worse, and you know it. You know what needs to be done, brother." Raphael said, and I had no idea what he was referring to.

"You will keep your fucking mouth shut. Keep your filthy hands off her, Raphael. This isn't over." Raziel spat. The sheer anger that resonated from him was sickening, engulfing me in its toxic waves. I knew he wasn't mad at me, but boy, was he fucking mad.

Then he materialized us away from Raphael before he could mutter another word.

Chapter 31

He sat me down on his bed, moving the gold and black pillows from behind me. Sitting next to me, he took me into his arms. "Thank you. I'm so sorry, I don't know what happened." I said with sincerity in my voice. "Shhh darling, it's ok. You're alright." He said softly, while running his hand through my silver hair. His demeanor was very different from the Raziel that I usually deal with. All snark and cockiness was absent, replaced with deep concern. It was very strange, but I was too distraught to really focus on the changes. He snapped and produced us both drinks of liquid gold. "Drink, you'll feel better." He said.

I drank the liquid, sipping it this time rather than taking it as a shot like I had the drink Raphael had given me. Raziel was right. It did make me feel better. Besides the uncomfortable burning of my mark, I was definitely feeling less anxious. My hands weren't tingly, I didn't feel like I was accidentally calling The Shadows.

I wasn't even really panicking thinking about what other powers I might end up with by accident. The sheer burning of my mark was almost a comfort at this point, telling me that I was right where I needed to be… in Raziel's arms, and far the fuck away from Raphael.

"Now tell me about The Shadows, darling." Raziel asked. "I'm not sure where to start. I'm not even sure how I called them… but it was like they came from everywhere and nowhere all at once." I recanted. He listened intently. "They whispered to me in a multitude of voices. They told me they would obey my wishes for a price. I asked them to remove the mark, and they asked for my mate bond. I said no, but I didn't even know that I had a mate bond still... Raziel, how do I have one if I'm like you?" I stammered.

He looked at me and I couldn't read his expression. It was as if he was trying to find the best way to explain this to me.

"You were born outside of a Coven, and never introduced to one. You grew up thinking you were just a Wolf and thus you have the same abilities as a Wolf. Call yourself a Reaver with Wolf focused abilities. Your Reaver abilities cannot break through unless you are in a Coven and have been trained to use them. There are a plethora of Reavers out there in the world that will never know what they are for this reason. Why you came into your powers with no Coven influence, is beyond me." He said, confusion clouding his golden eyes.

I remained silent, trying to take in all that he had said. "I knew what you were the first time I laid eyes on you, in the forest at the wishing well. I knew you were special. I've kept track of you ever since then, hoping that when you turned 21 you would be ready to leave your pack and choose me. Little did I know you actually had a mate bond, or that you would come into these powers. I'm sorry Rayne, I should have done more to protect you." The sadness in his words slowly seeped into my bones and settled in my very core.

I locked eyes with him, and I could feel his pain. "Don't do that... you had no way to know." I stammered.

"But as young as you were, I was wrong by taking you to a pack. I should have brought you to one of my Covens where you could have learned to hone your powers. I thought I was helping you not subjecting you to the torture of learning so late in your life. But I see now that all it did was hinder you, and for that mistake, I am truly sorry." He said.

"Raziel, I don't think that is something you need to be sorry for." I said, and it was then, randomly, when what Alpha Drake had said flashed through my mind. As much as I wanted to continue to console Raziel, I had to know what the fuck he was thinking making a deal like that. "But I do need an explanation for this… why would you make a deal with Alpha Drake that if I wasn't mated to you he could have me as Luna? Especially if you didn't even know I had a mate bond?" I tried not to be upset with him over this. I could see the emotion in his face shift. He smiled as we locked eyes.

"Rayne, I made whatever deal he would accept in order for your protection all these years. He needed power and numbers, I needed you safe. I went into the deal knowing full well that I wasn't going to let him make you Luna of The Obsidian pack. I fully intended on winning you over, then marking you myself and making the bond permanent. You couldn't be a Luna if you were mated to another." He said, and flashed me another dazzling smile.

I scoffed. Of course he had a plan. The thought of me being by Alpha Drakes side was infuriating, to say the least. I wanted nothing more than to never have to deal with him again. Sadly, I was sure I hadn't seen the last of him, even with my newfound situation.

"Thank you, and like I said, don't you dare be sorry, Raziel. You have done more than enough for me. More than I could ever ask for just by being here for me. When my mother passed away, I was lost. And even though I hate Alpha Drake, I was never mistreated by him. Nowadays he's a bit more brutal with me, but he has never truly hurt me. Thinking back, I don't know where I would have gone, or where I would be now without you." I told him.

I locked onto his golden eyes, placed one hand on the side of his face, and the other hand on his chest over his heart. "Promise me that this is real. Promise me that *we* are real. Mark or not, mate bond or not… promise me that you won't give up on me." I said, knowing in that moment that I had made up my mind completely. I was exactly where I wanted to be, and I wasn't going to let a stupid mark or a frustrating mate bond change anything.

"I will promise you, darling. But before I do, I need to tell you something… something rather important. I had every mind to keep it to myself and handle it… alone. But I think you deserve to know." His words were a bit solemn, and honestly had me panicking internally. I inhaled and nodded, without saying anything, silently urging him to continue.

"A very, very, long time ago, my brothers and I had a conversation regarding Reavers who came into their powers outside of a Coven. To make a long story short, having no control over your powers can be extremely volatile. You could unknowingly hurt a lot of people. Hurt them and possibly even do more damage than just that. It takes a lifetime to hone in your powers, starting from birth. What I'm trying to say is, you, in your current state, are more than a threat... you are a danger to yourself and every living creature on this side of the continent."

His words sunk into my chest like a poison arrow, digging deeper and deeper until it penetrated my heart. "But... but I would never... I... I couldn't..." I stammered before he stopped me with a finger on my trembling lips. "I know your heart, and I know you would never intentionally hurt a soul. But unbridled power to the extent that we have... you wouldn't even realize it before it was too late." He said.

I swallowed whatever words would have come out next in favor of a ragged breath that was burning my throat. "I didn't ask for this. But... but what is the solution? What did you and your brothers decide when you spoke of this?" He inhaled slowly through his nose and briefly looked away. I took that as a bad sign, which made my anxiety spike. He looked back and we locked eyes.

"The moment I realized you were coming into your power, I should have killed you. I should have ripped your heart clean from your chest." He said, placing his hand over my heart softly. I gasped under my breath, but I found myself not as surprised as I thought I would be by his answer. It was almost as if I knew he was going to say that already. Even Wynter was quiet in my mind.

"No one ever said I was a good man and I'll never claim to be. Call me selfish for being willing to risk the lives of all of my Covens, and this entire half of the continent just to have one more chance to take your breath away... but I would do it again in a heartbeat. I promise, darling. I promise that *we* are real, that *this* is real. I promise that no matter what life throws at us, I will never give up on you." He purred.

And pulled me in for another kiss, more feral this time. The feeling of his lips on mine succeeded in completely taking my breath away. He pulled away far before I wanted him to, but I soon realized it was for a good reason. "I need to speak to my other brothers about you... I don't know how they will react and frankly, I don't give a damn." I chuckled under my breath at his snarky attitude, but deep down I was terrified of what they would say.

What had Raphael said besides what I heard earlier? I don't know why these things mattered so much to me, but suddenly, I was desperate for his brothers to accept me. Desperate to be able to someday form a bond with them all individually, and live together in peace. Somehow, that was the most important thing to me at that moment.

"When will you speak to them? What will you say?" I questioned. "Actually, I plan to speak to them now, and you will be accompanying me." I gasped out loud this time. "But... what if somethi..." I began before he captured my lips with his, effectively stopping my next set of panicked words. "They will not lay a single finger on you, lest they want to lose it." He growled against my lips before pulling away.

"Now that I have you, truly have you, *nothing* will get in my way. Not a rule, not a pact, and sure as hell not any of my brothers. Get dressed, we leave in 20 minutes." He said, snapping to produce me a shimmery gold and black sundress with matching strappy sandals. He left the room to allow me to change.

I scrambled to the mirror once the outfit was on to admire it. The fabric of the dress felt like silk and shimmered as I moved, even in the lack of light. It was absolutely gorgeous. The sandals while black and gold were less shimmery and more chameleon, changing color between black and gold as they hit certain lighting. I held in a silent gag when I saw Raphael's mark on my face in the mirror. The silver just clashed with my entire outfit, but I wasn't about to change colors to appease it.

I left my hair in the pony that it was already in and checked in with Wynter. I realized she hadn't said much and her opinion was important to me. "Well, what are your thoughts?" I asked Wynter. She sighed and I could tell she was troubled.

"Have you felt the unbridled power Raziel spoke about? Can you tell when it's going to happen? Because I have either been oblivious to it, or I really can't feel it... and if I can't feel it then you likely can't feel it either. And if neither of us can feel it, then how are we supposed to know when it's becoming too much and we are about to be a danger to ourselves and others? I'm really trying to be positive here. I couldn't be happier about being with Raziel and you know that as fact. But I'm scared, Rayne. I'm truly scared of what he said... I don't want to lose control and hurt people. Can you imagine what happens if we destroy Raziel's Covens, or worse... this entire side of the continent. Think of how many people would die."

I had been so distracted by Raziel that I hadn't fully grasped the severity of what my unbridled powers could truly do. My head was spinning. "Listen, I know this is scary, terrifying even, but we need to trust that Raziel will have some sort of solution. I mean, he has to, right? Do you think he would honestly let me live if he didn't think there was a way around this?" I replied.

"I truly hope that you are right, Rayne. I hope that this doesn't come back to bite us in the ass. As rough as Eric's death has been on both of us, I couldn't imagine multiple people's deaths being on our shoulders too." She said, and then I felt her move to the back of my mind on her own.

That simple reaction from her made my stress levels increase exponentially. I didn't have much time to ponder it before Raziel knocked on the door. "Are you ready, darling?" He asked before opening the door a crack. "Yes, I am." I replied heading towards the door. He stepped in and I saw his whole demeanor change as he looked at me. I watched his eyes trail over every inch of my entire body before he looked back into my eyes.

He said nothing but he walked right up to me and crashed his lips into mine. Again, heat flooded my cheeks, draining throughout my entire body. My mark was burning as if to chastise me, but I didn't care. I reciprocated, and pulled him closer to me.

"Fuck, you are so fucking incredible. My intentions were to make it to meet with my brothers, but at this rate we'll be lucky to make it out of this bedroom." He growled. He buried his face in my neck where he was planting aggressive kisses and nips trailing down to my collarbone. When he suddenly stopped and pulled away from me I could see a very annoyed look on his face.

"I suppose I should have waited to mind link them and let them know I was coming until we were ready. They are inquiring as to my whereabouts. As much as I would love to ignore them and focus all of my attention on you for the rest of the foreseeable future, I am nothing if not a man of my word. We need to go." He said, taking a small step back and holding his hand out for me. We weren't even a foot apart, but I took his hand anyway and we materialized.

Chapter 32

I expected to become sick like I had the last time, but the nausea was brief and barely caused me any issue. I didn't recognize the brilliantly lit city that we were standing in, but it was gorgeous. It gave a vibrant and electric feel with its plethora of grand mansions and ornate ironwork. By the lack of lighthouses and coastal themed buildings, I could tell we weren't in Maine anymore.

There was a very old looking medieval Tavern sitting directly in front of us. I was in awe because it looked like something straight out of a fantasy novel. The weathered timber and cobblestone that makes up the main structure seemed a bit worn. Chipped stone and peeling paint off the wood gave it quite a charming, quaint feel.

The roof, while more modern, still had a thatched appearance and I could see moss making its way across the south corner and down the exterior. Long, leaf covered vines strung the expanse of at least two thirds of the entire building.

A large wooden sign that read 'TwentyOne' in large Old English lettering that was burned into the wood, hung off a set of chains that were centered across the top peak above the door. The door itself looked to be oak, and it was completely solid. There was a large iron knocker in the center of the door that looked like a Griffin.

Faintly glowing lanterns were strategically placed around the covered entryway and along the wooden fence that surrounded the property, allowing a soft glow to engulf us. It was breathtaking. I followed Raziel as he walked up and pulled the door handle. The door creaked as it opened, alerting all of the patrons inside to our presence. A warm golden light, matching the light tones that were set on the exterior, spilled out as we made our way inside. The murmur of hushed conversations infiltrated the air, followed by the scent of sweet meats and liquor. The ceilings here were high, and rows of wooden tables and benches lined the walls.

You could tell the interior was updated but still made to look old and weathered. There was a large stone fireplace crackling off to the right hand side, and directly in front of us was a solid wood bar with every type of alcohol you could imagine, in a locking glass case behind it. To the left was another solid wood bar, with glass and drinking accessories littering the stone wall. Behind the bar was a door that was closed. The place was inviting and beautiful, I longed to spend more time here than I knew we would be.

Three beautiful, dark haired, blue eyed women were bartending and assisting the plethora of customers that requested their help. I saw one of them notice us, but she did not acknowledge. Raziel didn't seem to be looking for her acknowledgement anyway. He looked around for a brief moment before he must have found what he was looking for, because he began to walk towards a booth in the far back corner.

I followed blindly, unsure of what his brothers even looked like. I assumed we were meeting them here, or why else would we be here? We stopped in front of the booth and I looked down, locking eyes with a pair of rose gold beauties. The man had brown hair and striking features.

A light stubble danced along his square jawline and seemed to accent his high cheekbones. He was wearing a suit that was mostly black but accented with rose gold. He raised an eyebrow at me, but didn't say a word. I knew he was a Reaver, it was very easy to tell.

I looked over at the other man, who had fiery red hair that was a bit unruly, and bright bronze eyes to accent his also perfect jawline. He was gorgeous, and had the most perfect teeth that he was flashing in what looked like a genuine smile at me. He was also wearing a suit, but he had surrendered the jacket and was just wearing a black vest over a metallic bronze button down. The pants were the same shade of bronze and I swear they were glinting, even in the low lighting of the Tavern.

"Brother, you didn't say you were bringing a... friend?" The red haired Reaver said. I watched as his eyes landed directly onto my face, focusing on the large silver mark that shone oh so brightly there. "Raphael?" The rose gold Reaver questioned. I didn't have to look at Raziel to know that he had rolled his eyes.

He motioned for me to take a seat and he took his place next to me. The air was thick with tension as I settled into the silence, my senses heightened as I became acutely aware of the formidable presence that surrounded me. The weight of their collective power was a palpable force, a dense, heavy energy that pressed in on me from all sides. It was as if the very atmosphere had grown thicker, more charged, as these four individuals converged in a single space.

I felt small, insignificant, in the face of such concentrated authority, my own presence seeming to shrink in comparison to the towering figures that loomed beside me. Still, I remained silent, and truly, for the first time, understood the sheer amount of power that sat between the 4 of us. "We have a problem." Raziel said, and I knew he was referencing me.

"You think? You have Raphael's chosen mate in your presence and he wasn't even invited to this meeting... I'd say we have a fucking problem." The red haired Reaver chuckled. He seemed very light hearted, though there was an undertone of seriousness there. A very slight undertone, but one, nonetheless. Raziel sighed.

"Ramses, Rowen, meet Rayne." He said, looking at the red haired Reaver first then sliding his gaze to the rose gold Reaver. "Hi." I said softly, hoping they couldn't hear the shaking of my voice. "Well, hello there. And I take it that you are not supposed to have that mark on your face, now are you?" Ramses said. I shook my head and then he nodded. "Brother, you brought us here to discuss a beautiful woman with Raphael's mark? Couldn't this have been handled in a more... private setting?" Rowen asked, looking from me to Raziel.

"Rayne is a Reaver with Wolf focused abilities." Raziel finally said. Neither brother said anything, but the slow inhale from Rowen, and the subtle seat shift from Ramses, told me everything I needed to know. These tiny, nonverbal cues conveyed a wealth of information, hinting at the complex, simmering tensions that lay just beneath the surface.

"Smooth, brother. Fucking smooth to bring us to a very populated, very public place to release this information. My only question is, what is she *still* doing here?" Rowen asked. I held back my offense but was still astonished that they were speaking of me as if I wasn't even present for the conversation. Ramses looked at Rowen and scoffed. "She's marked. Clearly, Raphael isn't going to allow her to be... well, he will not allow it." Ramses said.

"This has absolutely nothing to do with Raphael, or he would be here. Let's be real." Rowen retorted. "Oh, this has *everything* to do with Raphael, which is why he isn't here. Clearly, he's put his fucking mark on her and it definitely doesn't belong, now does it?" Ramses snipped. "Enough!" Raziel growled, instantly bringing the two bickering brothers to silence. They looked between myself and Raziel with wide eyes.

"I've brought you both here today to introduce you to Rayne and to inform you that her fate will not be the one previously decreed. I'm fully aware of the risks and dangers involved, and I want to assure you that I've made this decision with eyes wide open. I'm not naive to the potential consequences, and I'm not going to make excuses for my failure to uphold the oath I swore all those years ago. However, I refuse to let a centuries old promise, one that has never been acted upon, stand in the way of what is rightfully mine. I'm taking control of this situation, and I won't let anything or anyone come between me and what belongs to me."

I felt that he handled that relatively well and by the way his brothers were both looking between him and I, I'd say neither of them were too keen on arguing with him. "Raphael is already aware and has already voiced his opinions. Would either of you like to put in your 2 cents? Or are we at an understanding?" He asked.

Neither of the brothers jumped at the opportunity to speak. I have no idea what came over me next. Maybe it was my insistent need for them to accept me, but I had to plead my own case. "Rayne, don't you fucking dare... these men are the most powerful men in the world. Don't get in the middle of it!" Wynter cried, practically begging me to keep my mouth shut, but when have I ever succeeded in such an endeavor?

I didn't even have a chance to respond to her before all 3 of the brothers locked their eyes on me. "You have something to say, sweetheart?" Rowen purred. Panic flooded into my chest, how did they know? I wasn't ready to be put on the spot, but I didn't want to seem weak in front of them, so I pushed the erratic thoughts from my mind and began to speak.

"Look, I know you are all leery of me, and I can't blame you. A Reaver with Wolf focused abilities? According to Raziel, this has never happened before. It's not possible for a Reaver to develop powers outside of a Coven, but here I am. You're going to tell me that in all the time you guys have been alive you've never once seen anything like this, and you don't think that there is a reason for it?" My words were shaky, but I kept the appearance of confidence.

"A reason?" Ramses questioned. I nodded. "Yes, a reason. Why else would my powers develop? I am hard pressed to think that I am just special, or a random anomaly. I don't believe in coincidences, I never have. This happened for a reason. Everything that I have been given has been given to me for a reason. What is the reason? I have no idea. But I can't sit around and be afraid, waiting for something bad to happen. The Gods decided that I am to have these powers and we can't change it. So outside of killing me, you guys only have 1 option. Teach me… train me to use these powers so I don't hurt anyone." My words became stronger this time, my conviction less wavering. Rowen opened his mouth to speak but I cut him off.

"I know what you're going to say. I understand that these skills are honed from birth and I just so happen to be 20 years behind, I am *very* aware of this fact. But I believe that I can do it. I am willing to put in the work. I know I can harness these powers and use them for good. I've already resisted the mate mark, and if I can do that I can do anything." I said. Both Rowen and Ramses looked at me with wide eyes. "The mate mark, what?" Ramses questioned. Raziel nodded next to me.

"It's true. She called me to come and get her after Raphael had taken her to his home. This was after she was marked, and the bond would have been in full force with their skin to skin contact. She pushed him away from her with the green flame and mind linked me." Raziel explained.

Just then I could feel a slight tingling in my hands. I looked down expecting to see a green flame but it was absent. I could feel it though, I recognized the feeling from the few times it's happened before. I took a slow breath in and willed the flame to appear, small and dainty, in the palm of my now opened hand. I withheld a gasp of surprise when it worked. I closed my hand around it, but it didn't dissipate. It wasn't until I willed it to go that it actually disappeared.

That was it? My will? The magic was basically like an animal, and my will was a command. Somehow, it clicked and I knew I could use this as a bargaining chip.

Chapter 33

I tuned back into the conversation just to hear the tail end. "And if she can't control them?" Rowen inquired. Raziel began to speak. "She ca..." but I cut him off too. "I can." I said, opening both of my hands on top of the table. Two small green fireballs were dancing within my palms. Rowen gasped. "Well I'll be damned." Ramses said with a chuckle.

"How long have you been teaching her for?" Rowen immediately asked Raziel. "He hasn't. Look at his face, he's just as surprised as we are, brother." Ramses retorted. "How are you doing that?" Raziel asked.

"I'm willing it to happen. Magic does what it is commanded, but telling it isn't going to work, you have to *will* it. You have to speak the same language as the magic, in essence. Look." I said, willing the fireballs both to grow larger in my palms.

Now that it had clicked, it was easy. The fire did everything I wanted. Once I was done I willed it away and the fire dissipated. Not once did I waver in the belief that the magic would do as I commanded.

"I refuse to allow the magic to control me. So again, teach me to use this magic, and maybe together we can figure out why I was gifted with it." My words were much stronger now than when I started. I was feeling very confident in my abilities to learn and control this power.

Rowen and Ramses looked impressed, and I didn't look at Raziel next to me. I wasn't trying to plead my case to him because I knew he already had my back. His brothers needed convincing, not him. "Look man, you know best and if you think she is worth the clear, excruciatingly intense consequences of unbridled Reaver power, then I have your back." Rowen finally said. Ramses nodded. "I mean, she is... something. There really might be a reason for this. I'm inclined to think that she may be onto something. Plus, I trust your judgment, brother." Ramses said, locking his bronze eyes and perfect smile onto me. I tried to keep the blush from invading my cheeks, but I was miserably failing at the task.

Raziel nodded and then stood, holding out his hand for me. I took it and he helped me out of the booth, pulling me to his chest by my waist. My mark was burning like crazy but I tried my best to ignore it. "Now that we are all on the same page, I expect both of you to stay out of the drama between Raphael and I. Things might get... ugly." Raziel said before he materialized us back to his bedroom.

"I'm sorry for interrupting you, and Rowen, but I really think that went well..." I said, looking up at Raziel. He hadn't released his grip on me yet and it didn't feel like he planned to. We locked eyes and he was smirking at me.

"You are fucking incredible. The way you take control of a conversation, plead your case and show how serious you are with actions... you are a natural leader." He said. "No." I laughed. "I just knew they wouldn't want to hear it, they would want to see it. Proof that I am capable of doing what I say is key." I replied, brushing off the compliment.

"You know nothing of my brothers, and yet, you've already entranced them both. I expected much more tension but you seemed to ease a majority of their concerns, and so easily. You now have 4 very powerful men wrapped around your little finger and you've barely done a single thing. Maybe there is a reason you were gifted with this. How did you learn to control the fire, anyway?" He asked.

I began to grasp the full extent of my unintended allure as I processed what Raziel had said, and then registered that he asked me a question. "I just used my will. I don't really know the exact process, but I willed it to happen, willed the fire to listen to me, and then I commanded it.

219

Once it clicked that this is how you get it to work, then it was easy." I replied. He finally released me and walked over to his nightstand. "Incredible." He murmured under his breath.

Then he snapped, and produced a pair of gold shorts and a black tank top. He then motioned for me to go to the bathroom to change. I looked at him with a raised eyebrow. "You want me to stay the night?" I asked, realizing it was actually pretty late according to the way the oranges and purples danced along the skyline. I could see the beautiful scenery from the windows in his room. We clearly had spent more time with his brothers than I realized.

He made a sound that was somewhere between a scoff and clearing his throat. "If you think I'm letting you out of my sight again, you're sorely mistaken." He said, but I couldn't tell if he was joking or not. I was leaning towards not.

"You'll be lucky if I ever let you out of this bedroom." He laughed. He was joking… I think. I shook my head at him. I was surprised that I didn't really hate the idea of it. I then headed to the bathroom to change. I came back out to lay down and I must have been exhausted because I don't even remember falling asleep.

The moment Raziel pulled me into the crook of his arm, I was out. For the first time in a while, I had a peaceful, calm, dreamless sleep. No dreamwalking, no crazy dreams or nightmares, nothing. Just sleep. When morning came, my eyes fluttered open, and it took me a minute to remember where I was. In Raziel's room.

I could see the gold and black silks lining the top of the four-poster bed. He had his arms around me, and my mark was burning, but it seemed like it was less painful than usual. *I must be getting used to it,* I thought. Wynter was still sleeping in my mind. I turned to face Raziel and admired his beauty. I loved being awake before him so I could admire the ethereal aura he exuded.

I can't believe I used to be so afraid of him. But, considering how dangerous he is, I guess I can't blame myself. My thoughts were a little out of sorts. Being with him goes against everything I was ever taught. But I am just like him… I'm a Reaver too. The thought sent chills down my spine. How could I be the very thing I was taught to fear? And why didn't my mother tell me? She had to know, right? I don't understand why she would have kept it from me.

She had the same color eyes as I did, so did that mean she was also a Reaver? But maybe she just didn't know? I wish she was still alive so I could speak to her. I shook the thoughts from my mind and instead, looked down at Raziel. I smiled as I took in all of his features.

His eyes were closed, and he looked so serene, so peaceful. It was much different from the turmoil that clouded his eyes as of late. His strong jawline was accentuating his perfectly symmetrical features. I could see his chest moving in and out as he took each breath. This was something I could get used to.

His eyes suddenly fluttered open, and after a second, he shot me a million dollar smile. It had me thinking… in fact, I had seen him smile more this past little bit than I ever had in my entire life. The thought made butterflies swarm my stomach.

"Good morning, darling. Did you sleep well?" He asked, as he pulled me in close and our lips met. The sensation awakened my inner Wolf. Pushing my carnal desires to the top with this simple move. It was more than a physical reaction, it was a mind, body, and soul reaction. Regardless of my current situation, I knew this is where I belonged. My mark, of course, was burning at my indiscretion. I noticed again that it wasn't burning as much, or as painful as before.

"I slept better than I have in a very long time. Is my mark going away?" I asked, running a hand across my face like I would be able to feel it even if it was. "It's too soon, it won't be fading yet, darling." Raziel said, but he moved my hair behind my ear and turned my face with his fingers on my chin so he could get a better look. "Wow, but it doesn't make sense." He mumbled. "So it is going away?!" I exclaimed, jumping from the bed to go look at it in the bathroom mirror.

"It has to be because you were able to resist it. The mark can't regenerate itself. So once portions fade, they are gone forever. You can't be re-marked either until the mark, in its entirety, is gone." Raziel said. He was excited, maybe even more excited than I was. I looked back at him as he stepped up behind me.

"Will you ever stop impressing me?" He said with a smile. I shrugged, unsure of how I had even impressed him thus far. He snapped and produced me a black and gold sports bra, black leggings, gold panties, and gold combat boots.

"You have got to teach me that snap thing." I chuckled, as I shooed him out of the bathroom so I could change. I, of course, wanted to wear anything that he picked out. He always knew exactly what I loved, what I always wore.

And honestly, even if it wasn't something I usually wore, I would wear it for him. I jumped in the shower, and then put on the new clothes Raziel had picked out. I let my silver hair fall pin straight to dry. Raziel had on a black pair of slacks, a gold button up shirt, black dress shoes and a black tie. His hair was tousled but perfect, like usual. We matched perfectly which made my heart flutter.

Everything about him was perfect. "Are you ready to go, darling?" Raziel purred. "Yes, but where?" I said. "It's a surprise." He replied with a smile. My heart fluttered as Wynter swooned in my mind. He took my hand and we headed out the door.

~

(Raphael)

"How did she do it? How did she resist the marks pull?" I asked Axel. "She is strong. Having unbridled power affects her differently. She is not a normal Reaver, and she is ours." Axel growled. "I know she is… she just doesn't know it yet. My brother may think he is top dog, but this will be a battle he will not win. As long as my mark adorns her beautiful face, I still have a chance. And I will not give up that easily." I told Axel.

I reveled in thoughts of Rayne ruling by my side. "She is perfect, she is exactly what I need. Can you imagine it? High Priestess, Rayne, by my side and ruling my Covens?" I pictured her wearing the High Priestess crown and standing strong by my side.

I could see her wearing a long, silver and black dress with a crisscross back. It had a slit from the floor to her upper thigh on one side. She looked so beautiful standing there with my mark adorning her face, sparkling in the sunshine.

No one would dare step to her, especially by my side. She would be a fierce leader, and not to mention absolutely beautiful on my arm. I had never really been interested in women, or anyone really. It seemed that they all were too eager to please... too, what's the word? Obedient?

Very few had piqued my actual interest in thousands of years. None since my Roxy. What was so special about Rayne? Why was I so drawn to her? I know she's a Reaver, but that shouldn't make a difference.

Maybe it's the fact that she came to me in my dreams? Or maybe the fact that she shares my color, although hers is more of a platinum while mine is just silver. But others have had my color and didn't get my attention either...

I couldn't place it, just something about her draws me in and I can't seem to walk away. It's as if she marked me and doesn't even know it. I had to get my hands back on her.

Such a beautiful, fiery little thing she is. Her fighting my mark just makes me want her more. Her fire attracts me, pulls me in. I just felt like I had to protect her, like I had to keep her safe ever since the first time she unknowingly dreamwalked into my dream.

Raziel or not, unbridled Reaver power, or not, I wasn't going to go down without a fight. I refused. I threw on a black button-down shirt with a silver suit vest over it. I grabbed a pair of black slacks, and my silver dress shoes. I ran my hand through my already messy hair, and I vanished. I needed to have a meeting with Alpha Drake, it was time to make a new deal.

Chapter 34

~

(Alpha Drake)

"Fucking Reavers. Always ruining my plans. There is no way that motherfucker is going to let Rayne go if he isn't her mate, who am I kidding? And now, with Raphael in the mix, and his mark..." I spewed to Samael, who was silently listening. Just the thought of my beautiful Rayne sporting Raphael's mark infuriated me.

I was already preparing for the fact that she may be mated to that fucking Reaver, and if so, I'd have to accept it. A deal is a deal, and I wouldn't go back on my word. But to have the chance at having her as my Luna... the Luna of the Obsidian pack, the largest, most well-known, and ruthless pack in the world? Even if she hated me? I would give anything.

I was pacing back and forth in my office at the pack house. There had to be another way. In fact, I made the deal with him... he never said anything about another Reaver in the mix, nothing about Raphael. This changes everything. The deal is broken. My only issue was I can't mark her myself. I can't choose her just like she can't choose me. A Wolf's mate is predetermined. I couldn't make her stay if she didn't want to.

"We can worry about that later, let's get her away from those filthy Reavers first." Samael snarled. "Sean." I called out to my Beta. He was just as large as the rest of my warriors. Rippled muscles lined his body and Jagged scars ran down his arms and throat. Most of them with no rhyme or reason. We had definitely seen some battles in our day. The sacrifices that were made were not to be forgotten.

My men wore their battle scars proudly, as did I. He was 6 feet tall and had sandy brown hair with blue eyes that sparkled in the right lighting. He always held a hardened look on his face. War does that to a man. He was my second in command and would take the pack over if anything were to happen to me.

"Yes sir." He reported. "Start readying the troops, the Reavers have Rayne and we are going to get her back." I snapped. It looked like he was going to say something, but he chose not to. Good, I wasn't about to take any other answer than, yes sir, at this point. This was fucking war! Rayne would be mine, whether she liked it or not.

I picked up my phone, about to call a couple of neighboring packs who owed me a favor for letting them live, and ask for warriors to join us. I knew we had the largest pack in the world, but it couldn't be big enough when we were talking about Reavers. I needed every nearby pack to join our fight, or the effort would be futile.

Honestly, I was nervous. No pack has ever taken on a Reaver, let alone possibly multiple Reavers and lived to tell about it... I had the phone up to my ear and my eyes trained on the book I had been reading regarding coping with the loss of a loved one.

The phone rang once and I trained my eyes on the photo of Reya I kept in my office on my desk while I waited for an answer. God, I missed her so fucking much. My little sister didn't deserve to be murdered. I was lost in my own thoughts when the next thing I knew, a Reaver, who I had never seen before, appeared in my office. "Wolf." He spat. "Reaver." I growled, as I hung up the phone. I eyeballed him for a moment and assumed he was Raphael. Why else would a Reaver approach me, of all people?

That is, unless he had business with someone in my pack... Rayne. "You must be Raphael... can I help you?" I spewed. Yes, he was terrifying, but I wasn't about to show weakness. I never did with them, and I never would. I looked him dead in the eyes. My gaze didn't falter in the least. I noticed this Reaver seemed to be different from the other. His demeanor was calm and collected, not fiery. He seemed like he may be more of a man of business than his counterpart, who seemed to love violence over anything else. I mind linked my pack, to alert them and have them on standby in case this went bad.

"Indeed, I am Raphael. No need to alert the pack... I'm here to make a deal." Raphael said, with a glint in his eye. How did he know I alerted the pack? *What the fuck? Could they hear a mind link?* I realized at that moment that I didn't really know that much about Reavers. Only what I had read, and a few things from Mr. Kane, but not enough to know the true extent of their powers.

I shook it off. "A deal you say?" My lip turned up into a devious half smile. "And what do you propose, Reaver?" I said, a little more nicely, but not much.

"My brother, Raziel, foolishly believes he has a claim on the woman I've chosen, Rayne, a member of your pack. I'm willing to make a deal with you. I want you to hand deliver her to me. What is your price? Name it, and I'll make sure it's worth your while." He said. *Brother? They are brothers?* And how did I know it would have to do with her? *God damnit!* She was the only thing I didn't want to give him.

"Don't fucking make a deal with him. He can't have Rayne, she is ours." My Wolf said protectively.

"I can see your Wolf doesn't like the idea... I will ask again. Name your price." Apparently, he could hear my Wolf, which made me a little uncomfortable. "Are you speaking of Mr. Kane?" I asked, just ensuring that there wasn't a third Reaver in the mix. Raphael raised an eyebrow. "You know him by his surname which we all share... odd. The Reaver in gold is who I speak of." He replied.

It struck me as strange that he would use a surname, but the others didn't. Maybe it was too difficult to know who was being spoken to if they all shared it. I shook the thoughts away. "There is no price, she is mine." I enunciated every word through gritted teeth. I swear I saw a change in Raphael's eyes, but his face remained still and calm.

He definitely was different from his brother, I thought. He took one elongated claw and sliced his hand open. "Drink." Raphael said, as he held his hand out. I looked at him with confusion in my eyes. In an instant, the room plunged into darkness, and an unholy chill descended, colder than anything I'd ever experienced. It was as if the very essence of cold had seeped into my bones, leaving me shivering.

Shadows began to writhe and twist, seemingly materializing out of thin air, their dark forms slithering across the floor like living serpents. They swirled around Raphael's feet, their tendrils rising like snakes to ensnare his hand, drinking in the blood that he eagerly offered. "What the fu…" I started to say, but shut my mouth when Raphael shot me a glare.

What in the fuck was going on though? At this moment I was not sure I would be making it out of this office again. I didn't let my fear show, I wouldn't. I would rather die a fearless leader than a coward, no matter what the situation entailed.

Once The Shadow tendrils had their fill, they retreated to the floor, writhing around his feet with the others. "These are The Shadows, they will grant any wish, for a price. Name your price for Rayne, Wolf." Raphael growled. I thought about it for a minute. Anything I wanted? I could literally have anything. More power, more wealth, more pack members, more status… but I wouldn't have her.

"If you don't make a deal with them, I will, and my outcome might not benefit you as much as yours would." He said with a smirk. "I can't make a deal for Rayne. I want her as well and I can't just give her up that easily." I said. At the same time I summoned my pack through the mind link, and lunged towards Raphael, hoping I didn't just sign my death certificate.

Wolves came rushing into the pack house surrounding my office. "Shadows restrain him." Raphael commanded. I was violently jerked from my ascent and slammed to the ground, the impact knocking the wind out of me. The Shadows erupted into a frenzy, their dark tendrils wrapping around me like chains, holding me down with an ironclad grip. The more I fought the more Shadows seemed to trap me. I may not have been winning, but I was giving them a run for their money.

"Tsk tsk tsk." Raphael clicked ever so calmly as he walked my way. He waved his hand at the door and covered it in Shadows, effectively holding back the Wolves threatening to enter from the other side.

"You have no choice, Wolf. What is your price?" Raphael spewed. He was definitely getting pissed and I could tell. I was at a loss, the only thing I really ever wanted was my little sister, Reya, back from the dead. Everyone else could stay dead for all I cared.

Everything I have done in all these years since her death... every deal I have made... every life I have taken... it's all been for her. In her honor. "Can The Shadows bring back the dead?" I questioned. "They can, although giving me Rayne alone will not suffice for that want. Their price may be a little more than you expect." He said.

"What is the price?" I asked. "The pricccee is steep... a lifo for a life. You do not get to choossseee the life, or when it isss taken." The Shadows hissed in a multitude of voices. "I get Rayne, and you help deliver her to me. The Shadows will have their fill of my sacrifice for this ask, as well as yours. That will be enough to satiate them." Raphael replied.

I didn't say anything for a moment. I never wanted to give up Rayne, even knowing I would likely never have her. But I could have my sister... "Do you accept the price?" Raphael asked. I could see the tendrils writhing around anxiously at the thought of their sacrifices waiting to happen. They seemed anxious, and excited for the fact. They seemed ready to pounce at his every waking call. "A random death to bring back my sister?" I said. Raphael nodded. *I would lose Rayne but I would have my sister.*

What could go wrong? Samael was in my mind begging me not to agree. The price was too steep. But he knew my past, he knew how many innocents I had killed, what was another?

"I accept your price." I said with a steady voice. Raphael's face lit up, it was the first time I saw him show outward emotion during this interaction, and that scared the fuck out of me. *What have I done?* I thought, as The Shadows split and went all kinds of different ways, seething and writhing out of the room. No doubt they left to collect their bounties.

"I will let you know when the time comes, Wolf." Raphael said as he was leaving. "Do not disappoint me, as The Shadows can take what they have given just as easily." His tone was deadly.

The Shadows were only gone for a few moments when they returned with Reya. She was 13, literally, exactly how I remember her. She was wearing that same black and white polka dot dress down to her knees. It had absolutely no blood stains, and she had black slip-on shoes adorning her feet.

Her eyes were ocean blue just like mine, and her brown hair was cut short, in a bob cut. She hadn't aged a day. I definitely had, but she still recognized me nonetheless. "Drake?!" She exclaimed, as she ran straight into my arms.

"Oh Reya, I've missed you so much!" I said, pulling her tiny figure into my arms. I held onto my little sister, afraid that this was just a dream and if I let go she would truly be gone again.

And for the first time since she was killed, I cried real tears, and I didn't even care who saw me.

Chapter 35

~

(Raphael)

 $\mathcal{I}$ stood there in Alpha Drake's office, Shadows writhing at my feet. Alpha Drake had taken his newly risen little sister into his arms, and I could see the tears glistening from his cheeks. I knew calling The Shadows would work. It's a deal too good to pass up, that is, if they don't ask for the ultimate sacrifice… which they often did. Unfortunately for him, he was not excluded from this.

I, of course, was reluctant. I was not as friendly with The Shadows as Raziel. None of us brothers really were. You had to be willing to give up quite a bit to work with them, and the price usually wasn't worth the prize.

However, The Shadows seemed to be my only option because Alpha Drake wasn't budging. He loved Rayne as well, and I couldn't help but think of how special she had to be to get the attention of all these people. There was something more about her, something we were missing, there had to be. Anytime I was around her she seemed so innocent and eager to learn something new. I felt like I had to protect her. Maybe everyone else did too?

I knew Alpha Drake would eventually cave. Everyone has a weakness, something they want more than anything else, even Rayne. The Shadows asked for a life in return for his sisters. Luckily, they did not ask for a life for my end of the bargain. They did however ask for something else from me.

They wanted a love for a love, the ashes of my chosen mate, for Rayne. She had been dead for many years now, but I kept her ashes in a beautiful silver and black urn upon my mantle. She was Human, and she died Human. She refused to let me change her into any Supernatural being... said she didn't want to live a cursed life.

No matter how much I begged her she wouldn't budge. I contemplated turning her anyway, multiple times over the years. But I would have risked her hating me for it. I couldn't lose her, and as much as it hurt me to see her grow old and wither away, I knew it was what she wanted.

Her name was Roxy. She had a head full of medium length brown curls that couldn't be tamed if she tried. She had beautiful olive skin that tanned easily in the sun, and light brown eyes that seemed to burn into my soul with every glance. She was about 5 foot 9 inches and had the most beautiful curves. I loved her from the day I met her when she was 16, until the day she died at 92, peacefully in my arms.

Her brown hair had turned shades of gray and white. Her curls had slowly straightened. Her curves faded as she aged, and her olive skin slowly lost its luster. But those beautiful brown eyes never lost their fire. Not even when she spoke her last words. "Thank you for giving me such a wonderful life, I will always love you." It was like she knew it was time to go. She stared deep into my eyes, burning a hole into my soul. Then she closed her eyes and exhaled her last breath.

I remember the torment it put me through, and how angry I was at her for not letting me turn her, for not letting me preserve her fragile life. I spent a good part of 20 years or more, hating myself for not just turning her anyway. Having her hate me, but still being here would have been a fate better than what I've endured. I had to cling to the good memories, the good times in order to get myself by.

I recalled the time we first met, she was so damn young. She was walking along the river trail on her way to school. She was alone. I was sitting on a park bench nearby reading, which was something I have always loved to do. I was in the midst of a Necromancer and Cryomancer battle of sorts, and was trying to calm my mind.

She was wearing a levi mini skirt, with some pink tennis shoes and a pink shirt. Her curly hair was a mess, of course, falling only to her shoulders at the time. She was a bit young for my taste, but even so, I couldn't tear my eyes from hers. She walked by and flashed me a million dollar smile. I remember my heart fluttering and thinking *how? She is simply Human, how can she make me involuntarily react like this?* The next thing I knew a Vampire had appeared out from the woods and grabbed her, not realizing I was sitting close by.

He was about to sink his teeth into her neck. She was screaming when I materialized in front of them. I used my fireball to engulf the Vampire and throw him across the trail into an adjacent tree. He got up and ran at the sight of me. I still to this day wonder what he was doing here? This far from home. Vampires never frequented my territories. That was something I never was able to figure out. Her eyes were wide with fear, and at first, I wasn't sure if she was more afraid of me, or the Vampire. "Are you ok?" I asked, looking into her beautiful brown eyes for any trace of fear towards me, but there was none.

"Yes, thanks to you…. what are you?" She asked me. The curiosity in her curious eyes sparkled, just begging for knowledge. I ignored her question. "What is your name?" I asked. "Roxy." She said.

I knew right then and there that she was the one. She was my chosen mate. Period. We had spent literally every single day of the rest of her life together. That was only one of many. The memories we shared would never be replaceable. The years had passed, at least 100 by now. I had lost count, honestly. I hadn't even tried to look for someone new. I hadn't cared. To be honest, I hadn't even looked for her, she found me.

No one ever piqued my interest anyway. No one until Roxy. And even now, no one could live up to her, I had thought, until Rayne. What was giving up the ashes of someone I once loved many, many, years ago, to get a chance with someone new? After all of this time? It was time to move on… it had been a century, after all. I materialized to my home with The Shadows in tow as we approached the mantle. The silver and black urn was sitting right in the middle.

It was adorned with glittering filigree and vines that when the light hit them, sparkled, casting reflections across the room. The sight of the urn had more memories flooding back. I was standing at the mortuary, urn in hand. My face was solemn and void of emotion. I couldn't breathe, let alone speak to anyone. I was surprised I was even able to remain there long enough to hear the assistants last words before I materialized at home in front of the mantle. I had just enough time to set the urn down before I completely and utterly lost it.

I fell to the floor in a crumpled mess. Tears streamed down my face for what seemed like an eternity. Every emotion I had been holding in since she passed just released into the open. My entire life was pointless, worthless without her. The sound of her laugh, the sight of her smile. The memories flashed into my mind as if I were watching them on a television screen.

It was as if every molecule of air was sucked from my lungs. It was all I had to try and suck air in only so I could keep shedding tears like a waterfall. My heart was completely shattered. My every being was torn into a million pieces. I had never been this distraught, never been this overwhelmed. I wasn't even sure how I could ever live on without her. I was nothing without her…

I don't even know how long I laid there on the floor at the mantle, before I fell into a deep, and thankfully, dreamless sleep. After I woke, I swore I would never show outward emotion again. The urn remained on the mantle in the exact spot I left it before my breakdown. I had never touched it once in 100 years.

I tried to justify my actions anyway I could. I had to make it seem like it wasn't such a big task, like it wasn't such a

234

big sacrifice. Whatever I had to do to tell myself that this was ok. Samael was in my mind howling at the thought of losing her ashes. He was not happy with me, but I had to do it, I *had* to do this. It was time to move on...

The Shadows convulsed and oozed towards the urn with a ravenous intensity. But before I could change my mind, they engulfed it... shattering it into 1,000 pieces. Silver and black shards exploded into the air, piercing my chest and scattering across the room like a dark, malevolent rain. I fell to my knees as my heart shattered, once again, the shards piercing my very soul. I clasped my hand over my heart, struggling to draw breath, and fought to stem the tide of tears that threatened to overwhelm me.

The anguish swelled inside, my chest heaving with sobs, as I battled to contain the emotional storm raging within. The Shadows devoured every last ash before they were gone. They abandoned me amidst the carnage, surrounded by the razor sharp remnants of the urn. My body reduced to a crumpled mess in the fetal position on the cold, hard floor.

The shattered fragments seemed to mock me, their jagged edges gleaming in the dim light, as I lay there, lost in a sea of despair, my world reduced to a broken, bloody mess.

I wasn't sure what hurt worse, the urn shards protruding from my chest... or my shattered heart.

Chapter 36

~
(Rayne)

With the lessening of my mark I was feeling a lot more confident in my abilities to resist Raphael, should the time come, and I was sure it would. No way he was giving up that easily. He was very patient, and the man was persistent to a T. I may not know much about him, but if he was anything like his brother… he wouldn't give up so easily. Luckily, I didn't have to dwell on it because Raziel was great at distracting me.

He had gotten us all dressed up in matching attire and told me he had a surprise for me. I was excited but had no idea what to expect. I didn't really know him, after all. The short interactions I had with him growing up were more terrifying than anything else, and left little room for anything more serious..

So, to take a guess what he might be planning wasn't something I even attempted. I figured I would just be along for the ride. We left his house hand in hand, which was new to me as well. Us being openly affectionate was something I had never thought would ever be a thing, until now. This also irritated the hell out of my mark.

We didn't have a title. I wasn't sure what we were, but I knew how I felt, and that was all that mattered to me. I followed him outside and around his property to the backyard. There were multitudes of trails leading every possible way.

We chose a path that was slightly overgrown, its grasses and wildflowers nudging the edges of the trail, as if nature was reclaiming it. The trail was increasingly overgrown, with thick bushes and vines encroaching upon the path. While it was clear that the trail had seen use, the frequency seemed low. The vegetation had begun to reclaim the route, as if nature was slowly erasing the signs of human presence.

I heard my phone go off as we made our way through the trail, but I ignored it. I pushed the sinking feeling from my chest. I had an inkling the message was about Eric. I had been waiting for this, but now was not the time to check it and stress myself out.

We walked for about 10 more minutes through the winding path. As we ventured further, trees began to emerge on either side, their trunks and branches gradually immersing us into a narrow walkway between the trees. Raziel kept looking over at me with anticipation in his golden eyes, making me smile every time he did. As we rounded a bend, a shining golden gate suddenly swung into view, its radiant hue glowing like a beacon in the soft light.

The gate's intricate filigree seemed to dance across its surface, casting a mesmerizing pattern of light and shadow on the ground below. It stretched across the path, a shimmering barrier that seemed to separate the ordinary world from what I assumed to be a realm of magic and wonder.

Raziel stopped us here, then he took a single golden key out of his pants pocket and put it in the lock on the gate. With an audible click the lock opened, and Raziel pushed the gate, motioning for me to go inside. I walked through the gate with him following me. He stopped to shut it and relocked it with the little golden key. He put the key back in his pocket then grabbed my hand, much to the dismay of my mark. Luckily, I had been learning to ignore it. Not that it was easy to do, but it helped the tiniest bit.

"Are you ready?" He purred, letting go of my hand to run his hand through his hair. "Yes." I said with anticipation. "I'm always ready for anything he asks." Wynter smirked. I saw a smile creep up on his face as if he heard her. He then grabbed my hand again and I ignored the searing pain across my face. As he guided me through the winding tunnel, its entrance was veiled by a tapestry of hanging vines and vibrant purple flowers. With a gentle gesture, he parted the vines, revealing a hidden passage. As we emerged from the tunnel, I stepped into a realm unlike anything I had ever seen.

The air was alive with radiant light, and every detail seemed to shimmer with an essence of magic. My eyes widened in awe, drinking in the sheer beauty of my surroundings. The scenery unfolded like a canvas of enchantment, with every element harmonizing in perfect symphony. I felt as though I had entered a dreamworld, where the boundaries of reality blurred and the magic was palpable.

Before me was a vast lake, its shimmering waters stretching far and wide. In the lake's heart, a gentle mound rose, cradling the most magnificent willow tree I had ever laid eyes on. Its branches, robust and graceful, stretched out in every direction, spanning at least 50 feet. The leaves and colorful flowers that adorned these branches danced in the breeze, creating a mesmerizing spectacle.

Some branches swooped down, their tips kissing the water's surface, sending tiny ripples across the lake. The tree's branches also shimmered with a dazzling, glitter-like substance that sparkled and twinkled, as if infused with stardust. But what caught my attention was that this same glittery essence wasn't just limited to the tree, it was also suspended on the lake's surface.

Amidst this shimmering expanse, giant lily pads floated serenely, each one crowned with a majestic tulip. These blooms came in a kaleidoscope of blues, magentas, and purples, their delicate petals unfolding like silken sails in the breeze. Some tulips stood tall, their cups open to the sky, while others remained softly closed, as if hiding the secrets of the world beneath their delicate, soft exterior.

The lake's edges were fringed by vast, seemingly endless forests, their canopies a vibrant tapestry of greens.

Meandering trails and paths, lined with lush shrubbery, crisscrossed the landscape as far as the eye could see. Looking further, I spotted vibrant patches of colored mushrooms dotting the forest floor, clustering around tree bases, and peeking out from within the shrubbery.

Dotting the shrubbery and nestled within the tree branches were charming, tiny cottages. Every inch of ground not covered by the lush, bluish-purple grass was ablaze with a vibrant tapestry of flowers, showcasing a dazzling array of colors and types. Petals of every hue, soft pinks, radiant yellows, delicate lavenders, danced in the breeze.

The entire area was bathed in that same radiant, glittering substance that seemed to infuse every aspect of the landscape with an ethereal shimmer. I stood there, awestruck and entranced, my senses overwhelmed by the sheer beauty of it all. Time itself seemed to stand still as I struggled to take in the majesty of this mystical place. I never wanted to leave this place, whatever it was.

As we ventured deeper, the landscape came alive with tiny, iridescent creatures that darted and flitted about, weaving in and out of the lush bushes and delicate tree branches. Their gentle hum and soft chirping filled the air, creating a soothing melody that harmonized with the rustling leaves and whispering wind. Were those?

"Oh my god!" Wynter shouted. "Pixies?!" I exclaimed, turning to Raziel. His smile was the biggest I had ever seen. By the look on his face, I could tell he was pleased with my reaction. "Yes, darling." He purred. "But, I thought they were extinct? How are they here?" I exclaimed.

I had always heard the stories of Pixies and Pixie Dust. They used to frequent the world, living in trees and shrubbery. Mostly found in forests and hidden grottos. They liked to remain secret, hidden from the world when at all possible.

They were considered extinct after they were being hunted for their Pixie Dust, which was rumored to grant any wish, and could heal even the most terminal ailment. I had always wanted to find them, which is why I was so apt to explore as a child. I thought the more places I could see, the more chances I could see a real Pixie. I never did, but always looked. How did he know?

"This enchanted colony is protected by powerful magic, rendering it inaccessible to all without the key. The gate is hidden by magic, so I am the only one who can find it, or allow another to find it. About 300 years ago, I found a small colony of Pixies on the outskirts of a town that had just been eradicated by a neighboring Wolf pack. I stumbled upon it by accident. The Pixies were all but extinct at this point, and I knew if I had just left them there, that they too, would meet an untimely demise. Compelled by a desire to protect them, I spoke to them in hopes that they would trust me. It took time and coaxing, but they finally agreed to come with me. I had, in the meantime, been preparing this grotto, in hopes that they would agree someday, and make this their new home. I agreed to protect them and let them thrive. They took my once small grotto, and over the past 300 years, turned it into this magical place." He explained.

I took another look around. I couldn't believe that this started 300 years ago with a small group of Pixies. I took his face in my hands, ignored my annoying mark burning, and looked deep into his eyes. "You are a wonderful person, you know that?" I said, as I kissed his lips softly. My mark started on fire at this point, and I didn't even care. He picked me up and I wrapped my legs around his waist, deepening our kiss.

This place was so magical, it was like you could feel the magic radiating off everything. Every bush, every tree, every Pixie. It was as if the land itself was whispering ancient secrets, and the Pixies were the guardians of this mystical realm, their presence infusing every moment with a deep sense of enchantment.

Raziel set me down gently, our hands entwined. He guided me to a serene spot beside the lake, where a beautifully crafted gold bench was nestled among the lush

240

shrubbery. The gentle lapping of the water against the shore created a soothing melody, as if nature itself was serenading us.

The bench, adorned with intricate carvings, seemed to glow with a warm, inviting light, beckoning us to sit. We obliged and he snapped to produce us 2 golden drinks. He handed mine to me, and he put his arm around me. I leaned into him, placing my legs across his. I sipped my drink and just enjoyed my view. This really gave me a perspective into another side of Raziel. Underneath his fiery, but collected composure, he truly cared about others. Preserving a whole species? It's just unheard of. My entire life my mother taught me to be afraid of Reavers. She told me they were ruthless killers. That they were not to be tested or trifled with.

She told me that if a Reaver ever requested something from me, no matter what it was, I was to oblige or lose my life. I grew up terrified of Reavers, especially of Raziel.

Though my interactions with him were brief, it didn't help that I had first handedly witnessed him being ruthless and a murderer. I know all species have their moments, but I couldn't deny that a lot of what I thought about him wasn't actually based on facts. I realized this after seeing this place. How could a ruthless, hardened, killer save an entire species? Why would he if he was everything my mother had said?

"Raziel?" I asked, looking up at him. He pulled back a tiny bit so we could lock eyes. "Yes, darling?" He replied. "Do you think my mother knew? Do you think she knew that we were Reavers… assuming she was too with her eyes and all. I've just been thinking about it a lot lately and how could she not know? Why wouldn't she have told me?"

My questions danced around his highly educated mind and His eyes lit up with a warm, intellectual curiosity, as if the questions themselves were an intriguing puzzle to be solved, and he was eager to unravel their secrets. "I cannot guarantee that she knew if she did not, in fact, know that she was one herself. The eyes should have given it away,

241

but tell me little Wolf, how did you not know either?" He questioned. "Ok, you make a good point, and I… I'm not exactly sure. I guess because I can shift… and the stories my mother used to tell me about Reavers, I never thought about it." He hummed in response before actually answering.

"Unless your father is a Reaver, then it's very possible she had no idea of either of your origins. The other possibility is that she knew, and knew full well, which is why she acted the way she did. Living outside of a pack, and ensuring that you were afraid of our kind. It's possible she never wanted you to know and this was her way to ensure it. Call it a failsafe. Had she lived, you'd be none the wiser until you started coming into your powers." He said. I thought about his answer for a moment, allowing the possibility of it to dance along the edges of my mind. "It makes sense, honestly. I wish I could ask her." I replied.

He seemed lost in thought and I briefly wondered what he was thinking, but refrained from asking. "Your mother… she was… a character." He finally said, caution lacing his careful words. My eyes lit up. "You knew her?" I questioned. I had known that he was watching me after the wishing well incident, but I never knew that he had ever spoken with my mother.

"You could say that, in a sense. Let me explain. Once I had put my claim on you I approached her to speak of it. I knew she wouldn't be happy and would most likely forbid it, which she did, but I thought it best to alert her to my intentions and at least allow her to feel like she was getting her way. Of course, I continued to watch you from afar. The fury emanating from her face when I told her that I had an inkling that you may be my mate… she was a very protective woman." He explained.

I exhaled a breath I didn't realize I was holding as I looked up at him in all of his glory. "I… I had no idea. The way she spoke of how dangerous Reavers were, and especially you after the wishing well… I never in a million years would have guessed that she had ever spoken to you again." I stammered, unsure of what to even say.

"My point was never to scare or anger her. I only ever wanted her to know that you were safe, that I would protect you. She shunned my offer, and refused to acknowledge me the singular other time I approached her. Understandably so. I left her with only one reassurance, and I've kept my promise." His words were filled with reverence.

Each phrase was a tender, mournful whisper, heavy with the weight of memory and respect, as if the sheer act of speaking was a sacred tribute to the past... to her. I rested my hand on his forearm and we locked eyes. "Thank you for sharing this with me." These faint whispers were all I could muster, my voice cracking with emotion as I struggled to hold back the torrent of tears that threatened to overflow from my brimming eyes.

Raziel cupped my cheek in his palm and I closed my eyes, leaning into his soft caress. "I promised her that I would never allow a single thing to ever happen to you. And I refuse to let her down. I will keep this promise until I have taken my last breath." He said, and then he leaned in and pressed his lips to mine.

His kiss was electric, igniting every nerve ending in my body. "Plus, you belong to me." He growled against my lips. I pulled away and raised an eyebrow at him. He smirked in response. "I belong to no one, and you infuriate me!" I snapped, crossing my arms. He chuckled. "There she is, my feisty little Wolf."

I shook my head, but I also smiled at him. I was still getting used to seeing this softer side of the man in gold. We sat together for who knows how long, just chatting and drinking golden drinks. We laughed together and talked about my childhood, and the places he had traveled to.

As we delved deeper into conversation, the boundaries between us began to dissolve, and I found myself revealing parts of myself that I had long kept hidden. Raziel, too, shared his own fears and doubts, and I listened with an open heart, feeling a profound connection to this complex, multifaceted individual. The hours slipped away, unnoticed, as we explored the depths of each other's souls, our words flowing like a gentle stream, carrying us to places of vulnerability, trust, and ultimately, profound understanding. It was a truly transcendent experience, one that left me feeling seen, heard, and deeply connected to another human being, a feeling I hadn't known in years.

Before I knew it the sun was setting, and we were in the perfect spot to watch it go down. I wondered if he had planned it this way. The man never seemed to do a single thing without a reason, but I wasn't complaining. I was perfectly content watching as the sky changed to a kaleidoscope of beautiful colors. Soft oranges, pinks, purples, and, of course, golds, filled the sky before us.

We had just gotten up to leave when I felt the venom wash over me, Alpha Drakes mind link. I shuddered as his voice infiltrated my mind.

"Rayne, you are still part of this pack. I expect to see you at training tomorrow morning." And then he closed the link.

Chapter 37

*P*art of me thought Alpha Drake sounded, sad maybe? I couldn't really place it. This wasn't his usual venom, and I wondered what might be bothering him, but didn't think about it too hard. He was right, I was still part of the pack until I turned 21 at least, and I had an obligation. "You don't have to go if you don't want to." Raziel purred, as he flashed me a perfect, cocky smile.

"You could just stay here with me, forever. In fact, why don't you just move in? I'm sorry, that might be fast, but the offer stands." He smirked. I was flattered. "You know I would love nothing more than to spend every day for the rest of my life with you. But I do have an obligation to my pack. For now, I still have pack duty, and I can't let my pack down." I said as I looked up at him.

Once I turned 21 I would be free of my pack obligations. I would find out who my mate bond had chosen for me, and I would definitely not be Luna of The Obsidian pack. My life was going to change drastically, and I was preparing for it every day. I had put a lot of thought into what I would do if my mate wasn't Raziel.

Honestly, the chances were very slim that it would be. I had been thinking a lot about how I would reject my intended mate, and choose Raziel instead. I had practiced the lines in the mirror, trying to stay strong and hopefully be able to fight the mate bond.

I had dreamt of this day, hoping that it would be a quick and easy process. I had hoped I was able to do it with conviction, and 100 percent certainty that I wasn't making the wrong choice. To say my nerves were shot over it, was an extreme understatement. "The choice is yours, darling. I can pull any strings needed." Raziel said.

I looked up at him and smiled. "I would not doubt that in the least." I replied. "Good. You should, honestly, never doubt me." His words were full of pride and cockiness. I laughed before standing from the bench. "I am beginning to realize this."

We left the grotto, much to my dismay, and headed back to the house. We got inside and into his kitchen when he started grabbing literally everything from the cupboards. Pans clanged, spices wafted, and the sizzle of cooking food filled the air as he worked his culinary magic. Raziel didn't tell me he was a master cook. He was cooking like he was a top chef. You couldn't have convinced me otherwise.

He cooked top sirloin steak with garlic asparagus and mashed potatoes. I took one bite and knew I had to keep him around. It was literally the best thing I had ever eaten... maybe in my entire life. "Well, I definitely have to keep you, this is amazing! Where did you learn to cook so well?" I asked. "When you've been around as long as I have, you learn a thing or two." He said with a wink. He just kept amazing me.

Once we were done eating, Raziel snapped and produced me a gold sports bra and gold shorts to sleep in. I didn't really have anything at his house and hadn't been home in 2 nights, so I appreciated the gesture. I went into the bathroom and took a quick shower.

Then I brushed my teeth, changed, and climbed into Raziel's bed. He took me into his arms burying his face into the side of my neck. He then took a deep breath inhaling my scent. I could feel the peace rolling off him, like he was right where he was supposed to be. I shared the feeling.

His fangs elongated and I felt him brush them against my neck. My body reacted on its own to his advance, my nipples hardening, and arousal making its way in between my legs. He pulled me around so I was facing him and he looked deep into my eyes, tracing my jawline and lower lip with his thumb. As his fingers traced over the remnants of the mark on my skin, it erupted into a fierce blaze, a fiery reminder of where my loyalties should lie, but didn't. Our lips merged in a tender, yet passionate embrace, as he cradled my head in his hand, drawing me closer.

His tongue danced across my lips, seeking entry, and I surrendered, granting him access. Our mouths united, our tongues entwined, and a primal fervor awakened within me.

My mark, again, seethed with a fierce intensity under his touch, as if a spark had ignited a blaze beneath my skin. The burning sensation was almost unbearable, yet I craved more of him. I was consumed by an insatiable hunger for his touch, my body yearning for the next brush of his fingers, the next whisper of his breath.

Raziel's passion intensified as he shifted his weight, positioning himself atop me. With a swift motion, he removed my sports bra, his fingers brushing against my bare skin. His lips descended upon my neck, leaving a trail of tender kisses as he traversed the curve of my shoulder. His mouth continued its gentle exploration, meandering down to my breasts, where his warm breath sent shivers coursing through my veins.

With deliberate slowness, Raziel savored each moment, his lips enveloping my nipples as he tenderly sucked and gently nibbled. His touch was a delicate balance of softness and firmness, leaving me breathless. He continued his sensual journey, pausing to place a reverent kiss on my belly button before his hands grasped my shorts, ripping them away with a primal growl that sent shivers down my spine.

Despite the mark's persistent burning, I focused on Raziel's gentle descent, his lips tracing a path onto my inner thighs. His warm breath caressed my skin, sending shivers up my spine. As he drew closer, his exhalations danced across my sensitive flesh, teasing me with anticipation. I gasped softly, my body betraying my excitement, as his breath whispered against my clit.

"Do you want it?" He whispered, his voice low and husky, each word an intricate spell that sent shivers down my spine. His warm breath danced across my skin, teasing me with promise, as he spoke directly to my deepest, darkest, desires.

"I want to hear you say it. You know the drill, darling." He purred, his voice low and sultry. "I want it." I breathed, my voice barely audible, as a soft moan escaped my lips. "Please." I whispered, my eyes locked on his. I bit my lip, the gesture a subtle invitation, as I surrendered to his every whim. Something about the way he spoke to me was like a gentle command, his words weaving a spell of submission around me.

I saw the passion and lust flash through his gaze like a lightning strike, illuminating the dark depths of his irises and leaving me breathless. With a gentle yet firm grasp, he held my hips in place as he buried his face between my thighs. His warm breath danced across my skin, again, sending shivers up my spine.

I arched my back, surrendering to the pleasure, and let out a soft moan. The sound seemed to fuel his passion, driving him to explore every inch of me as if he would never be able to taste me again.

His tongue traced a path of fire, leaving no corner uncharted, and I was lost in the sheer ecstasy of his touch. I tangled my fingers into his golden blonde hair, anchoring himself to the bed. Every movement of his tongue had my body writhing with pleasure.

I was dancing on the edge of ecstasy, my pleasure almost to the tipping point, when he paused and gazed deeply into my eyes. The sudden stillness was electrifying, as if time itself had halted, leaving only the two of us, suspended in a moment of raw connection. "Don't come until I tell you to." With that subtle command he resumed, sending me tumbling toward the peak of pleasure. The problem was, I was already so close.

I was already dangerously close to the edge, my moans growing louder and more insistent. As I struggled to maintain some semblance of control, I found myself torn between the desire to obey and the overwhelming urge to surrender in defiance of his command. Just when I thought I wasn't going to be able to stop it he allowed me the permission I so desperately seeked. Within seconds I was at my climax. My orgasm tore through me like a fucking tornado, destroying any semblance of peace I may have had. Raziel put his fingers on my clit continuing the stimulation, and with elongated fangs he bit right into my inner thigh.

My mark erupted beneath my skin, unleashing a mixture of pleasure and pain that ravaged my body. As his bite amplified the sensations, I was utterly consumed, my cries echoing through the air as I surrendered to the intensity of the moment.

My screams of pleasure echoed through the room. He allowed me to ride the entire orgasm out before he stopped drinking from me. Then he quickly healed my thigh, and buried his face back between my legs. I gasped, my breath catching in my throat as the sensation surged to a nearly unbearable intensity.

He remained between my legs for a few more seconds before he finally stopped, and I could see his stubble glistening with my fluids. As my tremors subsided, he returned to eye level and smashed his lips into mine. The delicate blend of our flavors, my own essence mingling with his, was utterly intoxicating. Time stood still as we surrendered to the pure, unadulterated bliss that consumed us.

He pulled back, his gaze piercing mine with an intensity that made my heart skip a beat. "Good girl." He whispered, his voice dripping with satisfaction, as he wrapped a strand of my hair around his fingers. A devilish grin spread across his face as he began to toy with my locks, his eyes never leaving mine.

He looked at me with a look of absolute enchantment. As if I were the most beautiful thing in this universe. Like he had never seen anything as interesting or intoxicating in his entire life. Then he enveloped me in a tender embrace, pulling me close to his chest. "Rayne?" He whispered in my ear. "Yes?" I replied. "I want you to know that whatever happens when you turn 21, whoever you end up mated to… I'll kill him, but then I'm going to be here for you." His whisper turned to a growl.

My jaw dropped. "Raziel!" I cried, attempting to pull myself from his ironclad grip. He didn't allow it, which figures. "I'm kidding, darling." He chuckled, kissing my cheek softly. "Are you though?" My accusation caused him to feign offense, but then he shrugged. "I knew it! You ARE going to kill him!" I said. His playful features hardened as we met eyes.

"My actions will depend solely upon his actions. Should he attempt to touch what is mine… my hands will be tied." He replied. I rolled my eyes, knowing that he was completely serious. "You know how the bond works, you know how strong it is. Please, do not do something stupid. We can deal with it, just… in a more… humane way." I replied.

"Fine, but know that if he so much as looks at you wrong there will be hell to pay." His words were full of truths that I didn't want to believe. He leaned in close, our lips almost touching. "I will kill anyone who tries to get between us, and I mean that in the worst possible way."

Then he captured my lips with his before I could reply. His intensity blew me away, as he pulled my lower lip into his mouth. He bit down hard enough to cause me to moan out before he released me and pulled back. My mark was burning out of control and I shook my head, realizing, for the first time, just how honestly conflicted he made me feel. And with this conversation, I realized how much my birthday looming was truly affecting him.

"You are awful. Completely and utterly fucking awful… but I want you to know that I choose you. No matter who my mate is. I choose you, Raziel." I spoke playfully at first, ending in a hushed whisper, my voice barely audible.

"Yes, yes you will. You've no choice if I'm being honest. But it's nice to hear you finally admit it, darling." He purred playfully. I scoffed and shook my head at his antics. He gazed down at me with a radiant smile, one that I knew was reserved only for me, and wrapped his large arms around me again. He pulled me down so my head was on his chest. My mark seared out of control, as if chastising me, but I ignored it.

I felt his heartbeat sync with mine, our connection strong and unbreakable, as we drifted off to sleep tangled in each other's embrace.

Chapter 38

My eyes fluttered open to my alarm going off at 6am, time to get ready for pack training. I turned to face Raziel and just took a minute to admire his beauty. He looked so peaceful just lying there with his golden blonde hair a mess and not a worry in the world. His chest was rising and falling slowly as he slept.

I got up carefully and planned to head to my house to get ready when I realized that Raziel had already laid out a set of clothes for me to wear to training. A black sports bra, gold shorts and gold combat boots. He knew exactly what my style was, and I couldn't help but feel butterflies at the fact that he paid so much attention to what I wore.

I threw on the clothes and threw my hair into a messy ass bun. On my way out I grabbed a stick of beef jerky and some cheese. I didn't eat much in the morning, I found myself rarely hungry. It was a little further to the training grounds from here than from my house. I didn't mind though. That's when I remembered that my phone had gone off yesterday and I hadn't looked at it still. I snatched it from my side pocket and unlocked the screen.

I tried to hide the oh shit look on my face when I realized I actually had 3 messages that I hadn't looked at. 2 were from Jae and 1 was from Brett. I knew they were Eric related. My stomach didn't sink as badly as before. I clicked open Jae's message first.

'Rayne, I hope you are ok! I'm really worried about you since everything happened with Eric. Let's meet up and get lunch or something, ok?'

I didn't reply, and instead clicked open the second message from her.

'It was him… Rayne. It was Eric at the bottom of the ravine. The coroner has identified his remains and dental records proved it. Plus, they were able to retrieve his car. I'm so sorry! I don't even know what to say, I really thought that maybe it wasn't him… I'm sorry it was.'

I replied to her so she didn't think I was completely ignoring her.

'Thank you for letting me know. I had a really bad feeling that it was him. I am happy they found him though, I think we all need closure. And I am down to meet up for lunch soon, I've just been working a lot lately trying to distract myself so give me a little time, ok?'

I hit send and knew she would understand my need for time. Then I clicked open Bretts text.

'You are not in the clear just yet. There is a candlelight vigil on Friday night, and then we are burying Eric on saturday. Plan to be at both, I'll pick you up.'

I knew exactly how it would look if I wasn't there at either event. I was forced into this, but at least after these events were over I wouldn't be obligated to attend another Human function if I didn't want to. I could handle 2 more, no matter how sad and guilty they made me feel. I hit reply.

'Ok, let me know the times when you know and I'll be ready.'

I closed my phone and shoved it back into my pocket, opting to jog the rest of the way there. I was trying to get my heart rate pumping, but mostly I was trying to distract myself from my Human problems. Fucking Humans…

I arrived at the training grounds just in time to see Roman. "Hey Rayne." He said and his face lit up when he saw me. "Hey Roman!" I replied. I could tell he was staring at my mark. And by the slight burning sensation, my mark didn't like it one bit. I just ignored it, knowing he couldn't help it. No one could, the mark was just so powerful.

We all lined up for training and my mark was burning a little more persistently with everyone's gaze upon it. I just

kept a straight face and ignored them all. Alpha Drake
came out and paired everyone off like usual, but he paired
himself with me. I rolled my eyes, of course he would. "He
needs to back the hell off." Wynter huffed. "I know. No is no,
ugh." I scoffed. My Alpha was glaring at me intently as if I
had wronged him in some way. I raised an eyebrow, but
ignored his weird, uncomfortable stare.

I was just about to lunge and start training when Alpha
Drake grabbed my hand and yanked me to him. "Come
with me." He whispered. My mark started burning out of
control at his gesture. It never liked being touched by Alpha
Drake, and I didn't either.

I reluctantly followed, not like I had a choice in the
matter. He led me out of the stadium where we trained, and
into a smaller arena we used for meetings and things. He
stopped when we got to the middle of the arena and turned
to face me. He kept his grip on my hand, completely
ignoring my attempts to pull my hand free from his. We
locked eyes and I could see a plethora of emotion
swimming across his face. Worry, fear, guilt, and regret.

What could have him so upset? I wondered. He finally
let go of my hand and put both of his hands on my
shoulders. "Rayne, I need you to know that I am so sorry. I
had no choice. I was forced into it." I could physically hear
the sadness lacing each and every word. I could tell he was
being sincere, not one ounce of venom in his voice.

"What are you talking about, Alpha?" I asked, as an
uneasy feeling started to form in my stomach. "You'll know
soon, but just know I was forced into it. I literally had no
other choice... Reya, dear, come here, would you?" He
almost whispered that last part, with a little sparkle in his
eye.

A young girl, maybe 13 or 14, came running into the
stadium. She had the same olive skin and ocean blue eyes
as Alpha Drake. Her short brown hair was in a bob cut and
perfectly curled under towards her neck. She was wearing
a red dress with no sleeves and some black sandals. She
ran right up to Alpha Drake, and he pulled her into a bear

254

hug. Then he looked up at me with tears in his eyes. This, coming from a man who, in the 8 years I had lived in this pack, never showed emotion, hardly even a smile. I instantly began to panic and took a step back. "Rayne, this is Reya... my little sister." He said. Shock flooded my face. "Oh my God." Wynter shrieked.

"His little sister that was murdered in front of him? The same little sister that he murdered multiple entire packs over, including what used to be this one? The same little sister that he killed a multitude of innocents to avenge her death?? That little sister??" Wynter shouted. Cold chills racked my entire body as I fought to make sense of what Alpha Drake had just said.

The pieces of the puzzle started to come together in my head. I realized what kind of price he would have had to pay to get her back from the dead. But he couldn't access The Shadows. Someone accessed them for him... but why would he be sorry to me? What did any of this have to do with me?

I was torn from my thoughts when Alpha Drake closed the gap between us, took my face in his hands causing an unwanted reaction from my mark, and looked straight into my eyes. "I truly am sorry Rayne, but I want you to know I wouldn't have done it if I had any other choice. I'm so sorry." He said, and then he tried to kiss me, but I didn't allow it.

I pulled away from his advance and took a couple of steps back. I could feel the sincerity and regret in his words, he really meant what he was saying. "What did you do, Alpha??" I stammered, taking another couple steps back.

"I'm so sorry." He said. I could see sadness and regret filling his face, and I swear I saw another actual tear fall down his cheek. That's when I felt it, my mark erupted with a fiery intensity, unleashing a torrent of lightning that coursed through my veins. A wave of unbridled ecstasy swept over me, sending my body into rapturous convulsions, as pleasure pulsed through every fiber of my being. Raphael was here. "Son of a bitch." Wynter howled.

She knew resisting the mark was going to be hard, and at that moment I understood what Alpha Drake was talking about. My Alpha gave me one last glance. "Please forgive me." He mouthed, and then grabbed Reya and left the stadium. Of fucking course he fucking did. "Ugh, I'm going to fucking kill him!" I said to Wynter.

"Come here, beautiful." Raphael's pearly voice sent chills down my spine. I turned to face him. He was wearing all black with silver shoes, and a silver suit vest. His hair was neat and perfect, as usual, with a little stubble on his chin. His facial features were calm and collected. They were void of outward emotion, like always, but he had absolute hellfire burning in his silver eyes.

He really was fucking gorgeous, but I thought that about him before I was marked… I couldn't help but admire him. As if on command, my legs started walking towards him and I was helpless to stop it. I walked right into his arms, and the second we touched, my mark ignited, and a kaleidoscope of pleasure coursed through my veins. My mind was cloudy besides the calm of his presence washing over me.

Soon, I was focused on nothing else but the mark and Raphael, the complete source of my ecstasy. Inside, I knew I wasn't supposed to be there, but my body would not react. As much as I fought it, I couldn't move a muscle. "I've missed you, beautiful." He said, sending another pleasure filled chill down my spine.

He then pulled a beautiful silver bracelet from his suit jacket and placed it on my wrist. As soon as he clasped it, a pink orb surrounded my wrist and absorbed into the bracelet. Magic, I assumed? It sparkled and glittered on my wrist, acting as if it belonged there.

"I've missed you too." I said, involuntarily. *Why can't I fight it? What is happening?* It was like I was watching myself from the sidelines. I already knew I was there, and I wasn't supposed to be. And now, my body was doing whatever Raphael wanted, and I was completely helpless to stop it. Panic crept up my neck, settling just at my nape.

"You are so beautiful." He whispered in my ear, amplifying the torrent of sensations surging through my veins. As he drew me nearer, our lips merged in a tender, yet electrifying kiss. It was as if the universe itself ignited, unleashing a bolt of lightning that intensified our connection, forging an unbreakable bond between us.

I could feel the connection between us solidifying, and I wanted to pull away, but I couldn't. I was screaming inside to fight and break away like I did before, but my cries for help fell on deaf ears. Instead, it was like the more I tried to resist him, the more my body didn't. I wrapped my hand around the nape of his neck, pulling him closer as our lips devoured each other. The kiss intensified, unleashing a torrent of lightning that crackled with explosive energy.

Our tongues danced, entwined in a sensual exploration, as if seeking to satiate a hunger that only grew more ravenous with each passing moment. Raphael reluctantly pulled away, while tracing what was left of his mark on my skin. His eyes were still full of fire.

"Fuck, I'll never get enough of you." He murmured before we materialized in front of a breathtakingly beautiful blue lagoon. It shimmered like a sapphire gem, its crystal clear waters inviting and serene. Vines and colored flowers adorned the spaces between the trees, hanging down as if they were a canopy.

The water in the lagoon was the same beautiful turquoise from the river, and wishing well, from my childhood. A majestic and very old looking willow tree sat right on the edge of the water. Its branches reached towards the sky like nature's own cathedral. Some branches protruded far enough out and were long enough to almost touch the water, creating a secluded cove that beckoned visitors to enter. Within this mystical haven, time seemed to stand still.

A little further back there was a cottage inlay within a bed of silver rose bushes. The cottage blended seamlessly into the forest surroundings. The cottage's dark exterior allowed it to sink into the shadows.

Silver accents, a glinting chimney, a shimmering door handle, and a delicate filigree of metalwork around the windows hinted at the magic within. A winding path, barely visible through the underbrush, led to the cottage door, which was adorned with a silver knocker in the shape of a large infinity symbol standing diagonal.

The door itself seemed to blend seamlessly into the wall, as if it might disappear altogether if you didn't look closely. Smoke drifted lazily from the chimney, carrying the scent of burning wood and something sweeter… vanilla, perhaps, or honey. The sound of soft music, like the gentle plucking of a harp, seemed to emanate from within, adding to the enchantment.

As we made our way inside I realized that even the interior of the cottage was a beautiful blend of cozy warmth and elegance. Everything I saw was shades of black and silvers. Soft, golden light spilled from candles and lanterns, casting a warm glow on the plush furnishings, illuminating their rich textures. The air was thick with the scent of old books that I'm sure all had silver spines.

Plush armchairs and velvet cushions in deep, silver and blacks invited relaxation, while the walls, lined with towering bookshelves, seemed to hold the secrets of the ages. Tomes bound in leather with silver spines sat on the shelves.

Some of the books were adorned with strange symbols and glowing runes, all of which weren't present in Raphael's home. I wondered if this was where he kept the secret books that he wanted no one to find, and suddenly I had the urge to pluck each one from the shelf and read it in its entirety.

Upon reaching the upstairs foyer, we found ourselves enveloped in a library of sorts, with floor to ceiling shelves encircling us. The shelves were adorned with an impressive collection of books, their black and silver spines seeming to shimmer in the dim light.

What struck me as strange, however, was the absence of the glowing symbols that had been so prominent on the books we'd seen earlier, leaving me wondering exactly how significant they truly are. Upstairs, two bedrooms awaited, each with its own unique charm.

The guest bedroom, in particular, caught my attention. A black and silver bed, covered in a plush black feather duvet, stood as the centerpiece. A black dresser with subtle silver accents across from the bed added a touch of sophistication. I was surprised by the room's lack of silver embellishments, a definite change from the cottage's typical whimsy.

Raphael led me into the other room which was more of a master suite. The room's centerpiece was a stunning 4-poster bed. Its silver and black posts were adorned with intricate carvings of mystical symbols, matching those I saw glowing on the books downstairs. The bed's canopy was a deep, rich black, embroidered with silver thread that shimmered like the moon.

Off to one side there was a mini bar that reminded me of the night sky itself with as deep of black as the marble top looked. It was fully stocked with an array of premium spirits, wines, and champagnes. Looking to the other side, there was a walk-in closet full of black velvet, lace, and silver silks hanging alongside silver-embroidered jackets, trousers, and dresses.

None of this was my style, but it did create a dazzling array of elegance. Delicate, beaded evening gowns sparkled like the night sky, while sleek, high-collared coats, much too expensive for my taste, shimmered in the low lighting.

Shelves and drawers were filled with an assortment of accessories. Silver-buckled belts, black feathers, and gemstone-encrusted brooches that seemed to be from all different eras. A selection of black and silver hats adorned the shelves, from fedoras to top hats. It looked as if he had a hat from every age, maybe even from every year. It seemed he liked to collect old relics like these.

259

Nestled between two bookcases, sat a snug reading nook, surrounded by black and silver books that shone with an ethereal glow. The symbols on their spines matched those downstairs, fueling my curiosity. I promised Wynter I would ask about those soon.

Nearby, a closed bathroom door concealed its interior, but I imagined a space that matched the color scheme of the cottage, and assumed there would be some sort of reference to the night sky here as well. This cottage was a bit differently themed than Raphael's home, but it was charming and beautiful.

"This is where we will be staying for a while, beautiful." Raphael stated. "This place is amazing." I exclaimed. *Wait, why are we here? What is this place and why can't I speak up? I shouldn't fucking be here...*

I tried so hard to fight back, to say no, to walk away... but my body just wouldn't budge. My thoughts were screaming for me to run... and run fucking far.

Raphael closed the bedroom door and started walking back towards me. Panic flooded into my chest as I realized that I was trapped in my mind, and my body was completely under Raphael's control.

Chapter 39

~

(Alpha Drake)

"I'm so sorry." I said, and tried to press my lips to Raynes. She, of course, pushed me away, like I figured she would. I wanted her to feel my regret though, and I hoped I had gotten the message through. Even if it hurts me to do it. "What did you do, Alpha?!" Rayne said, with fear in her voice. Guilt flooded into my chest when I saw the look in her beautiful silver eyes. "I'm so sorry." I stammered as a stray tear fell down my cheek.

I couldn't believe I had been forced to agree to this. I just wanted to yell for Rayne to run... but I knew I couldn't. If I did, The Shadows could take Reya. After everything I was forced into that ended up giving me her back, I couldn't risk it. I honestly never thought I would be willing to give Rayne up, but I also never knew about The Shadows... and I certainly never thought they could bring someone back from the dead.

No wonder Reavers are so powerful, they literally have every supernatural power at their disposal. It's just insane, there had to be a way to stop them... I was snapped from my thoughts when Raphael materialized behind Rayne. I could tell that she knew he was there just by her reaction, which I'm sure was courtesy of the wretched mark adorning her beautiful face.

I hadn't noticed the first time, but as soon as Raphael was within a few feet of her, that mark started glittering. It was actually really goddamn beautiful. It was positioned perfectly on the side of her face, and as much as I hated it,

261

because I wanted her for myself, that mark really did suit her.

I locked eyes with Rayne. "Please forgive me." I mouthed silently, as I grabbed Reya and we left the arena. I took one look back as Rayne walked right into Raphael's arms. A sharp stab of guilt pierced my heart, coursing through my veins like a river of regret, as my eyes landed on the scene, but I knew I couldn't do anything about it. I had chosen my path, and there was no going back now.

I had just ruined any chance I ever could have had of being with her, or making her Luna of The Obsidian pack, and I knew it. Overwhelming guilt and regret flooded my soul, their dark waters threatening to drown me in a sea of sorrow and remorse.

I looked down at Reya just to remember what sacrifices I had made to get her back. This had to be worth it. It *had* to be. I had to tell myself this otherwise I would never forgive myself. I still may never forgive myself...

That's when it hit me, they said a life for a life and I didn't get to choose. The Shadows hadn't chosen what life yet, I was sure of it. I suddenly got nervous, wondering who they might take and when. It was as if my thoughts had awakened The Shadows from their slumber, and they responded with an unnerving swiftness. An unholy cold descended upon us, seeping into our pores. Reya and I shivered in unison, our hearts racing with a primal fear that seemed to emanate from the very essence of The Shadows themselves.

"Reya, get to the pack house right now, find Beta Sean and tell him I said to watch you until I return." I shot at my little sister. "No, I'm not leaving you alone." Reya snapped. "Go, now!" I yelled, making her flinch. I felt bad, I didn't mean to scare her, but I didn't want her anywhere near The Shadows, not again.

I mind linked Beta Sean. "Reya is on her way to the pack house, watch her until I return." I spat to my Beta. "Yes sir." He said, and then I closed the mind link. "GO!" I shouted, and she ran off towards the pack house reluctantly, leaving me ensnared in a dark tangle of writhing Shadows and icy cold. These dark entities encircled my feet and torso, their icy chill seeping straight into my bones. The Shadows whispered in a cacophony of voices, each one distinct and unsettling, their tones ranging from menacing growls to mournful sighs.

"A life for a life, a price you must pay." They slithered. Their words gave me chills. It seemed like more of them kept appearing as the seconds went by and I had a terrible feeling something extremely bad was about to happen.

"Who have you chosen to take?" I asked them reluctantly. I honestly didn't even want to know, but The Shadows dissipated, and within minutes returned with a woman. She had her back to me, but I would recognize those blonde space buns anywhere.

My heart plummeted, sinking like a stone in my chest, as my mate bond erupted into a frenzy of anguish. Its primal wail echoed through every fiber of my being, desperately crying out for her. The intensity of the bond's distress mirrored the depth of my own despair. Samael was howling, begging me to somehow spare her life as if I could possibly change a single thing. Angel was in my old pack, this was before they were slaughtered and absorbed into The Obsidian pack. When I turned 21, I found out that Angel was my intended mate.

Her medium length blonde hair was a wild tangle of curls that perfectly complemented her porcelain skin and striking baby blue eyes. She was a petite powerhouse, standing at just 5 foot 4 inches, but her small stature only added to her allure.

I, on the other hand, was significantly taller, but I'd always been drawn to petite women. She was the epitome of elegance and grace. The bitter truth was that she had already given her heart to someone else. Though the mate bond urged me to claim her, she rejected me. I struggled to come to terms with her decision, replaying our interactions in my head, but I couldn't bring myself to accept her rejection. Instead, I tried every conceivable way to win her heart, hoping to prove my worth.

Sadly, all that I did just wasn't good enough. Her heart belonged to another, and she refused to budge. Eventually, she made the difficult choice to leave our pack and start anew with the man she loved. I allowed it, opting to cater to her happiness over anything else. But I was left to nurse my broken heart, a constant reminder of the pain that came with loving someone who would never be mine.

My longing for my mate never really went away and I know hers hadn't either. Late at night when I was alone, my heart would reach out for hers. I knew she felt it too, because there were times when hers reached out for mine, and I could feel it. It was in those moments that I contemplated just running to her and scooping her up in my arms. But I had to fight the urge to save her chosen happiness.

I knew I would have to accept her rejection when I took Rayne as my Luna, and I was fully prepared for it if the time came. But nothing could have prepared me for the gut wrenching reality in which I found myself stuck in. It caught me off guard, leaving me reeling and exposed. I was not fucking prepared for this level of pain and heartache.

"No!" I yelled to The Shadows. "Anyone but her. Please..." I begged. "You do not get to choose." The Shadows whispered.

"Drake?" Angel said, fear engulfing her voice. "What is going on? What are these creatures?!" She stammered, her voice trembling as tears welled up in her eyes. I felt the knot in my stomach constrict, as a sense of dread and helplessness washed over me. Frozen in time, I knew the reality was stark and brutal. I was about to witness the love of my life being taken from this world, and I was powerless to stop it.

"Angel, my dear, I'm so sorry. This is all my fault, please forgive me." I stammered. She made a frantic dash towards me, her face contorted in fear. I was able to predict her actions because I knew I was her safe space at this

264

moment. Samael was unhinged, his growl thundering through my mind as he begged me to intercept her. But my body was rigid with dread. I knew the tragedy that was about to occur.

The moment her foot lifted, The Shadows pounced, their dark tendrils snapping around her small figure like a vice. They writhed and seethed around her, their malevolent presence suffocating. I felt an explosive pain in my chest, as if my heart was being ripped from my ribcage. My hands flew to my sternum, clawing desperately at my chest as if that needless action would calm the immense agony that flowed through me.

Her blood curdling screams of terror and agony echoed through the air. I was paralyzed, unable to tear my gaze away from the gruesome scene unfolding before me. Tears streamed down my face for the third time that day, as The Shadows mercilessly sliced into her fragile body, draining her of every last drop of blood.

The brutality was unlike anything I had ever witnessed and I knew the trauma of that moment would stay with me like a constant, nagging, reminder of the darkness that I was forced to endure.

After satiating their dark appetite, The Shadows carefully placed her lifeless form on the ground, as if they were suddenly concerned for her well being. With her lifeless form laid to rest, The Shadows dissolved into the nothingness, dissipating the icy grip that had held me captive.

Bile began to rise in my throat, but I forced it down, refusing to allow The Shadows yet another win. As the frozen grip on my heart began to thaw, it left behind complete and utter devastation. Time seemed to stand still as I struggled to process the finality of what had just occurred.

The world around me faded into a blur, leaving only the stark, haunting reality of her lifeless form etched into my consciousness. I longed to rush to her side, but I knew nothing I could do would comfort her, she was already almost gone. As she drew her final breath, I felt as if my very soul was being torn from my body. The mate bond that had once connected us so deeply now shattered into a million pieces. It was as if the bond had been a physical entity, and I could feel it being violently torn from my body leaving a searing, oozing, wound. And at the same time, my heart was ripped from my chest, shattering into a thousand pieces that left me breathless.

The pain was so immense it brought me to my knees. I was trapped in a living nightmare, my head pounding in tandem with my racing heart. My chest was burning with a fire that seemed to scorch my very soul.

It was as if every fiber of my existence was being mercilessly shredded, leaving me a broken, quivering mess. In that moment, I knew I had entered a realm of suffering so debilitating, it would forever alter the fabric of my being. On top of that, Samael's anguish echoed mine, if not exceeded it. I was forced to bear the weight of his sorrow, which felt like a crushing burden that threatened to consume us both.

I had to summon every last ounce of strength I possessed to crawl to her side. As I gathered her delicate body in my arms, I gently moved a stray strand of hair from her face. Even in death she looked so still and serene. The contrast between her beauty and the brutality of her fate was a cruel mockery. Tears continued to stream down my face as I held her close, mourning the loss of my beloved mate.

"I'm so fucking sorry. Fuck... Angel, God, please forgive me. God dammit!" I growled. The pain of losing my mate was a living hell, a torment that defied words. I kissed her forehead softly, uncaring that her blood stained my lips, nor that what little was left of her life force now drenched my suit. My eyes closed as I fought to breathe.

Each breath felt like razor blades, slicing through my chest and abdomen. In the silence, I mourned alone, my tears spent and my soul exhausted. I refused to let anyone see me like this, broken and defeated. My grief was a solitary prison, one I would forever tackle alone.

Finally, I set Angel's body down in the arena, and I used my mind link to call Beta Sean. "Leave Reya with our Omega and meet me in the arena." I said, then shut the mind link down.

I was unable to utter another word, my voice lost in the abyss of grief. I needed another moment to collect myself, to rebuild my shattered facade. I consciously pushed Samael's presence out of my mind. I knew he was struggling possibly more than I was, but he was affecting my composure, and I needed to get my shit together.

I never fathomed that losing my mate would cut so fucking deep. I am the Alpha of the biggest, most ruthless pack in the world. Showing weakness or losing my composure was a luxury I couldn't afford. Ever. I had already lost it 3 times today, and that was my limit. I didn't have any more room for weakness, it's been expended. It was time to get my head back on, and be the Alpha that my pack needed. The Alpha that my pack deserved. I didn't get here because I lost my shit at every negative event that's happened to me, and I wasn't about to start now.

Just then Sean entered the arena and headed my way. I took a deep breath and put on a straight face, no emotion showing, like usual. Sean, however, was the only one in our pack who knew what Angel was to me. I gauged the emotion in his eyes as he took in the scene. It was clear that he recognized her immediately.

After a moment he assessed me, looking for any hint of emotion. I showed none. "The Shadows?" Sean asked. "Yes. Had I known the price wouldn't just be some random innocent, I never would have made the deal." I replied. I knew that sounded harsh, as if a random innocent's life was less valuable. But in this moment, it was, it truly was. I'd have rather watched 100 innocents meet the same fate than the reality I had to endure.

Sean looked at me with a sense of understanding. That was one thing I loved about my Beta, his unfaltering knack to listen without question, and do as I asked, regardless. I had never once regretted choosing him as my Beta.

"Clean this up, return her body to her lover. Make up a story, a Vampire attack, I don't care. Let them give her a proper funeral." I said. Sean nodded and went to work. I didn't look back as I left the arena, afraid that doing so would tear down my carefully placed facade, yet again.

I returned to the pack house, checked on Reya, and apologized to her for my brash behavior. I held her tightly, and though I didn't say it out loud, just having her here, physically in my arms, reiterated the fact that she was worth every life lost, even that of my mate.

Then, after I talked myself into believing my own words, which was a feat in and of itself, I headed for the bar. After the fucking day I had, I was going to need something strong.

Chapter 40

~
(Roman)

I hadn't needed to be on Rayne duty for quite some time as she was spending most of her time with Raziel. This was much to my dismay, of course. So, when I saw her this morning I was super excited! Maybe a little more excited than I should have been, but I couldn't help it.

She was wearing gold and black in her normal getup. A black sports bra, that I swear accentuated her upper body perfectly, (I could be biased though) and gold shorts that hugged her every curve. Plus, the gold combat boots, which she never zipped all the way up.

These seemed to be her chosen colors now, and to be honest she was beautiful in anything she wore. I hated that stupid fucking mark on her face though. It reminded me of her infatuation with Raphael. I know it's forced infatuation, from the rumors I've heard, but I was still jealous as hell.

I'll be damned if the mark didn't make her that much more appealing though. It was perfectly positioned and the perfect size adorning her gorgeous face. Even partially faded, the remnants glittered in the sun and caught my eyes every single time she moved. It was the perfect accent. I couldn't help but be infatuated, and as much as I tried to hide it…

I knew she noticed. It was like she was magnetic. My eyes were just taking in every bit of her beauty. Looking at every curve, every smile… and as much as I tried to look away, I couldn't. Luckily, she was great at ignoring my stupid obsessive stares. I appreciated that. At least I wasn't physically trying something, I was just paying extra attention to her. So, this morning when Alpha Drake took her to the arena, away from training, I was a little worried. Given his feelings for her and his unwanted advances I had personally witnessed multiple times, I felt it was my duty to protect her.

There was a straggler who was late to training so I quickly paired him up with my partner and headed towards the arena. There had been hushed talk that Alpha Drake made some sort of deal to bring his little sister back from the dead. Rumors had been flying and while I wanted to ignore it, I had an inkling that if anyone would achieve a feat this large, it would be him.

I was intrigued, of course, but still, it was nerve wracking to think about it. No one fucks with the dead unless you go through a Necromancer. But we haven't seen or heard of one of those in decades. I was sure they still existed, but few and far inbetween if so. I knew something had happened though, because I had seen her, Reya, around the pack house. But what did he do to get her back? The price had to be extremely high to raise the dead and I was worried about just what he gave up. I had a feeling it had to do with Rayne, but I couldn't be sure. I also wasn't about to alert Raziel if it was nothing, so I decided I had to find out first.

I walked up to the arena entrance and stood just inside the door off to the side, out of their sight. I could see Alpha Drake. He had a hold of Rayne's hand dragging her to the middle of the arena. It looked like it was against her will, really. But everything he did was against her will. I noticed they stopped but then they were talking. I couldn't really make out everything they were saying, but it didn't seem like a fight.

Then Alpha Drake called out a small girl that I realized was his long since dead little sister, and introduced her to Rayne. I had carefully gotten closer to them by now and I could see the shock fill Rayne's beautiful face and I imagined it looked just like mine in that moment. I continued to watch her as fear clouded her features, which made my body tense up. Then he grabbed her shoulders, and it looked like he was sad, or maybe extremely upset? It sounded like he was apologizing to her. But for what?

What would he have to apologize to her for? Unless it was for his behavior. But he wouldn't apologize for that. Hell, he wouldn't apologize for anything. He must have done something pretty bad if he was apologizing. In fact, was that a tear he just shed? I couldn't even believe what I was seeing.

This was the strangest situation I had ever been witness to. Alpha Drake was not a force to fuck with. He literally was the baddest and most ruthless Alpha in the entire world. He had no reason to fear anything, or even care. He would kill you for disobeying and not even blink an eye. He even tried to kill Rayne once... or so I heard.

What could he have done that is worse than what he's already done to her so many times before? What could be so bad that it would warrant an actual apology? Then it hit me, and my heart absolutely sank when I saw Raphael materialize behind Rayne. I fucking knew it had something to do with her! *God damnit!*

I stood there paralyzed. I couldn't match up against a Reaver. I wouldn't even attempt that. I'm not stupid. There was literally nothing I could do. I watched as Alpha Drake grabbed Reya and left the arena. Then as soon as Raphael told Rayne to come here, she turned and walked straight into his open arms.

I knew it was the mark, and I knew she didn't want to be there. I mind linked Raziel right away and he appeared just as Raphael disappeared with Rayne. "Where is she?!" He roared, and I wondered if this was about to be the end of my life. I was feeling guilty because I could have mind linked him sooner, but I froze and panicked.

"Raphael took her. I'm so sorry Raziel I didn't know what was happening until it was too late." I stammered. The fear and regret was clear in my voice. His eyes were fuming, it looked as if they were molten gold. I had never seen them like this before which was terrifying. "Tell me everything you've witnessed." He shot. So I told him about Alpha Drake and his obsession with Rayne. I told him how Alpha Drake suddenly got his sister back from the dead and then went into the events from this morning leading up until now.

I could see the fire changing in his eyes. His glare hardened as I was talking. I couldn't help but feel the fear building. He was going to explode, and I definitely didn't want to be around when he did. He was the most terrifying man I had ever met, hands down, and I knew I was just pissing him off more and more by the second.

Once I was done talking, he looked me dead in the eye and put his hand on my shoulder, causing me to flinch involuntarily. "Thank you Roman. I will get this shit sorted out but I'm going to need to get to Rayne first before he makes that mark permanent. If he does, I'm not sure we will ever be able to get her back." The urgency in his voice was crystal clear, and then he disappeared.

I let out a breath I was holding and took a step back, trying to process what he had said. Damnit, how did a simple job in return for a favor turn into all of this? "We can't control who we fall for, sadly." Ace pouted.

"I know buddy, I know." I said to my Wolf, as I turned and headed out of the arena. I wished there was something more I could do, but I was helpless when it came to this specific situation. Guilt engulfed me, ripping its claws into my lungs as I thought about the fact that I was supposed to be protecting her, and I had failed.

I tried, and mostly failed to forget about it as I headed home. I wasn't about to stick around when Raziel got to Alpha Drake, where I assumed he would go next. That man had a hell of a temper, and I knew all hell was about to break loose. I didn't want any fucking part of it.

~

(Raziel)

272

I materialized to Alpha Drake. To say I was upset, was the epitome of an understatement. I was fucking furious. Knowing how much Alpha Drake cared for Rayne, even possibly loved her, I couldn't believe he would be a part of this betrayal. Our deal was for him to protect her, not surrender her to the goddamn enemy. He was sitting alone at the bar in his pack house, drinking brandy on the rocks. It seemed as if he expected me, but how could he not?

Even despite knowing I was right behind him, he didn't turn around or say a word. He just kept drinking his brandy. "What the fuck did you do?!" I exclaimed as I slammed my hand down on the bar next to him making the liquid in his glass ripple. Much to my surprise he didn't even flinch.

He just picked up his glass, took another long drink of brandy, and set it back down. He finally turned to me, and we locked eyes. While his face was solemn and void of emotion, I could see the emotions swimming in his darker than normal blue eyes. It was anger, sadness, animosity, loss, but mostly regret. "Raziel, I had no choice." He said softly, and I could feel his anguish. I could tell he was struggling with an internal battle of some sort.

"Explain." I spewed, uncaring of his current anguish. He then went into the story of how Raphael had cornered him in his office and asked for his price to deliver Rayne to him. He told me he didn't want to do it and refused the offer multiple times before Raphael called The Shadows and forced him into it.

He said if he didn't make a deal, Raphael would, and his outcome wouldn't be favorable. He told me he was too nervous about what deal Raphael would make on his behalf, so he did it to avoid a worse outcome.

"I had no other choice. The only thing I could have possibly wanted, besides Rayne herself, was my little sister Reya. I had no idea The Shadows existed, let alone that they could bring back the dead." He stated.

I took a breath in slowly, knowing far too well how The Shadows and their prices worked. "What was their price? I know Raphael manipulated you into making a deal with them in trade for Rayne, but that alone wouldn't have been payment enough to bring someone back from the dead." I scowled. I was very familiar with The Shadows, having used them often. I definitely knew they had extremely steep prices. I've always been willing to pay, but not everyone was as willing as me. In fact, no one seemed to be quite as willing as I.

I could see the emotion in his eyes turn to grief, and then heartbreak. "What was the price, Wolf?" I growled, over enunciating every word for theatrics. "They wanted a life for a life. They took my intended mate, Angel... she rejected me years ago, but I never accepted her rejection and so she moved away to be with the one who held her heart. They killed her in front of me."

I understood fully what he experienced. The Shadows have killed a multitude of people in front of me and it's always the same. Slicing their bodies open to drain them of every last ounce of their blood. It's a slow, painful, traumatic death. I did not envy him, but I could tell he was about to break down before me. I also knew how important the mate bond was to a Wolf. It was the single most important thing in their lives.

Reavers never had a specifically intended mate, we were free to choose our own. Wolves, however, were different in the fact that they found their chosen mate upon turning 21. The Gods paired them from birth, and they couldn't escape it even if they wanted to. This is not to say that a Wolf's intended mate wouldn't be a Reaver, though interspecies mating is looked down upon and hasn't even been truly seen in thousands of years.

Some say they could feel the bond after they turned 21, even if their intended mate wasn't of age yet, but others said they had no idea until the day their mate turned 21. It varies, and the bond they share is extremely strong.

I had heard stories about the mate bond breaking and the grief and pain it caused, even causing a Wolf to become suicidal, but I had never witnessed it personally. As I said before, a Wolf could be mated to any species, even

Humans if that was what fate intended. Given that possibility, the option to reject a mate was present. If the mate were to accept the rejection it would cause the mate bond to shatter. That would then put them back into the mating pool, and the possibility of them becoming mated to another, someday, was there.

Not every Wolf found their mate on their 21st birthday, they just had the opportunity to. The bond was so important and so strong that many Wolves spent years, or even their entire lives, scouring the world for theirs. I couldn't imagine what he was going through, losing his mate just prior to this conversation.

As much as I loathed Alpha Drake, I understood the situation he was forced into. I put my hand on his shoulder, calming some of my prior rage. "I am sorry, Alpha." I said sincerely. His demeanor changed a little, and I thought I saw something change in his eyes, but I wasn't sure what. "I need to get to Rayne. Raphael will pay for this, all of it." I sneered, my face hardening.

"We… we need to get to her." Alpha Drake said with conviction in his words. He gulped the last bit of his brandy and slammed his glass down on the bar so hard it shattered, sending shards of glass scattering across the marble surface.

"This is fucking war!" He yelled. We locked eyes and I knew I had an ally, for now, at least. "Very well, Alpha. I will call you when I need you." I stated. He nodded his head in understanding, then I materialized to the front gate of Raphael's house.

"Raphael." I roared. "Don't you fucking touch her, or so help me, brother." I yelled, as I blew his silver gate off the hinges, once again, and stalked towards his front door. It was unlocked. "Ha, he probably didn't want to fix it again." Nero spat.

"I wouldn't mind destroying this whole place again and again if it would get Rayne out of his grasp." I retorted. "Raphael, where are you!" I roared. My patience was thinning by the second. I searched the main floor areas of his home that he frequented, but he wasn't down there. "I don't think he's here." Nero said.

I traversed my way up the right side spiral staircase and made my way down the hall to Raphael's bedroom. The doors were open and there was no sign of either him or Rayne. No sign that they had even been there recently. Panic started to settle into my chest as I paced back and forth in my brother's room. "If it were me, and I were trying to keep Rayne away from myself I would have taken her to a place only accessible by magic. Somewhere that no one knew about and would be extremely difficult to find." I said to Nero.

"My brother must have a place like my Grotto that only he knows how to access. Which means it would be on his property so he could keep a close watch and be able to keep the magic flowing to it." I said, mostly thinking out loud.

Not that I spent much time with my brother to know something like this, Raphael and I were never the closest of us 4. But as alike as all of us were, it would be naive to think he didn't have a Grotto of his very own.

I tried to mind link Rayne, which was my next course of action, but I was blocked from her. This made my blood boil, but confirmed my suspicion. He definitely had her in a place hidden by magic.

Now if we could only find the gate.

Chapter 41

~
(Rayne)

$\mathcal{J}$ tried to run as Raphael walked back towards me, but I wasn't able to move a muscle. As hard as I tried, my legs didn't even budge. It was like I was frozen in place just waiting for his next command. It was so much different than before, and this pissed me off to no end. He strolled up to me and took me in his arms. My mark exploded in approval, sending unwanted chills down my spine.

It was like my body wasn't my body. I tried to mind link Raziel and wasn't able to. It was blocked, somehow. That sent immense panic flooding through me. I have never not been able to reach him. Raphael laid his lips onto mine with a soft sort of hunger. I reciprocated easily, as if it was what I wanted. But I didn't, I didn't want this. I didn't want him. He pulled away none the wiser. "What would you like to do, beautiful?" He asked. *I want to leave, actually.*

My mind was perfectly intact right now, but my body was fuzzy. It was the opposite feeling from before. Like I was being controlled rather than being in control. "Whatever you want to do, my King." I said with a smile.

Which in turn made him grin and spin me around in the middle of the floor. I acted as if I were happy to be here, flashing him another smile and I could feel my mark sparkling in approval. All of this infuriated me. I felt so helpless.

I tried to contact Wynter, but she was starstruck. She was willing to give Raphael anything and everything he wanted, and she was willing to do it right now. I was alone in not wanting this, and she was not willing to help me. I had to figure out a way to get out of here. I needed to get the fuck away from him.

'If you complete the mating process the mark will be permanent, forever.' Raziel's words swam through my head making me dizzy. I was so frustrated because I couldn't figure out what the fuck was going on, or how to stop it. I just knew I needed to get away, needed to get out of this. *Now.*

"Well, I can think of a few things." He said with a smirk, pulling me from my internal banter. "Why don't we work on making this mark permanent? Would you like that, beautiful?" He asked, while tracing what was left of my mark with his finger. His touch sent lightning bolts through my entire body.

No, no, no! I was shouting in my mind, but what came out was so different. "Of course, my love." I said with a wink. *What the fuck? No! Body, why the fuck are you doing this?!* I was screaming in my mind for this all to stop. I then noticed a slight burning on my wrist. It hadn't been there before… or maybe the mark being so powerful was overpowering the feeling so I didn't notice, but I definitely could feel it now that I was focusing on it. I looked down and could see a slight pink glow.

I felt like such an idiot when I realized it was magic. *Fucking magic!* He's using magic to trap me, to control me and force me into completing the mating process. I had to get this fucking bracelet off. But how? I had absolutely no control of my own body. My actions were not mine.

My body wasn't in my control when he was near, not at all. My head was absolutely spinning and I didn't know if I was more pissed at him, or myself for ever dreamwalking into his dream.

Raphael picked me up and took me over to the bed. He gently laid me down and positioned himself on top of me. I pulled him down into a feral kiss, which he very greedily reciprocated. *God damnit!!* I was so enthralled with pleasure, thanks to my mark, I was temporarily immobilized and unable to think about anything else but his lips on mine, and the weight of his body on top of me. Raphael pulled away, took his shirt off, and flicked his wrist. I gasped as my combat boots went flying off.

He, for some reason, left my top and bottoms on, thankfully. Then he made his way down my body kissing every inch of me and exploring with his hands. My body was enjoying every single second. Every kiss was sending lightning coursing through my veins. My mind, however, was lost in thought trying to find a way to get free.

He started rubbing my inner thigh causing my body to react in his favor, and I took a sharp breath in. "You are so beautiful. You will make a perfect High Priestess." He whispered into my ear, causing cold chills to rack through me. I honestly couldn't help but be attracted to him. As much as I didn't want to be with him, I couldn't deny his sheer beauty.

Maybe it wouldn't be so bad being mated to Raphael. *No!* Oh my god, it was getting harder to resist him in my mind now. It was like even my mind was caving. *This can't be… if this happens, I will be with him forever!* I said to myself. *Well, would it really be that bad?* I thought. *Yes, yes it would! I want to be with Raziel!* I shot. This internal dialogue went nowhere because Wynter was also, unfortunately, on his side. This was fucking hopeless.

Then I thought about it. I can't use magic. I can't mind link anyone. But what about The Shadows? You can't tell me that magic is powerful enough to block The Shadows… nothing can block the Shadows!

I started focusing on calling them forward, which was a lot harder than it was the first time. I chalked it off to this fucking bracelet. Just as Raphael sat up and went to flick his wrist, no doubt, to remove my remaining clothes, a curtain of relief showered over me. The familiar icy chill to the bone washed over us both.

The plethora of tendrils came snaking out of nowhere and everywhere all at once, and for the first time since Rahael had taken me, I had some sense of body clarity. It was an invigorating feeling being in control of my own actions once again.

I elongated a Wolf claw, which was also a feat harder than I expected, and I sliced my hand open. "Drink." I said to The Shadows. I locked eyes with Raphael as the tendrils snaked their way past him and up my arm to happily oblige. I saw the terror form in his eyes, then it changed to confusion. I was able to maneuver myself away from him and off the bed. He stood up at the end of the bed and didn't move a muscle.

"How… how is this possible?" He asked The Shadows. "We are here to make dealsss. We made a deal with you to get Rayne. We fulfilled our part, you have her. Now ssshe isss here to make a deal with usss." They hissed.

I could see his confusion turn into anger. "You were supposed to stop her from being able to use any magic and give me complete control!" He spewed. He was fucking pissed. So that's what he did, he made a fucking deal with The Shadows!

What a damn snake! I thought. "We did, you have had complete control, ssshe cannot usssse mosssst of her magic." They hissed. "Then how are you here?!" Raphael growled, his teeth clenched in frustration. His patience was wearing thin.

"We are not sssummoned by magic. We are not bound by ssspellsss. We are The Shadowsss… we are omnipresssent, yet invisssible. We are the unssseen forccceee that permeatesss every corner of exisssstencccceee."

The Shadows seemed to shift and writhe as they spoke. Their slithery words dripped with venom, and their presence seemed to grow more menacing with each passing moment. "We are not controlled by magic, and we will not be contained."

"You slimy fucking…" Raphael started to say but was suddenly silenced by The Shadows. "Enough!" They roared, sending a blast of icy wind throughout the room causing us both to flinch. They turned to me. "What isss it you wisssh for, Princesss?" They questioned in a much calmer tone.

I tried to stay strong in front of them. As much as I didn't want to admit it, The Shadows scared the ever living hell out of me, but I didn't want to find out what would happen if they were aware of this fact. "First, I want this magic barrier removed." I said.

They had already drunk my blood and that must have sufficed their price because they suddenly surrounded my wrist and shattered the bracelet into tiny pieces. The impact sent dainty shards flying all over the black and silver room. I grabbed my wrist and rubbed my opposing hand across it. I instantly felt the body fog completely dissipating. As soon as it was all gone, and I was back to normal I could feel the familiar tingling in the palm of my hand.

My magic was back! My body was my own again. I was able to freely move and react. My mark was still tingling in proximity to Raphael, but it was something I could now withstand. I looked at Raphael with pure, unbridled hatred in my gaze. "I'll have you know that I do not belong to anyone, and not even magic can change that." I snapped at Raphael before looking down at The Shadows.

I was beyond pissed and feeling very fucking violated. I could feel the hint of unbridled power flowing through my veins, and I contemplated unleashing it all directly at Raphael. But I refrained after the meeting between Raziel's brothers and myself played though my mind. I was suddenly more worried about letting them down than getting revenge on Raphael, but none of this would ensure that I could stay away from him until this mark was gone.

I had never experienced something so utterly consuming as trying to fight the marks pull. That's when I made the impossible choice to rid myself of Raphael once and for all.

"Shadows, remove this mark from me!" I commanded. "The pricccceee isss steep, a bond for a bond... you already know... do you accept?" They slithered. "No!!" Raziel shouted from somewhere behind me as he reached for my arm.

"I accept!" I snarled, before I even realized he was there.

Chapter 42

~

(Raziel)

I was pacing in my brother's room trying to figure out how I could find the gate to the hidden location and stop my devious brother from completing the mating ritual with the woman I loved, when suddenly, I felt it... Rayne was using magic! That meant the barrier was down, she was no longer hidden.

I materialized to her in an instant, just in time to hear her ask The Shadows to remove the mark. I knew the price. It was a bond for a bond. A price that was too steep, especially if I were her intended mate. Even though the chances were so slim, it was a possibility I wasn't willing to give up.

"No!!" I screamed, desperation echoing through my voice as I lunged for her arm. But my attempt was futile. "I accept." She snarled. Panic surrounded me, but it was too late. With those 2 fateful words she sealed her fate. Before I could reach her, The Shadows enveloped her, their dark tendrils wrapping around her like a shroud.

The darkness lingered for only a moment, but that fleeting instant was all it took for The Shadows to extract the most important part of who she truly was. They took it with no remorse, no afterthought, and no care as to the consequences.

Then as quickly as they appeared, The Shadows began to vanish, dissolving into the nothing and everything from which they came. I materialized before her, my eyes scanning her face with urgency. Her features were flawless, with no hint of Raphael's mark remaining. It was as if it had never existed. But her eyes told a different story. A deep emptiness had formed behind them, and she crumpled to her knees before me. The pain of her mate bond shattering was crystal clear in her anguished screams.

Tears cascaded down her face in relentless waves. She clutched at her chest, her breaths coming in short gasps, as if all the air had been drained from her lungs. I stood there, helpless and in agony, knowing I was powerless to ease her suffering.

She had just surrendered her mate bond, the most sacred and fundamental aspect of a Wolf's existence, for me. The weight of her sacrifice hit me like a tidal wave. The mate bond was more than just a connection, it was the essence of a Wolf's being, the source of their identity, and their very purpose. And she had given it up, willingly, for me... I should have gotten here sooner. I should have stopped her. I should have stopped my brother. I should have done more...

She let out another heart wrenching cry, and I felt it, the searing pain of the bond shattering, as if I were experiencing it alongside her. The sensation was like a jagged edge tearing through my very being, leaving a trail of despair in its wake. I caught her in my arms, cradling her as she collapsed, her body trembling with sobs. I held her close as she mourned the loss of her future mate. There was no stopping the guilt that was tearing and ripping its way through my body.

I could hear Wynter's agonizing cries and realized that she was not only dealing with her own loss, but Wynter's too. She put her hands on her head, covering her face while she mourned. Raphael's eyes were wide in shock at the scene. He hadn't moved a muscle from the space he was standing in. He was shirtless, which intensified my rage.

Though, I was more worried about her than to even mention it. Raphael walked over. "Rayne, I'm... I'm so sorry." He said, as he fell to his knees in front of us. She didn't acknowledge him. She was too lost in her agony to even realize he was there. I locked eyes with him, my glare was deadly.

"You did this! You are the cause of this!" I snarled. She began to shake in my arms and I realized my anger seemed to upset her as she began to weep harder. I stopped and took a deep breath in, trying to calm myself, while also trying to calm her.

"You've made a grave mistake. You've been tampering with forces beyond your control, invoking The Shadows, and entangling yourself in their dark dealings. I'm sure it didn't end well for you. And to use their sinister influence to manipulate an innocent into loving you? And not just any innocent, *MY* innocent! Who do you think you are, Raphael?" I hissed.

"I swear, Raziel, I honestly never once thought she would give up her mate bond to rid herself of my mark. I never would have done this had I known she was that attached to you. I honestly thought she was just a fling, or maybe her feelings were easily swayed. I didn't know her feelings for you were this deep. I swear, brother." Raphael stammered.

I could tell he was being sincere but it didn't make me feel any better. "This isn't over, brother." I snapped, and materialized myself and Rayne to the only place I could think of to keep him away from us. The gate to the Grotto. I took the golden key and opened the gate. I picked Rayne up, closed the gate, and headed inside. She was still weeping, but softer now. I walked the short path with her in my arms, and moved the vines overhanging the entrance.

I carefully brought her inside and set her down on the vibrant, purple and blue grass. Her eyes, red from crying, and her cheeks, stained with tears, only added to her haunting beauty. In that moment, I was reminded why she was, without a doubt, the most stunning woman I had ever laid eyes on.

"I'm so... so... sorry." She said softly as more tears fell from her eyes. "I couldn't let him make the mark permanent.

I couldn't be with him." She whispered. "He used The Shadows to stop me from being able to use magic, and they gave him complete control of my body. My mind was there, but my body wouldn't do anything I wanted it to, only what he wanted. I know it was drastic, but I had no other choice." She said with longing and sadness in her eyes.

I could tell she was distraught over the entire situation. My blood was fucking boiling. I have always been my brother's keeper, but I was so upset over this I wanted to materialize to Raphael and slit his throat right then and there… brother or not. I didn't even fucking care. But I couldn't leave her right now, not after this.

She buried her face in my chest again, and wept. I told myself I never wanted to witness a mate bond shatter, ever again. It was the most excruciating experience. I was helpless, watching the woman I love hurt so badly.

My mind instantly went to Alpha Drake and wondered if this is what he felt like too, how he acted when it happened. When I got to him, he had a stoic expression on his face, but I could see the hurt and emotions in his eyes. I wondered if Rayne would eventually have a hardened look on her face too, and how long this would continue to affect her.

I snapped to speed up time, in hopes that it would lessen the amount of time she had to endure this agonizing pain. After what seemed like forever, and she couldn't have possibly had another tear to shed, she stood up.

I snapped to return time to normal. She grabbed my hands and helped me up so we were face to face. She still looked distraught, and I bet if she had any moisture left in her body she would still be crying. She did however have something new in her eyes, a fire? Something was different.

"I don't regret it, and I would do it again if it meant I could be with you." She stated. It was in that moment that I realized just how deep her feelings ran. I already knew that she would eventually come to love me. Not that she ever had a choice, I wouldn't have stopped until she decided to choose me. But this confirmed that we were already there.

Even after knowing how it felt to lose her mate bond and being in this kind of agony, she was still willing to do it again. She had feelings for me, and she knew it now. Giving her mate bond to The Shadows means she wouldn't be eligible to find a mate when she turned 21. It was gone for good. No getting back in the mating pool later on. The guilt gnawed its way through my bones. I couldn't help but feel that it was all my fault and the acknowledgement of this was suffocating.

My fucking brother, I could strangle him. "I know you would, darling. But you'll never have to go through this again." I said, caution lacing my voice. I wanted to comfort her, but I couldn't shake the feeling that something about her just felt different. I was feeling a different type of energy flowing from her delicate body.

My mind instantly jumped to the fact that she was dangerous. A Reaver who was coming into her powers outside of a Coven. I didn't want to trigger her to explode, not when she was in such a fragile state.

"I want you to mark me, Raziel." She said, with more conviction. "I want the world to know just who I belong to, and I want to make sure that Raphael can *never* fucking mark me again." She spewed that last part, her words laced with venom and revulsion at the mention of his name.

My heart sank straight to my feet. Of course I wanted to mark her, but I never wanted to mark her like this. Short of forcing her to love me, I had hoped that this moment would be much more… enchanting.

"Darling, wouldn't you like to wait a while? You know, until you start feeling better?" I asked curiously. I mean, she had just been through an extremely traumatic experience due to being marked and losing her mate bond. I had thought she wouldn't want to jump right into it again this quickly.

"Now, Raziel, fucking mark me!" She commanded. Her tone caught me off guard, but also kind of turned me on.

She had never been this daring. I smirked and looked deep into her platinum silver eyes. This was hardly the time for me to completely destroy her, but I couldn't ignore the fact that the way she commanded me, as if I would just cower down and obey, had me feeling objectively primal. Immediately I wanted to hunt, and she had already unknowingly triggered my deepest, darkest, instincts.

I stepped closer to her and slowly wrapped my hand around her throat. She stood still, but she didn't fight me like I thought she would. "You think your words, even as angry and commanding as they are, will sway me?" I questioned, running my nose along the side of her cheek. I could hear her labored breathing as I nipped on her earlobe. She swallowed hard enough it made an audible sound.

"Y-yes…" Her voice was shaking and I knew she hadn't forgotten *who* or *what* I was. The apex predator, and right now she was my prey. I released her neck and circled her, keeping my fingers on her chest and dragging them across her shoulder to the back of her neck.

"Oh little Wolf, regardless of your current state of mind, you are in absolutely no position to be making demands." I purred, resisting the urge to sink my now elongated Vampire fangs straight into the soft tissue of her slender neck.

"Fine. But when Raphael tries again, and succeeds, you'll lose me forever. And Raziel? That will be completely on your fucking shoulders." She growled. "That little fucking Siren." Nero hissed. She was trying to manipulate me, and even though her intentions were crystal clear, it was working.

I tilted my head, cracking my neck without touching it then I narrowed my eyes on my prize. "You belong to me… and no one, not even my own brother will stop me from collecting my prize. You would *dare* insinuate that I wouldn't destroy this entire fucking world, and watch it and every creature in it burn to the fucking ground just to get you back if that were to happen?" I growled.

Her breath hitched in her throat again as I threaded my fingers through her hair starting at the nape of her neck. I closed my fist once I had a decent handful of silver locks and pulled her head back exposing her perfect neck. My lips touched down on her delicate skin and I softly placed kisses in all of the places I would prefer to be biting. She gasped and whatever words she would have said became lost in the moment. It wasn't until I stopped and allowed her to speak that she finally admitted her reasoning.

"I… I know you would save me. But… Raziel, please. I… I can't be with him, I just can't be away from you… I just can't do that again…" She whimpered softly. And that's what did it. She begged me in the softest, most innocent tone I had ever heard coming from her, and I came completely undone. My entire demeanor softened and I wanted nothing more than to comfort her.

I instantly wanted to hold her and tell her everything would be ok, tell her that I would never allow him to put his hands on her, ever again, and grant her every vice and wish. "Your wish is my command, darling…" I said, trailing off as I released her hair and licked her bottom lip softly.

I pressed my lips to hers, and at the same time cupped her right cheek in my hand and placed my mark upon her beautiful face. She fell head first into my kiss and even when I knew she was gasping and needed air, I didn't allow her lips to leave mine, not quite yet. I wanted just one more taste.

When I had finally had my fill of her luscious lips, I pulled away and stood back to admire my work. Fuck, she was so goddamn beautiful. Even an angry, dark, empty mess, my mark glittering along the side of her face just made her that much more beautiful. And she was all mine now.

My mark was a golden crescent moon, adorned in filigree and vines that flowed around the crescent and down her neck. It was large on her face, much like Raphael's mark, but different in many ways. It was glittering as she moved around in the sunlight, and I couldn't help but fall more in love with her knowing that someday that mark would be permanent. "Your will is done, darling."

I thought I saw a sparkle in her eye for a second, but it quickly returned to the darkness that I was already starting to grow accustomed to. I knew what the mark did to her and how it affected her. Especially when I was around, so it didn't surprise me when she pulled me in for another deep kiss.

I knew the marks pull was strong, but I wasn't prepared for the intensity of what came next. It was as if lightning bolts coursed through my very being, igniting a fierce passion that left me breathless. I gripped onto her harder, pulling her to my chest.

She was unaware, but the mark works both ways. The feelings she feels, I also feel. The mark intensifies what's already there and from the way I was feeling now, I could confidently say that both of us were infatuated before this moment.

I originally intended for her to fall for me on her own, though I know I didn't make it easy for her to do so. Though, marking someone did ensure that even if their feelings faltered in the future, they would be replaced by false feelings. I was trapping her, in a way. But isn't that how the mate bond worked too? Like a thick cord that attached two beings, and forced their lives together? *The mate bond...*

A searing blade of guilt sliced through my conscience, reawakening the heavy burden of my regret. My thoughts were interrupted when I felt that familiar tingle of Rayne using magic. She pulled away from the kiss and looked at me, both hands burning with green flames.

"Raziel, how difficult will it be to teach me to control my Reaver powers? I mean… will it be as difficult as your brothers made it seem?" She asked softly. For a brief minute, it sounded like she was back to her old self, but the darkness returned immediately, and she was gone.

I looked into her eyes and she was in there, but there was also an emptiness, a darkness brewing. I could feel it before, but now I could physically see it. She was fighting an internal battle that I wasn't sure she would win. I knew a storm was coming, and imminent danger or not, I was planning on being there for her through it all.

Having this amount of unbridled power at her disposal while she was in this fragile state scared the hell out of me. But who was I to tell her no? Regardless of her mental state, she needed to learn to use her magic... to control it. There was no getting around this and I knew it. She was a Reaver, and honestly, she deserved this much and more.

"It will be difficult, and you will fail, many, many times. But I'll never give up on you, darling." I said softly, as I took her hand in mine, palms up, and we started her first real lesson.

Chapter 43

~

(Rayne)

hen Raphael marked me, it was as if he was just touching my face. I didn't feel anything for him, I didn't feel anything at all, really, except a slight tingling. Which was still there in the morning, and that is why I checked the mirror. That must be what happens when you are marked and there are no feelings there prior. The fake feelings take a little time to manifest.

When Raziel marked me, it was as if every fiber of my being exploded into ecstasy! The sensation transcended words, speaking directly to my core in a language that echoed through my soul. As his mark claimed me, it felt as though every inch of my being was enveloped, every nerve ending awakened, and every fiber bound to his. In that moment, our connection was sealed, forging an eternal bond that linked us for eternity.

I watched him step back after he was done and admire me. I had no idea what his mark actually looked like, but I was assuming it was similar to the crescent moon on the golden gate at his house.

Raphael's was the same as his silver gate, so I was just guessing. But from the look of it, Raziel definitely approved. I couldn't even fight this mark. The pull of it was so much stronger than Raphael's. So fucking much stronger. I swear I couldn't resist this even if I wanted to.

I pulled Raziel in for a kiss, and intense lightning exploded between us. He grabbed me and pulled me closer. Just that simple maneuver had me reeling with pleasure. It wouldn't be long until this mark was permanent, that was a fact.

Then I felt the tingling in my hands. I pulled away reluctantly to inspect it. I held my hands out palms up to see they were engulfed in magic and green fire. I was nervous, but excited at the thought of learning to control these powers."Raziel, how difficult will it be to teach me to control my Reaver powers? I mean... will it be as difficult as your brothers made it seem?" I asked softly.

For a minute I didn't feel the icy warmth, but then I felt it wash back over me. It was the weirdest thing, that icy warmth. I couldn't place my finger on just what it was, or why it was here. All I knew is when it was gone, I felt like I was on the verge of breaking again. I couldn't break, not again. I needed the icy warmth.

Raziel locked eyes with me, and I could see worry in his molten golden orbs. He was worried about me, but I was just fine. I just needed to learn to control this shit so I didn't accidentally do anything I would regret.

"It will be difficult, and you will fail, many times. But I'll never give up on you, darling." He said softly, as he took my hands in his, leaving my palms up, and we started my first real lesson.

"Magic isn't something you can force. It has to flow free. It's all energy, my love. You know some of this, as you explained it to my brothers at TwentyOne. You can't force it, you must *will* it. I know you have a small grasp on what that entails, but this might help. Imagine your energy as a light flowing through your body. Let's use green light since the fireball is already green. You need to channel the energy into your palms. Close your eyes." Raziel explained.

Just hearing his voice was sending chills down my spine. This mark really had a different effect when there were actually feelings involved. I had to concentrate extremely hard to get my mind to quit focusing on Raziel and start focusing on channeling energy.

After a few failed attempts I was getting frustrated. The mark was just too powerful. I couldn't concentrate with him so close to me. "Back up, would you? Just enough so the mark will stop interfering with my concentration." I asked Raziel with a wink. I didn't want to hurt his feelings, but our connection was so extreme, it was really hindering my learning.

Desire flashed through his golden eyes as he turned around and walked back about 40 feet. Once the marks' effects had dimmed down, I was able to think. "Whoa, that shit is intense." I said to Wynter. "You know what else is intense? The sheer size of Raziel's dick bulging in his pants." She cackled.

"Wynter!" I squealed. "What? You're telling me you've never looked down there? Don't even." She retorted. "Stop!" I cried, her commentary made me blush and even from the distance we were away from him, I could see exactly what she was talking about. Redness filled my cheeks and I immediately averted my eyes. "I can't believe you made me do that!" I cried to my Wolf. She just snickered before I pushed her from my mind so I could concentrate.

Of course I had looked, I had felt it, I knew how big it was. But now was not the time to focus on that. I exhaled, clearing the embarrassment from my cheeks. I closed my eyes to regain my focus and took a slow breath in. Once I felt calmer, I held my hands about a foot apart, facing each other. I imagined the green light flowing through my body, similar to how blood flows but through rhetorical energy veins, and I willed all of the green light into the palms of my hands.

I could see it sucking itself out of the rest of my body and moving directly into my palms. It felt a little strange to imagine it all, almost as if it was all make believe. I opened my eyes when I felt the mark tingling to find Raziel right by my side. I gasped when to my surprise, a larger than I expected, green fireball was floating between my hands. My heart started to race. It worked... imagining it worked...

Excitement swirled through me like a whirlwind, its energetic vortex coursing through every vein. I couldn't force it, it had to flow freely and I was starting to realize that visualization was apparently key. I thought back to when I was so upset at Alpha Drake, and also at Raphael, I must have been unknowingly willing my energy. Which is why when I tried to force it on my own it didn't work. Forcing it would never work. "When you want to get rid of it you can either throw it, or just imagine the green light disappearing from your hands. Will it away." Raziel said.

I imagined the light dissipating out of my hands and becoming sucked back down into the earth. Then I watched as the fireball slowly shrunk and disappeared, taking the tingling in my hands with it. "Good, let's go again. Make it bigger this time." Raziel said.

I nodded and shooed him away from me. The marks pull was too distracting for me to fully focus. Once he was far enough away I closed my eyes and began. I wasn't actually sure how I had gotten it to be as big as it was the first time. Raziel didn't instruct me on how to change the size, but I remembered how I willed it to change while speaking to his brothers, and opted to do the same thing.

Once I could feel the fire in between my hands I opted for it to grow in size. The issue was I didn't know how to get it to stop growing. It was twice the size of the first one and it was still growing. Fear enveloped me, as dark tendrils wrapped around my heart, suffocating me with an overwhelming sense of dread and anxiety. All the words Raziel and his brothers had said regarding how dangerous I would be, came flooding back.

"Stop it, Rayne… will the fire to stop growing!" Raziel shouted, but I couldn't focus. Everything just seemed so loud, so inherently distracting.

"Rayne. I don't like where this is going, make it stop!" Wynter whined, and I could hear the fear in her voice. "I don't know how!" I growled, not meaning to bark at her but my emotions were all over the place.

"Try harder!" She snipped. At this point the fireball was large enough to engulf a person, or two. I was struggling to imagine the fire dissipating like I had last time. Emotions swirled around me, a cacophony of feelings that threatened to consume me whole. And in the midst of the turmoil, I could feel the void's insidious presence, its dark tendrils probing for a way to reclaim its hold on me. That's when I felt it, the silky caress of the icy warmth. It enveloped me, its gentle, soothing touch a mesmerizing paradox of comfort and chill.

Like a soft whisper on a winter's night, it wrapped around my senses, calming my mind and stirring my soul. Immediately my mind came back into focus and I was able to compartmentalize my emotions, casting out those that didn't serve my purpose. I exhaled in relief as the fire stopped growing and remained still. I was finally in control again. I looked at Raziel who was nodding to me. "Good. Now dissipate." He said.

I was surprised at how easy it was to control the fire once I was in control of my own mind. Within moments it was gone, as if I had never conjured it to begin with. Raziel had me in his arms before I could make eye contact.

"You are doing exquisitely well, darling. Your progress in this short of a time is truly impressive. Please know that you will struggle and you will fail on your journey to control your magic. It's ok, so long as you can regain your control. Try not to panic, as that will make things worse. The moment you lose control of your will is the moment your magic begins to control you. Don't let it. *You* are in charge, *you* make the rules."

I heeded his words and for the next hour or so we went over the different ways to channel energy. Raziel showed me how to use the energy to become an extension of myself. He let me engulf different objects in flames and move them, as I've seen him do many times before.

We practiced on some of the boulders around the Grotto until I was feeling much more comfortable with the fireball. He then attempted to teach me how to materialize to another place. This was marginally harder than channeling energy. "Materialization requires dedication and finesse. It's not just a matter of wishing yourself somewhere, you need to cultivate a profound mental connection. Imagine a metaphysical rope that bridges your consciousness with your desired destination. Envision attaching this rope to the target, whether a place or person. Begin by focusing on that nearby bench. Visualize the rope extending from your mind's eye, wrapping around the bench, and anchoring itself. As the connection solidifies, you'll feel the familiar sensation of materialization, and suddenly, you'll find yourself standing there." Raziel stated, as if it were the easiest thing in the world.

"Ok, here we go." I said. I imagined a rope and threw it to the bench, visualizing it wrapping around and anchoring itself like he said. I suddenly felt as if I were being ripped from my place and abruptly hurled through the air. I was not prepared for this level of force. Then, suddenly, I landed with a jarring impact on my knees. Dazed and disoriented, I struggled to regain my bearings, only to realize I had merely covered half the distance to the bench. "Shit, what happened?" I gasped.

Raziel was right at my side, helping me up. He was laughing, and once I regained my senses I couldn't help but laugh with him. "That was an epic fail!" I said, while still laughing hysterically. This was going to be harder than I thought. He took me into his arms, and we laughed together for a few minutes. I had never heard him laugh before, and the sound was like music to my soul.

It was as if the warmth of his joy had melted the icy reserve that usually shrouded him, revealing a glimpse of unguarded happiness. I felt like I could die right here, in his arms, and be happy about it.

My mark was exploding at his touch, causing my body to shudder and for the first time since I had lost my mate bond, which, granted, was only a few hours ago, I felt normal. I felt like I hadn't just lost a huge part of myself...

We locked eyes, and I couldn't help but notice how beautiful Raziel's eyes really were. I mean, I had been admiring them for years, but something about them in this moment was mesmerizing. The way the various shades of

297

gold seemed to swirl and dance within their depths, like molten metal in a state of constant transformation. As if their very essence was mutable, ever changing, and hypnotically beautiful. Staring into the chasm that was Raziel made my heart sing.

Suddenly, worry flooded his face, and at the same time I felt the icy warmth taking over. It felt as if it were coaxing me out of my safe space and pushing me into the unknown. I suddenly had a feeling of urgency. We couldn't be fucking around, we had to get to work. This was important. I stepped out of Raziel's arms. "Let's keep working." I shot.

Raziel nodded his head and stepped back. I couldn't help but notice the worry was still resting on his angelic features. He was overreacting, though. I was fine. Clearly, I was perfectly fine. The icy warmth washed over me again, reassuring me that I was, indeed, ok. I ignored his worry and continued working.

I closed my eyes and threw the rope to the bench again. This time, I felt as if I were being pulled, rather than thrown. I fell again, hard on my knees. But, I was in front of the bench this time. "YES!" I cried, ignoring the pain. I got up and walked back to Raziel so I could keep trying.

Soon, I had mastered the ability to materialize but my landings were still awkward, leaving me on my knees as if I were paying my respects to the ground I'd so recently traversed. I continued to go back and forth from Raziel to the bench, then back to the Raziel, until I finally was able to partially anticipate my landing.

I couldn't land like Raziel, who didn't even stumble. It was as if he was there the whole time. I was more like a baby colt learning to walk for the first time, stumbling and falling. But at least I was there! I knew I would get better, someday. But for now, I was happy to just be able to get from point A to point B at all.

Next, Raziel showed me how to materialize items like he always did. "It's a similar principle to hurling the rope to the bench, but this time, you're harnessing the power of your mind. Visualize the object you desire, reach in with your thoughts, and grasp it. With a swift snap of your fingers, the manifestation should materialize in your hand. Essentially, you're bridging the gap between your mental realm and physical reality, bringing your desires into being with a mere thought and gesture." He explained. He made it sound so easy, but I knew it was going to take me a moment to pick it up.

"Imagine a crisp, vibrant apple suspended in your mind's eye. Envision every detail. The radiant red hue, the subtle sheen on its skin, the delicate stem protruding from the apple's core. Hold this mental picture with clarity and precision. Now, with a swift snap of your fingers, reach out with your mind and grasp the apple, as if plucking it from the ether." Raziel said. I saw the apple.

I pictured myself grabbing the apple, and I snapped, but nothing happened. "Shit, I lost the apple." I huffed. I was already frustrated and this was only my first attempt. This was much harder than I anticipated. "It's ok. Rome wasn't built in a day, my love." Raziel chuckled.

"Envision the apple hovering in the air before you, its vibrant red color and precise details suspended in the space outside your mind. See it floating, tangible and real, as if you could reach out and touch it. Now, with a swift snap of your fingers, extend your hand, and as if capturing the apple, enclose it within your grasp. It's all in the mind, and the will. *Will* the apple into your hand." Raziel stated.

I took a deep breath, focused my intentions, and tried it again. This time I visualized the apple floating in the air before me. With a quick snap of my fingers, I reached out and, to my utter astonishment, felt the cool, smooth skin of the apple nestled in my palm! I was actually holding it!

The rush of success swirled around me as I gazed at the tangible fruit of my mind's creation. So, this was definitely going to take more practice but I felt much better about it now. Over the next hour Raziel had me snapping and producing all kinds of random items. We went from more fruits and vegetables, to pens and paper, notebooks, to clothing. I was seeming to get the hang of it pretty well, which surprised me as it happened a lot quicker than I had anticipated. It was becoming easier the more I did it.

Time seemed to warp and bend within the Grotto's mystical confines. I lost all sense of its passage. Hours, minutes, seconds, it all blurred into an eternal present. So, when Raziel's strong hand grasped my arm, halting our intense training session, I felt a jolt of surprise similar to waking from a dream.

I looked up at him with wide eyes as the mark on my skin ignited with a sudden burst of radiant energy. The lightning-like sensation coursed through my veins, electrifying every fiber of my being. I looked up and met the fire flowing through his eyes.

"That's enough for tonight, we can continue the training tomorrow." He said. I didn't want to go, but I knew we still had other obligations. We couldn't spend all of our time here training, no matter how much I wanted to. We walked to the gate, opened it, then locked it behind us. He then reached for me, and materialized us to his room. I half expected him to make me materialize us.

As we got ready for bed, I realized we hadn't eaten anything. I didn't even know how long it had been since I ate last, but honestly, I wasn't even feeling hungry. It was as if my very essence had been sustained by the secrets and wonders of the Grotto. "I mean, if you think about it, you haven't really eaten much since you found out you were a Reaver." Wynter said. I shrugged it off because things had been so chaotic since then. I just didn't really think about it.

"Reavers are exempt from the mortal necessity of sustenance. We can indulge in the pleasure of eating, savoring the flavors and textures, but our existence is not bound by the need for nourishment. As you awaken to your inherent powers, you'll discover that your body will transcend the requirements of hunger, freeing you from the cycles of sustenance as well." Raziel answered, as if he had heard Wynter talking. "Oh, and yes, I did hear Wynter. That is something you will develop as well. I can hear any

Wolf or mind link if I am close enough." He said to me, as he flashed me that million-dollar smile that I loved. It sent chills through my entire body, courtesy of the mark. Wynter gasped at the realization, and I almost did too.

So many things made sense now! How he knew about certain things, and the way I would see him snicker or smile when he was near me. He was hearing Wynter's internal swooning! My cheeks flushed at the thought of him hearing her insistent obsession with him, but I knew I couldn't change it now and she sure as hell wouldn't watch her mouth. I would just have to get used to it.

We got into bed and Raziel took me into his arms. My mark invaded the deepest recess of my soul, staking its claim with a sultry intensity that left me breathless. I wanted to rip every shred of clothing he was wearing off of him. However, my body was so exhausted after today's events that I fell into a deep sleep almost immediately.

"Rayne... Rayne..." My eyes fluttered open to find that I was sitting in complete darkness. "Who's there?" I asked. Then I felt the familiar icy warmth wash over me. I suddenly felt confident in my surroundings and in my abilities to protect myself should the need arise. "I said who's there?" I snarled. My voice resounded with an unshakable assurance, as if my very being had been infused with an unwavering conviction.

"You may call me The Darkness, my dear. I am here to help you." It said. Its voice was female and seemed to reverberate through me, penetrating deep down to my core. "Help me with what?" I questioned. "I come when the need arises. I'm sure you've felt me comfort you today, have you not?" It asked. I shuddered as a small chill ran up my spine. "I have felt something… but I didn't know what it was." I stammered.

I was now getting a little nervous that I may be playing with something I probably shouldn't be. Then I felt the icy warmth wash over me again, and like a comfort blanket my confidence was back, pushing any doubts I may have had out of my mind. So, this is what it was. *This* is what has been helping me today, keeping me from breaking into a thousand tiny helpless pieces, all over again. This is what I had been channeling to keep my strength up while training. It was The Darkness.

I started to feel myself slipping back into a deep sleep, out of the grasp of The Darkness, and I couldn't help but wonder just what The Darkness actually wanted.

Nothing comes without a price...

Chapter 44

Once morning came, my mind was reeling with my newfound abilities. I was going over all the practices in my head from yesterday and I was ready to start the day training. I threw on a black pair of leggings and a flowing gold tank top then headed to the bathroom to put my hair up in a high pony.

Raziel, of course, was matching, with his black and gold suit. I loved that we always matched. It made me feel like we were actually a couple. I mean, we were actually a couple… but I had never experienced anything like the relationship we had, and I loved it.

He pulled me into his arms and kissed me before we left. The touch ignited a wildfire within my mark, sending shivers of delight coursing through my very essence. The sensation was exhilarating, as if the spark of our connection had awakened something deep and carnal within, leaving me breathless and yearning for more.

It took every last shred of my self control to simply walk alongside him, our hands entwined, and our clothes still intact. But I had other things on my mind as well. The Darkness... I hadn't forgotten the meeting we had… or my dream, or whatever that was last night. I allowed myself to become distracted thinking about it. I knew there would be a price, there had to be. But The Darkness was literally the only thing keeping me together, keeping me from cracking into a thousand tiny pieces of pain and regret.

I knew Raziel wouldn't understand because he would never have to lose his mate bond… he didn't have one. Not like a Wolf, at least. It had to be different for Wolves when fate brings us together. But for a Reaver? He was able to choose whoever he wanted. I was certain it was different, it felt different. The loss of that bond left an unrelenting void, a chasm that yearned to be filled by anything, any sensation, any connection. The ache was a constant reminder of what could have been, a bittersweet echo of a future love that I would never get to experience now.

And when the cruel truth sinks in, that the void will forever remain unfilled, the torrent of emotions returns, as a relentless tide of grief and longing. That's when The Darkness swoops in, its frosty warm embrace enveloping me like a shroud and fills the void. It happens more often than I want to admit. But even Wynter is thankful when it comes. We may be playing with fire, but it's better than dealing with the grief and agony. I told myself that it was better. It *had* to be better, right?

I decided I wasn't going to say anything to anyone about The Darkness. I didn't think it mattered, and honestly, I thought I might be going a little crazy anyway. It's possible The Darkness wasn't even real. Merely a construct of my own fragile mind. A phantom comfort born from the depths of my psyche.

Maybe it was a coping mechanism, a desperate attempt to find solace in the face of unimaginable trauma. Yet the memory of the icy warmth felt all too real. I didn't want to seem crazy, so, to save what face I had left, I figured this was the right way to go. I told myself it was. It *had* to be, because I had no other options.

Just as I was feeling doubt, and the emptiness of the void was creeping back in, The Darkness washed over me and brought out a new confidence. Construct of my imagination or not, I needed this. I needed The Darkness... whatever it was.

I locked eyes with Raziel as we started training. I could see the worry flood his face and I wondered why he was so worried? I was literally fine. I hadn't even broken down since the major break when it all happened. He didn't know about The Darkness, and we were together. I was training and learning, getting stronger. I was fine! I ignored his worried look and kept moving on with training. I was able to create a fireball with ease today. It was much easier once I had done it a few hundred times. I could dissipate it and I perfected how to throw it today, as well. I was able to materialize anywhere in the Grotto, but still stumbling on my landing, of course.

Still though, the rope was easier to throw and anchor to anything I wanted. I learned to imagine the end point in my mind being closer to me, to make the rope travel a shorter distance. A trick I figured out on my own. I was able to materialize items from my mind a lot easier today. Raziel taught me about dreamwalking, which is when everything clicked. That's what I had been doing when I was with Alpha Drake. It wasn't just a dream. It was my dream, and I was manipulating it.

When I was in Raziel's home, I was dreamwalking to his dream. And that's how Raphael fucking got to me. I was dreamwalking to his dream. So really, I started it all, but I just didn't realize it. Now, how I got there was unknown. I must have just been thinking about his name, or something that I read after the first time I started researching, and that must have caused it to happen. The second time I knew I had gone there on purpose, and that was when he marked me. I just didn't realize it was real. I was so eager for knowledge that I did whatever I had to do to get it, even if that meant completely disregarding caution.

Anger flooded through my body at the thought of Raphael marking me. It was my fault for playing with something I didn't understand. I just didn't know what I was doing at the time. I hadn't even realized but I had stopped everything I was working on, and I was standing there reeling in anger. This wasn't just anger, it was deeper. It seeped into my very essence, settling deep within my core. Here, it simmered with a ferocious intensity, poised to erupt at any moment.

Raziel materialized in front of me and grabbed my shoulders. "Rayne, are you ok? What happened?" He said, with an exasperated breath. I saw his face, again worry flooded over him, and again, The Darkness flooded over me. But this time, rather than filling the void with The Darkness to keep my composure, it was like the darkness fueled my rage. Like it was just there, egging me on, begging me to take my anger out on someone... on the person who hurt me.

It was a sinister whisper in my ear, tempting me to surrender to my basest instincts and indulge in a vengeful frenzy. I felt a sudden rush of confidence but this time it was stronger, pulsing through my veins with an insistent need to obey. Every fiber of my being at that minute wanted nothing more than to materialize to Raphael and make him pay for what he did to me.

To make him pay for forcing me to use The Shadows... for making me give up my mate bond. Giving up my mate bond was second, only to the ultimate sacrifice, that's how I was feeling. The emotional turmoil was so intense that I crumpled to my knees, overcome by the sheer force of my emotions. As I closed my eyes, I could feel the anger and hurt coursing through my veins like a vortex, threatening to consume me whole. I felt like I was drowning in a sea of pain, my consciousness slipping away with each passing moment, as if the sheer force of my emotions would short circuit my very existence... and then I heard it. The Darkness, it was speaking to me.

"Rayne, get up. You are strong, get up on your feet!" It shot. Alarmed at the tone The Darkness had used, I did as directed. I stood back up to my feet. "Good. Now you have a choice. You can let the anger take over you, as it just did... or, you can let the anger fuel you, as it previously was." I compared the two instances in my mind.

"Feed off the anger, feed off the rush, and use it to make those who harmed you pay!" The Darkness exclaimed. I could feel the icy warmth rushing through my veins. It was shuddering as if it were excited. This was something I had seen The Shadows do before, and I wondered just how similar The Darkness and The Shadows truly were.

"All you have to do is let me in, I can help you." It said. I was suddenly jolted out of my trance-like state, my mind snapped back to reality when I realized Raziel had me in his arms. Apparently, I did pass out, because he was lightly smacking my face.

"What... what happened?" I asked softly, still somewhat confused. "You passed out. Are you ok, how do you feel?" Raziel exclaimed, worry was ringing clear in his voice. "I'm fine. I just worked too hard... I think. I'll be fine, I just need to sit down for a minute." I said, as I got up out of Raziel's arms. This was much to my marks dismay, of course.

I went and sat up on the bench that was nearby. My head was swirling with everything The Darkness had just said. 'All you have to do is let me in.' Wasn't The Darkness already in? I was so confused but I shook it off. Confused or not, The Darkness wasn't going to train for me.

I got up, brushed myself off, and got back into training. I was determined to master my abilities and learn to control them. Then I would deal with Alpha Drake, and Raphael. Even saying his name made my whole body shudder. The icy warmth instantly washed over me like a soothing blanket, confirming my intentions.

There was no doubt in my mind that Raphael was going to fucking pay for what he did

Chapter 45

I wasn't asleep, but I was lying in bed with my eyes open. I was realizing for the first time that the underside of the top of the canopy on Raziel's bed was peppered with small gold flakes that almost resemble stars. I had been on his bed multiple times, but never once had I looked up and truly paid attention to the fine details. Yes, I was more distracting myself from the void that I could already feel beginning to creep back in. It wasn't until my phone went off that I truly succeeded in that distraction.

'I'll be there in an hour to get you for this vigil.' Brett wrote.

I groaned out loud because I had completely forgotten about it, and secretly, I hoped he had too. I couldn't be so lucky. "What is it, darling?" Raziel purred, rolling over and wrapping his arm around my waist. "It's just Brett is going to be here in an hour to get me so we can go to Eric's vigil. He's making me come, saying that my absence would be weird to the Humans given mine and Eric's relationship." I huffed, reciting words Brett had previously said to me.

"I hate to say it, but the Humans are right. It would be strange for you not to show up." Raziel replied. I gave him a side eye that he couldn't see. I couldn't believe the sheer audacity of him to agree with the Humans. "This is your fault, you know." I scoffed.

That got his attention. He moved his arm off of me and used it to prop himself up. His golden eyes met mine and a sly smile crept onto his lips. "My fault? You think that this mess you're in with Eric, is *my* fault?" He hummed. By the look on his face I had the feeling that I had already lost this argument and we hadn't even started it. I decided to try and prove my point anyway. "Yes I do! *You* killed him... If you hadn't kill..." I started, but was cut off by his finger to my lips. "Let me correct that sentence for you. If *you* hadn't been allowing him to place his lips on *my* property, and in places they didn't fucking belong, then I wouldn't have taken them from him... along with his life." He growled.

I glared at him while he smirked. "You have to take responsibility for your actions!" I scoffed. "Do I though? As inhumane as you think the act was, you know I'm right, darling. I will admit that I may have overreacted, a tiny bit. But you are the entire reason I even cared what a measly Human boy was doing to begin with. Had he not touched what is mine he would still have his life. You can be upset all you want, but he deserved it and I will not apologize for it." I rolled my eyes at him and then attempted to get out of bed. He pulled me back by my wrist and pinned me down underneath him. I gasped as he placed his hands over both of my wrists and yanked them above my head.

The mark exploded with lightning and cool fire at his touch. It coursed through my veins and settled deep within my bones.

"You are *mine*, Rayne. You belong to me. You have *always* belonged to me, and I will not share." He growled, before roughly taking my lips in his. The sheer ecstasy of approval radiating from my mark had wetness dripping through my panties. I pulled him to me and deepened our kiss, allowing his tongue access. I smiled against his lips as he drug his teeth across the bottom of mine. I smiled, pulling my lip from his teeth before smashing my lips back into his.

I moaned out in the most seductive way I possibly could hoping he would take this much, much further. "Rayne." He warned, the word vibrated against my swollen bottom lip but I didn't stop. Threading my hand through his hair I pulled him down closer to me. He allowed it, and slipped his hand underneath the small of my back. I took advantage of the position and pressed my hips up into his leg. "You will be the death of me." He growled, before materializing away from me.

I giggled knowing he didn't want to stop but I had to get ready to go. After he devoured me with his eyes and effectively avoided taking me right then and there, even with my shirt completely off, I gave up. "Fine." I fakely pouted, before getting off the bed. He made a sound as I walked past him but he resisted the urge to reach out. I kept walking and didn't look back until I was in the bathroom with the door shut behind me.

I exhaled as Wynter lost her shit in my mind. "Ok, ok, maybe you were right about him... a little." I said, as the hot water ran over my face. "Of course I was! What do you take me for?" Wynter replied. She sounded almost offended that I would even question her. "Hey, you haven't always led me in the right direction, ok. Mostly, yes, but not always. I had a right to doubt your opinion." I replied. She laughed.

The shower was quick, with the hottest water I could handle, as if the heat would wash away the guilt that was creeping into my chest. I had to go to this vigil, knowing that Eric's death was mostly my fault, and I had to act like I missed him. I had to keep a straight face, even after everything he did... the thought made me want to vomit, but I knew this was necessary.

The nausea soon turned to tears that fell unnoticed under the water streaming down my face. I wanted so badly to rip the tear ducts from my eyes so I never had to shed another tear for this man. I could feel the void beginning to creep in and I knew I wouldn't be able to hold it off for long if I didn't distract from it right now.

The outfit Raziel had laid out for me was perfect for a vigil. A medium length black pencil dress with a slit up the right side. It had an asymmetrical neckline with cutoff sleeves. It was simple and would give off the right impression. Paired with the soft black flats that were on the ground by the end of the bed, it was perfect.

Once dressed, I blow dried my hair pin straight and the moment I walked out of the bedroom Brett pulled up. It was perfect timing. Raziel met me at the door and walked me out. As I got into the passenger side of Brett's car I heard part of their conversation. "If she comes back with a singular hair out of place, I'll have your head." Brett made an uncomfortable sound while trying to clear his throat. "Understood." Was all he replied before he got in and closed the door. "He's fucking intense." Brett said as we headed out.

~

(Raziel)

I couldn't help but worry about Rayne. Something was different about her ever since she lost her mate bond. There were times when she was perfectly fine. When she seemed normal, like her old self. Then there were times when I could feel something, something dark. Like a darker energy trying to push its way through her.

I had never encountered this before, but when making deals with The Shadows you never know what you will really get. I could only assume they took much more than she bargained for. I tried my best to conceal my worry, but every time it threatened to take over, I could see it in her platinum eyes. She didn't know, but there was a tell tale sign. A dark, serpentine smoke. It seeped in, flooding her platinum orbs slow and snake-like, shrouding them until they were eclipsed. The sight always worried me.

I was torn from my thoughts as I watched the Black Audi R8 back out of my driveway and speed down the road in the opposite direction. I fought the urge to materialize in front of them and force him to slow down with Rayne in the car, but I refrained. "She will be fine." Nero said, but I could hear the unease floating through his voice. Neither of us liked her in anyone else's care.

She was not happy with me making her go to the Human boys vigil, but she needed to save face and this was the only way. Sure, I may have exasperated this entire

311

mess, but that will teach her to disobey me. I chuckled internally at the thought. Maybe I was just as fucked up as she thought I was.

I had a few things to complete today and hoped that it would distract me from worrying about Rayne. Not that I didn't trust the Human/Wolf Hybrid that I allowed her to leave with, but... no, that's a lie. I didn't trust him as far as I could throw him. Even knowing that he is the son of Aries, the Wolf that is close with my brother. For that small fact I may have a different outlook... *if* he didn't currently have possession of something that belongs to me.

"Go get her, Raziel. Fuck the Humans and their perceptions. They will be long gone and we will still be here, living and thriving. Who cares what they think?" Nero growled.

I shook my head at my Wolf, even though he had a very valid point. The short time in which a Human lives in this world is but a mere speck in the whole of things. 70 to 100 years to make an impression and then be forgotten forever... that, versus our infinite lives was nothing. Had I not been such a prideful person, I would have materialized and snatched her from the car while it was in motion.

However, I made such a big deal of this, making her go... I couldn't go back on my word now, and what? Look weak? Not a fucking chance. She would have to survive this on her own.

The afternoon passed by slowly, just as I expected it would. Time always seemed to when I wasn't watching my prize. I had made it to my 7th Coven, and was just about to walk through the main doors to meet up with my Priest, when I felt the familiar tingle of Rayne using magic. Confusion riddled my face. She was surrounded by Humans, this should be the last place she should be using magic.

I materialized to her location and we locked eyes from across the field where the vigil was being held. Tears were streaming down her face and it only took me about 3 seconds to realize the extent of the damage which she had done. I remained calm as I surveyed the area. Multiple trees, their trunks snapped like twigs, lay shattered with their branches strewn across the grassy expanse. The once beautiful pavilion, formerly a proud centerpiece that stood strong in the middle of the clearing, was reduced to splintered beams of wood and twisted bars of iron.

To the left of the shattered pavilion a massive crater yawned open, its edges charred and blackened as if a ball of fire had engulfed it only moments prior. Tendrils of wispy smoke floated upwards, dissipating into the sky. Humans were screaming and crying, holding their injured family members and friends.

I looked down at Rayne's feet to see her friend, Jae, lying lifeless with blood running from her nose and mouth. Her only error? Being far too close to the epicenter of the damage. To the right of her I could see the once proud and cocky Wolf/Human Hybrid.

He suffered a similar fate, but he was breathing, albeit barely. The multitudes of Humans either covered in blood on the ground, or running around in a complete panic, was enough to drive any sane man to drink. And even through all of this, my only concern was Rayne and how she looked so emotionless… so unconcerned. Had it not been for the tears steadily streaming down her cheeks I would have thought she had only walked up onto this horrific scene and wasn't the ultimate cause of it.

Instinct had me wanting to mind link my brothers, but my rational mind told me I needed to handle this myself. I refused to have a single one of them tell me, 'I told you so.' I'm much too prideful to allow that. I snapped and froze the entire park. Every single Human was instantly still. The chatter ceased, and an eerie silence engulfed me, wrapping its tendrils through my mind. The peaceful silence settled deep within my chest, like a very welcome summer breeze.

"Anthony, I need you and only you, now." I said calmly, keeping an eye on Rayne as I mind linked my second in command. He appeared before me within seconds. It was mere moments before he realized just what kind of mess we were in. "Sir?" He said. I just nodded, he knew what needed to be done. Fixing the trees, pavilion, and crater deep within the earth were the easy parts. It was covering up the multiple deaths, and replacing the Humans' memory of this specific event that was going to take more time. It wasn't impossible and it could have been worse. We were lucky it was contained to only this park and these specific Humans.

I let Anthony begin as I walked over to Rayne and put my finger under her chin, forcing her to look up at me. As I figured, the haunting black smoke was softly curling around her silver orbs. Though I found it strange that her face showed absolutely no emotion, even as her friend, whom I knew she cared for, if only a little, lay lifeless at her feet.

This sheer lack of emotion made me uncomfortable. I knew she wasn't ok, but I had no idea how to fix this. I shook my head trying to clear the worry as I put my pointer and middle finger on her forehead, catching her before she hit the ground.

Chapter 46

~
(Rayne)

Red, that was the only thing I could see. The anger, it was so much... too much. Betrayal, that was the one and only emotion coursing through my veins. The words Eric had said to me that night floated through my head. The way he had manhandled me, trying to force himself on me. And here I was, pretending to care that he was dead. He fucking deserved it and we all knew it.

I knew that his family was faking it just as much as I was. I could tell in the way they held themselves and in the words they carefully crafted when speaking his name. The audacity of his mother to ask me to speak on his behalf. Me, the woman he said he loved, yet would have raped without a second fucking thought. The woman he treated like a sidewalk whore...

The anger grew within my chest, spewing from the cage I tried so desperately to lock it into. I had kept to myself, remained visible, and ensured to look distraught. I hugged people and spoke so highly of Eric. Everything Brett and I had spoken about, but none of that was going to save me, or anyone at this vigil. Not when I was this upset.

The strange thing about it? I didn't even feel the magic until it was too late. It wasn't until trees were shattered, metal was groaning and bending, and the very earth below us was shooting 100 feet into the air, did I realize that I was the cause of this... of all of this.

And when Jae tried to stop me, I stopped her. And when Brett tried to help her, I stopped him too. And others... but the worst part? I felt *vindicated* doing it. I felt like they *all* deserved it for being part of his life, for not warning me of the type of pig he was, for not helping me. When Raziel showed up it changed absolutely nothing. The utter rage coursing through my veins wasn't satiated and I felt that maybe it never would be.

My thoughts were feral and rabid, as if I were foaming at the mouth. I would kill him too, if I was able… and maybe I was now. Cold and lifeless, that is how I would explain the emptiness inside of my chest. The void with its tentacles of darkness crept its way back up and completely engulfed me in its barbed snare.

For a brief second, the icy warmth flooded into my chest, forcing the void back down to the depths of my shattered mind. Strength coursed through me, snapping me from my void ridden state, but it was too late.

I looked around briefly in horror as I realized that the damage had already been done. There was no saving this, no fixing this… I looked down at Jae lying lifeless at my feet and I wanted to vomit. Anger returned to my chest full force, but it wasn't the void this time. I was angry at myself for what I had done, what I had allowed to happen.

So many emotions were coursing through my veins but I was in shock so badly that I couldn't even figure out how to show a single one of them. A blank stare, that's all that I could muster while I completely shattered on the inside. I felt Raziel touch my forehead and before I could register what he had done the black circles within my vision engulfed me.

My eyes fluttered open and I groaned as I came to and realized that my head was absolutely fucking pounding. I couldn't even keep my eyes open due to the severe brightness of the lights around me. I squeezed my eyes shut immediately, forcing the pillow next to me over my face.

I heard footsteps and pulled the pillow off my face just enough to peek out with one eye cracked. My beating heart stilled when I realized it wasn't Raziel. "How is your head?"

316

Anthony asked. I pulled the pillow back over my eyes and groaned out loud. "It's fucking killing me. What happened?" I asked. I heard him pull a chair up and assumed that he took a seat. "That isn't important, what do you remember?" He replied. I racked my brain trying to think back but I was drawing a blank.

"I… I don't know. I… ugh, this headache." I groaned, pushing the pillow even further into my face, if that was even possible. "Here, let me." Anthony said, pulling the pillow from my face. He put his hand over my eyes and I felt a slight tingle before the raging migraine dissipated. I exhaled out loud as I opened my eyes. "Better?" He asked. "Yes, thank you." I replied.

"Now, what do you remember?" Anthony asked me again. I thought it was strange that Raziel wasn't here. "Where is Raziel?" I asked. "Rayne, this is important." Anthony said a bit sternly causing me to focus back on him. I had never really looked at him this closely. He was very attractive with his dark hair cut short and neat, and a crescent moon tattooed on the side of his face. I followed the vines as they disappeared below his shirt.

I thought his tattoo resembled a Reaver mark, but I wasn't sure what his actual mark even looked like. His dark, bronze eyes narrowed on me making me feel very small in this large bed. I looked away from him and up at the ceiling, trying to remember anything from before this very moment.

"I… I remember getting ready for the vigil. I was in a car, oh, yes, I left with Brett. He drove me and Jae there. And then…" I stammered, before memories slammed into my mind like a tidal wave. Jae and I were laughing on the way there over something stupid Brett had said. He looked back at me in the backseat with a cheesy grin but he was going too fast, and the turn was too sharp.

Panic clawed through my chest as fragmented memories flashed through my mind. The car's relentless rollover left me confused. I vaguely remembered the sickening crunch of my head as it slammed into the side panel of the door, followed by a cold darkness. When I came to, I was upside down, struggling to free myself from the seatbelt. Brett was still in the car, his breathing labored and shallow. Jae was nowhere to be seen.

My memories blurred as I fell from the seat and frantically tried to pry open the mangled door next to me, but it refused to budge. Even with my enhanced strength it wasn't moving. My nostrils burned with the scent of blood, a gruesome, coppery smell, that etched itself into my consciousness. It was overwhelming.

Black spots began to form in my eyes as I fought to keep my eyes open, but that was all I remember before I succumbed to my own injuries. As the memories impeded my mind my breathing became more erratic. I looked up at Anthony.

"Where is Jae?" It was the only thing on my mind as I don't remember seeing her in the aftermath of the accident. Anthony's face remained stoic and calm, giving me false hope that she was ok. "Rayne, she didn't make it."

His words were soft and careful but it didn't do anything to quell the pain that sunk its sharpened teeth straight into my heart. Blood, even more gruesome than what I remember from the accident, filled my chest and gave the illusion that I was suffocating. Tears streamed down my face as I tried to come to terms with my loss. She was the only Human I actually enjoyed spending time with, and now I would never see her, hug her, speak to her... ever again.

"Rayne?" Raziel said, pulling me from my inner turmoil. I looked up at the god-like man standing before me with tear stained cheeks. I hadn't even heard him come in. He sat down on the bed next to me and pulled me into his arms while I cried.

~

(Raziel)

I felt guilty as fuck but I couldn't allow her to know the truth, not yet. In her fragile, yet extremely volatile state,

318

there was no telling how much more damage she would inflict. This outburst seemed to be contained, somewhat, and while not easy to clean up, it was doable. Next time I may not be able to fix it.

I refused to allow her to attend the funeral of her friend or Eric, not telling her that not one of Eric's family or friends even remembers her. I made sure to take every single memory they ever had. No one would even realize she existed.

And though she was very upset about Jae's, she understood. I had her thinking that I was worried about another 'accident'. Another guilty moment for me as I pushed my agenda into her fragile little head, explained just how important she was to me, and how she wasn't immortal like I am. She can be killed, just like any other Reaver. Shit move, I know… but I used it to my advantage. I had no other choice if I wanted to repair what was left of her fragile psyche.

As the weeks passed and we trained, she seemed to heal from losing her friend. I knew that pain would pass, and I also knew that someday I would have to reveal the truth, and the pain would come back tenfold. She would probably hate me for lying to her too, but for now, I was more worried about her mental state and the effect it would have on her unbridled powers.

She was progressing amazingly with her Reaver abilities though. I was impressed, and honestly I wasn't sure what I expected. I thought maybe she would lose control more often. Even seeing the destruction with my own eyes, I was starting to doubt the fact that her unbridled magic was really as much of a danger as we had expected for all of these years. One mishap over 3 months? Was this possibly the start of a new branch?

I recognized Rayne's exceptional nature the instant I met her. I knew what she was and I knew she wasn't in a Coven. I never worried that she would develop powers. In fact, I never even thought twice about it. There was absolutely no way I could have known. Not a tick or tale to

319

be found. I had a sense that she was destined for greatness, and that her life would eventually be filled with remarkable achievements.

But I never thought we would be here, doing this very thing... me training her to control her powers so she doesn't spontaneously combust and kill us all. And all of this under my brother's noses. I shook the thoughts and focused back on the not so fragile woman I called mine. She had been focusing extremely hard the past few months and keeping busy in her training.

I was impressed with her drive to succeed. I thought it was good for her to get a distraction, something to focus on rather than Raphael and losing her mate bond. Training this intensely, seemed to be doing well keeping her mind off it. I had thought that not seeing him for this long would have helped her to heal, but I never quite felt that she was truly over what he had done.

There were times, though, that I could see her starting to get an empty look in her eyes. It was like she was there, but she wasn't really there. Like she was somewhere else in her mind, but her body was still here, sort of. Those are the times when the black smoke flooded into her eyes. And immediately after it did, she snapped back to reality and continued working. The black smoke is what I was most worried about.

There's no telling what it could be, or what it could end up being... I was snapped from my internal chatter when I noticed Rayne had stopped training and she was just kind of standing there for a second. She then fell straight to her knees. I rushed to her side immediately. I looked into her eyes and they were completely black, which was very different from what they usually do. Then she just passed out. I panicked, and grabbed her before she hit the ground.

I was holding her in my arms, shaking her, trying to get her to wake up but she was not responsive at all. I turned on my Vampire hearing which I did not use often, too many noises to tune out, but I made an exception and used it to listen closer. I could hear her heartbeat. It was slow and steady, matching her breathing. So she was alive, and she wasn't in distress either. She was just... unconscious? That didn't make any sense to me. Why would she just lose consciousness out of nowhere?

I slapped her face softly trying to wake her, and the panic was really starting to set in until she finally started moving in my arms. "What... what happened?" She asked softly. "You passed out. Are you ok, how do you feel?" I exclaimed. I tried to keep the worry from my voice, but it was crystal clear.

"I'm fine, I just worked too hard, I think. I'll be fine, I just need to sit for a minute." She said, but I could tell she was weary of the situation she found herself in. She seemed like she was not quite sure how she got there, and that made two of us. She got up and climbed out of my arms, then walked over and sat on the silver bench.

She sat there for just a minute. I could see an internal battle in her facial expression, but Wynter wasn't speaking, so I had no idea what she was experiencing. She then got up, brushed herself off, and got right back to training.

Every thought possible was going through my mind. Had she called The Shadows? No, that's impossible. I've been with her the entire time since she'd lost her mate bond, she'd never called them. I couldn't fathom just what she may have done to cause her eyes to cloud over with that black smoke. And when they went solid black, that was absolutely terrifying.

I think she is playing with something she shouldn't be, and not knowing what it was, was killing me. I was so worried about her, and lost in my own crazy thoughts, that I didn't even realize she was talking to me until she materialized right in front of me.

"Oh my God, Rayne! You didn't even stumble that time! You materialized, and it was as if you were already here! You did it!" I exclaimed. Her face lit up with joy! She started jumping up and down screaming, which made me laugh, and for a second, I forgot why I was even so worried to begin with.

Chapter 47

~
(Rayne)

"I did it!!! I did it! Yessssss!!!!!!" I exclaimed, while jumping up and down in place. I had been practicing that for months, and this was the first time I hadn't stumbled when I did it. I was finally getting better. I was feeling stronger and more in control. I felt the icy warmth wash over me as if in approval of my progress. This is exactly what I was planning on. I needed the control. I needed to be able to control my abilities. Mostly for myself, and of course, my vendetta for revenge. But also, because it was my birthright. Being a Reaver, I fucking deserve to have these abilities. Those thoughts startled me for a second. That was The Darkness talking, and I knew it.

All of my newfound confidence and cockiness was The Darkness. I can't say I didn't like the feeling, though. It was doing more than just filling the void in my heart and soul. I felt powerful and magnificent, like a Goddess when The Darkness was with me. Who wouldn't want to feel this way all the time? Wynter hadn't said much since we lost our mate bond.

I know she appreciated The Darkness filling the void, but she wasn't ready to move on yet. She was still mourning the loss of our future mate, and the bond. I assumed it was always harder on your Wolf when something like this happens, and I could only do so much. I was there for her, and just let her know when she was ready, I would still be here. She had recessed to the back of my mind more often than I'd like to admit, and I guess The Darkness helped fill her void as well.

As the days went on of training and learning, I was getting used to the quiet in my mind. Something I hadn't had since I was 15. I rarely had quiet after I turned and Wynter came to the forefront of my mind. It was as if the quiet helped The Darkness grow. I hadn't spoken a word about The Darkness to anyone still, not even Raziel.

I realized I wasn't crazy, and The Darkness was real, but I didn't care if it was dangerous. Without it, I was nothing. I was weak, with a void and an insatiable sadness. I refused to be weak... to be that girl who couldn't protect herself. I needed The Darkness... and in the past week I had learned how to call The Darkness when I needed it, rather than waiting for it to find me.

I could tell that Raziel had no idea what was going on, but he could tell there was something. I could tell by the way he looked at me sometimes. The worry in his face gave him away. He did his best to push it away and support me no matter what, but he could tell something was off and he didn't like it. It made me feel guilty, hiding things from him. But how was I supposed to tell him? I wasn't even sure what I was getting into myself.

I didn't deserve him, though. He was loyal to a fault, always right at my side if I needed him. He wasn't prying or pushy and did not force me to talk if I didn't want to. He was a damn godsend and that just made my guilt even worse. I had to continually push it from my mind and ignore it. The Darkness also helped me numb the effects of the mark when I wanted so I could focus. I couldn't have my feelings for Raziel getting in the way of my training. Plus, I knew he wasn't ready to make the mark permanent yet, he said so himself.

It had already faded completely twice, and I made him re-mark me. It was halfway gone again now anyway. I was sure I wanted him, wanted this mark. I just wasn't about to let anyone else have the chance of marking me again. This is why I made him keep marking me once it faded. I wanted the mark to be permanent, but he wasn't ready yet. I wondered what his hold up was, but never bothered to ask. I had been so busy dealing with training and The Darkness, that it wasn't really at the forefront of my mind.

What was though, was the fact that some parts of me were different now thanks to The Darkness. Some parts of me I now reveled in. Others? I wasn't so sure about, but I seemed to be getting used to the new me. I was feeling rather confident in my abilities at this point. I decided it was time to make a trip back to my pack and speak with my Alpha. It had been about 2 months since everything happened, and I hadn't said a single word to him since.

Honestly, I didn't care if I ever did, but he wasn't going to get off scot free... hell no. He would pay for his part and I was going to make damn sure of it. I waited until Raziel left for his Coven meeting and then I got up and got ready for the day. I had big plans today. Oh, trust me, I had huge plans, actually.

I was careful to make sure Raziel didn't notice anything different. I couldn't have him asking me any questions. I always had trouble lying to him. It would just be better if I didn't even have to. I did one last mirror check before I materialized to Alpha Drake. He was sitting, alone, in his office, mulling over some papers.

He was wearing only a pair of red gym shorts without a shirt. His hair was messy as if he had been running his hand through it recently. I couldn't help but notice his perfectly olive colored skin was reflecting every muscle that rippled down his chest and arms in the glow from his desk lamp. He had a glass of brandy on his desk, but it looked like he hadn't touched it.

The ball of ice in the middle was halfway melted causing the honey colored liquid in his glass to be a bit translucent. He looked up at me and we locked eyes. He didn't move a muscle, but I could see a slight flicker of emotion dance across his brow.

Confusion first, then curiosity, followed by fear mixed with desire. He was a conundrum in and of himself, and I

324

knew exactly how I made him feel. You'd be wrong if you thought I didn't dress up for this. Oh, I can assure you, I definitely did. I was wearing a black mini skirt, with thigh high black and silver boots. I had a silver crop top hoodie that almost showed my breasts when I put my arms up, but stopped just before it did, as a tease. I had my hair down in those beachy waves which I knew he loved.

I knew Alpha Drake's feelings for me, and I decided it would make it that much more satisfying to toy with him... just like he's been toying with me all these years. This entire idea was thanks to The Darkness, of course. Once I learned to call The Darkness forward, I realized we could communicate, much like myself and Wynter used to.

She was still hibernating, and with such a devastating loss, I wasn't sure that she would ever recover. I was still pretty upset about her absence, but The Darkness did an alright job of replacing her. It wasn't the same, really, but it would have to do. I just hoped Wynter would come around, eventually.

"Alpha'.' I said coldly. He stood from his chair and I followed his gaze. His large stature was casting a towering shadow onto the desk as he took a step towards me. "Rayne." He replied, less cold than I, but still cold. This was how we were, always cold to each other, always throwing tension back and forth like a softball.

I could see him eyeing my figure, which made The Darkness revel. Our plan was working. The Darkness was writhing around me, anticipating my next move. I had him exactly where I wanted him at this moment.

Just the sound of his voice made my blood boil, even after all of this time. Flashbacks of that night came racing through my mind. Alpha Drake apologizing. His gaze filled with sorrow. I saw the regret flooding through his eyes and dancing along his face when he spoke.

I remembered the tear I saw fall from his cheek, and his little sister Reya. I remember him fucking throwing me, basically, directly into Raphael's goddamn arms. The memories incited rage which fueled me... fueled us. I called

The Darkness forward and reveled in the icy warmth it showered over me.

The memories were playing over and over in my mind, and they just continued to fuel my rage... which ultimately continued to feed The Darkness. "Can I help you?" Alpha Drake snapped, and that was all it took for me to come undone.

Before Alpha Drake even knew what hit him, I had him by the throat and slammed him up against his office wall. I could hear his men scrambling to get to the door once they heard the sounds of a struggle emanating from within.

With one big sweep of my hand I used magic to slide his desk, and everything else in his office, in front of the door. That would keep them out. I looked back, and locked eyes with Alpha Drake. While his face was still solemn and he wasn't moving a muscle under my grip, I could see the fear burning within his expression.

"You didn't think you would get away with it did you?" I snarled. My face was inches away from his. The Darkness continued to fuel me as much as I was fueling it. "My fucking god Rayne, you are sexy as fuck right now." He growled under his breath. I could feel the lust rolling off him in sickening waves.

My mark started burning like hellfire at his advance. "Am I? Oh, I hadn't noticed." I replied. I then brushed my lips against his ever so slightly. I could feel his body tense at my interaction. Good, this is exactly what I wanted. I wanted him to want me. I wanted him to want me so badly that it physically hurt.

Then just when he thought I was going to give in, and ultimately give him what he wanted, I was going to fucking kill him. I used my other hand to run my finger down the side of Alpha Drake's face. He'd done this to me so many times before.

I used my thumb to pull his bottom lip down a little. Another move I'd stolen from his playbook. The Darkness was using my own memories to guide me. We had been in this position many times before, always with him as the antagonizer. Well, it was my fucking turn now. I could tell by his eyes Alpha Drake was scared as fuck, but he was also extremely turned on. I placed my other hand on my Alphas inner thigh, just close enough to his, now hard cock, and squeezed tightly. I felt his whole body tense up.

I could practically hear him begging me for more. Then I moved my hand and placed it on the center of his chest. I could feel his heart beating out of control, and just before I could reach in there and fucking rip it clean out of his chest, I was suddenly engulfed in a green flame.

"Rayne, no!" Raziel shouted. *Son of a bitch.* I thought. He succeeded in getting me away from Alpha Drake, but he couldn't keep me contained. Feeling the icy warmth of The Darkness I threw my arms down and out to both sides. This destroyed Raziel's fireball, and released myself, allowing me to land gracefully in front of him on one knee.

I looked up and locked eyes with Raziel. My mark erupted in a frenzy of euphoric sensation with his proximity. I took a second to admire him, taking in every feature. He was fucking magnificent looking, standing there in a fiery blaze of glory. He was furious, and I mean fucking furious. I couldn't help but think he looked like a fucking God. One worthy to stand by my side, with his tousled golden blonde hair, and his powerful stance. The *only* man who would ever be worthy of my affection.

I was still fucking pissed, but he was equally pissed. The Darkness was feeding off my anger, begging me to make another move. I looked back at Alpha Drake and then returned my fiery gaze to Raziel and we locked eyes. I could see a small hint of fear dancing along his irises. Destroying his fireball was something he didn't know I could do. I knew I was going to get drilled about it later, but I didn't care. I stood up and faced the God standing before me.

"He deserves everything he fucking gets." I spat through gritted teeth trying to justify my actions. I could feel The Darkness swirling around me like a tornado as I spoke.

Sucking me in, and egging me on, with every ounce of hostility in the room feeding the unruly whirlwind. "He had no choice, Rayne!" Raziel shouted. I turned my glare to my Alpha. "You ALWAYS have a choice." I spewed. It was clear that I was on the verge of an explosion at this point.

"Did you?" Raziel asked, as he narrowed his eyes at me. I turned and looked back at him, then stopped for a minute and thought about it. God damnit, why does he always have to be right? "I don't care!! He doesn't know what I lost. He doesn't know what happened!" I snapped at Raziel. My confidence was starting to dwindle. I knew I was losing this battle, but I didn't want to admit it.

"I know Rayne, I know. But he was forced, just like you were. You don't have to do this." Raziel pleaded. His voice was like molten gold, healing my every ailment and chasing The Darkness from my mind. He closed the gap between us and took my face in his hands.

The instant his skin made contact with mine, my mark detonated in a blaze of euphoria, triggering an uncontrollable response as a bolt of electric sensation seared through my entire being. I hadn't used The Darkness to dim the fire from his mark because I didn't actually think he would follow me here. I closed my eyes, and I could feel The Darkness slowly dissipating. I knew Raziel was my safe space, and he could calm The Darkness. He always did, even if he didn't know what he was doing.

No! I need The Darkness. My thoughts were more like screams, and the internal battle between Raziel's mark and The Darkness felt like the cataclysmic clash of fire and ice. Heat versus the cold pulsing and coursing through my veins. The mixture of temperatures was ravaging my already weakened body, bringing me straight to my breaking point.

I stepped out of the comfort of Raziel's grip, threw my arms down and out to my sides again, and screamed as loudly as I possibly could. The Darkness reveled in my release. The extreme energy pushed everything in its path, including Alpha Drake and Raziel, across the room and into the adjacent wall. They both looked up at me from the floor where they lay in a crumpled mess. Pure, unadulterated shock flooded both of their gazes. I felt the icy warmth wash over me again, reassuring me that I was in the right, and that was a deserved action.

"You're fucking lucky, Wolf." I spat, not caring that I also was considered a Wolf my entire life, and then I turned to leave. But before I could materialize away, my legs buckled, sending me crashing to my knees as a debilitating dizziness seized my head.

The telltale signs of impending unconsciousness began to manifest. Black spots danced across my field of vision, and my surroundings began to blur and fade. Then I heard The Darkness. "You can do so much more Rayne, so much more with our power."

"I know, I have been practicing, I'm learning." I replied. My voice cracked as I spoke, and it was then that I realized just how scared I really was of The Darkness. Terrified even, but I had to pretend that I wasn't afraid because I needed it, whatever it was.

"If you just let me in, I will take the reins, you just have to say it." The Darkness said. I could feel the icy warmth leaving my grace, sending me into an empty void, a pit of despair and longing.

A feeling I had been trying so hard to escape these past months. I felt like I was drowning, being sucked down through an abyss of agony with no one to help me out. I had been doing anything I could to get away from the emptiness, the pain. I had been focusing on training, focusing on The Darkness, plotting my revenge, staying extremely busy. Too busy even, but I knew deep down that I would never get away from this feeling. Not truly.

I had no other choice if I wanted to be able to maintain my composure ever again. Another rush of agony and emptiness engulfed me. It was like withdrawal, but worse. So much worse. The pain was like a living, breathing entity, writhing inside of me like a serpent, refusing to release its deadly grip. This is what I had to look forward to, this is what I would have to deal with every day for the rest of my life…

I called for Wynter, but she wasn't there. Tears began to form in my eyes as I realized that I was completely and utterly alone.

Nothing else mattered to me in that moment except my freedom from the looming agony that threatened to take over my body and soul.

"I accept." I said.

Chapter 48

*I*n an instant, I was enveloped by The Darkness. I felt myself being lifted off the ground, suspended midair, as a swirling vortex of dark smoke encircled me. The Darkness wrapped around me like a shroud, its icy warmth seeping into my very being, threatening to consume me whole. I closed my eyes and took in every ounce of the icy warmth, feeling it remove any remnant of the void I had once felt. This time the icy warmth didn't dissipate leaving me gasping for air. No, this time it felt permanent.

I was exhilarated, electrified by an endless surge of power. The dark energy flowed so easily through my palms, and it felt as if anything I wanted, I could have. I felt like a Goddess… no, I *was* a Goddess. Suddenly, I felt the familiar pull away from The Darkness and I regained consciousness as Raziel gently slapped my face. "Rayne, Rayne, come on, wake up!" He spoke with a panicked tone. My eyes fluttered open and Raziel immediately gasped. I could see my reflection in his golden eyes. My eyes were completely black…

I shook it off, and materialized into a standing position, but I realized I wasn't standing, I was floating just above the ground. I looked down at my feet to see a layer of black smoke curling at my feet. It was in between me and the ground. I held my hands out, palms up and manifested 2 black fireballs with ease. These were quite different from my normal green ones. These felt darker, more powerful even.

"Now finish what you started, Rayne!" The Darkness spewed into my mind. I locked eyes with My Alpha. Fear flashed in his gaze, its intensity rippling through his eyes like a hurricane. Regardless, he stood strong and proud, never faltering, as always. I threw both fireballs at Alpha Drake with a slight flick of the wrist. It was effortless. He dodged my attacks and rolled out of the way. He knew how to fight. He trained me and countless others in our pack.

I snickered as the portrait that was on the wall behind Alpha Drake, crashed to the ground. Such a small area for a battle, and I wanted a fucking battle! I flicked my wrist, and transported all 3 of us to the arena where my Alpha had betrayed me. I was surprised at how easily these powers were to control and manipulate. I thought it, and it happened.

I raised my palm and summoned a tumultuous swarm of dark clouds, their thunderous growls and flashes of lightning electrifying the air above us. As the tempest raged on, I couldn't help but feel a thrill of excitement. This storm would undoubtedly make our encounter far more intriguing.

I was floating on my cloud of black smoke, throwing black fireballs at Alpha Drake. He was fast and kept dodging me, but I was relentless and wasn't about to give up. It wasn't until I noticed green fireballs heading my way that I realized that Raziel had joined the fight… against me.

I should have been upset that he chose the wrong side. He should be next to me fighting *for* my cause, not against it. But what he was doing was the least of my worries. It was easy for me to block his fire with a simple wave of my hand. In fact, it felt too easy. He then materialized behind me and put me in a headlock. I know his intentions were pure, he was probably worried for my safety but I didn't care about his reasoning at this point.

I threw my hands down to my sides, and the force of The Darkness sent Raziel hurtling through the air. He materialized to the ground on his feet with a look of utter defeat on his face.

"You can't beat me. I am infinitely stronger than you." I sneered. I hated being like this towards him, but he was getting in my way. He didn't know how much I wanted this… *no*… how much I *needed* this. I snapped and produced a set of silver bladed fans. I snapped again, and sent a sword over to Alpha Drake. I had to make the fight somewhat fair. Before he even picked it up, I closed the gap between us, fans in hand. I jumped into the air, spun around, and sent both fans slicing through Alpha Drake's torso with one fluid movement.

Although the cuts weren't excessively deep, the force of the impact sent blood spraying outward in a wide, crimson arc, splattering everywhere. He started to heal instantly, thanks to his Wolf genes. He picked up the sword and blocked my next fan maneuver, which in turn caused me to throw one of my fans and slice into his arm. I snapped and it appeared back into my hand. My Alpha was good with a sword which is why I gave him one. I loved a challenge.

He stepped in towards me with force, and swung his blade around almost slicing my midsection, but I materialized back a foot and he missed. I was clearly aware this was an unfair fight, but I was having fun. It almost looked like he was too. *Too bad I have to kill him.* I thought. "Rayne, stop this!" Raziel growled, and I could hear the anger in his voice. "Raziel, stay out of this!" I snapped.

I never wanted to talk to him like that, but in the state I was in, I honestly wasn't sure if I could stop myself if he were to get in the way. It wasn't him I was angry with, but collateral damage wasn't out of the realm of possibilities. I was hyper focused on my task, and nothing, not even the great Raziel Kane, was going to get in my way.

I threw my fans to the side, closed the gap between myself and Alpha Drake slamming him into the ground by his throat, just as a huge clap of thunder hit. This was a move he had done on me, many times before. His sword flew from his hand, and I heard bones breaking upon impact. Good thing Wolves heal quickly, this was not going to be a quick process.

"Rayne, I'm so sorry. Please understand I would never hurt you intentionally." Alpha Drake gasped, spitting up blood. I tightened my grip, his words only fueled my rage.

"Rayne, I love you... please forgive me." He stammered. My mark did not appreciate his declaration, burning and seething along the side of my face. This angered me even more.

"You have no idea what I lost, you have no idea what it feels like! The pain, the suffering... the void that I'm feeling every single fucking day." I spat. The fury burning in my eyes was barely visible through the solid black. "Rayne, yes he does, darling." Raziel said, his breath whispering against my ear as he appeared beside me, and rested his hand on my arm.

I still had my hand on Alpha Drake's throat. I shot an icy glare at Raziel, and if looks could kill... he didn't even flinch, he remained calm and stoic as he spoke his next words. "The Shadows killed his mate, Rayne. She was the price for his sister coming back... a life for a life. They killed her, drained her of all the blood in her body. It was slow, and her screams of agony are the last sounds he will ever remember of her. They forced him to watch it. They took her right in front of him." Raziel stated.

A sudden pang of sadness, or was it guilt? Shot through my chest, softening my gaze. I knew exactly how he felt, but in a very different way. It was the void I desperately fought to fill... I wouldn't wish this torment on my worst enemy. I released my Alpha and took a couple of steps back, creating some distance between us.

"What are you doing, Rayne?! Finish this!" The Darkness spat, as another wave of icy warmth swirled around my figure. My face hardened. The Darkness was pushing every instinct in my body, basically begging me to rip my Alphas throat out, but I was fighting like hell to resist the urge. *What the fuck was I doing?*

Reality hit me like a fucking freight train. He was suffering the exact same as I was. Maybe even worse because he witnessed her actual death. But he didn't have The Darkness to help fill his void. He was literally just suffering... alone, in the void. A fate far worse than death. The Darkness was fighting to get to the forefront of my mind, and I continued to fight like hell to push it back out. For a second, I thought I succeeded.

I could feel the icy warmth leaving my body, taking with it all the power and confidence I had gained. But the void was returning. The emptiness, the pain... it all came flooding back like a river. I felt my legs give out, and to my surprise, my Alpha caught me before I hit the floor.

I burst out into tears. I was completely myself again. I could feel no trace of The Darkness at all, just the void, the emptiness. The reminder of my sacrifice swirling in my mind. My shattered mate bond, my loss... the ultimate loss... I laid in Alpha Drake's arms and wept while he tried to console me.

I didn't even deserve his comfort... I almost killed him. But the only real thoughts were internal agony, and the never ending void threatening to suck me under with every ragged breath. My mark was burning furiously at my Alpha's touch, but also tingling due to the proximity of Raziel, who was kneeling right next to us.

I heard Raziel snap, but I wasn't sure why. And after what seemed like hours of weeping, and I literally had no more tears left to cry, I sat up and locked eyes with my Alpha. I could see sorrow and understanding dancing along his face.

"I'm sorry. I don't know what came over me." I said softly, knowing I didn't deserve any of his sympathy. "I deserved it, Rayne. I really did." He said, looking down, before locking eyes with me again. "But I meant every single word. I never would have hurt you intentionally. The last thing I ever wanted was to see you in pain, or to be a part of the cause of it. I may not act like it, but I truly do love you... and I'm always going to." Alpha Drake said softly.

I saw Raziel's body tense at Alpha Drake's words, but he didn't move. It was no secret that Alpha Drake was in love with me.

He made it very known, not caring who was around when he made his numerous advances at me. It was probably the most known fact in the entire pack, I just didn't expect to ever hear him say it out loud. "I know." I finally replied, fully understanding the conviction of his words. I had never seen this side of my Alpha before, and somehow, I felt that his sheer vulnerability only helped to begin to mend our broken relationship.

I was still feeling myself, no sign of The Darkness at all. I crawled from my Alpha's arms and stood up, locking eyes with Raziel. I could see the worry in his face.

My eyes were still solid black in the reflection of his golden orbs. He hesitated briefly, then pulled me into his arms. My mark finally had peace as flashes of pleasure and soothing waves of cool fire coursed through every fiber of my being. I needed this. I needed to feel his arms wrapped around me. It was an intimate action, and it was something I had been neglecting for months now.

"I'm sorry... I'm so sorry, Raziel." I stammered. "We are going to fix this." Raziel said with conviction, ignoring my apology.

Still, a wave of relief washed over me, and I felt some of the stress I had been carrying suddenly melt away. I exhaled slowly, wanting to believe him. But I knew this release of stress was temporary. This wasn't over, not yet.

Chapter 49

After my breakdown Raziel and I went home. I was expecting him to drill me with a million questions about my newfound powers, my black eyes, or anything that had just happened. But to my surprise, he didn't. I knew he wanted to know, and he wanted to ask. I think I was in such a fragile state that he figured it would be better to just let me talk when I was ready. I was thankful for this.

The truth is, I was never going to be ready. How would I explain this? *Oh sorry, I was so sad that The Darkness came to fill the void, and I, like an idiot, agreed to let it in knowing this was a bad idea? Oh, yea and Wynter hasn't been present in my mind in at least 3 months, so I'm just, you know, dealing with this shit alone? I know, I know. I almost killed my Alpha, but The Darkness just makes me feel better, so that makes it ok, right?*

How do you even say that? I wouldn't even know where to begin. Plus, the fact that I had power superior to his… I knew his brothers were afraid of me too. And with him already allowing me to live, when by all the rules he and his brothers had made, I should be dead… he had a lot on the line here with me, and I wasn't making this easy.

I knew we needed to discuss this and maybe he could even help me with it, but I just didn't know how to bring it up. I didn't know how to tell him how stupid I had been when I was vulnerable. I also didn't know how to stop it now that I had already let it in…

While The Darkness wasn't in my mind right now, I could continually feel the icy warmth trying to wash over me. I had to fight to push it away. The void was ever so present though, and sometimes I didn't want to push The Darkness out... I just didn't want to hurt anymore.

I was so lost in a turbulent sea of thoughts and confusion, that I didn't even register Raziel's embrace until my mark burst into radiant life. "I know you're going through a lot right now, darling. Why don't we forget it all for a while?" He purred. His voice was so silky and golden, it sent chills throughout my entire body. How could he be so perfect? I didn't deserve him. Especially not after all I had put him through.

The guilt of this realization singed every single nerve ending in my body. He lightly traced my mark with his fingers and the calming wisps of pleasure that danced along the edges of my skin worked to calm my erratic mind. He looked at me like I was the most beautiful woman in the world. Like he couldn't get enough and being in my presence, holding me in his arms, wasn't and never would even be enough to satiate his need for me.

I hadn't felt the real effects of the mark since I was able to communicate with The Darkness. I was using The Darkness to dim the marks effects so I wouldn't get distracted from my training... and more importantly, my mission to get revenge. I had almost forgotten what it was really like to be marked. I had almost forgotten the unrelenting yearning to be by his side, the unshakeable need to feel his touch, and the deep seated craving for the sense of completion that only he could offer.

I was so insistent that Raziel continued to mark me every time it faded so that Raphael could never mark me again, I had almost forgotten what the entire point of the mark was.

It was a bond. It was a tether linking two souls, in this case mine and Raziel's. For me it was protection, a way to ensure that no one could ever force me into something I wasn't willing to adhere to, ever again. But for him, the mark was important, sacred even. And I was forcing him to use it against his will. The thought sent guilt cascading through my chest. To him, the mark was something you truly didn't fuck around with.

He was not like Raphael, who marked anything he could for any reason. They were two *very* different people, but a lot alike as well. The thought of Raphael had me plunging back into the emptiness of the void until Raziel pressed his lips to mine. His touch sent pleasure reeling through me and pulled me from the void, momentarily.

I had been so distracted this past few months with training I hadn't even taken a minute to appreciate Raziel. Guilt forced its way back into my chest. He was such a perfect addition to my chaotic life. Always there when I needed him, so understanding, never prying or judgmental. He offered unconditional love, always. And here I was, a Darkness filled mess of chaos and anger fueled revenge. Selfishly forcing my foolish agenda on him... and everyone around me.

I needed an escape. I needed to forget about everything, even if it was just for a moment. I reciprocated his kiss, putting my hand into his messy hair and deepening our connection. My mark was going wild, and I let it, no using The Darkness to dampen the effects. I wanted to feel everything, I *needed* to.

I materialized us onto the bed, myself sitting on his lap facing him. Both of my hands were on his face. Our tongues softly explored each other's mouths, as if looking for just another taste of something they had previously missed. We broke from our kiss, and I took his shirt off. He went to move me to a different position, but I, instead, pushed him down on the bed. It was my turn to please him. I scoffed to myself as he laid back, placed both hands behind his head, and smiled at me.

I started kissing my way down his neck and spent time at each of his nipples. I made sure I was biting and sucking on them with just enough pressure to cause them to harden and stay hard. I continued making my way down his chest through his abs to his stomach. I could tell the mark was affecting him as well by the chills running through his body at my every touch. I paused briefly to remove his pants and underwear, then continued onto his inner thighs.

My cheek brushed against his throbbing cock, and I felt it pulse. I could hear his breath sharpen as I made my way to his hardened length, taking it into my mouth a little at first but letting more and more slide in as I went. He was moving in rhythm with me, as I was allowing just what I could handle with each thrust.

His light moans were like ecstasy to my body, courtesy of the mark. He had, at this point, wrapped his hand into my hair, and was guiding me with each movement in rhythm. I had gotten to the point where I had allowed almost all of his length into my throat, only breathing as he pulled out, and I could feel him pulsing with each movement.

"Mmm, just like that." He moaned. I could tell he was getting close. I didn't stop, I kept moving in rhythm with him, using my free hand to pinch his nipples. Within a few seconds of this gesture, I felt him contract and his body started to spasm.

He moaned my name at his release and I was completely awestruck with how he tasted. It was everything I had ever imagined it would be. Sweet, like an over ripened persimmon, which sent pleasure and lightning coursing through me as I swallowed and let him ride the entire orgasm out on his own terms. He slowly moved in and out of my mouth a few more times while pushing the rest of his seed out into my mouth.

He honestly tasted like fucking heaven, and I was surprised that I didn't struggle as much as I thought I might due to his sheer size. Proud of myself I sat up and smiled at him. "Fuck, darling... you're fucking incredible." He purred while pulling me up to lay with him. I put my head on his chest and he put his arm around me.

I was content in our relationship, never having questioned his loyalty or love for me. Even after everything, I was feeling lucky that I would never have to. He kissed the top of my head and traced his fingers along my shoulder and arm. I knew he wanted to ask me about The

340

Darkness but he was keeping it to himself, trying to savor every last moment of ecstasy we had shared. But it was time. I needed to tell him what was going on. I never should have allowed myself to get to this point with The Darkness in the first place… it was time to open up and get help. I was sure as hell going to need it.

"Raziel." I said softly, as I attempted to sit up. He put his finger to my lips, silencing me. We locked eyes and I could see the understanding in his eyes. He knew we needed to talk about this, but he didn't want to ruin the moment.

I smiled and laid back on his shoulder. Just another minute wouldn't hurt, right? But I ended up falling into a deep sleep.

Chapter 50

found myself floating on top of a cloud of black smoke, just like I had before. This time was different though. I wasn't me. I mean, I was me, but it was like I was someone else, and I was watching me from the sidelines. I looked like a dark Goddess. I wore a flowing black and silver gown, its intricate design seeming to shimmer and writhe like living shadows.

Slits on either side of the dress rose to mid-thigh, imbuing my every step with a sense of subtle, mysterious power. The sleeveless top plunged low, framing my cleavage in a sumptuous, jewel toned curve. Atop my head, a crown appeared to be forged from the very essence of The Darkness itself, its twisted, nightmarish beauty seemed to draw the light out of the air around me.

My silver tresses cascaded down my back in sleek, pin-straight folds, framing my face with icy elegance. My makeup was a deliberate, dramatic statement, a rich, dark smokey eye, bold winged liner, and a deep, mysterious black lipstick. In my hand, I grasped a staff of dark, polished wood, its tip crowned with a globe of black obsidian that seemed to absorb the light around it.

The orb was wreathed in flickering black flames, their eerie, dancing light casting an otherworldly glow across the surrounding space. It seemed to pulse with a malevolent energy, as if the black flames that danced across its surface were feeding off some hidden power.

I looked fucking enchanting. I looked powerful, magical, and equally terrifying. I was commanding an army of what looked like new Vampires... maybe it was the dead? I couldn't really tell, but they were all lined up in rows. There were hundreds of them, maybe thousands. Their voices wove together in a hypnotic, velvety chant, my name echoing through the air in a flawless, rhythmic cadence that was almost melodic – a dark, haunting ballad that sent shivers coursing down my spine.

Raziel materialized beside me, his movements eerily silent. He carefully raised my hand to his lips, his kiss sent a shiver through me. Then, in a gesture that left me taken aback, he bowed deeply, his golden locks inclined in a show of deference. Instead of Raziel reigning by my side, it was as if he was bound to serve me. As he straightened, he fell into step behind me, positioning himself off to my right, a subtle yet unmistakable acknowledgment of my dominance.

He stood at attention as if waiting for me to call him forward. I would never put him behind me, or below me. We are equals... he is my partner. I was so appalled at this darker version of myself. How could I do this? Why would I do this to him? With a sudden, fierce gesture, I slammed my staff onto the ground, unleashing a deafening explosion that sent black flames erupting in all directions. The sound was like a thunderclap, echoing off the walls and reverberating throughout the entire room.

Instantly, every one of those new Vampires, or dead, whatever they were, split into groups. I watched expecting chaos, but found none. With eerie synchrony, they sprang into motion, their movements fluid and practiced, as if they had been conditioned to respond to that specific sound, a Pavlovian reaction that sent them flowing into precise, predetermined positions.

There were about 10 per group and at least 300 groups, if I were to guess. I held my hand out to Raziel. He took it and locked eyes with me. They were speaking without speaking out loud, using the mind link, no doubt. Still, one of my Reaver powers I couldn't seem to connect to. I still couldn't hear anyone's Wolf or mind links, which was frustrating as hell. So, I had no idea what they were saying, but then he disappeared.

I observed, detached, as I raised my hand in a languid gesture, and the legion of dark entities responded with military precision. With unwavering discipline, they formed orderly ranks and filed out of the area in synchronized groups, their departure a testament to the unyielding control I seemed to wield over them. I had no idea where they were going but it looked like they were prepared for war.

The scene shifted, and I found myself suspended above a battle-scarred expanse, an open plain transformed into a gruesome arena. Below me, a ferocious conflict raged, a no-holds-barred struggle for survival pitting precision army against the Wolves. The combatants clashed with savage intensity, tearing each other to pieces with frenzied abandon. Blood splattered everywhere, a ghastly rain that accompanied the sickening crunch of severed limbs and the chilling screams of the dying.

Throats were ripped out, leaving gaping, bloodied chasms, while bodies were mauled beyond recognition, reduced to mangled, lifeless husks. The dark me didn't even seem to notice or care that they were murdering each other. I was just there, admiring my work as if it were any regular day. The landscape below me was a vision of unmitigated devastation.

Flames engulfed multiple areas, casting a hellish glow over the carnage. Scattered ruins, once perhaps homes or dwellings, now smoldered and partially burned. As I gazed out upon the desolate scene, I realized that this was not a random field, but instead, the pack lands, now transformed into a graveyard.

The ground was littered with lifeless bodies, their faces frozen in a perpetual mask of cold, dead shock. Their eyes, wide and unblinking, seemed to bore into my very soul, as if they were aware of my presence, watching me with a haunting, accusatory gaze. As I continued to observe my dark counterpart, a disturbing realization began to dawn on me. It seemed that I was not only witnessing the carnage, but also willfully perpetuating it. It was as if I had deliberately manipulated the Wolves into conflict, orchestrating their destruction in a ruthless bid to eradicate the entire species.

The scene shifted, and I found myself in a dank, foreboding dungeon. Raphael was chained to the cold stone wall, his slender form sagging against the restraints. What struck me, however, was the haunting gauntness of his features.

Despite being a Reaver, an entity that didn't require sustenance, he looked starved, his body reduced to a wilting, withering mess. His dark hair was matted and filthy, while his torn and bloodstained shirt hung loosely from his frame, revealing the stark prominence of his ribcage.

The sight of Raphael's gaunt form stirred a mixture of emotions within me. I couldn't help but wonder what dark, malevolent magic was being employed to reduce him to this state. His appearance was a testament to the suffering he endured, a suffering that seemed to have shattered his spirit.

When his silver eyes met mine, I saw a haunting blend of terror and resignation, a look that seemed to scream that his mind had long since surrendered, even if his body still clung to life. And yet, as I gazed upon his broken form, I couldn't shake the question, why was I keeping him here? I mean, I understand I'm upset, and I want him to pay for what he did. I want him to pay for all this pain he caused me. But this was extreme... to keep him prisoner and hold him in such a way that he deteriorates like this? How could I consciously treat someone like that?

My scream tore through the darkness, a raw, anguished sound that seemed to shatter the very air around me. I jolted upright in bed, my heart racing with a frantic intensity as the vivid, disturbing images still seared my mind, refusing to relinquish their grip on my reeling senses. Within seconds Raziel was at my side, his presence a comforting anchor amidst the turmoil. My chest heaved with ragged breaths, and my heart thundered in my ears, racing with a frenetic intensity.

Memories of The Darkness came flooding back, its suffocating grip, the way it had consumed me during my battle with Alpha Drake. I recalled how desperate I was to reclaim control, to banish The Darkness and take back control. The weight of responsibility settled heavy on my shoulders. I knew I was the one who had opened the door, who had invited The Darkness in. The blame rests solely with me, and I couldn't shake the crushing knowledge of my own responsibility.

Are you okay?" Raziel asked, his voice laced with concern as he held me in his arms. But I was too lost in thought to respond. I was torn apart by the scene that had just unfolded before my eyes. Was this a vision of the future?

Was this the reality that awaited me if I surrendered to The Darkness? The thought sent a shiver down my spine. I vowed to myself that I wouldn't let it happen. I would keep fighting, resist The Darkness with every fiber of my being. I am stronger than it is, and I can continue to resist. No, I *would* continue to resist.

I promised Raziel no more secrets, so once I calmed down, I explained to him everything from my dream. I wasn't sure what he was thinking, but I could tell that he was worried. "Was it a vision?" He asked. I shrugged. "I have no idea, but it felt real Raziel… it felt *so* real. It was terrible, and you were just allowing it… I can't… *we* can't let it truly happen." I replied. He looked worried, more worried than he ever had before, but he nodded.

"We won't, darling." He murmured. I knew he had been contacting the Priests of his Covens to see if anyone had ever dealt with this situation or had any information at all. He thought I didn't know, but I paid more attention than he realized. Plus, it helps that I had heard him and Anthony speaking of it a bit back. He was determined to help me fight it, and I commended him for that. But I knew deep down that I was the only one who could do that. No one could truly help me, not with The Darkness.

I was really wishing Wynter was here right about now. The silence in my mind, now, with The Darkness gone too, was driving me mad. I felt the familiar icy warmth washing over me and I fought to push it away.

"I don't want you. I don't need you. Go away!" I yelled internally. The truth is, I *did* want it. I was lying to myself, and to The Darkness, which made it that much harder to fight it. I felt so much better with its icy tendrils wrapped warmly around the expanse of my mind. It felt like I could do anything!

Then I remembered the dream, and I remembered why I was fighting The Darkness to begin with. My thoughts were so back and forth, and to be honest, each passing minute was an exercise in unrelenting torment... and the turmoil was growing more unbearable by the second.

Chapter 51

~

(Raphael)

*I*t had been about a month since The Darkness had made its presence known to me. Losing the ashes of my mate, Roxy… my only true love, had hit me much harder than I expected. I found myself wallowing in a pit of despair for months, yet seemed like eons before The Darkness arrived. I was sure it would never end on more than one occasion since the trade.

The fact that I didn't even get the prize I gave so much up to get, was the worst blow. It left me writhing in pain and agony trying to fill a void that was my own damn fault to begin with.

The Darkness swooped in so easily. It was an icy warmth that washed over me like a blanket, soothing my ailments and filling the void that my mishap had left me. With The Darkness I felt whole again. I felt free from the constant torture that was the void. Something that nothing else had been able to replicate thus far.

I had rarely left my home since I failed to claim the prize that I so sought, and I didn't really plan on leaving anytime soon either. Mere months in my infinite life was nothing. I didn't need to be outside around people while dealing with my bullshit anyway. I had no idea what The Darkness was or where it came from, but I was extremely grateful for its comfort.

I can't say the same for Axel though. He hates The Darkness because it pushes him to the back of my mind so it can be in the forefront. Without Axel, I am alone. But when The Darkness started to speak to me, I felt more comfort in his absence. He tries to break through once in a while. I can feel him fighting The Darkness to get his spot back in my mind, but it never lasts long. As many powers as I wield, even I am helpless to let him back in. If The Darkness doesn't want him there, then he will not be there. It's just too powerful to overcome... even for a Reaver.

I'm aware this is not a good situation to be in, but the pain and agony I've been dealing with feels a lot worse. All The Darkness has done for me so far is help me. So how can it be that bad? I had to tell myself this to justify my actions. I couldn't go to my brothers with this either. I was already on Raziel's bad side, for good reason, of course. I was always getting myself into messes that I needed their help to clean up. I'm sure they were sick and tired of it by now. This was my own doing, and I came to realize that I had to face it alone this time.

My thoughts regarding The Darkness were always a jumble. I sat in my newly finished reading nook and snapped to produce a book with a silver spine. I snapped again to produce myself a brandy on the rocks, which turned silver the second I touched it. A twinge of pain ran through my chest as I recalled when I sat here with my beautiful Rayne, and we read together

I recalled the wonder and surprise on her face when she saw my room. This was before she knew she was dreamwalking, or that she was even a Reaver. Her perfect smile and gorgeous silver flowing hair. Just the thought of her had me spiraling back into an endless abyss of agony and pain. All the memories of her, brief, but overwhelming, came flooding into my mind.

The very pain her memory caused was what I was trying to avoid. With memories of Rayne came memories of Roxy. It was just a domino effect. I couldn't escape the agony from either situation. Then The Darkness came and washed its icy warmth along my skin, caressing my every nerve, and filling the void with its delectable comfort. The Darkness gave me a false sense of security, and power that

349

I reveled in. It was infinitely better than the sorrow and pain I had been dealing with previously. "You shouldn't give up so easily on Rayne." The Darkness said. Its voice was like music to my ears.

"She's with my brother, bears his mark, no doubt. What's the point in even trying to pursue her, then? Forcing her to love me would be a hollow victory. I want her to choose me, to love me on her own terms, not because of some manipulation or coercion." I said, my voice laced with disdain.

I knew the effects of the mark were much more powerful when there were already feelings there. I remember what it was like with Roxy. The bond was so strong it almost drove us both mad, honestly. We gave in to it every chance we had. I wanted that again. I could have any plaything I wanted and mark them, but the sparks just weren't what I was looking for. I wanted real, I wanted more... I wanted Rayne.

"Then take her." The Darkness said. "Didn't we just go over this?" I huffed as I downed my drink in one gulp, then slammed the glass on my side table. "All you have to do is let me in. I can help you... we can get her back and she will fall in love with you on her own accord. Keep her long enough and she will come around." The Darkness stated. I shook my head. "Stockholm wasn't quite what I had in mind." I mumbled. "With our power, she will not be able to resist for long." It replied.

I felt the icy warmth wash over me, and suddenly, you know what? The Darkness actually had a pretty good plan. Maybe Stockholm was the way... I take Rayne and keep her hostage with me. Eventually, she would come around, she would have to...

I would be the only person she would interact with for however long it took to get her to fall for me. I would shower her with love and gifts, letting her do as she pleased so long as she stayed within the boundaries I have set. It would destroy any relationship I ever had with my brother... but the reward would be worth the loss. I would have to

350

make her stay, of course, with magic. But eventually she would get over my brother, and I would be here to pick up the pieces of her heart. She would *have* to love me after that. It was a great idea! I didn't care if it took another century, or longer. Why hadn't I thought of this before? What a great plan.

The Darkness always had good ideas, this one tops them all so far. I thought for a moment that I could hear Axel trying to break through. But the moment passed quickly. "I accept your offer." I said to The Darkness. Within an instant, I had fallen from the chair to my knees. The book I was holding clattered as it hit the shiny marble floor.

I felt as if I were about to pass out, blackness moving in and out of my field of vision. Then suddenly, I was floating in the air upon what looked to be a cloud of black smoke. I felt powerful and strong. I felt omnipotent, like a God unleashed. A primordial force pulsed through my veins, akin to a tempest straining to be set free from its confines. It was almost like a thunderstorm waiting to let loose, or a caged tiger, pleading to be free from its shackles.

I put both of my hands, palms up, and produced black fireballs. They were coursing with dark energy, begging to be used... taunting me, practically begging me to cave in and destroy something. I dissipated them, but it felt as if they were ready to return at any given moment. I was reeling in this newfound feeling of glory and power. Then my eyes fluttered open, and I was lying on the cold marble floor.

So, I did actually pass out. However, the feeling of power and energy coursing through my body, like a dam that had broken, remained. I stood up to find that I wasn't standing at all, I was floating just above the floor on a cloud of black smoke.

I glided rather than stepped, and just that small fact had me reeling with a very urgent need to go out and take what was mine. Rayne. There would be no way she could resist me now. My power would be far superior to hers, and I could take her... easily. I would kill anyone who got in my way, my brother included, if need be. I knew we were immortal, but could we withstand The Darkness? I suppose we would find out should he try anything stupid.

My thoughts seemed to please The Darkness. Anytime I had a negative thought, or something regarding murder or war, The Darkness seethed with pleasure. It was like it was feeding off my anger, off my torment. And I had enough of that to share. I didn't care that it was using my emotions. The only thing I cared about was her. And I wanted her, *now*.

Enough lying around in misery and enough counting on The Darkness to satisfy and fill my void. It was time to take my life into my own hands and choose my fate. I choose for myself what I want, or in this case, *who* I want.

This newfound cockiness was addicting. The more confident I was in myself and my powers, the more I felt dark energy pulsing through my veins. I was a fucking God, and I was going to get my prize. I'd dare anyone to try and stop me.

I thought of Rayne in my mind and materialized to her exact location. The Darkness was ready. It was time to collect our prize.

Chapter 52

~
(Rayne)

As crazy as it sounds, I was really missing my pack and pack life. The regularity of it all. The training and dealing with Alpha Drake, even. The past months I've spent here with Raziel were amazing, there was no doubt about that. I had learned so much about myself and my powers. Plus, our relationship had really grown and had been getting better every day. I couldn't deny that things had truly been wonderful. It's so funny to me to see Raziel and not feel fear around him. I remember when he used to scare the ever-living shit out of me, and I feel like that wasn't really that long ago.

I had a brief flashback of him killing Eric and his fangs dripping with Eric's blood. I recalled seeing Eric's lifeless body on the floor. Then I heard the words he spoke to me. 'No one may take your innocence but me.' A shudder ran through me causing cold chills to run down my spine. I guess there was still a little fear, but not for my own life, at least. My overall experience here has been good. This included my battle with The Darkness, which I was still fighting daily.

I just felt that this new life was different, you know? Like something was missing. I missed training. I missed my pack. I missed Roman, my only real friend. Even if he was hired by Raziel to be my friend. I even missed my Alpha… as much as I hated to admit it.

Alpha Drake was a huge part of my life for many years. We may have never seen eye to eye, but I knew as long as I followed his rules, he would protect me. I never faltered in that security. Ok, except, you know, the time I did break the rules and almost died by his hand. But that was my fault. I knew better. Handling grief was never my strong suit, as we can see, and I let it get the best of me. I would have deserved my fate. But he hadn't attempted to kill me again, and he had no reason to, as I was following the rules.

My anger towards him had dissipated once I realized he was forced into his decision just like I was. I couldn't blame him for being in an impossible situation. What would I have done if I were him? Probably the very same thing. Though, I would like to think I wouldn't have, who can really say unless they are in the situation. It was just a lot to take in. I had lived in my pack since I was 12. I grew up a Wolf, with a pack. A pack who was family, even if I distanced myself from them all. There was still a family type bond and that isn't easily broken.

I may have lived alone, but I always had Wynter once I turned and I always had my pack. The thought of me turning 21 in less than a year, just hurt. My grief and the void threatened to return at that very moment, and I had to think of something else to distract me.

"Raziel, can we go visit my pack today?" I asked him. I gave him my best puppy dog eyes, hoping he would allow it. I hadn't been outside much since The Darkness took over, just in case I couldn't control it again. I had been doing really well at keeping it at bay, but Raziel had yet to find out anything from any of his Covens regarding how to stop it. That worried him, and I know it did. I wish I had any kind of answers for him, but I honestly wasn't sure how to rid myself of The Darkness. Especially now that I had let it in. I was no help with this at all.

I looked up at Raziel and I could see the worry flooding his beautiful face. I knew he thought it was a bad idea. Especially, since my last interaction with Alpha Drake wasn't that long ago. "I promise, I will be ok! I am just really missing my pack. I'm really missing Wynter. Maybe being back in the pack setting will coax her to come out from her hibernation?" I said hopefully. The thought of Wynter being gone for this long was really starting to bother me. Now that my mind was clear, and I was in my own thoughts with no influence from The Darkness, I realized just how much Wynter being gone was affecting me. I hadn't really had time to think about her much previously… but now, all I had was time.

His face softened, he couldn't really ever tell me no, and that's something I loved about him. He was always looking out for my best interest, but also always trying to give me what I wanted. He was perfect and I didn't deserve him. A thought I had begun to think often once I lost my mate bond. He was wearing something casual, which surprised me. He always wore such fancy clothes.

Today he was in basketball shorts, gold, of course. With a black tee, that accentuated his muscular physique. His hair was perfectly styled though, not a hair out of place. This was usual for him, he never looked disheveled or worn. He always looked like he was chiseled from stone. Perfect. He took me in his arms and pressed his lips to mine. My mark went wild at his gesture, and I reciprocated. He pulled away. "Let me change." He said with a sparkle in his beautiful golden eyes. And he materialized in the closet.

How did I know he wouldn't go out in casual clothing? He wouldn't be caught dead not wearing a suit. I had never in my life seen a suit collection as elaborate as Raziel's. His side of the closet was bigger than mine and it was lined with a suit for literally every occasion. Solid colors, striped colors, spotted, animal print, gold, black, white, green, blue, pink. You name it and he has it in there, no matter how absurd.

My mind flashed to Raphael for a brief moment, and anger flooded into me like fire running through my veins. He always wore a suit as well. It must be a brother thing, but I immediately pushed the thought from my mind. I could feel The Darkness looming just around the corner, begging to be let in. Anytime I had a thought of anger, emptiness, or the void. Really anything negative or upsetting, I could feel

The Darkness looming just below the surface, threatening to explode.

The dark tentacles of comfort were swirling around my mind, begging to infiltrate and soothe with false pretenses. I couldn't even open the door for it to come in, or it would force its way through, and I knew this.

That door had to remain shut at all times, and boarded up from both sides. I was torn from my internal battle when Raziel came out of the closet looking like a million bucks. He had on a traditional gold suit, except this time the suit pants and jacket were solid gold. His shirt and vest underneath were black, same with his shoes.

I thought of Raphael and his solid silver suit, then I immediately regretted the thought. The Darkness was so close to rearing its ugly head and it was getting harder to push it away. Everything lately, for some reason, had reminded me of Raphael.

My anger was boiling, threatening to explode at any moment. It was like a shaken up can of soda… the lid was the only thing keeping the contents under extreme pressure inside. With every thought of Raphael, the lid was turned a little more.

I was like a ticking time bomb, and my minutes were almost up. I had to stay strong though. I fought The Darkness back again, for the third time this morning. Luckily, I was successful. "Are you ready?" Raziel purred, flashing me a perfect smile that had me melting.

My mark exploded with a cool, fiery energy, unleashing bursts of electrical intensity that crackled through my body like lightning bolts. It wasn't helping to calm my anger, but I couldn't resist the marks pull. Seeking solace, I flung myself into Raziel's waiting arms, hoping that the mark's influence would somehow temper The Darkness within me.

I was nervous because I was close to exploding… too close. Thankfully, it worked, as it always does. Raziel laughed as I pulled away reluctantly.As I reached out to gently touch Raziel's luxuriant hair, a shower of sparks erupted through my mark, the electrifying sensation coursing through my very being.

"I don't think I'll ever tire of this... of you." I whispered, my voice husky with affection, before gently pressing my lips to his in a soft, tender kiss. In this fleeting moment, I was free from the suffocating grip of The Darkness, and I reveled in the joy of being with Raziel. Then I pulled away, grabbed his hand, and we materialized to Alpha Drake.

Chapter 53

*A*lpha Drake was in his office talking to Roman. He looked up and I could see a brief flash of fear followed by worry, snake through his eyes. My smile seemed to calm his mind though. "Hi Alpha!" I said excitedly. I ran up to him and threw my arms around him. He stood there for a moment in complete shock. I had never done anything like that before, especially not in front of another Wolf from the pack.

I was a little worried what his reaction might be knowing he had an image to uphold. But then he slowly wrapped me in a bear hug, calming all of my previous worries.

My mark raged out of control, its fiery energy surging to a fever pitch. I couldn't help but wonder if it was somehow attuned to the emotions of those around me, burning brighter in response to their feelings. I wondered if it burned worse when they were in proximity as a warning, or if it just didn't like Alpha Drake.

I ignored it, pulled away and smiled, then looked over and locked eyes with Roman. I could see his face light up, but also a look of worry washed across it.

"Rayne!" He said, then he grabbed me and threw me into a tight hug, causing the same type of reaction from my mark. I had never thought of Roman romantically before. I had never even noticed if he liked me like that or not, but my mark was burning just as badly now as when Alpha Drake touched me, so now I had to wonder.

I didn't say anything, of course, and just pulled away. "What happened to your eyes?!" Roman stated, disrupting my train of thought. He was the first one since I had allowed The Darkness to take over completely, to say anything about my eyes. Go figure, he would be the first one. Friends always break the awkward ice. I took a deep breath in. "It's a long story." I said and then I looked over at Raziel who nodded at me. "But I promise I'm ok." I said, looking back at Roman. I could tell he understood that we would talk later, but not right now.

"What are you doing here, Rayne? Are you ok? Do you need something?" Alpha Drake asked. He, of course, was wondering because he thought I had moved for good. I couldn't blame him. After that long of not being here I would have assumed the same thing. I took no outward offense to his barrage of questions, but deep down it did kind of hurt my feelings. I probably deserved it after everything I did though... *Yep, I deserved that,* I thought, and then pushed it from my mind.

"I just missed you guys so much! I miss training. I miss the pack. I miss my house. Basically, I wanted to come back because I just really miss you guys." I said, fighting back the tears threatening to flood from my eyes. "Well, your home has remained untouched. I've made sure of that." Alpha Drake said. I didn't realize just how much I missed my life, until I was back here. It may seem stupid or trivial, but I really needed normalcy... I needed my pack.

I couldn't help but feel a slight flutter of butterflies when Alpha Drake said that he had made sure my home was untouched, probably hoping I would return. I know he loves me, but to keep my house untouched for months, not even knowing if I would return or not? That really hit me hard. I tried to stay focused, there was another reason I was here, after all.

"Also, um, Wynter hasn't been in my mind for a few months. She's hibernating due to the loss of our mate bond..." The mere utterance of those words summoned a searing agony that shot through my very core. As the pain threatened to consume me, I felt The Darkness stir, its icy warmth whispering false promises of comfort and solace. I pushed back against its insidious influence for the 4th time today, avoiding becoming trapped within its treacherous allure before focusing back on my Alpha.

"I was really hoping that being back home would maybe coax her out." I stammered, trying to gain my composure and stay out of the void. So far, I hadn't felt her so much as make a sound or move, so it didn't seem to be working. I could see the regret flash through Alpha Drake's eyes when I mentioned Wynter.

He, of all people, understood how important our Wolves were. They were a part of us. A Wolf without a Wolf spirit wasn't a Wolf. You had no internal dialogue. No conscience, you could call it. No help through hard times, and you couldn't shift. Sure, you might be able to heal unnaturally fast, and keep your muscular figure without working out or eating right, but what was all that without your Wolf? I knew exactly how that felt as I had been living it since I lost my mate bond. I was torn from my thoughts.

"She's not in your mind?" Roman said curiously. "No, it's just quiet in there. And honestly, it's been driving me a bit mad." I said. He seemed to be thinking really hard about something. "Does it have anything to do with your eyes?" Roman questioned. I honestly hadn't even thought about that.

It was strange to me that Wynter would abandon me during this rough patch... she never had before, why would she suddenly abandon me now? I mean, even through the trauma she wouldn't want to face it alone. What if it was due to The Darkness? The realization hit me like a freight train. *Oh my god, how could I be so fucking stupid?!*

"I'm... I'm not sure, but it's not out of the realm of possibilities." I stammered. I couldn't believe I could overlook that... "How could I have been so blind?" I asked, my voice laced with a mix of frustration and desperation.

"What can I do to get her back?" For the first time in what felt like an eternity, a tiny spark of hope flickered to life within me, casting a faint glow over The Darkness that I had allowed to consume me. Raziel was sitting in a chair in the corner, watching intently. He rarely stuck his nose where it didn't belong, but just him being here helped me stay calm. In the midst of my panic, my gaze frantically sought out Raziel's, and our eyes locked in a flash of understanding. He offered me a subtle, reassuring nod, and in that instant, my mark responded with a gentle, soothing warmth.

Soft sparks danced across my skin, calming my frazzled nerves and restoring my composure. With newfound clarity, I regained control, my senses sharpened and my focus renewed. The Darkness was lurking right below the surface, and the thought of The Darkness being why Wynter was gone had my blood boiling. Although, that in turn fed The Darkness, making it push harder to break free.

Dealing with The Darkness was a conundrum, in and of itself. Nothing I did was truly Darkness free. There was always some reason for it to try and rear its ugly head. Even in the simplest of situations The Darkness tried to break through. I only hoped we could figure out a way to get rid of it before I lost control again.

"Have you attempted to turn since Wynter went dormant?" Alpha Drake asked, pulling me from my internal dilemma. I actually hadn't even thought about turning. I rarely turned outside of patrol or training as it was. So, to think about turning the past few months? I definitely hadn't. "No. I have been so distracted lately I haven't even tried." I said. Hoping my Alpha had an idea that might work.

"Let's go to the arena so we can test it out." He said, and he grabbed my hand as we made our way to the door. My mark and Raziel didn't quite like the idea of Alpha Drake holding my hand as we walked. I, however, knew he was doing it to make sure I didn't lose my control over The Darkness. He had witnessed it firsthand, and I'm sure he never wanted to witness it again. I couldn't blame him… I mean, I did almost kill him the last time.

I swear I thought I saw Roman smirk sarcastically, then mumble something under his breath at the gesture. Then Raziel shot him a death glare, and it looked like they may have been communicating via mind link, but I just ignored it. There were too many men in this room who wanted to be with me, apparently, and I was only now noticing. My mark, however, was fully aware... it definitely made sure I was too.

Testosterone flowed through the room in thick waves, dancing on my skin anytime anyone made a move, so I was happy to be leaving the confined space. After what seemed like forever, we got to the arena. It was just me, Raziel, Roman, and Alpha Drake. "Shift. You know how to do it Rayne, it's like riding a bike." Alpha Drake said.

"You're right, I can do this." I replied and I called Wynter forward. I tried to shift, but nothing happened. Wynter never came to my call. She didn't even rustle in my mind. "She's not there." I said with a frustrated sigh. "Try again." Alpha Drake said with conviction. He was treating me now like we were in training. As brutal as he is, I realized I actually missed this. Something about his tone snapped me right into training mode.

"Yes Alpha." I said with the same conviction, and I tried again. "Wynter, come on! Where are you!? I know you're still in there. Please come forward!" I begged her in my mind. I was a little harsher than I usually would be, but this was a dire circumstance. I thought I felt a tiny stirring, but it was gone before I could tell you if it was really anything or not.

"Nothing. I thought I may have felt her, but it was gone before I could tell." I said, exasperation filling my voice. "Stop stressing, Rayne. Concentrate. You know how to do this. You've done this 1,000 times! Now shift!" Alpha Drake sneered. This was the Alpha Drake I was used to. His conviction gave me power, made me feel strong. I could do this, I *would* shift.

"Wynter, come to me, now!" I sneered. I could feel her stirring, like I had awoken her from a deep slumber. "That's it, come on girl!" I said to her. "Come forward." I coaxed. "Rayne?" Wynter stammered. "Wynter?! You're here!" I cried. "I don't know how long I'll be here for... The Darkness, Rayne! It keeps me trapped! It pushes me back and keeps me quiet. It suppresses my powers... Rayne... we can't shift." She cried.

"The Darkness is doing it? I'm so sorry, Wynter... I did this... please forgive me!" I begged. "I'm going to fix this! I swear I will fix this!" I promised.

Tears began to form in my eyes as Wynter was pushed back to the far recesses of my mind. I had hoped she would have been able to say anything else, but it was too late.

I was frantically trying to call her back when suddenly Raziel was by my side, and I could see a look of terror flash through Alpha Drake's eyes. I looked up to see why the sudden change when I heard it...

"Hello Beautiful."

Chapter 54

$\mathcal{A}$s much as I didn't want to see him, Raphael was honestly looking like a gorgeous, dark God. I couldn't deny that I was attracted to him. It was impossible not to be. He had on a solid black suit with a silver suit vest and silver shoes. His dark hair was perfectly positioned on his head in a neat short cut. He never had a hair out of place. He had stubble on his chin, which made him look a little gruff. His silver eyes were solid black, as black as night.

He was absolutely breathtaking in this form. But what caught me off guard was the unexpected, visceral pull I felt towards him. It was a sensation that was decidedly absent before. This newfound attraction was unmistakably sensual, igniting a spark of desire within me that I neither welcomed nor understood.

My frustration mounted as I struggled to come to terms with this unwelcome development. My mark reacted out of its own volition. It must have sensed Raphael's feelings for me, and responded by burning with an intense, uncontained ferocity.

Ignoring these conflicting feelings the best I could, I looked over at Raphael. I could see that he was engulfed in The Darkness. It was writhing under his feet and flowing around him in waves, just like it had been when I let it in. But this time, it seemed as if my Darkness wanted to get to his Darkness. The pull was so strong I was having trouble not running straight into his arms. And I did not like that fucking shit, not at fucking all.

A torrent of anger and resentment came surging back, memories of the past boiling to the surface as I recalled how his actions had propelled me into the abyss of The Darkness. The weight of that bitter history crashed down on me with the force of a freight train, leaving me breathless and reeling. The Darkness within me stirred, its presence growing more insistent as it begged to be unleashed, to claim dominion over my soul. But what sent a chill down my spine was its twisted longing to seek out Raphael and surrender to its darkest impulses in his presence.

I didn't want to let The Darkness back in… I couldn't. Not after how well I had been doing keeping it out. Plus, I was just able to contact Wynter for the first time in months! I couldn't lose all of my progress…

but the emotions The Darkness stirred within me were so raw, so extreme, that I found myself locked in a fierce, physical struggle against my own desires. My body trembled with the effort of resisting The Darknesses insidious allure, as I fought to override the primal urges that threatened to consume me.

My gaze drifted automatically to Raphael, our eyes meeting in a flash of mutual awareness. A single, searing glance was all it took to unravel my self-control. The moment our eyes met, my body seemed to betray me, responding to some primal, irresistible call. I struggled to shake off the unwanted sensations, to silence the treacherous whispers in my mind, but my heart refused to be swayed.

Every fiber of my being yearned to surrender, to abandon all restraint and run to him… to flee into the sanctuary of his arms, where I could lose myself in the warmth of his embrace. We could leave this place, these people, and just go.

I didn't even care where we went as long as we were together. It had to be The Darkness drawing me to Raphael. Mere moments passed before the pain hit. It was unlike anything I'd ever endured. It was a chasm of unutterable despair, a bottomless pit of desolation that yawned open, ready to swallow me whole. The emptiness was suffocating, a crushing weight that pressed upon my soul, threatening to consume me. Its poisonous tentacles were deep, dark, and dreary as they pulled me into its empty depths. There was no escaping it, not this time...

I held my breath as it took me under, into its soul crushing waters. I drew one last, shuddering breath, but it proved to be the fragile thread that snapped, unleashing the pent up torrent within. The Darkness, sensing its moment, surged forward with an unstoppable force, shattering the remnants of my control and engulfing me in its inky, abyssal depths.

I raised one of my arms up and above my head, palm up, and surrounded myself in a whirlwind of black smoke. I felt the familiar icy warmth washing over me, filling the void, and calming the empty that I was facing. And for the first time in what seemed like ages, I was no longer hurting. I was no longer feeling the void... the pain.

In an instant, the anguish was extinguished, replaced by the eerie, numbing solace of The Darkness. Its icy, velvety embrace enveloped me, and I succumbed to its soothing balm, reveling in the sweet release from pain. But as the calm deepened, a new awareness began to stir within me. It started as a spark, a flicker of empowerment that swiftly grew into an uncontainable flame.

Power, confidence, and, most tantalizing of all, control... the very things I had been desperately seeking, now coursed through my veins like liquid fire. I levitated eye level with Raphael and sneered. I was still pissed, clearly. "Rayne, you look... ravishing. The Darkness suits you. What I wouldn't give to have you rule by my side, to replace that mark with mine... forever!" His voice was like liquid silver pouring into my entire core and agitating my mark to no end.

Something about his words fueled the excitement in me, filling my body with a rush of butterflies. Yet, a simmering ember of resentment still glowed deep within me and it felt like all those butterflies suddenly burst into flames in the pit of my stomach. I didn't move an inch, but beneath the surface, a tempest of conflicting emotions seethed and churned, threatening to shatter my fragile composure.

"Together, we would be fucking unstoppable!" He roared. I still hadn't said a word and this sexual attraction was really getting on my nerves. The thoughts were so intense, I just wanted to fuck him. To ravage his body until he was screaming my name and begging me to stop... and then I wanted to kill him. The Darkness was toying with my emotions, weaving a complex web of conflicting feelings that left me reeling and disoriented.

I could tell Raphael was feeling the same, though. Trapped between two extreme wants, one was sure to boil to the surface. The rage ultimately prevailed, its pent up fury exploding into uncontrollable chaos. With a snarl, I unleashed a black fireball that shot toward Raphael's chest with deadly precision. He vanished, reappearing an instant later to counter with an identical blast of dark flame.

I, too, materialized out of harm's way, the fireball dissipating harmlessly in the space I'd just occupied. From the corner of my eye, I saw Roman, Raziel, and Alpha Drake scatter to different sides of the arena. Smart move, knowing that they were no match for us consumed in The Darkness. I regained my composure, lifting my hand to unleash a torrential thunderstorm, reminiscent of the tempest I had summoned before.

My Darkness seemed to delight in manipulating the environment, turning the skies against us. Rain lashed down in sheets, as if poured from celestial buckets, while lightning crackled and thunder boomed, casting an ominous, electric glow over the turbulent landscape.

I, of course, wasn't getting wet at all. I couldn't ruin this perfect hair. I did have magic, after all. Raphael, however, wasn't so lucky. He was drenched, and for some reason the sight of him with water rolling off his muscular form in waves, seemed to make him that much more attractive to me. This in turn pissed me off, angering my mark and feeding The Darkness. The air was electric with the fury of our clash, as if two deities were locked in a struggle for supremacy.

The cacophony of our attacks colliding with the thunderstorm's fury drew the attention of the entire Obsidian pack, who converged upon the arena with eager curiosity. Raphael and I danced across the arena, exchanging blasts of fiery energy and employing our mastery of magic to weave intricate defenses, materialize and vanish with breathtaking speed. Then we took our battle to the ground. I snapped and produced a staff with a black obsidian orb at the top of it.

Tongues of dark, velvety flame erupted from the obsidian, their inky depths seeming to swallow the light around them as they danced and licked at the cool air. This was the same staff I saw in my vision. I should have been nervous from what I saw in my dream, but I wasn't. Despite the ominous foreboding of my dream, I felt a strange sense of calm. Something about this moment didn't resonate with the dark premonition that had haunted my subconscious.

My gaze snapped back to Raphael, my attention refocused. With newfound determination, I grasped the staff, aware of its limitless potential. It was an instrument of my will, capable of unleashing any power I desired. With a swift motion, I pointed the staff at the earth, and the ground began to shudder. The air grew heavy with the stench of decay as I summoned an unholy legion: an army of the damned, risen from their eternal slumber to do my bidding.

"Per manum meam, et mortui resurgent." I chanted in Latin. I couldn't recall when or how I'd acquired knowledge of Latin, but I suspected it was yet another mysterious gift from The Darkness, which seemed to be imbuing me with secrets and abilities from beyond. I looked up as about twenty twisted, undead forms emerged, their bodies contorted in agony as they writhed within dark, ethereal shrouds.

My eyes locked onto Raphael's, and I was taken aback by the unbridled horror etched across his face. I couldn't fathom why the mere presence of these resurrected souls would evoke such a visceral reaction from him. Perhaps, I mused, my prolonged dalliance with The Darkness had inured me to its darker aspects, leaving Raphael unprepared for the unholy spectacle unfolding before him. As the undead horde began their relentless march toward Raphael, his eyes remained fixed on me, filled with a mix of terror and bewilderment.

The undead legion unleashed a diverse array of dark assaults upon Raphael. Some hurled black fireballs that exploded with malevolent force, while others spewed forth twisted, stringy flames from their mouths, as if their very souls were being consumed by the inferno. Those wielding staves eerily similar to mine channeled a multitude of dark magic spells, each one bursting forth with malignant energy as they assailed Raphael from all sides.

Raphael countered with fierce determination, unleashing fireballs and wielding magic to pick off my undead minions one by one. Yet, with each successive wave of casualties, I simply raised my staff, and a fresh legion of the damned arose to replace the fallen. My army swelled, its numbers doubling with each resurrection.

The relentless horde stumbled forward, driven by some malignant force, their progress illuminated only by the erratic flashes of lightning that cut through the turbulent darkness. The tempest raged on, thunder booming and rain lashing down, as Raphael stood firm against the unyielding tide of darkness.

They were surrounding him, overwhelming him. I could hear Raziel yelling for us to stop. I know Raphael is his brother and he still cares about him, but this was not his fight.

The sheer weight of the undead onslaught eventually proved too great for Raphael to withstand. His defenses began to falter, and still, I showed no mercy, refusing to halt the relentless tide of dark, reanimated bodies that threatened to engulf him.

In a sudden, desperate bid to turn the tide, Raphael flung his arms wide, palms downward, unleashing a

369

cataclysmic blast of energy that shook the very foundations of the arena. The shockwave ripped through my undead legion, annihilating them utterly, and sending the shattered remnants of the damned hurtling through the air, scattering them across the desolate expanse of the arena and back to the hell from which they were summoned.

I, of course, used my hand to create a shield to block any of that shit getting on me. No way I was about to ruin this perfect outfit. If The Darkness taught me anything, it's to always be confident and presentable. I thought about just creating another army, but what's the fun in letting them fight my battles?

I snapped my fingers and materialized a gold set of double-bladed fans. These were my go-to weapons. My favorite, even. Raphael's voice cut through the tumult, his words dripping with persuasion. "Rayne, let us end this futile game of power and wills. Join me, and together we shall rule. Be my queen." His hand extended, an invitation to seal our fate.

The Darkness within me stirred, its presence urging me to accept his offer. My own desires, too, seemed to lean in that direction, which only served to ignite my anger and mistrust. Yet, I knew this was the opportunity I had been waiting for.

With a calculated smile, I grasped Raphael's outstretched hand, allowing him to believe I was surrendering to his proposition. Instead, I used his hand to steady myself, my grip firm but deceptive. In a swift, deadly motion, I flung open my fans and struck, slicing through Raphael's chest and abdomen with precision and ruthless intent.

The wounds were deep and savage, mortal blows that would have felled any ordinary Human. Raphael's body crumpled to the ground, broken and bleeding. Yet, The Darkness that dwelled within him refused to let him succumb, its power coursing through his veins to heal the grievous wounds. With an unnerving swiftness, Raphael rose to his feet, his eyes blazing with fierce determination.

The Darkness seethed within me, its malevolent presence churning with discontent at my defiance. but I didn't care... I was here for one thing, and that was to make Raphael fucking pay for what he did.

Chapter 55

aphael barely had time to regain his footing before I launched both fans at him with deadly precision, hoping to connect with flesh once again. He materialized out of the way, but he was still a second too late as one of my fans bit deep into his calf muscle. A triumphant smirk spread across my face as I watched my fans, with almost sentient loyalty, boomerang back into my waiting hands, ready to be wielded again in our dance of vengeance.

The Darkness once again asserted its influence, healing Raphael's wounds with an otherworldly swiftness. But what happened next caught me off guard. With a sudden, sharp motion, Raphael clenched his fist, and my fans were torn from my grasp, flying toward him as if drawn by an unseen force.

I expected him to catch them, but instead, he unleashed a black fireball that struck the fans with incredible accuracy, shattering them into a hundred glittering fragments. Blades and shards of gold spun through the air, suspended for a moment in a deadly, whirling dance, before clattering to the ground between us.

Raphael's bold move signaled a decisive escalation in our battle, and I welcomed the challenge. "It's about time," I thought, a fierce grin spreading across my face. With a swift, decisive motion, I slammed my hand downward, summoning a black bullwhip that erupted with dark, flickering flames.

The whip cracked through the air, its fiery tip wrapped around Raphael's throat with unerring precision. In one fluid, ruthless motion, I yanked him off his feet, slamming him to the ground with a force that sent shockwaves through the dark, scorched earth. With a sharp, brutal motion, I wrenched the whip free from Raphael's throat, its flaming tip leaving a smoldering gash in the earth beside him. I recoiled, preparing to strike again, but Raphael rolled clear just in time. My whip cracked down, smashing into the ground with explosive force, sending shards of dirt and grass flying in all directions.

Undeterred, I spun the whip above my head in a blurring arc, its flames cast eerie shadows on the surrounding terrain. As I released the whip, it shot forward with deadly precision, aimed squarely at Raphael's torso. But he vanished, reappearing a foot away, and my whip struck only empty air, its flames hissing in frustration.

A feral growl tore from my throat as I launched the whip at Raphael once more, its flames blazing with fierce intensity. But this time, he was ready. With a swift, powerful motion, he snatched the whip from the air, his grip like a vice. Then, with a sudden, brutal tug, he yanked the whip towards him, exploiting my momentum.

I felt myself being dragged forward, helpless to resist the force. A deafening crack of thunder boomed through the sky, and I stumbled into Raphael's arms, our bodies colliding just as a brilliant flash of lightning illuminated the darkened arena, casting us as its centerpiece. As the light faded, I found myself gazing up into Raphael's black, piercing eyes, our faces only inches apart. The air between us was charged with tension.

The Darkness within me recoiled in a mixture of shock and exhilaration, its malevolent presence sensing the proximity of its desired union. This was the very outcome I had desperately sought to prevent, and yet, here we were, bound together by some unseen force.

Despite my struggles, I found myself unable to break free from Raphael's grasp. It was as if The Darkness had become a palpable, magnetic force, drawing us inexorably together the moment our skin made contact. Dark energy pulsed through me, thrilled to have finally brought us to this point. I could feel its power surging, eager to claim dominion over me once more.

Raphael's drenched form seemed to radiate an otherworldly allure, the relentless rain only adding to his dark, brooding charm. I cursed myself for entertaining such treacherous thoughts, but they persisted, flooding my mind with unwanted visions.

I imagined the gentle brush of his fingertips, the soft caress of his lips, and the shiver-inducing sensation of his mouth on mine. My mind's eye conjured images of myself beneath him, arching in ecstasy as he awakened sensations I'd never known. The Darkness within me reveled in these depraved fantasies, refusing to relinquish its hold on my imagination.

Despite my revulsion, I found myself helpless to shake the vivid, disturbing images that haunted my every waking thought. The thoughts were repulsive at best, but The Darkness wouldn't stop... and I couldn't either. Raphael's finger trailed along the golden crescent moon mark on my cheek, sending a jolt of pleasure intertwined with a searing burn coursing through my body.

It was as if The Darkness within me had found a way to bypass the mark's protective influence. Then, with a swift, economical motion, Raphael flicked his wrist and closed his palm, unleashing a dark energy that shattered the mark on my face. The golden symbol dissolved into shards of fury, its fragments dissipating into a burst of fiery radiance. Without the mark's stabilizing presence, I felt my defenses crumble, leaving me vulnerable to the turbulent emotions that The Darkness stirred within me.

As the mark's influence waned, I found myself powerless to resist Raphael's advances, my senses reeling under the onslaught of his dark allure. Raphael's thumb grazed my lips, sending a maelstrom of pleasure coursing through my body, courtesy of The Darkness's insidious influence.

His warm breath danced across my ear as he whispered. "My God, I want to take you right here, right now." The husky timbre of his voice sent shivers cascading down my spine. My resolve was crumbling, my desire to surrender to his cravings threatening to overwhelm me. The fantasies I'd tried to suppress since his arrival now taunted me, tempting me to relinquish all control. What a fragile thread of restraint holding me back…

Without the mark's protection, I was exposed and vulnerable, a fact I knew all too well. Despite the intoxicating allure of Raphael and the Darkness, a spark within me refused to be extinguished. A deeper, more resilient part of my being yearned to break free from the Darkness's grasp, to escape Raphael's mesmerizing pull. I knew that spark was still smoldering, buried beneath the surface.

I needed to fan it into a blaze, to harness the anger and resentment that had been simmering within me. By focusing on those emotions, I could channel them into a counterforce against the Darkness's manipulations. Its influence was potent, but I knew it was a facade, a cruel deception designed to ensnare me. As much as the pull of The Darkness was trying to force us together, I knew deep down that wasn't real. It was just The Darkness, toying with me.

I reached my hand out, summoning my flaming staff I had discarded earlier in place of my fans. The staff soared from the arena floor and into my hand. With a fierce cry, I plunged the staff into the ground, unleashing a tremendous shockwave. Raphael stumbled backward, his feet scrambling for traction, while the surrounding crowd struggled to maintain their balance.

The impact was colossal, like a plane crashing into the arena, shaking the very foundations. The deafening boom reverberated through the air, its echoes thundering through the stunned silence.

I observed as Raphael regained his footing, his expression twisted in a mixture of anger and determination. "Rayne, join me," he growled, "or I'll start slaughtering those you hold dear." His patience had worn thin, and it

375

was clear that our stalemate had reached a critical point. Neither of us could gain the upper hand, our powers locked in a fierce standoff. The Darkness had ensured that our conflict would remain a brutal, unending cycle. I spat out a defiant retort.

"You wouldn't dare," but my words were laced with a desperate hope that he was bluffing. Raphael's response was swift and merciless. He soared into the sky, his gaze locking onto Alpha Drake, Raziel, and Roman who were below us.

With a sudden, deadly motion, he unleashed twin black fireballs, their massive size and intensity dwarfing his previous attacks. Alpha Drake and Raziel barely escaped the inferno, dodging out of the way just in time. But Roman, inexperienced in the chaos of battle, was caught off guard. Without hesitation, I vanished and reappeared in front of him, positioning myself to absorb the full fury of the twin fireballs.

The impact was catastrophic, like being struck head-on by a speeding semi-truck. A deafening crack resounded through the air, the sound waves piercing my eardrums. The Wolves in the crowd erupted into screams of horror as the blast sent me crashing into the ground.

The force was so intense that it ripped the air from my lungs and propelled my body through the earth, sending chunks of dirt and debris flying above me. Pandemonium broke out, with everyone screaming in terror.

Raziel's anguished cry echoed through our mind link, "Rayne, no!!!" That was the last thing I remembered before everything went black.

Chapter 56

~

(Raziel)

his battle had been ruthless, and knowing that it was pointless to even try and intervene, I was somewhat enjoying the show. Things seemed as if they were coming to a head, but what would that outcome entail? These were the questions I wasn't sure I wanted the answers to. I looked up at my brother and we locked eyes just as he sent multiple giant black fireballs hurtling my way.

Beside me, Alpha Drake dodged to safety, and I instantly materialized to the side, narrowly avoiding the inferno. But Roman remained paralyzed, frozen in shock, utterly helpless. I knew I couldn't reach him in time. That's when I witnessed a selfless act that would haunt me forever.

Rayne materialized directly in front of Roman, positioning herself to bear the full force of the attack. I watched in unspeakable horror as the twin fireballs struck her with unrelenting ferocity, the blast slamming into her chest with devastating precision. My heart plummeted, sinking like a stone into the depths of my stomach.

The moment the fireballs struck Rayne, she was catapulted into the ground, sending dirt and grass flying in a chaotic explosion. The impact was deafening, its thunderous crash drowning out the storm's own cacophony. In a bizarre, synchronized movement, Raphael, standing on the opposite side, was also hurled through the air, as if he too had been hit by the fireballs. The symmetry of their movements was unsettling, like two puppets jerked by the same invisible string.

It took a heartbeat for the reality of the situation to sink in. "Rayne, no!!!" I screamed at the top of my lungs, my voice piercing the anguished cries of the Wolves in the arena. The moment Rayne was struck, the thunderstorm's fury abruptly dissipated, as if her magic had been extinguished along with her life force. The sudden stillness was oppressive, a haunting reminder of what had just been lost.

A scorching agony tore through my chest, threatening to buckle my knees beneath me. The anguish was suffocating, an unrelenting weight that crushed me with the merciless force of a steamroller. My chest felt heavy, constricted, as if the very air had been squeezed from my lungs. Each breath was a labored feat, every movement a Herculean effort. In my endlessly long lifetime, I had never encountered a pain so piercing, a grief so overwhelming. It defied comparison, an anguish that shattered all precedence.

But no matter the anger I was feeling towards my brother, and the despair I was feeling right now with Rayne lying lifeless in a sinkhole, I knew I couldn't lose her. I would make whatever deal was necessary to bring her back, I didn't care the price, nor the consequence.

I tried to materialize to Rayne, but I was blocked. Magic was stopping me from getting anywhere close to her. Panic surged through my chest as I grasped the implications. Something was wrong. I should have been able to reach her and the fact that I couldn't sparked a growing sense of dread.

This wasn't contractual magic, with its predictable rules and boundaries. What, then, was the source of this obstruction? The uncertainty ignited a burning urgency within me, and I strained against the magical barrier, desperate to break through and reach Rayne's side.

Roman's anguished cries echoed behind me, but I tuned them out, my focus solely on Alpha Drake. Our gazes met, and while his face remained a mask of stoic calm, his eyes betrayed a flicker of alarm. My chest tightened, panic threatening to overwhelm me once more. Grief consumed me, its intensity fueling a desperation that would stop at nothing. I had to save Rayne, no matter the cost.

As a regular Reaver, she wasn't blessed with the same immortality as my brothers and me. She could be killed, and the thought sent a chill coursing through my veins. I knew I was on the cusp of making a deal that would likely haunt me for eternity, but I didn't care. The only thing that mattered was bringing Rayne back.

I materialized at the edge of the chasm, peering down into its seemingly bottomless depths. The darkness was absolute, a void that swallowed all light and hope. I extended a Wolf claw, preparing to slice my palm, when an unsettling chill crept over me, signaling the arrival of The Shadows. They emerged from every direction, and none, their dark tendrils writhing like living serpents.

The Shadows had come, though I hadn't summoned them. I exchanged a puzzled glance with Alpha Drake, who shrugged and shook his head. Roman, meanwhile, whimpered softly to himself, equally bewildered. As The Shadows deepened the arena's darkness, I watched in rapt attention as their slimy, slithery tendrils burrowed into the earth, seeking out the spot where Rayne had vanished.

The Wolves encircling the arena shifted restlessly, their uneasy murmurs and whispers weaving a nervous tapestry. I suspected that most of them had never laid eyes on The Shadows before, and the unfamiliar sight left them bewildered and apprehensive.

My gaze drifted across the arena, where Raphael was slowly stirring, regaining his footing. For now, he was the least of my concerns. My attention remained fixed on the chasm, where The Shadows eventually reemerged, their dark tendrils cradling Rayne's lifeless form.

I attempted to materialize beside her once more, only to be rebuffed by the same unseen barrier, its presence a cold, unforgiving reminder of my helplessness. I attempted to rush to Rayne's side, but my feet felt rooted to the spot, as if heavy chains had been anchored to the ground, immobilizing me. The helplessness was suffocating, forcing me to bear witness to the agonizing scene unfolding before me. Tears streamed down my face, a rare and unsettling phenomenon. I had always prided myself on my ability to navigate even the most treacherous situations with composure, but this was different.

This was a pain that shattered my defenses, leaving me vulnerable and broken. As The Shadows continued to writhe and seethe, levitating Rayne's lifeless body in the air, I crumpled to my knees, overwhelmed by the weight of my grief.

"A sssacrificcceee wasss given," The Shadows whispered in eerie unison, their voices a chilling sigh that sent shivers through the air. "An innocent life wasss ssspared, thanksss to a ssselflesss act of extraordinary bravery. A life for a life, the balanccceee hasss been struck, but the true cossst wasss never a mortal life. A debt wasss never incurred, and repayment doesss not need to be collected. And though it may ssseem paradoxical... sometimessss, Shadowsss sssshow mercccy." They slithered.

As the last word dissolved into the air, The Shadows rippled and slithered, their dark tendrils undulating like living serpents. The Shadows' voices thundered through the air, reverberating deep within my soul.

"Come back to the world of the living, Rayne!" They chorused in a cacophony of echoes. "Come back to usss now!" The words shattered me, their icy shards dancing across my skin like a maelstrom of frozen needles.

And then, in an instant, Rayne was bathed in a blindingly radiant white light. Its intensity was almost palpable, a physical force so piercing it felt like a blow to my eyes, forcing me to recoil from its brilliance. The light expanded rapidly, erupting outward in a blinding flash, before being somehow absorbed into Rayne's body, as if her very cells were drinking in its essence. The phenomenon was both mesmerizing and terrifying, leaving me awestruck.

The Shadows gently descended, cradling Rayne's limp form, before setting her down on the ground with an unsettling delicacy. As they released their hold on me, I felt my paralysis lift, and I instantly materialized beside her. Dropping to my knees, I gathered her into my arms, holding her close, intent on never letting her go.

The Shadows swirled around us, their dark tendrils pulsing with an otherworldly energy, but I ignored them, numb to their presence. Their icy chill seeped into my bones, but I didn't flinch, my focus solely on the fragile, precious form in my arms.

"Rayne, please, darling... wake up," I whispered, my voice trembling with desperation. Though The Shadows had revived her, I knew better than to assume it came without a price. My mind racing with worst-case scenarios, I feared she might be trapped in a perpetual slumber. Yet, even as panic and frustration threatened to consume me, I couldn't help but be struck by her ethereal beauty.

Her face, serene and peaceful, even in death and resurrection, was a stark contrast to the turmoil that had ravaged her for months. I gently brushed the hair from her face, tucking it behind her ears, my fingers grazing her skin with a tender reverence.

"Don't you dare leave me," I snarled, my voice low and menacing. "Don't you fucking dare. I'll traverse the very cosmos, tearing it apart brick by brick if I have to in order to bring you back. Do not make me do that, Rayne." I growled, hoping against all hell that my words would pierce the veil of her unconsciousness and rouse her. But she remained still, unresponsive.

I took a slow, deliberate breath, pulling her closer to my chest, holding her tight as if I could somehow bring her back to life. The distant chatter of the crowd filtered into my awareness, a muted hum that only served to heighten my sense of desperation. "Why isn't she waking up?" I snapped at The Shadows. They writhed and slithered before us, but didn't reply.

A soul crushing weight pounded down on my chest as I struggled to get any singular word to flow from my mouth. "Rayne, darling... I need you to fight. I need you to pull yourself out of whatever cavern you are in, and make your way back to me. I swear if you don't, I'll come in there and pull you out myself. I won't rest until I have successfully retrieved your soul from whatever hell you are currently in... I need you... please..."

I'd built a reputation as a man impervious to vulnerability, a master of my emotions. Yet, Rayne had a way of chipping away at that façade. She'd caught me off guard with her presence, and before I knew it, I'd found myself smiling more often, feeling depths of emotion I'd thought were long dormant. She'd awakened something within me, and I'd come to realize that she made me a better, more whole person. The prospect of losing her was unbearable, a thought that shook me to my core.

Time seemed to stretch on forever, each moment an eternity, until I sensed her presence beside me. It was a sensation I'd grown accustomed to over the millennia... the ability to feel and see the dead from The Otherside when they drew near. A secret I'd kept hidden, even from my brothers. It was a part of me I'd never shared with anyone. I turned, my gaze meeting Rayne's spirit as she took in the scene around her.

Her eyes finally met mine, and I felt a jolt of electricity run through me. "You can see me?" She asked, her voice barely above a whisper. I nodded, a smile spreading across my face, no longer caring what others might think. "Come home, darling," I whispered, my voice filled with longing.

As Rayne's spirit hovered, a single tear escaped her eye, and she reached out to reclaim her lifeless body. The moment their forms reunited, her spirit merged with her physical self, and she began to stir in my arms.

Time suspended as her eyes fluttered open, and I exhaled a shaky breath of relief. "Thank God," I whispered, my voice barely audible. But it was the sight that greeted me next that left me breathless. Rayne's platinum eyes sparkled back at me, radiant and unblemished. The Darkness that had once shrouded them was gone. Nothing, no swirling black smoke, no obsidian irises, no dark wisps remained.

"Rayne, oh my god, are you alright?!" I asked her, My voice trembling with concern. "Raziel? I'm fine..." She stammered, catching her breath. I brought her close to my chest and held her tightly as I fought to calm my racing heart. Then, my gaze shifted to The Shadows, my eyes narrowing. "What is your price?" I demanded, knowing they never acted without expecting something in return. "She hasss paid the price. A life for a life. A selflesss act. We owed her thisss time." They slithered.

"And what of The Darkness?" I pressed, my eyes locked on The Shadows. Their collective voice whispered back, "It isss destroyed. The Darknesss cannot survive itsss own magic. Thisss isss why it isss drawn to itself, a self-destructive force.

When Raphael wielded The Darknesss against Rayne, it proved fatal... but also sealed its own fate. The Darknesss shattered into fragmentsss, dissipating into the void, consumed by itsss own power." The Shadows' ethereal voices trailed off, their words hanging in the air like a promise.

And without letting us ask another question they slithered back into the everything and nothing from which they came. I could finally breathe again as they took their icy chill to the bone cold with them.

"The Darkness, it's gone!" Rayne exclaimed suddenly, as she jumped up out of my arms. I could hear Wynter howling in Raynes mind. "Wynter's back too! It's really gone, all of it!" Rayne's voice trembled with emotion. "The void, the despair of losing my mate bond... it's gone too!"

Tears glistened in her eyes as she spoke, her hand instinctively rising to cover her heart, as if searching for the familiar ache that had once resided there. Her gaze turned inward, her expression a mix of wonder and curiosity. Meanwhile, Raphael approached us with a slow, deliberate stride, his eyes cast downward in shame, his head bowed in a gesture of contrition. For a moment, I worried that Rayne's emotions would get the better of her, but instead, she took a calm, deliberate step forward. She opened her arms and enveloped Raphael in a warm embrace.

I watched in surprise, touched by her capacity for compassion and forgiveness, a side of her I'd grown familiar with before The Darkness had taken hold. Raphael's arms slowly encircled her, and he whispered something in her ear. Rayne's whispered response was met with a soft murmur of agreement from Wynter.

Rayne stepped back from Raphael's embrace, and their eyes met in a tender, searching gaze. Raphael's fingers gently brushed the hair from her face, and a soft smile spread across his lips. "Thank you, beautiful," he whispered, his voice filled with gratitude. Turning to me, his expression turned somber, and he spoke with heartfelt sincerity.

"Brother, I'm deeply sorry for my actions. I was wrong to interfere, and once The Darkness consumed me, I was powerless to stop myself. I know that's no excuse for my behavior, and I don't expect forgiveness easily. I know that is not an excuse for my unacceptable behavior… but I hope that someday you'll be able to find it in your heart to pardon me." Raphael's words were laced with genuine remorse, and I could sense the depth of his regret. With a quiet nod, he vanished into thin air, leaving the arena behind. Rayne's attention turned to Roman, who stood frozen in a mix of anguish and shock.

She approached him with compassion, and he swept her into a crushing bear hug, his apologies tumbling out in a heartfelt torrent. Rayne's soothing voice calmed him, her words a gentle balm to his frayed emotions. "I would do it again if the need arose." She said. I could see tears in Romans eyes. "Thank you, Rayne." He stammered.

Rayne released Roman from her embrace and met Alpha Drake's gaze. A subtle smile played on his lips, and they exchanged a silent understanding, their eyes conveying a wordless message. It wasn't a communication born of their mind link, for I remained oblivious to their unspoken exchange.

With a quiet nod, Rayne turned and walked back to me. Her eyes shone with gratitude as she spoke. "Thank you, Raziel. Thank you for never giving up on me, even when it seemed impossible." I smiled, my voice taking on a low, rumbling purr. "I haven't followed you to the literal ends of the earth since you were 9 years old, just to give up on you now, have I?" I purred.

Rayne's eyes sparkled with amusement as she chuckled. "Fair enough," she said, "but now that the drama's subsided, who's going to clean up this mess? We can't just leave a gaping hole in the middle of the arena." I responded with a swift snap of my fingers, and the arena instantly restored itself to its former state, as if no destruction had ever occurred. Rayne's soft, delicate chuckle escaped as she turned from me, leaving me with a knowing smirk etched on my face.

I turned to Alpha Drake, our eyes locking in a silent understanding. "I trust you'll handle the pack?" I asked, nodding toward the crowd still seated in the stands, their faces etched with confusion and concern.
"You can spin the story however you see fit, but they deserve some explanation." Alpha Drake's expression was resolute. "I will handle it, don't worry." I nodded, accepting his assurance.

My gaze then shifted back to Rayne, who was watching me with a discerning eye. "Raziel, do you have something you need to tell me?" She asked, her voice tinged with a hint of curiosity. I feigned nonchalance, attempting to conceal the guilt that had begun to simmer within me.

"In regards to?" I replied, already aware of the direction her inquiry was headed. Being dead, even if only briefly, meant Rayne had likely crossed into The Otherside, where

385

the boundaries between realms were blurred, and interactions with others were possible. I already knew exactly where this was going.

Rayne's gaze held mine, her expression unreadable. "Let's speak at home," she said finally, her voice low and measured. I nodded, a sense of trepidation settling within me. Rayne's hand intertwined with mine, and in an instant, we vanished from the arena, reappearing in the serene confines of my room.

The soft glow of the luminescent accents and the plush textures of the furnishings seemed almost jarring in their tranquility, a stark contrast to the maelstrom of emotions churning within me.

Chapter 57

~

(Rayne)

I felt weightless, as if suspended in mid-air. It was disorienting, considering I could've sworn I was just being propelled through the earth at breakneck speed. But when I finally materialized, I found myself standing in a familiar yet unsettling landscape. The scenery around me seemed to match the area just outside the pack arena in Maine, but something was off.

A gaping hole, which I was certain I had just emerged from, was nowhere to be seen. Instead, I stood amidst an eerie stillness, the sky above tinged with an ominous reddish hue that cast an unnatural glow over everything.

There were many Wolves here training, and I could hear them being led by an unknown male voice. He sounded powerful, with conviction. I made my way to the arena and looked inside. I was right, a strong looking male figure was teaching about 25 Wolves. I leaned on the side of the arena bleachers and watched.

Some of the Wolves training looked young, like children. Others were full blown warriors, covered in tattoos and scars. The scene felt eerily familiar, like a parallel version of my own pack. As I stood there, I was suddenly enveloped by the unmistakable, bone-chilling presence of The Shadows.

Though I couldn't see or hear them, their icy aura sent a shiver down my spine. I glanced around, wondering if anyone else sensed the ominous presence, but the Wolves continued their training, seemingly oblivious. As I approached the trainer, the Wolves continued their drills, but his attention snapped toward me. He strode forward, meeting me halfway, his massive frame looming larger than it had from a distance.

Sweat-drenched and imposing, he towered over me, his muscles rippling beneath his skin like a living, breathing entity. A jagged scar sliced across his chest, its edges twisted and raised, giving the impression that it had been carved by some brutal, unforgiving force. His dirty blonde hair clung to his forehead, matted and damp, while his piercing hazel eyes seemed to bore into my very soul.

Initially, his expression had been open and welcoming, but the moment he realized what I was, his demeanor shifted. His eyes narrowed, and his voice dropped to a low, menacing growl. "A Reaver?" He snarled, his massive body tensing into a defensive stance, as if poised to strike.

"I'm a Wolf." I snipped, but no matter how hard I tried I couldn't get my Wolf claws to elongate. He scoffed, and I could tell he didn't like me much. "I am Rayne from The Obsidian pack. Alpha Drake sends his regards." I growled, getting into a defensive stance as well. At the mention of Alpha Drake he calmed down. "Drake, huh? He's still running things up there?" He asked. Confusion clouded my face. "Up where?" I asked cautiously.

A look of sudden comprehension washed over his face, followed by a swift change in demeanor. "Oh, uh, how did you get here, Rayne?" he asked, his tone tinged with a hint of evasiveness. I paused, reflecting on the events that had led me to this place.

But as I replayed the memories, I realized that I had no clear recollection of how I'd arrived. My thoughts were shrouded in a haze of uncertainty. "I… I was fighting with Raziel's brother, and then The Darkness consumed me," I stammered, my voice trembling as a terrifying realization dawned on me.

"Am I… am I dead?" The words tumbled out of my mouth, the only explanation that seemed to make sense in the face of my inexplicable presence in this strange,

388

unfamiliar place. "You're no more dead than the rest of us, if that helps." He said, motioning to the still practicing trainees. A pang of guilt flooded through me as I thought about Raziel, and all the pain I must have caused him. Even more so now, if I was actually dead. I couldn't control The Darkness, but it was my own fault I let it in to begin with.

"I... no, I can't be... dead..." I stammered, taking a few steps back. "It's always hard at first, but it gets easier. Why don't you go find your home, relax and process." He said. His words barely registered as I replayed the past few months in my mind, an exasperated sigh escaping my lips. I had been a complete and utter failure in so many ways. Allowing myself to be controlled by The Darkness, and even inviting it in... why the fuck would I do that? I felt so stupid for being so damn weak.

An icy chill swept through me, leaving me shivering and rubbing my arms in a futile attempt to ward off the creeping cold. It was as if The Shadows had closed in around me, their presence suffocating, yet they remained frustratingly invisible. My mind began to reel, but I forced my thoughts to narrow, to focus on one person: Raziel. The image of him crystallized in my mind, and I felt the sting of unshed tears. But I refused to let them fall. If death was my reality now, I would accept it.

With a resolute nod to the trainer, I turned away from the arena, leaving its familiar sounds and the warmth of the sun behind, and stepped into the unknown. As I walked, I realized just how childish I had acted. I was so naive to mess with powers I didn't understand and look where it got me. 6 feet underground, literally.

I replayed the past months events in my mind, going over every moment where I acted out of turn, and every situation where I allowed the intrusive thoughts to win. I held my head down in shame, noting that those instances were not few and far inbetween.

A wave of shame washed over me as I reflected on the frequency with which I had succumbed to The Darkness.

389

Yet, I knew that regrets were futile now. The past was etched in stone, and I couldn't alter its course. A solitary comfort flickered to life amidst the shadows of my regret: Roman was safe, and I had saved him. That selfless act now stood as a beacon of redemption in the darkness. It was a small solace, but it was enough to lend my eternal rest a hint of purpose.

In this desolate landscape, I clung to the knowledge that my final act had been one of goodness, a lasting testament to the spark of decency that had once burned within me. I looked up and noticed I was almost to my house when I heard a very familiar voice from behind me.

"Rayne?" Jae said carefully. I turned and locked eyes with my friend. And for that moment all my other stresses were gone. "Jae?!" I cried, running into her arms. Tears streamed down my face as I held my friend, whom I never thought I would see again. "Oh my god, Jae, how are you here?!" I cried, releasing her so I could get a good look at her.

She was crying and trying to wipe her tears so I wouldn't see, but I didn't care. "I guess being killed by magic tethers you to The Otherside, which is where we are… but how are you here?" She asked, trying to change the subject. It didn't work because her words caught me off guard. "What do you mean being killed by magic?" I asked. Her deep brown eyes softened as she looked up at me. "You… you don't remember?" She asked. "No, I do. I remember the car accident, but that wasn't magic." I said.

She looked uncomfortable, and after exhaling slowly she shook her head. "That's not what happened, Rayne. I don't know how to… you… you killed me." She finally said. An unbearable anguish consumed me in the form of a gut-wrenching torment that threatened to destroy me from the inside out as I tried and failed to process what she had just said.

"No… no, I never would have done that!" I cried. She tried to console me but the pain was too heavy, the burden of guilt was suffocating me. I fell to my knees before Jae as she put her finger on my forehead and the memories came flooding in. I had done so much more than just kill her, I had killed others, and hurt Brett...

I had destroyed the entire vigil, the surrounding forest, and pavilion, and left a gaping hole in the grass. The memories of the car accident faded, replaced with the truth that was being kept from me. I was upset that I was lied to, but I understood why they did it. I was in such a fragile state I would have lost control again. "I'm so fucking sorry. I never meant to hurt you or anyone." I cried, tears streaming down my face.

Jae leaned down next to me and took me in her arms. "It's ok, Rayne. I forgive you." She said, squeezing me a little more tightly. "You had so much life left to live, so much to experience. I took it from you... I... I took it all." I stammered, looking up at her. She wiped my tears gently.

"Rayne, you didn't take anything from me. You gave me more than I ever could have wanted." She said, her voice filled with emotion. Again, confusion dotted my face. She stood up and gestured behind me. I turned and looked to see the large Wolf from training as he sauntered his way towards us. He walked right past me and pulled Jae into his arms, kissing her deeply. "I missed you, love." I heard him say to her once their lips parted.

"I missed you too, babe. I just put dinner on the table, go wash up." She said. He turned with her in his arms and looked at me. "Rayne, I see you've met my mate, Jae. Join us for dinner?" He asked. It was only then that I realized that both of them shared the same mark.

Perched on the Wolf's neck, right where his shoulder met the curve of his collarbone, was a delicate, deep orange dove in mid-flight, its wings outstretched and frozen in time. Beneath the dove, two circles intertwined, forming an elegant, harmonious design.

I was struck by how I had overlooked this intricate marking on both Jae and the Wolf during our previous encounters. He turned and headed towards the house behind us which was only 2 doors down from my house on the same block. "Your mate? How?" I cried. She shrugged.

"I... I don't know. I just ended up dead and very close to here. Call it weird but I was on my way to your house afterward because I was confused and didn't realize I was dead. But on my way here I ran into Jordan, and we both felt it instantly. I never knew any of this was real... I never knew it existed. But if I had to die to find him, and remain dead to be with him, then I never want to live again." She said.

"Well, I'm going to feel guilt for the rest of my life over killing you, but I'm glad that you are happy here." I said, following her into her home. We had only sat down for a brief moment when I felt a strange tugging on my body. It felt as if someone had a rope connected to me and they were pulling on it. Gently, but still firm. "Jae, say goodbye to your friend, it seems that someone in the land of the living wants her back." Jordan said.

Jae got up and wrapped her arms around me again. "Don't worry about me, I promise I am happier than I've ever been. Thank you, thank you so much for sending me here. I love you girl! Now get back to whoever is missing you." She said, and before she could let me go I was being forcefully yanked from The Otherside.

As the strange sensation dissipated, I found myself back in a familiar setting, my own arena. A sea of somber faces surrounded me, their eyes fixed on a lifeless form cradled in Raziel's arms. My heart sank as I realized the body was mine. I felt a shiver run down my spine as I approached my lifeless form, a sense of detachment washing over me. It was then that I understood the horrifying truth... I was invisible to the mournful crowd, a silent spectator to my own demise.

My gaze fell upon Raziel, and my heart ached at the sight of his tear-stained cheeks. Though his eyes were dry now, the tracks of his earlier tears told a story of unbearable grief. I shifted my attention to Alpha Drake, whose somber expression seemed chiseled from stone as he watched us with an unyielding gaze. Nearby, Roman stood frozen in shock, his body trembling visibly as he struggled to process the scene before him. The weight of their sorrow was crushing, and I felt a pang of regret for the pain I had caused them.

I glanced down at Raziel, and my eyes met his. To my astonishment, he was gazing directly at me, his eyes locking onto mine with an unmistakable intensity. "You can see me?" I asked, my voice barely above a whisper. Raziel nodded, a gentle smile spreading across his face.

"Come home, darling," he whispered, his voice filled with longing. A solitary tear escaped my eye as I reached out to touch my lifeless body. The moment my spirit reconnected with my physical form, I felt a surge of energy course through me. As I adjusted to the sensation, my eyes fluttered open, focusing on Raziel's relieved face.

His expression held surprise, but not fear, and I realized that my eyes must have returned to normal. More remarkably, I couldn't sense The Darkness within me at all... Finally, its presence had vanished, leaving an unsettling yet welcome silence..

"Rayne, oh my god, are you alright?!" Raziel exclaimed, his voice laced with worry, as he helped me sit up. I nodded, still catching my breath. "Razlel? I'm fine..." I stammered, my words barely above a whisper.

I wanted to ask about Roman, but I had already seen him from the Other Side, and I knew he was safe. Raziel's arms enveloped me, holding me tightly against his chest.

"What is your price?" He demanded, his voice firm, as he addressed The Shadows. I noticed then that The Shadows were everywhere, their dark forms swirling around us like a living entity.

They spoke in hushed tones, their words indistinct, but I caught snippets of their conversation. It was something about a life for a life, the price being paid, and a debt owed to me. But my attention was divided, my mind rejoicing at the realization that Wynter was back, and The Darkness was truly gone. "The Darkness, it's gone!" I exclaimed suddenly, jumping up out of Raziel's arms. Wynter's triumphant howl echoed through my mind, a sound I had deeply missed. Tears of joy pricked at the corners of my eyes as I exclaimed, "Wynter's back too! It's really gone, all of it!"

My gaze drifted inward, and I reached out with my senses, searching for the familiar ache of the void. But it was as if it had never existed. The despair that had once threatened to consume me, the anguish of losing my mate bond... all of it was gone.

I pressed my hand over my heart, seeking any lingering remnants of the pain, but there was nothing. It was as if I had been reborn, restored to my former self. The realization left me stunned. *How is this possible?* I thought. My gaze shifted as Raphael approached, his eyes cast downward in a clear display of shame.

His slow, deliberate steps seemed to weigh heavily on him, as if each footfall was a reluctant admission of guilt. I waited, expecting the familiar stirrings of anger, fear, or resentment to rise up within me.

But instead, a profound sadness settled in, accompanied by an unexpected urge to forgive him. The emotions swirled within me, a bittersweet mix of sorrow and compassion that left me feeling hollow, yet somehow lighter.

I walked up to him and took him into my arms. He slowly put his arms around me pulling me into a tight embrace. "Rayne, I am so fucking sorry. I have no idea what came over me. I just... you are just so incredible... I just couldn't help myself. I never wanted to hurt you."

Raphael's voice caught in his throat as he struggled to articulate his thoughts, the words faltering on his lips like a hesitant confession. His eyes, still downcast, seemed to bore into the ground, as if seeking solace in the earth itself.

The air was heavy with his unspoken emotions, and I could sense the weight of his remorse, like an unshed burden waiting to be released. "I'm so fucking sorry," Raphael whispered, his voice trembling with a mix of worry and sincerity. "Can you ever forgive me?" His eyes, red-rimmed and pleading, searched mine for a glimmer of absolution. I took a deep breath, Wynter's gentle hum of agreement echoing in my mind.

"Raphael... I understand," I said, my voice softening. "And while I'm still upset with you, I do forgive you." He brushed a strand of hair behind my ear, his fingers grazing my skin, and smiled weakly. "Thank you, beautiful," he whispered, his voice filled with gratitude. Then, he turned to face Raziel, a hint of trepidation in his eyes.

"Brother, I'm deeply sorry for my actions. I was wrong to interfere, and once The Darkness consumed me, I was powerless to stop myself. I know that's no excuse for my behavior, and I don't expect forgiveness easily. I know that is not an excuse for my unacceptable behavior... but I hope that someday you'll be able to find it in your heart to pardon me." He said. He sounded sincere, then he materialized away from the arena.

I decided it was time to comfort Roman. He looked like he had been crying, hard, and I could tell he was still in shock. I walked over to him and took him into a bear hug. "Rayne, I'm so sorry! I froze, I didn't know what to do. I never meant to get you killed... I'm so sorry." Roman stammered, tears filling his eyes again.

"I would do it again if the need arose." I said. And that was the truth, I definitely would. I wouldn't even hesitate. I would do anything for my pack members, even give my life, again, if that were the cost. I felt the conviction pulsing through my body while I thought this. I let go of Roman as he thanked me again. I looked behind him and locked eyes with Alpha Drake.

We didn't say anything because there was nothing to be said, but I knew he was proud of me. I knew my sacrifice was something the Luna of The Obsidian pack would have done for her people. I may not be the Luna of this pack, but I would fiercely protect it as if I were. I knew he knew that, and we nodded to each other in understanding.

I headed back towards Raziel. I was so utterly grateful for him, and I wanted to ensure that he knew this.

"Thank you, Raziel. Thank you for never giving up on me, even when it seemed impossible." I said. He smiled, and I knew that the smile was something only reserved for me. "I haven't followed you to the literal ends of the earth since you were 9 years old, just to give up on you now... have I?" He purred.

I chuckled. He literally had done exactly that, though the full extent of his stalking, I may never truly know. He was sleuth in his ways. "Fair enough, but now that the drama's subsided, who's going to clean up this mess? We can't just leave a gaping hole in the middle of the arena." I said, realizing that Raphael and I had really made a mess of things.

Raziel snapped, and the arena looked as if it was never even damaged. I wanted to say that I was surprised that he could do that, but I was beginning to think there was nothing outside of the realm of his powers. He then looked at Alpha Drake. "I trust you'll handle the pack?" You can spin the story however you see fit, but they deserve some explanation." He said, motioning towards everyone who was still in the stands.

"I will handle it, don't worry." Alpha Drake replied. Raziel then nodded to him and then looked back at me. "Raziel, do you have something you need to tell me?" I asked, referring to Jae, but I didn't want to give him details right here. I thought this could wait but it was really pressing in the back of my mind.

"In regards to?" He replied. I could feel the guilt in his words, though he didn't show it outwardly. I knew he was aware of what I was referring to.

"Let's speak at home." I said, and he nodded. I grabbed his hand and materialized us to his room.

Chapter 58

O nce we made it back to his room I sat him down on his bed and looked into his golden orbs. But before I could speak he took my face in his hands. "I am sorry I lied to you about Jae and what happened. I know this is what you refer to because this is the only thing I have ever hidden from you and regardless of my intent, I know it was wrong. I promise never to hide anything from you, ever again."

There wasn't even a moment when I thought I wouldn't forgive him, but this made it even more clear that I was willing to go through a lot for this man. "Thank you, for keeping it from me.

Honestly, I wasn't in the mindset to handle such a devastating loss. But I am now, and I'm ok." I said. I figured I would tell him about Jae and Jordan, but not right now. I was exhausted. Dying, and then being reincarnated by The Shadows, really took its toll. As tired as I was, my mind was still racing. Although I was still upset at Raphael, the hatred I was feeling before was completely gone.

The Darkness's influence lingered in my mind, and I couldn't shake the feeling that it had manipulated my emotions, amplifying every negative sentiment until it became almost unbearable. Anger, grief, despair, and fury… all these feelings had been magnified, distorted, and twisted to serve The Darkness's sinister purposes. Its presence had been a constant catalyst, fueling my pain and nudging me toward destructive choices. And it worked, exploiting my vulnerabilities with devastating precision.

But now, with The Darkness gone, I realized that its absence had brought me a sense of relief that was both profound and unsettling. It was as if I had become so accustomed to the weight of my pain that I had begun to crave the intensity of those emotions, even as they consumed me. The thought sent a shiver down my spine... had I become addicted to my own suffering?

I was lost in thought, my mind still reeling from the aftermath of my ordeal, when Raziel's arms enveloped me, pulling me close. As our bodies touched, a sudden jolt of electricity coursed through me, like a spark of lightning illuminating the darkness. I felt a shiver run down my spine as I wondered how this was possible. After all, I no longer bore the crescent moon mark that had once symbolized our bond.

Raphael's brutal act, fueled by The Darkness, had shattered that mark, leaving me feeling lost and disconnected from Raziel. Yet, here I was, feeling the familiar thrill of his touch, as if our bond had never been broken.

Raziel's eyes locked onto mine, his gaze piercing as he searched for any lingering remnants of The Darkness. I could sense the turmoil of emotions swirling within him, but his eyes remained steady, scrutinizing me with an intensity that was both captivating and unnerving. Just as it seemed like time was suspended, Nero's voice whispered in my mind. "Ours." The sound of his voice was like a key turning in a lock, and I felt a surge of wonder.

For the first time, I had truly heard him, and it was exhilarating. This was the one power I had struggled to grasp, and now, like a door creaking open, it was finally within my reach. "Yours." I whispered in response to Nero, my voice barely audible. Raziel's eyes widened in astonishment, a radiant smile spreading across his face.

"You heard him?" He asked, his voice filled with delight. He chuckled, the sound low and husky, and swept me off the bed, spinning me around in a joyful circle. As he pulled me close, his lips claimed mine in a kiss that sent shivers coursing through my veins. At that moment, I knew that I didn't need the crescent moon mark to know where I belonged. My heart, my soul, and every fiber of my being knew that I was his, and he was mine.

Raziel guided me back to the bed, settling me into the crook of his arm, where I felt safe and protected. As we lay there, I knew it was time to confront the elephant in the room. "I've been thinking," I began, my voice barely above a whisper. "I realize now how childish I was acting while under The Darkness's control. I'm so sorry, Raziel. I wish I could explain the emotions that were swirling inside me, but it's hard to put into words."

I took a deep breath, hoping to convey the turmoil I had endured. "I was terrified to talk to you about it, afraid of being vulnerable and weak. And The Darkness... it just fueled those fears, making me believe I was better off alone, that I didn't need anyone else." I glanced up at Raziel, his eyes watching me intently, and I hoped that my words would help alleviate some of the questions and concerns that had been plaguing him.

Raziel's voice was low and soothing, his words dripping with conviction. "Listen, darling." He said, his eyes narrowing onto me as he spoke. "I've never been one to pry, and I never will be. I believe in you, completely and utterly. You're a strong, capable, and determined woman, and I've had the privilege of watching you grow into the incredible person you are today."

He paused, his gaze burning with intensity. "I've never doubted your ability to take care of yourself, and I never will. You're a warrior, little Wolf, and I have every faith in you." Raziel's words ignited a warmth in my chest, and I couldn't help but smile. My fingers absently traced the contours of his shirt, following the defined lines of his pectoral muscles. "Thank you for believing in me." I whispered, my voice filled with gratitude.

"Even if I had asked for your help, I realize now that there was nothing you could have done. The Darkness had taken hold, and no amount of coaxing or reassurance could have dislodged it from my mind. I was clinging to it, unwilling to let go." I admitted, the truth finally dawning on me, as I truly acknowledged it for the first time.

"I know, darling. I had never heard of The Darkness before, and I've lost a great many things in my life, yet I have never been face to face with something like this. I'm sure it chooses those who it feels are vulnerable enough to let it in. Had you never lost your mate bond, it never would have chosen you. I know this for a fact, because you are anything but vulnerable." He said.

I let out a skeptical snort, feeling a pang of self-doubt. "You have such a high opinion of me, but look at all the harm I've caused due to my own naivety. I was so blind, so vulnerable..." My voice trailed off, defeated. Raziel's expression turned fierce, and he wrapped me in a tight embrace, holding me close to his chest. Then, he gently grasped my chin, his fingers guiding my face upward until our eyes met. His gaze burned with intensity, as if he could see right through to my soul.

Raziel's voice was low and soothing, his words infused with a deep wisdom. "No one in this life is perfect, my love. We all stumble, we all make mistakes, and we all learn from them, often the hard way. You're no exception to this rule, nor am I. But don't let this experience break you. That's not what defines you. What matters is how you rise after you fall. It's a lesson I've learned from centuries of living, and it's one that I've seen play out time and time again. Your failures don't shape you, it's how you respond to them that does."

He paused, his gaze drifting away from mine as a faraway look crept into his eyes. For a moment, I thought I saw a glimmer of wistfulness, a hint of nostalgia for a time long past. His eyes, like two golden suns, seemed to hold a deep sadness, a knowledge that came from having witnessed the passage of ages.

Raziel's gaze snapped back to mine, and our eyes locked once more, sending a flutter of butterflies through my stomach. His voice took on a sense of urgency, as if he was imparting a secret that only he knew. "You'll continue to walk this earth, witnessing the passage of time, but there will come a day when you'll feel like you've learned all there is to learn. Don't be fooled, my love. The truth is, you'll never exhaust the depths of knowledge, no matter how long you live. So, take every experience, every triumph and every failure, and dissect it. Tear it apart, analyze it, and learn from it. Never let a lesson slip through your fingers, no matter how painful or difficult it may be. Because in the end, it's not the years you live, but the lessons you learn that truly matter." His words ignited a fire within me, shifting my perspective and filling me with a newfound sense of purpose.

I smiled, feeling a sense of gratitude and love wash over me. "Thank you, Raziel," I said, my voice barely above a whisper. "I'm ready to face whatever life has in store for me, as long as you're by my side. With you, I feel like I can conquer anything." My eyes locked onto his, and I saw the warmth and adoration reflected back at me, filling my heart with joy and contentment.

Raziel's voice dropped to a low, husky growl, sending shivers down my spine. "I have said this before, and I will say it again. I haven't followed your every move since you were 9 years old, just to let you go now. You are mine, Rayne." He growled. The air around us seemed to vibrate with his possessiveness, wrapping me in a warm, intoxicating embrace.

Red flags would have waved wildly for anyone else, but for me, Raziel's words were a siren's call, drawing me deeper into the depths of our passion. Instead of fear, I felt a thrill of excitement, my heart pounding in anticipation.

As the night wore on, I poured my heart out to Raziel, sharing every detail of my experiences under The Darkness's control. I recounted the intoxicating rush of power, the twisted thoughts that had consumed me, and the complicated emotions that still lingered. I spoke of Raphael, and how I currently felt regarding him. I shared the story of Roman's rescue, and the motivations that had driven me to save him. I even delved into the mysterious realm I had visited after death, a place that had felt like nothingness, yet somehow seemed connected to the origins of The Shadows.

And finally, I spoke of Jae and Jordan, and the sense of peace I had found in knowing that Jae was at rest. Raziel listened attentively, his eyes never leaving mine, as I laid bare my soul. When I finished, he asked, his voice tinged with curiosity.

"Why did you forgive Raphael?" I paused, collecting my thoughts before responding. I chose my words carefully, not wanting to inadvertently stir up any lingering emotions in Raziel. "Raphael didn't intentionally mean to harm me," I began.

"He wasn't motivated by malice, he was driven by a desire to find happiness again. I understand that feeling, that deep-seated need to fill a void. And I believe that if The Darkness hadn't consumed him, he would have left us alone. He wouldn't have continued to pursue me." I paused, collecting my thoughts before continuing.

"I'm still frustrated that he didn't accept my rejection the first time, but I see now that his actions were rooted in pain and desperation. He was trying to fill the emptiness within him, and I empathize with that." I glanced up at Raziel, hoping that he would understand my perspective.

Raziel's expression softened, his eyes filled with adoration as he gazed at me. "I understand," he whispered, his voice filled with emotion. "You're incredible, Rayne. Your capacity for kindness, forgiveness, and empathy is truly inspiring." He pressed a gentle kiss to the top of my head, his lips warm and comforting.

"You have a heart of gold, and I can only aspire to be as thoughtful and compassionate as you are," he added. The sincerity in his words wrapped around me like a warm hug, filling me with a sense of love and gratitude.

Raziel and I lost ourselves in conversation, the hours slipping away like grains of sand in an hourglass. I was determined to savor every moment with him, feeling a deep sense of guilt for having neglected him during my battle with The Darkness. For months, my focus had been solely on myself and the evil that had threatened to consume me. Now, I was eager to make amends, to spend quality time with Raziel and reconnect with him on a deeper level. As the first light of dawn began to creep into the sky, I finally drifted off to sleep, safe in the warmth of Raziel's arms.

The next six months were a journey of healing and redemption, as I worked tirelessly to repair the relationships I had damaged during my darkest hours. I began the process of mending relationships by reaching out to Alpha Drake.

After some discussion, we came to a mutually beneficial agreement. I would continue to participate in training and patrols, but I would have the freedom to come and go as I pleased, without being bound to the pack lands. Alpha Drake's words, spoken with a new type of warmth, touched my heart.

"Your home within the Obsidian pack will always be here for you, should you want it or need it." I never thought I'd hear him say something like that, and it was a testament to how far we'd come in such a short time. Raziel's words about growth and change echoed in my mind as I smiled, feeling a sense of gratitude. "Thank you, Alpha," I replied, genuinely moved.

Alpha Drake chuckled, a mischievous glint in his eye. "And, of course, the Luna position will always be available to you... whenever you're ready." I laughed, playfully rolling my eyes. "In your dreams, Alpha." He smirked, his expression confident. "You can bet on it."

Despite our rocky start, I was glad that Alpha Drake and I had developed a genuine relationship, one built on mutual respect and trust. His alliance was a valuable one, and I knew it would serve me well in the future.

Next on my list was Roman, and although we had never had a falling out, I wanted to check in on him and see how he was doing. I had heard rumors that he had left the pack, so I decided to reach out to him through our mind link. "Hey Roman, just wanted to touch base and see how you're doing. I heard you left the pack, hope everything is okay!" I asked. I had hoped he could hear the concern etched in my mental voice. Roman's response was immediate, and it was infused with excitement.

"Rayne! Hey, I did leave the pack, but only temporarily. Alpha Drake granted my request to join the Obsidian pack permanently, and he's allowed me to bring my family with me. I'm actually on my way to pick them up now, and we'll be heading back to the pack in a few days."

I felt an overwhelming surge of joy at his news. Roman was finally free from the contractual bond that had tied him to our friendship, and yet, he had chosen to stay. Some bonds, it seemed, were stronger than any contract.

"Roman, I'm so damn happy for you!" I exclaimed, my mental voice bubbling with excitement. "I Can't wait to meet your family when you get back!" Roman's response was equally enthusiastic. "Me too, me too! See you in a few days, Rayne!"

I felt a sense of harmony returning to my life. The bridges I had once burned were slowly being rebuilt, and I was finally starting to feel a sense of contentment.

The ache of losing my mate bond still lingered, a constant reminder of what I had lost. But somehow, after facing and overcoming so many other challenges, the pain didn't feel as overwhelming as it once had.

It was still there, a dull hum in the background of my mind, but it no longer consumed me. I had learned to live with it, and as I looked out at the new chapter unfolding before me, I felt hope.

Chapter 59

~
(6 Months later)

Things had been going well in the pack. I had been helping with training and doing other side jobs for Alpha Drake. Our relationship had really blossomed into something amazing. I was no longer afraid of him or disgusted by him. We were strictly professional, with an occasional flirty comment from him, that I mostly just ignored. Nothing too wild though. It was more fun than anything. I realized that he was only this way with me, and usually only without the presence of others. He still had an image to maintain and I understood that.

Since moving in with Raziel, I'd learned that being part of my pack was an essential part of who I was. The brief period of separation had left me feeling restless and unfulfilled. But now that I'd settled back into a routine with the pack, I felt a sense of contentment wash over me. I was grateful that Raziel understood and respected my need for balance in my life. He didn't mind that I was still deeply connected to the pack, and his unwavering support meant the world to me. I felt lucky to have found a partner who accepted me for who I was, pack and all.

Speaking of Raziel, he had been mysteriously absent for much of the week, popping in and out without revealing what had been keeping him so busy. Whenever I asked, he'd just smile and say it was a surprise. I had a feeling it was related to my birthday preparations, though.

My thoughts drifted to my birthday. It's tomorrow, and I will be turning 21. The excitement of my upcoming birthday was tempered by the lingering ache of losing my mate bond. It felt like an eternity since it had been severed, leaving an unfillable void within me. I tried to convince myself that the bond itself wasn't what truly mattered, after all, I still had Raziel by my side.

But the truth was, the loss of that sacred connection still stung. Last year's birthday was amazing. This year, however, felt different. No matter how wonderful the festivities might be, I couldn't shake the feeling that something essential was missing. I struggled to keep these melancholic thoughts at bay, but sometimes they became overwhelming, even for someone as resilient as myself.

When the ache of losing my mate bond became too much to bear, I made a conscious effort to shift my focus away from the pain. Dwelling on it wouldn't change the past, and I knew I had to accept the loss and move forward. That's exactly what I planned to do. I was determined to have a wonderful birthday, no matter what it took. If I told myself that enough times then it had to come true, right?

That night Raziel arrived home early and I was surprised to see him as I had been asleep before he got here for the past few days. "Rayne, darling, come here." He said while I was in the bathroom brushing my teeth. I rinsed my mouth and stepped out of the bathroom, a smile spreading across my face as I took in the sight before me.

Raziel stood in the bedroom, a dozen exquisite golden roses cradled in one arm, while the other held a champagne bottle, a large elegantly wrapped gift, and a smaller, intricately boxed one. "What's all this?" I asked, my curiosity piqued, as I walked towards him, my eyes locked on the thoughtful gesture.

Raziel's eyes sparkled as he handed me the stunning golden roses. "I know it's early, but tomorrow's going to be a whirlwind for you, and I wanted to steal some quiet time with you tonight, just the two of us," he said, his voice low and intimate.

As I breathed in the sweet fragrance of the roses, Raziel set the champagne, gifts, and other treats on the bed. He then leaned in, his lips brushing against mine in a gentle, tender kiss. I wrapped my hand around his neck, drawing him closer, careful not to crush the delicate flowers. The world around us melted away, leaving only the two of us, lost in the sweetness of the moment.

"Thank you. But you know this is all unnecessary, right?" I said, pulling away from his embrace. He chuckled. "You tell me this every year, but does it ever change?" He asked. "Ok, that's fair. Your love language is giving gifts, I get it." I said, and with a playful snap of my fingers, a beautiful vase filled with water appeared. I gently placed the golden roses into it, their delicate petals unfolding like tiny rays of sunshine.

I stepped back to admire the roses, now beautifully arranged in their vase, and turned to find Raziel already expertly opening the champagne at the bar. He poured two glasses with a flourish, then walked over to me, handing me one with a smile. Our glasses clinked together in a gentle toast, and we both savored the crisp, effervescent wine. Raziel then took my glass from me, setting it beside the roses, and presented me with the larger, elegantly wrapped gift.

"Open it." He said, handing it to me. With a resigned smile, I decided to humor Raziel and opened the package. Inside, I found a stunning silk tank top and matching shorts set.

The black fabric was exquisite, adorned with intricate gold lace that shimmered in the light. The overall design was elegant and sophisticated, with a touch of luxury that hinted at the high end quality of the garment. I couldn't help but feel a flutter of delight at the thoughtful gift, despite my initial hesitation.

"Put it on." He said, his voice low and husky. I stood to head to the bathroom but he stopped me with a hand on my bicep. "Right here, Rayne. Put it on, right here. I want to see your perfect body as you do." He reiterated. My cheeks flushed with a warm blush as I felt a shiver run down my spine. Raziel had seen me naked only during intimate moments, and I wasn't one to walk around undressed. This was a new level of vulnerability, but there was something about Raziel's gaze that made me feel safe and desired.

Our eyes met, and I flashed Raziel a subtle smile before slowly pulling my shirt over my head. My shorts followed, sliding down my legs and pooling on the floor. Standing before him in my matching black lace bra and panties, I felt a thrill of excitement as Raziel's gaze devoured me. His eyes roamed my body, drinking in every detail, and I could sense the hunger in his gaze.

I reached for the silk tank top he had given me, but he shook his head, his eyes never leaving mine. "Take the rest off first." He whispered. My cheeks burned with an intense flush as I hesitated for a moment, my fingers on the clasp of my bra. I looked up at Raziel, and our eyes locked in a charged moment. "Off," he growled, his voice low and primal, sending a swarm of butterflies fluttering in my chest. With a slow breath, I carefully released the clasp and slid my bra off, my arms moving slowly as I fought the instinct to cover myself.

The air seemed to vibrate with tension as I stood before him, exposed and vulnerable, yet drawn to the fierce desire burning in his eyes. "Fuck, Rayne... you're fucking perfect." He murmured. his gaze scorched me with its intensity. His eyes seemed to burn with a fierce desire, and I felt my heart skip a beat as he urged me on. "Go on now, continue," he whispered, his words dripping with anticipation.

I flashed Raziel a sly smile and teased him by pulling one side of my panties down my thigh, my hips swaying seductively. His eyes blazed with desire, and a low hum of appreciation rumbled in his throat. "Mmm," he murmured, his voice dripping with hunger. Before I could even finish removing my panties, Raziel closed the distance between us, his hand wrapping around my throat as he claimed my lips in a rough, passionate kiss.

"You drive me absolutely fucking crazy," he purred, his free hand sliding between my legs to rip my panties off. He tossed them aside, and in one swift motion, swept me into his arms, depositing me onto the bed. As Raziel settled on top of me, his hands cupped my breasts, sending shivers down my spine. Wynter swooned at the intimate touch.

Raziel was still fully dressed, but his tailored suit only added to his allure, making him look like a deity descended from the heavens. I tugged on his suit jacket, eager to feel his skin against mine, and he pulled it off without breaking our kiss. Our lips remained locked, the passion between us growing with every passing moment

I undid a button on his shirt but he stopped me. "No, tonight is about you." He pinned my hand above my head, his grip firm but gentle. His lips left mine, tracing a fiery path down my throat, leaving a trail of hickeys and marks on my skin.

I gasped, pleasure coursing through me, as he swirled his tongue around my left nipple, simultaneously pinching the right one. Raziel's mouth continued its sensual journey, leaving a canvas of marks and hickeys on my breasts and stomach before reaching my inner thigh

Raziel's teeth grazed my skin, a gentle yet thrilling bite that made me squirm with pleasure. He parted my legs, his eyes locking onto mine with a sensual smile. Then, he dipped his head, his face disappearing between my thighs as he began to lavish attention on me. I moaned out in pleasure as his tongue tantalized my clit.

Raziel's moans of pleasure vibrated against my skin, sending shivers of delight through me and pushing me closer to the edge. Just as I was about to succumb to the sensation, he abruptly stopped, and I heard a sharp snapping sound. I looked down to find that he had suddenly produced a bowl of ice cubes, the cold, crystalline structures glinting in the dim light.

I watched him take one of the icy squares from the bowl and I gasped as he gently rubbed it over my swollen clit. The sudden chill of the ice cube sent a jolt through my body, and I instinctively tried to close my legs, but Raziel's grip held firm, keeping me open to the sensation. He ran the ice cube down my folds and gently pushed it inside of me. I gasped again, unprepared for the unfamiliar sensation.

But before I could process it further, Raziel swiftly moved the bowl aside and flipped me onto my stomach. I turned my head, curiosity getting the better of me, and saw him slide into position beneath me.

He guided me onto my knees, positioning me so that I was seated above his face, his eyes locking onto mine with an intense gaze. I could feel the ice cube melting slowly inside of me, as he sucked and nibbled on my clit, drinking up all of the icy liquid that emerged.

Once the ice cube melted he soothed the cold by sticking his tongue up inside of me. My small gasps and moans of pleasure only made him more aggressive with me. He popped another ice cube inside of me and then pinned my pussy to his face with his hands on my thighs. I couldn't move if I wanted to. He allowed the ice cube to melt fully while devouring me before he began to focus on my clit, using his fingers to pump in and out of me.

As the pressure continued to build, I could feel myself reaching a critical point. Raziel's skilled movements pushed me over the edge, and I moaned out in ecstasy as an intense, overwhelming wave of pleasure washed over me. He continued to lick me and suck on my clit gently while I rode my orgasm out.

Once I was done he pulled me off of him and made me straddle him instead. I could feel his hardened cock as it rubbed against my swollen clit through his pants. I looked down, acknowledging it, and then back up as he met my gaze.

Raziel's warning, "don't get any ideas," hung in the air as he rolled over, gently placing me back on the bed before standing up. His back remained turned to me as he methodically removed his clothes, piece by piece, until he was left wearing only his boxers.

A sly smirk spread across his face as he turned to face me, his eyes gleaming with amusement. He sauntered towards the bathroom, and I instinctively got out of bed, attempting to follow him. However, Raziel's deep growl, "Rayne, don't even," stopped me in my tracks, and he shut the bathroom door firmly behind him.

I stood there, baffled, wondering why Raziel would refuse my intimate advances. "Why!" I exclaimed, frustration getting the better of me as I banged on the bathroom door with my fist.

Raziel's chuckle was a low, husky sound, and he opened the door just a crack. "There's a time and a place, but now is not it," he said, his voice firm but gentle. I pouted, feeling a bit rebuffed, and made my way back to the bed, flopping down onto the mattress.

I knew Raziel never acted without a reason, so I couldn't help but wonder what his motivation was for denying me. My gaze fell upon the black and gold silk lace pajamas he had given me, lying on the floor. I picked them up, slid them on, and was pleased to find they fit perfectly. Climbing under the covers, I turned my back to the bathroom door, still nursing my wounded pride.

The bathroom door creaked open, and soon Raziel slipped into bed beside me. I maintained my stubborn posture, keeping my back to him as a clear indication that I was still pouting.

Undeterred, Raziel wrapped his arms around me, pulling me close to his chest. He rested his head against the nape of my neck, his warm breath sending shivers down my spine. "You can pout all you want, I'm the master at ignoring it," he whispered, his voice low and seductive. His teeth gently grazed the back of my neck, sending a thrill through me.

I couldn't help but notice the frequency of these intense, almost primal reactions between us since The Darkness had dissipated. Yet, I was still confused. I wasn't marked anymore but our bond wasn't like anything I'd ever experienced.

I turned in his arms so I was facing him. "You infuriate me." I murmured, running my fingers through his wet hair. "I know, and I love it." He replied cockily, taking my lips in his.

"Now, get some sleep, you have a big day tomorrow." A frustrated groan escaped my lips, prompting Raziel to chuckle softly to himself. He tightened his hold, tucking me snugly into the warmth of his arms, and I felt my resistance slowly give way to the comforting sensation of being enveloped by him.

Chapter 60

$\mathcal{S}$leep had claimed me quickly, but waking up to an empty bed was a surprise. Raziel's absence on my 21st birthday seemed odd, but I pushed aside the doubt, assuming he must be busy with a surprise for me. I jumped into the shower, feeling a mix of excitement and anticipation.

As I stepped out, my eyes landed on the chaise lounge at the foot of the bed, where a stunning gold dress had been carefully laid out for me. The dress was a showstopper, its glittering fabric caught the light, and the daring slit that rose up one side to my upper thigh added a touch of sultry sophistication.

The backless design featured a delicate strap that wrapped around my neck, framing the higher neckline perfectly. I smiled, grateful for the thoughtfulness of my boyfriend. Red immediately swarmed my cheeks at the thought of Raziel and the way he touched me last night... I brushed it off and headed back towards the bathroom.

I styled my hair in loose waves, knowing it was a look Raziel particularly liked. I chuckled to myself, thinking it must be a sibling thing, briefly thinking about Raphael. Wynter caught my joke and burst out laughing.

"HAPPY BIRTHDAY, RAYNE!" She shouted, her enthusiasm was infectious. I smiled, feeling grateful for her excitement. "Thank you!" I replied, before turning serious for a moment.

"I'm sorry about the mate bond... I know today would be a whole different type of day if things were a little different." I said, surprised to find that discussing the lack of mate bond no longer filled me with the dull ache of the void. "I

413

know,Rayne… it's ok, everything will be fine. Who needs a mate anyway? We have Raziel." Wynter shot playfully. She wasn't wrong, we didn't need the mate bond. At this point it would honestly just cause more problems. I was now feeling lucky that I wouldn't have to reject my mate like I had practiced so many times before. That was one good thing to come out of this. A silver lining, if you may.

I slipped into the stunning gold dress, pairing it with the matching sandals that had been thoughtfully left out for me. My eyes landed on a note attached to the smaller box from the previous night, written in Raziel's distinctive handwriting.

'Happy Birthday, darling! Get dressed, you're going to breakfast with Roman. I had some business to take care of. I will meet up with you soon. Love Raziel.'

His words were written in 14k gold on a piece of parchment. I laughed out loud at my realization because of course they were. This man was the most extra person I had ever met. I admired the way his handwriting looked like that of an angel. Perfect calligraphy lined the note, making me question if he was honestly even real.

I gently set the note aside and opened the box, revealing a breathtakingly beautiful golden necklace. The pendant was a stunning crescent moon, adorned with intricate filigree and vines, mirroring the exact design of Raziel's mark.

The necklace was crafted from solid 14k gold, and its surface glittered radiantly in the light. My heart fluttered at the thought of being marked by him, but for real this time. I hadn't asked him to mark me again since everything happened. I knew when the time was right, he would mark me again.

This time it would be on his terms, and I was ok with waiting for that. I put the necklace on, and of course, it complimented my outfit perfectly. I did one last mirror check and I couldn't help but admire Raziel's taste in clothing and jewelry. "Well, here's to 21!" I exclaimed to Wynter, who responded with cheers and compliments on my outfit.

Feeling confident and excited, I headed out the door, where I found Roman waiting for me. I was taken aback by his sharp gold and black suit, which perfectly matched my dress. It was clear that Raziel had also chosen Roman's outfit, and I couldn't help but feel a sense of delight at the thoughtful gesture.

Roman's eyes widened in admiration as I approached him, and he looked like he was about to burst with excitement. "Happy Birthday!!! My God, you look amazing!" he exclaimed, his enthusiasm infectious. I smiled, feeling a little self-conscious but also pleased by his reaction. I playfully curtseyed to him, and we both dissolved into laughter.

We climbed into Roman's neon orange Toyota Supra, and he took me on a surprise journey outside of pack territory. I knew Alpha Drake wouldn't normally allow us to leave pack lands, but, of course, it was my birthday, and Roman must have gotten special permission. We pulled up in front of a quaint little mom-and-pop shop called Stix, and I'd heard whispers that their food was incredible. I couldn't wait to try it out.

As I sat down at the small café, surrounded by the enticing aromas of freshly cooked food, I realized that I wasn't feeling hungry. It was a peculiar sensation, one that I'd grown accustomed to without even realizing it. Now, as I reflected on it, I wondered if this lack of hunger was another aspect of my suppressed Reaver abilities.

Despite my lack of hunger, I was determined to enjoy the meal knowing that though I didn't need sustenance to survive, I could still eat, should I choose… and I was choosing. The waitress walked up to take our order and snapped me from my thoughts. I ordered an omelet, with a side of fresh fruit. Roman ordered bacon, eggs and pancakes, but he had like four sides of bacon. I couldn't help but laugh.

"What? I love bacon." He chuckled, taking a piece and shoving it into his mouth greedily. I took a second to appreciate Roman. He was still so young. Not that I wasn't,

415

but he had a lot of experience with life under his belt. Much more than I did. I laughed under my breath thinking about how we met and why. The world works in mysterious ways.

"Why did you decide to stay in the Obsidian pack?" I asked him. I was genuinely curious as to why he would switch packs. Most Wolves stay loyal to their pack their whole lives. It's rare that they change packs unless they are forced.

"To be honest... I'm staying because of you, Rayne. Originally, I was only here because of the deal Raziel's assistant, Anthony, made to save my pack from the Vampires. But once I got here and realized just how amazing you were, I just couldn't see myself leaving. Since then, I've become friends with Alpha Drake, and I've made other close friends in this pack. The Obsidian pack is my home now, thanks to you, indirectly, of course. I'm here for the long haul." He said.

I could tell he was confident in his reasoning. I smiled in response. "Well, I'm glad I had an overprotective boyfriend/not boyfriend who thought I needed a friend then." I said with a chuckle.

Raziel was a little out of control at first, but I was glad he led me to Roman. It was an unusual way to meet, but he became a great friend. Roman and I stayed longer than I anticipated at breakfast, just chatting away and hanging out. It was nice to just hang out and just spend time together. Nothing crazy, no battles, and no fighting The Darkness, no uncontrollable powers. I loved just feeling like myself again.

As the afternoon wore on, I estimated it to be around 2 pm, amazed at how quickly the time had passed. Suddenly, I felt the unmistakable presence of Alpha Drake's mind link, its venomous undertone was unmistakable. I sensed Roman's awareness of it too, and I realized that Alpha Drake must have intentionally linked us both.

"Rayne, Roman, report to the arena please." Was all he said, and then he ended the mind link. "Weird... I guess we have been summoned." I said dramatically, putting the back of my hand to my forehead and fake fainting. Roman and I both erupted into laughter. As we prepared to leave, Roman insisted on treating me to breakfast as a birthday gift, playfully swatting away my wallet when I tried to repay him.

We strolled outside, and I couldn't help but feel a thrill of excitement as we approached Roman's sleek, neon orange Supra. I had always been enamored with this car with its flashy design, impressive speed, and overall awesomeness. We slid into the Supra's sleek interior, and

Roman turned the key, bringing the engine to life with a smooth rumble that seemed to hum with anticipation. Roman's driving was as reckless as it was exhilarating, weaving in and out of traffic with a precision that contradicted the risks he was taking.

I couldn't help but think that he drove as if we had extra lives, a luxury neither of us actually possessed. As a Reaver, I was already living on borrowed time, and Roman, as a Wolf, was mortal. Wynter's amused laughter echoed in my mind, as if she found my observation entertaining. Wynter and I were both in such a good mood today that extra lives or not, driving with Roman was worth it.

We arrived at the pack house in record time, and Roman and I made our way to the arena. The pack's grounds were unusually quiet, devoid of the typical hustle and bustle of Wolves on patrols, working, shopping, or simply socializing. The eerie silence had me exchanging a curious glance with Roman.

As we reached the arena's entrance, I stepped through the doorway first, and suddenly, a thunderous shout of "SURPRISE!" filled the air. My heart plummeted through my chest, leaving me breathless and shocked. I leapt backward, my eyes wide with surprise, before erupting into hysterical laughter.

The arena was packed with familiar faces, all of whom were grinning from ear to ear, clearly thrilled to have pulled off such an epic surprise.

Chapter 61

My entire pack was here! Roman came in behind me yelling surprise and blowing into one of those little horns that made an obnoxious noise. You know, the ones with the streamers on the end. I couldn't help but laugh at his childlike nature.

I could smell the burgers and plethora of other grilled foods being prepared. Looking towards the mouthwatering smells I could see Wolves from the pack out cooking. Even though I swear we had just eaten, I definitely wanted to eat whatever it was they were making. There was an open bar on the other side of the arena that I spotted, which I was definitely going to partake in, and I noted that the whole arena was decorated in gold decorations.

As I scanned the crowd, I noticed that every single person was adorned with some touch of gold, whether it was a subtle accent or a more elaborate display. The synchronicity was striking, and I felt a thrill of delight as I realized that everyone's attire perfectly complemented my own gold dress. It was clear that Raziel had poured his heart and soul into planning this surprise party, and the attention to detail was truly impressive. I smiled at the thought.

The energetic beat of electronic dance music filled the air, and I couldn't help but move to the rhythm as I took in the lively scene. Wolves were dancing with abandon on the floor, lost in the joy of the moment.

The arena was transformed into a vibrant party space, with gold and black streamers and balloons clustered around the tables and throughout the area. Every detail was meticulously arranged, and it was clear that a tremendous amount of time and effort had gone into creating this unforgettable celebration. The sheer effort did not go unnoticed. I couldn't believe Raziel had made such a big deal out of my birthday. I had never celebrated it quite like this before, not to this extent. It was just a birthday... where was he anyway?

I was shaken from my thoughts when Raphael's smooth, velvety voice slipped into my mind. "Hello, Beautiful," he whispered. I sensed a hint of mischief in his tone as he continued, "I didn't think my presence would be... appreciated, shall we say, but I couldn't resist wishing you a happy birthday. You look absolutely breathtaking, by the way. Don't ask me how I know."

A low, husky chuckle accompanied his words, sending a shiver down my spine. I instinctively scanned my surroundings, searching for a glimpse of him, but I knew it was futile. Raphael's presence remained elusive, a whispered promise in the shadows. His final words, "I hope you have the most wonderful day," dripped with sincerity, bathing me in a molten silver casket.

I was no longer upset with him over his selfish actions, but the fact that he caused me to lose my mate bond still weighed heavily on my mind. I was getting over it, slowly. Still, I appreciated that he was trying to be civil. We had a long way to go if we ever wanted to repair what was broken, but this was a start. "Thank you, Raphael. I'm not going to ask how you even know what I'm wearing, but I appreciate your words." I said. He didn't reply, but I felt the mind link slowly dissipate, taking the feeling of falling silver glitter along with it.

Alpha Drake then came out of the crowd with Reya in tow, and scooped me into a big hug. "Happy Birthday, Rayne!" He said into my ear. And then pulling away he handed me a small box. "You didn't have to get me anything." I told him, and I punched his shoulder.

"I know, just open it." He said, with what I thought was *almost* a smile. As I lifted the bracelet from its box, I couldn't help but gasp in admiration. The delicate, twisted chain sparkled mesmerizingly in the light, its silver and gold hues blending together in perfect harmony. Unadorned by charms, the bracelet's understated elegance only added to its allure.

"Wow, this is beautiful," I breathed, my smile genuine and heartfelt. Alpha Drake's thoughtful gesture touched me deeply. As he fastened the bracelet around my wrist, I couldn't resist admiring it from every angle, turning my wrist to watch the way the light danced across its intricate twists. Exquisite was the only word to describe it. I knew I'd treasure and wear it often.

"Would you like a drink?" He said to me, "yes sir!" I replied enthusiastically. Alpha Drake put his arm out to escort me. I never thought we would have a good enough relationship for me to be comfortable on his arm, but here we were. I took it smiling, and we headed to the bar. I could feel the eyes of basically everyone on us as we walked. Knowing our history I was sure there would be rumors and questions, but I ignored it. Let the pack think what they will. When we got to the bar, he ordered brandy, of course, and I got a strawberry daiquiri. I liked the fruity shit better anyway.

"Sorry, I can't turn it gold for you." He said with a laugh. "For shame." I retorted, with an exasperated sigh. And then I burst out into laughter.

That time I know I saw a smile on Alpha Drake's face, even if it was only for a split second. Just then a slow song came on. "Would you do me the honor?" Alpha Drake asked. Then he bowed deeply and held his hand out to me. I briefly remembered the last time he asked me to dance, and what the outcome was.

Wynter was laughing so hard in my mind over our outburst back then that I couldn't help but smile. It was a stark contrast to the present moment, where the tension between us had dissipated, replaced by a sense of tentative harmony. As I smiled, mentally accepting his invitation, I couldn't help but think that I might actually grow accustomed to this newfound sense of camaraderie.

As I gazed at Alpha Drake, I couldn't help but notice the impeccable coordination of his outfit. His black suit served as a sleek backdrop for the gold vest, shoes, and pocket square, which sparkled with subtle sophistication. The overall effect was stunning, and I had to stifle a laugh as I recalled my previous efforts to avoid matching him. His dark hair was perfectly styled, framing his chiseled features, and his ocean blues seemed to hold a depth of emotion that hinted at a more vulnerable side beneath his usual stoic exterior.

"I would be honored to." I replied softly. I put my hand in his as he led me to the dance floor. He spun me around and pulled me in close. It was actually nice to be in close proximity with someone of the opposite sex, without the nagging of a mark going wild and burning the hell out of me.

Forget the history I had with my Alpha, we had patched the relationship over the past year and turned it into something much better. As we danced, I could feel everyone's eyes upon us again. Alpha Drake never showed emotion, or interest in anyone. Especially no one from the pack.

There were so many She-Wolves in our pack that adored him and wished they could be his. So many that wished they could be the Luna of this pack. But he barely gave them a passing glance, at least in public. I knew he could have anyone he wanted anytime, and no one could say anything about it.

In fact, I'm sure he had done this multiple times, but he wasn't public about it at all. Any relationship or courtship was in private when it came to him. So, for them to see him dancing with me, publicly, in front of the whole pack... I could practically feel the jealousy burning from their glares.

This is why I was so surprised when he used to pursue me, right in front of everyone. I recalled the times he'd challenged me during training, or the way he'd sought me out at the club. It was a behavior I'd never seen him exhibit with anyone else, and it made me realize that I must hold a special significance for him, despite his initial awkward displays of affection, if you could even call them that.

Ignoring the hostile stares, I let the music guide my movements, lost in the gentle rhythm of our dance. Alpha Drake's voice was low and smooth as he began to speak, "You know, if you ever change your mind..." But I didn't let him finish, interrupting him with a teasing smile.

"Not a chance," I said, my tone playful and lighthearted. Alpha Drake simply nodded, a hint of amusement dancing in his eyes, before he leaned in and gently pressed his lips to my forehead. I knew he would drop everything in an instant if I ever were to say yes to being the Luna of this pack, and that thought somehow comforted me.

Once the song was over Alpha Drake checked his watch. "It's 5:30 pm, it is time, my dear. Raziel told me to give this to you." He pulled out a piece of parchment paper that was folded in half and handed it to me.

"Happy birthday, Rayne." He said softly and stepped closer so he could kiss my cheek. I watched him head off the dance floor to where Reya was waiting for him. I opened the parchment and a small golden key fell into my hand. The message was a tender summons, penned in elegant script. Raziel's words, infused with affection and promise, seemed to whisper directly to my heart.

'Rayne, I'm waiting for you in the most magical place that exists. Come find me, my love. Always, Raziel.'

As I read Raziel's message, the Grotto immediately came to mind, and I recalled the key he had entrusted me with. A flurry of butterflies erupted in my stomach, and my curiosity was piqued. Having not seen Raziel all day, I couldn't help but wonder what he had planned. He knew the Grotto held a special place in my heart, its enchanting atmosphere was like a balm to my soul.

I had even requested training sessions there, just to soak up its magic. As I bid farewell to the others, Wynter's presence in my mind resonated with my own excitement.

422

We were both eager to uncover Raziel's surprise. This day had already been nothing short of incredible, filled with love, appreciation, and wonder.

I decided to walk to the Grotto, rather than materialize. The trek wasn't that far, and I could use the time to calm down and steady my racing mind. With Wynter's gentle presence accompanying me, I felt a sense of peace settle over me.

Our conversation flowed effortlessly, covering everything that had transpired since the loss of our mate bond. Although we'd discussed it at length before, the significance of my 21st birthday made it feel like a good time to revisit the past.

I reaffirmed the promise I'd made to Wynter, vowing never again to tamper with forces beyond my understanding. As we strolled closer to Raziel, I reiterated that promise, the words serving as a reminder of the lessons I'd learned and the growth I'd undergone.

As we wandered down the path to the Grotto, an irresistible aroma wafted into my nostrils, leaving me utterly entranced. The scent was a complex, alluring blend of forest musk, rich, velvety chocolate, and subtle citrus notes. It was a fragrance that defied easy description, but its impact was undeniable.

Wynter's excitement within my mind was tangible, and I found myself overwhelmed by an insatiable urge to track down the source of this intoxicating smell. My pace quickened as the golden gate of the Grotto came into view. Fumbling with the key, I struggled to contain my anticipation. The scent had grown stronger, teasing my senses and leaving me a little disoriented in my haste to uncover its origin.

As I pushed through the vines covering the entrance to the Grotto, the scent grew even more potent, leaving me breathless and dizzy with anticipation. I finally caught sight of Raziel, standing poised by the edge of the serene lake. He was positioned beneath a wooden white trellis adorned with twinkling lights that seemed to dance in rhythm with the gentle lapping of the water.

His back was turned to me, but the sheer sight of him took my breath away. He wore a stunning solid gold formal suit, perfectly complemented by black accents and shoes, creating a dazzling ensemble that mirrored my own dress. Even the golden glitter on his attire sparkled as he shifted his weight, as if beckoning me closer without a single spoken word.

The intoxicating scent had become almost overwhelming, fueling an unrelenting desire within me to draw closer to its source. As I took a few steps forward, the aroma grew even more potent, and I realized with a start that it was emanating from Raziel himself.

As if sensing my approach, he turned to face me, and our eyes met in a flash of mutual understanding. The excitement radiating from his god-like features was palpable, and I could sense the eagerness building within him, mirroring the anticipation that had taken hold of me.

In perfect synchrony, Wynter and Nero's voices whispered a single, unified word in my mind. "Mate."

The term resonated deeply, echoing the primal, instinctual connection that I now knew would bound me to Raziel forever.

Chapter 62

I mentally stumbled, reeling from the sudden revelation as I spoke to Wynter in stunned inquiry. "What??! How?!" Wynter's response was a mirror of my own shock, her mental voice rising to a shriek. "I have no idea, Rayne!! Oh my god!" Before I could further process this bombshell, Raziel had closed the gap between us and swept me into his arms, his eyes blazing with exhilaration. "I knew it!" He exclaimed, his voice trembling with emotion. "I fucking knew it, but I just had to be sure."

My mind reeled as I struggled to comprehend the impossible. "How is this happening?! I thought my mate bond was gone?!" I exclaimed, my words tumbling out in a chaotic mix of confusion and awe. And then, as if summoned by the turmoil of emotions, The Shadows emerged for everywhere and nowhere. Their dark presence coalesced from the very air itself to envelop us in an icy, unsettling chill.

The Shadows' emergence seemed to have a palpable, living quality to it, as if every Shadow that existed had indeed converged upon us, drawn by the tumultuous emotions and the rekindling of the mate bond. The air was heavy with their presence, making it hard to breathe. I could feel their collective gaze upon us, like a physical weight pressing down. The sheer number of Shadows was overwhelming, casting a suffocating gloom over the Grotto, and I couldn't shake the feeling that they were responsible for this unimaginable gift.

"Happy birthday, Princesss." They slithered. "You restored my mate bond?" I asked with a gasp. The

Shadows' collective voice was like a chilling whisper, their words dripping with an otherworldly intimacy as they spoke in unison. "We did, only for you though. Letsss keep thissss our little sssecret." The hissed promise sent a shiver down my spine, and then, as suddenly as they had appeared, The Shadows dissipated, their dark forms slithering away like living tendrils of night. As they vanished, the icy chill that had permeated the air lifted, leaving behind an unsettling sense of being bound to the Shadows by a secret known only to us.

My thoughts were racing with exhilaration, making it hard to catch my breath. The revelation was too enormous to process, and yet, it all made sense now. The Shadows' intervention, the void's absence... it was all connected. I turned to Raziel, my eyes wide with wonder, and asked the question that had been burning on my lips. "You knew?" His expression, a mixture of excitement and anticipation, hinted that he had indeed been aware of the truth, and I couldn't help but wonder what else he knew, and how long he had been keeping this secret.

"Of course, I did, darling. I'm very close with The Shadows. That's the reason I couldn't be with you today, I didn't want to ruin the surprise." He explained. Raziel's words poured out like a gentle brook, soothing and reassuring. The reason behind his absence earlier in the day now made perfect sense, and I felt a surge of gratitude toward him for preserving the surprise. But it was more than just gratitude, it was a deep-seated sense of contentment that seemed to swell from the very core of my being.

My heart felt like it was expanding, physically growing to contain the sheer magnitude of my emotions. The intensity of this feeling was almost overwhelming, threatening to spill out of me in a tidal wave of joy and appreciation.

"I knew there was only a slim chance that I would be your intended mate... Reavers do not have mates, but where you grew up suppressing your Reaver side, and honing in on your Wolf side, it would make sense that you would have one. Honestly, from the first day I met you and

426

looked deep into those beautiful platinum silver eyes of yours, I felt the pull. There was no way to know for sure if I was your intended mate. But I knew you felt something too, even if you didn't understand it and were terrified of me. I decided then that if there was a chance, it would be worth whatever risk I was taking to pursue you."

Raziel's voice was laced with vulnerability and sincerity as he shared his innermost thoughts and feelings. His words painted a picture of a deep and abiding connection, one that had been present from the very beginning, even if I hadn't recognized it at the time.

As he spoke of the pull he had felt, I couldn't help but recall the countless moments when our eyes had met, and the spark of attraction had flared to life between us. I had always ignored it, pushed the feelings away and fought the pull, but he knew... he'd always known. His continual acknowledgment of my fear and uncertainty only added to the sense of intimacy and understanding that flowed from his words now. With every sentence, I felt myself drawing closer to him, our bond strengthening as the truth of his emotions was laid bare before me.

He had loved me from the moment we met. And I couldn't deny the truth in his words, for I had felt the same inexplicable pull, the same undeniable connection. Though I had tried to resist it for so long. As if to underscore the intensity of our connection, Raziel's lips suddenly claimed mine, his kiss fierce and all-consuming, leaving me breathless and wanting more.

The mate bond pulled us together like a thick cord, uniting our Wolves, and our souls. Wynter knew exactly what to do, so she guided me. I found the perfect spot of flesh on the side of his neck partially on his shoulder and sank my canines in.

He gasped as pleasure racked through his body causing him to shudder. I was marking him as my mate, as my own, and his body reacted in turn. Then, with a gentle ferocity, Raziel reciprocated, his canines sinking into my neck, leaving an identical mark. The sensation was electrifying, an explosion of pleasure and warmth that enveloped me. But what happened next left me breathless.

The usual wait time for the mark to heal and reveal its permanent design was a week, but Raziel's touch accelerated the process. He placed his hand over the mark, and in an instant, it was healed. As he lifted his hand, a look of surprise crossed his face, and I caught a glimpse of wonder in his eyes. His awestruck expression hinted that the mark on my neck was absolutely stunning, but I had to see it for myself.

As I reached out to heal the mark on his neck, my Reaver powers flowed effortlessly, as if they had always been a part of me. With his mark now healed, I lifted my gaze to behold it, and my breath caught in my throat. The sight took my breath away, leaving me speechless and mesmerized.

The mark on Raziel's neck was a stunning, deep turquoise double crescent moon, its vibrant hue instantly transporting me back to the wishing well where our journey together first began. The larger crescent cradled the smaller one, forming a perfect, harmonious union. Delicate stars twinkled beside the moons, and the mark shimmered with an ethereal light, as if infused with magic.

I was entranced by its beauty, my fingers tracing the curves of the mark with reverence, sending shivers down Raziel's spine. The uniqueness of our bond was encapsulated in this exquisite design, a symbol that belonged solely to us. No other Wolf would ever bear this identical mark, making it a truly exclusive and precious token of our love. This was ours, and ours alone.

I fought to keep my composure as I gazed up at my mate. His eyes were burning with adoration and passion, and I couldn't help but smile. The curve of my lips felt like a betrayal of the turmoil that still simmered beneath the surface, but I couldn't deny the joy and love that radiated from my very core. Raziel's face lit up in response, his own smile a dazzling display of happiness and satisfaction. "Happy birthday, my beautiful Queen. Now it's my turn."

Raziel purred. Raziel's husky voice sent shivers down my spine as he wished me a happy birthday, his words dripping with affection and adoration. His hand cradled the side of my face, and I felt a surge of bliss as he marked me once more. The sensation was even more intense than before, our newly forged mate bond amplifying the pleasure to unbearable heights.

I was lost in the ecstasy of his mark, my senses reeling as I knew that this time, it would be forever. The permanence of his claim was a heady thrill, a promise of eternal devotion that once again left me breathless.

Raziel's gaze lingered on his mark, a look of satisfaction and longing etched on his face. The desire in his eyes was unmistakable, a burning intensity that spoke of unbridled passion and unrelenting need. I could sense the anticipation emanating from him, the knowledge that this time, nothing would be held back.

As he wrapped his arms around me, pulling me into a searing kiss, I felt my own desire ignite, our lips melding together in a frenzy of passion. The boundaries between us began to blur, our bodies merging into a single, pulsating entity. The mate bond and Raziel's mark pulsed in tandem, driving us toward a crescendo of pleasure and sensation that threatened to consume us whole.

Raziel's eyes blazed with an insatiable hunger as he tore my dress from my body, the fabric ripping apart with a soft whisper. I responded in kind, pulling his shirt off and discarding it carelessly. His lips seared a trail of kisses down my skin, sending shivers of pleasure coursing through me.

When he reached the barrier of my panties, he ripped them aside with a growl of impatience, his desire for me palpable. I tangled my fingers in his hair, holding him close as he lifted me up, my legs wrapping instinctively around his waist. The air was heavy with our mutual desire, a potent fog that drove us both to madness. As he laid me down on the soft, purple and blue grass, his hands moved to his belt, the sound of it snapping free from his pants echoing through the air. My breath caught in my throat, excitement coursing through me like a river of fire.

Raziel's hands moved with a deliberate slowness, wrapping the belt around my wrists with a gentle yet unyielding pressure. His fingers closed around my bound wrists, holding them in a firm grasp. At the same time, his other hand began a sensual exploration of my body, tracing a path of fire as he touched each of my nipples, sending shivers of pleasure through me.

His caress continued downward, his fingers dancing across my skin until they finally came to rest at the sensitive folds between my legs. He started with one finger until I was used to the motion then put in two. "Fuck, Rayne, you're so goddamn tight." Raziel's low, rumbling growl sent shivers down my spine.

His warm breath caressed my ear and ignited a spark within me. My body responded with abandon, surrendering to the tidal wave of pleasure that crashed over me, leaving me breathless and trembling in its wake.

The intensity of our bond and the mark's power was overwhelming, yet exhilarating. For the first time in my life, I felt a depth of emotion that was the absolute antithesis of the void and despair that had haunted me for so long. It was as if I was floating on air, surrounded by a soft, white haze that lifted me up and cradled me in its gentle embrace.

Every moment with Raziel was a thrill, a rollercoaster of sensations that left me breathless and wanting more. The butterflies in my stomach and chest swirled with relentless enthusiasm, refusing to settle, and I reveled in the sheer joy of it all. I never wanted this euphoric feeling to end, never wanted to let go of the pure, unadulterated happiness that I was experiencing in that moment.

Raziel then pushed my legs apart and positioned himself between them. I could feel the tip of his throbbing length against my slit. In that moment, I was completely swept up in the intimacy of our connection. The gentle, tender motion was all it took to send me tumbling over the edge, surrendering to the overwhelming sensations that had been building inside me. I was more than ready for this, I was eager. My entire being was yearning for the closeness and union that only Raziel could provide. Nothing else mattered. All that existed was this moment, this feeling, and the deep, unshakeable connection that bound us together.

"Do you want it, darling?" The husky, demanding growl that vibrated through Raziel's chest and into my ear sent shivers down my spine, igniting a fresh wave of sensations that coursed through my body. He was lightly rubbing the tip of his cock against my clit and I was sure I was going to come undone before he could even get it inside of me, but I knew the drill. "Yes, Raziel... yes, I want it." I moaned out hungrily.

Raziel's gaze blazed with a fierce, untamed hunger, his golden eyes burning with a primal intensity that stripped away all subtlety, leaving only a raw, unbridled desire that seemed to consume him completely. He released my hands, letting the belt fall loose and used one hand to steady my hips, as he slowly entered me.

I could sense the restraint in Raziel's movements, and tension in his muscles as he struggled to temper his passion with gentleness. His eyes, still burning with desire, also held a deep concern for my well-being. I knew it was going to hurt, I had never done it before, so I was expecting some pain, at least.

The expected discomfort was eclipsed by the overwhelming wave of pleasure that Raziel's touch ignited within me. His caresses were like a balm, soothing and calming, and I found myself becoming lost in the sensation, my mind and body focused solely on the delight he was creating rather than the burning sensation between my legs.

He wasn't all the way in yet, and I doubted with his sheer size that he would be anytime soon if he kept going as slow as he was going. I appreciated him trying to be gentle with me, but I wanted him. I wanted all of him, exactly how he wanted to give himself to me... without restraint. I yearned to unravel the mystery of Raziel's passion, to understand the depths of his longing for me.

I wanted to know if his desire was a flickering flame or a raging inferno, if it was a gentle whisper or a deafening roar. I was driven to uncover the truth, to explore the uncharted territories of his heart and soul. "Don't hold back. I want this... I want you, Raziel." I moaned. His name coming off my lips was the key.

As Raziel's lips made contact with the mark on my neck, a jolt of electricity ran through my veins, unleashing a torrent of pleasure that left me trembling. His warm breath danced across my skin, sending shivers down my spine as he inhaled deeply, his face buried in the sensitive spot where his mark pulsed with a life of its own. "As you wish." He growled, and then he thrust, hard, into me.

The sensation was nothing short of explosive, a maelstrom of pain and pleasure that detonated at my very core. I felt my body arch, my nails instinctively digging deep into Raziel's back as I struggled to anchor myself against the turbulent tide of emotions.

The moans that tore from my lips were a primal expression of the conflicting sensations, a raw and unbridled release of the pleasure and pain that threatened to consume me whole. Each moan fueled his fire, each thrust was harder and more feral. Slowly, the pain subsided, and turned into pure, unbridled ecstasy.

Raziel stopped momentarily, grabbed me and flipped me over so my back was facing him. He pushed me down to my hands and knees and positioned himself behind me using his knee to spread my legs wide open. He then wrapped his hand around my throat and forcefully re-entered my throbbing slit. "Fuck, Rayne." He moaned, while he had his way with me. Raziel's restraint had snapped, and he was now unleashing a fierce, unbridled passion upon me.

His movements were intense, almost savage, yet I was paradoxically enthralled by the brutality of his desire. My body writhed beneath his, not in protest, but in ecstatic abandon, as I reveled in the primal, all-consuming force of his love. The pain had become a distant memory, eclipsed by the overwhelming pleasure that threatened to shatter me into a million pieces. I was getting close to orgasm, and he could tell. He pulled me up to his chest by my throat.

"Don't you dare come until I tell you." Raziel's voice was deep and husky, dripping with a raw, unbridled lust that sent shivers coursing through my veins. The sound was primal, almost animalistic, and it seemed to speak directly to my very soul, awakening a deep, visceral response that left me breathless and wanting.

He kept thrusting deeply into my body while keeping an eerily even pressure on my throat. I was pinned against Raziel's broad chest, his arms wrapped tightly around me as he held me in place, angling me for a deeper, more intimate thrust. His gaze burned into my body, filled with a fierce, unbridled passion as he drank in the sight of me, his eyes scorching my skin with their intensity.

The position was exquisite torture, pushing me to the very precipice of endurance. Every sensation was amplified, every nerve ending screaming in ecstasy as Raziel's movements sent me careening toward the edge of a shattering release. I was poised on the brink, my body trembling with anticipation, as I struggled to hold on against the tidal wave of pleasure that threatened to consume me. His name escaped my lips multiple times as I fought to hold myself back. Time seemed to suspend itself, and I was trapped in a state of suspended animation, my entire being coiled and ready to unleash a maelstrom of pent-up passion.

The tension was almost unbearable, my senses heightened to the point where every breath, every touch, every whispered promise seemed to reverberate through my very soul. And then, in the midst of this exquisite agony, Raziel's movements became more deliberate, more calculated, as if he was savoring the moment, drawing out the anticipation, and pushing me ever closer to the edge of oblivion. "Come for me, darling." Raziel purred. In a moment of sublime mercy he granted me release, and my body surrendered to the overwhelming tidal wave of pleasure that had been building for what felt like an eternity.

As the waves of my climax crashed over me, Raziel's fangs descended, piercing the tender skin of my throat with a precision that was both exhilarating and terrifying.

The pain was fleeting, eclipsed by the rush of endorphins and the intoxicating sensation of Raziel's mouth sealed around the wound, his hot breath dancing across my skin as he drank deeply. The mark on my throat, and my cheek, his claims on me, seemed to throb in response, as if they too were alive and feeding off the primal energy that coursed between us.

The tempo of Raziel's movements had slowed, but the intensity remained, each deliberate thrust sending shockwaves of pleasure rippling through my core. The rough, insistent pace was a perfect counterpoint to the lingering aftershocks of my earlier climax, rekindling the flames of passion and sending me spiraling toward another precipice of sensation.

As Raziel's body tensed, his release exploded through him, a primal, visceral response that seemed to shake him to his very foundations. I felt the force of his climax, a scorching, all-consuming energy that merged with mine, creating a maelstrom of sensation that threatened to incinerate us both.

And in that instant, the marks that bound us together - the Reaver mark, and the Wolf marks - blazed with a fierce, permanent light, searing themselves into my skin, an indelible testament to the unbreakable bonds that now tied us together, heart, soul, and body. The sensation was indescribable. It was beyond description, a connection that resonated deep within my core.

As the marks pierced through me, I felt a profound, soul-deep connection forming between Raziel and me. It was as if our very essences were intertwining, merging into a single, harmonious entity. Every cell, every molecule, every fiber of my being seemed to vibrate in perfect sync

434

with his, creating an unbreakable bond that transcended the physical realm. The experience was both exhilarating and overwhelming, leaving me stunned, transformed, and reborn. As the intensity of the moment gradually subsided, it gave way to a delicate, tingling sensation, a gentle echo of the profound connection we had forged, signaling the completion of our mating bond.

As the last tremors of our passion subsided, Raziel gently released his grip on my throat, and with a tender touch, he healed the bite wound, erasing all evidence of his possessive touch. With a subtle smile, he guided me down onto the soft, vibrant grass, its purple and blue hues a surreal backdrop for the intimacy we'd just shared. I attempted to catch my breath while the echo of the experience we just shared was still rippling through me.

Raziel's gaze initially met mine, the intensity of our connection sparkling in the air. But his attention was soon diverted, his eyes drifting downward to explore the curves of my body.

I felt a flush rise to my skin as he took in the sight of the marks that now adorned my skin - the Reaver mark and the Wolf marks - his gaze lingering on each one before sweeping over the rest of me. His admiration was palpable, and I couldn't help but feel a sense of pride and possessiveness, knowing that I was his, and he was mine.

The sky transformed into a breathtaking canvas as the sun dipped below the horizon, painting the heavens with vibrant hues of orange and purple. The colors swirled and blended, a mesmerizing dance of light and shadow, casting a warm, ethereal glow over the landscape. The beauty of the sunset was almost surreal, a perfect backdrop for the intimacy and connection that Raziel and I shared. He looked back into my eyes with a smile. "I love you, Raziel."

As my fingers grazed the mark on his skin, a spark of desire ignited in his eyes, and his body responded with a subtle tension. Without a word, he sat up, his movements fluid and deliberate, and pulled me into his lap. Our faces were now inches apart, our eyes locked in a fierce, unyielding gaze. The air was charged with anticipation, the connection between us crackling with an almost palpable energy. I could feel the warmth of his breath on my skin, and his eyes seemed to burn with an inner fire, as if the flames of passion were being rekindled within him.

"I have always loved you, little Wolf... and I will always love you." He purred. Our lips met again, softly. "And so you know, you are mine now, forever. And you'll never be able to escape." He growled, nipping at my earlobe possessively.

A joyful giggle bubbled up from within me, and I let it escape, feeling carefree and unbridled. As I did, a delightful shiver coursed through my body, leaving a trail of goosebumps in its wake. It was as if my very cells were singing with happiness, and I felt a deep, abiding sense of completeness that I had never experienced before. Every part of me, body, heart, and soul, felt utterly, totally, and joyfully connected, and I knew in that moment that I was exactly where I was meant to be.

Raziel's voice was low and husky, filled with a promise of secrets and surprises, as he said, "I have one more gift for you, darling." He gently lifted me from his lap, and I felt a thrill of anticipation as he reached into the pocket of his pants. His hand emerged with a small, delicate container, which he held up to the fading light of day. The last rays of the sun danced across my face, illuminating the glittering powder within the container, and sending shivers of excitement down my spine.

My voice trembled with excitement as I stuttered, "Is that...?" but Raziel finished my sentence for me, a knowing smile spreading across his face. "Yes, it is," he said, handing me the small, delicate jar filled with the shimmering, iridescent powder. I took the jar from him, my fingers wrapping around it with a sense of reverence, and inspected the contents carefully.

"Wow... I... thank you," I breathed, my eyes full of wonder while meeting his gaze. Raziel's voice was filled with trust and confidence as he spoke. "I don't know what it can do, I've honestly never used it. But I know you'll take care of it, and use it when the time is right." As the weight of his trust settled upon me, I felt a surge of determination and pride.

I carefully lowered the jar, my fingers wrapping around it protectively, as if I could physically shield the precious Pixie dust from harm. I looked up at Raziel, my eyes locking onto his, and I knew that I would do everything in my power to honor his trust and safeguard this magical gift.

As our lips met, the world around us melted away, leaving only the two of us, lost in the magic of our love. The setting sun cast a warm, golden glow over us, infusing our kiss with a sense of promise and new beginnings. I felt my heart soar with joy, knowing that this moment, this love, was worth every trial, every tribulation, and every moment of waiting.

In that moment, time stood still, and all that existed was the two of us, suspended in a sea of promise and potential. Raziel's eyes, burning with adoration, met mine, and I felt my heart overflow with emotion. The world, with all its challenges and uncertainties, faded into the background, and all I could see was the radiant future we would build together. In that instant, I felt an unshakeable sense of certainty, a conviction that radiated from the very core of my being.

The promise of our future together shimmered before me, a dazzling tapestry of laughter, tears, and adventure, woven from the threads of our eternally intertwined hearts.

The End

About the Author:

Sesha Steele is the author behind The Reaver Chronicles series, as well as the spin off series titled Obsidian, and many other works. Helping Elon Musk to accelerate the world's transition to sustainable energy full time, she uses her free time to create the many characters and worlds that we have all come to know and love.

Where can you find her work?

Www.SeshaSteele.com
Amazon.com/author/SeshaSteele
Facebook.com/SeshaSteele
Instagram.com/SeshaSteele
X.com/SeshaSteele
Pinterest.com/SeshaSteele
Goodreads.com/SeshaSteele

The Reaver Chronicles:

Book 1:
Raziel (Complete)

Book 2:
Raphael (Complete)

Book 3:
Ramses (Complete)

Book 4:
Rowen (Complete)

Book 5:
The Keepers (Complete)

Book 6:
Rayne (Complete)

Obsidian:

(Spinoff based in the same universe)

Book 1:
Tryss (Complete)

Book 2:
Reya (Complete)

Book 3:
Raven (In Progress)

Duets:

Book 1:
The Hunter (Complete)

Book 2:
The Hunted (In Progress)

Standalones:

Shadow Seeker (Complete)

Sector 7 (In Progress)

Made in the USA
Monee, IL
14 January 2025